TWIST

A THRILLER

D L HAMMONS

ALSO BY DL HAMMONS

<u>Taggart McGill YA Series</u>
Prick
Jerk

<u>Silent Sleuth Investigations Series</u>
Knight Rise
Fallen Knight

Copyright © 2025 by DL Hammons

All rights reserved.

No part of this publication may be reproduced, distributed, or transmitted in any form or by any means, including photocopying, recording, or other electronic or mechanical methods, without the prior written permission of the publisher, except as permitted by U.S. copyright law. For permission requests, contact [include publisher/author contact info].

The story, all names, characters, and incidents portrayed in this production are fictitious. No identification with actual persons (living or deceased), places, buildings, and products is intended or should be inferred.

Book Cover Design by Christian Storm

ISBN: 979-8-9890231-6-5 (hardback)
ISBN: 979-8-9890231-4-1 (paperback)
ISBN: 979-8-9890231-5-8 (eBook)

First edition 2025

Trigger Warning:
Self-harm, suicide, or suicidal thoughts

While this book touches on the topic of suicide in a fictional setting, the problem is very real and should never be minimized. Suicide prevention is a critical need. Individuals in crisis who need help today can find it by calling or texting 988. The easy-to-remember 988 makes it easier for people in crisis to access the help they need and decrease the stigma surrounding suicide and mental health issues. Please spread the word.

National Suicide Prevention Hotline: 800-273-8255

*This is dedicated to readers searching for clues in books
at a time when the real world seems so clueless.*

"If you want to keep a secret, you must also
hide it from yourself."

George Orwell

Prologue

She paused putting away the groceries when she heard the front door open, her heart pounding with an overwhelming wave of apprehension. The flood of adrenaline coursing through her veins compelled her to take a deep breath to calm herself, then another. She listened to him go about his usual routine, imagining his movements in her head. She had watched him do the same thing day after day, week after week, year after year. First, he'd hang that ratty old thing he called a baseball hat on the peg in the hall. Then he'd toss the jean jacket he always wore, regardless of how hot it was, onto the chair against the wall. Next, he would check his pockets for anything to be deposited in the wooden bowl sitting on the shelf. Nowadays, there was hardly anything besides his keys to put in the bowl, yet he still diligently checked every pocket.

From the cupboard where she stood, she heard the refrigerator door open, where he undoubtedly would grab the first of three beers he'd drink throughout the night. Always three. Not two, not four, only three. It didn't matter what the temperature was outside. He drank the same thing in the same quantity every night. She made sure there was always enough beer to satisfy his curious habit. Not because it was a mother's responsibility to see to the needs of her children, but because she didn't want to face those black eyes again if they ran out.

When his heavy footsteps started making their way to the living room, where he would plop himself down on the couch in front of the television and zone out to a blank screen, it was time for her to become part of their daily ritual.

"Dinner is almost ready," she called out from behind the cupboard door. "I made your favorite, meatloaf."

He didn't respond. She didn't expect him to. It was one of several things that had changed recently. He used to be more communicative, at least making weak attempts to talk with her, but over the past year, he had become more and more distant. No matter what she tried or how she coaxed, her son was withdrawing further away from her.

She realized now what had changed, but not the why of it. That she would never understand.

She made her way to the kitchen and pulled their dinner out of the oven. She lifted the tinfoil from the steaming meat, squirted ketchup across the top, then carried the pan into the dining room. The mashed potatoes and green beans were already resting on the table, so she placed the meatloaf between the two bowls.

"It's hot and ready," she called out.

A minute later, her son came shuffling into the room. At five foot nine, he was six inches taller than her. He wasn't overweight, but he wasn't particularly fit either. His slack jowls and droopy eyelids made him look tired, but that was just his look. She'd given him a haircut the week before, still his chestnut brown hair still looked unkempt, sticking to his forehead as if he'd recently been sweating. The same bland overshirt he wore over the top of a plain white T-shirt smelled of rotting waste.

"Did you get the Thompson's junk taken care of today?"

A grunt and a nod answered her question.

She watched him slip into his usual spot, his back to her buffet sideboard. Across from the table, on the other side of the room, sat her ornate dish cupboard. She was very protective of that piece of furniture and the china inside. It had been in her mother's family for generations and endeared her a great sense of belonging. She had been born in this house and had lived her entire life here, never feeling the urge to explore the world. Her parents, rest their souls, never pushed her to do otherwise. Her china was a welcome reminder of that. Now, it seemed her son was going down that same path, with him showing little interest in moving out.

That was about to change.

She took her seat at the end of the table next to him, and then began dishing out the food. The two of them ate in silence. As she watched him dig into his plate, she reminisced about the times they discussed each other's lives while they ate. Those days were long gone. Tonight, it was probably best that they didn't talk.

After finishing, he pushed his chair back from the table and glanced at her plate. She had only picked at her food. When he looked up at her, she continued staring at him intently.

"You didn't eat anything," he said flatly.

"I'm surprised you noticed. It's just that I'm not very hungry. Was it good?"

He shrugged his shoulders, then finished the last of his beer.

"I bought a special dessert for you," she said, rising from the table.

"Why?" her son asked, using the nail of his pinky finger to pick a piece of meat from his teeth.

She moved to the sideboard and opened the drawer. "Because you deserve it, darling."

"If you say so."

She removed the handgun from the drawer, cocked the hammer, and placed the barrel against the back of his head.

"Goodbye," she said, then closed her eyes and pulled the trigger.

When the echo of the blast had faded, she cautiously opened her eyes. A wisp of gun smoke still hung in the air, filling her nostrils with the smell of burned earth. On the other side of the room, a mixture of blood and brain matter had splattered across the front of her mother's dish cupboard.

"Oh dear," she mumbled.

PART
ONE

One

Penelope Highsmith yanked the door open, then turned around and headed back into the room without bothering to greet the person who knocked. She navigated her way over to the desk and switched on the lamp. The light would make the pounding inside her head worse, but she couldn't stand not being able to see who was talking.

"Why is it so dark in here?" Penelope's personal assistant, Willa, remarked as she trailed her boss into the room. "And I thought you were cutting back," she added, referencing the drink in Penelope's hand.

"Is this really the largest hotel room you could find?" Penelope replied, ignoring her assistant's remarks.

She walked barefoot to the couch, the bottom of her flowing gown trailing behind her on the carpet. She sat down, shifting her carry-on bag onto the floor beside the sofa. Her puffy blonde hair glistened in the dim light because of the generous amount of hair spray she'd employed to keep it in place. For a woman in her mid-fifties, she didn't wear her age well, using makeup to compensate for the ever-increasing wrinkles invading her complexion. Moreover, the cosmetic procedure she endured years ago to make her lips fuller made her mouth look misshapen, like something you see on a washed-up ex-boxer. Except for her bare feet, Penelope appeared to be about to attend a fancy reception. Then again, she rarely looked any other way, especially when she expected visitors. The value of the jewelry she was wearing alone was worth more than a mid-sized sedan.

"This is the one that was recommended. The hotel has a four-star rating, offers room service, and I confirmed it has the largest room in town," Willa said, placing a thick binder on the coffee table in front of the couch and sitting down with a sigh. She was twenty years younger than her boss, but Willa constantly struggled to match the older woman's energy level. "This is Willow's Bane, not Seattle. You should know. You grew up here."

Penelope frowned, gesturing at Willa with her drink, causing the gin and tonic to slosh over the rim. "I lived here decades ago and although times have changed, your purple-tipped highlights and numerous ear and nose piercings won't do well here. What about Airbnb?"

"Again, not Seattle. This isn't that bad, though. Anyway, we won't be here that long."

"But there's not near enough closet space for my clothes," Penelope said, looking over at the four large suitcases beside the king-size bed.

Willa sighed. "You won't wear a quarter of that. You never do."

"Immaterial. I need options," Penelope pouted. "I never know what I'll feel like wearing until I wake. You know that."

Willa nodded, resigned. She had experienced enough versions of this conversation to know that further objections would be pointless. "I'll unpack everything in the morning, but your toiletries, makeup, and prescriptions are already in the bathroom. I'll make the rest work somehow."

"Yes, you will. Now, is everyone here?"

"I saw Susan in the lobby with your publisher."

"Good. And the invitations?"

"All sent."

"The local newspaper and other media?"

"I'm pretty sure Trent took care of that."

"I don't pay you for pretty sure. Follow up and make sure."

"Will do. You still haven't returned those messages I gave you earlier from Rolling Stone and Entertainment Weekly."

"They can both wait until after tomorrow. That goes for anyone else from whom you receive interview requests. I'm not talking to a soul until after the book launch, then I imagine it will be a journalistic blitzkrieg."

"Hello, anyone in there?" came a voice from the door, followed by a brief knock. A few seconds later, a woman about the same age as Penelope, stuck her head around the corner. "You left your door open."

"I did that on purpose, Susan. I knew you'd be coming by soon," Willa said.

Susan stepped into the room, her gaze taking in the surroundings. "Your room is much bigger than mine."

The beginnings of a smile appeared on Willa's face as she glanced at her boss, but Penelope remained focused on Susan.

"Have you been over to the bookstore?" Penelope asked.

"Just got back from there. Me and Trent both. Not very big," Susan said.

"It'll serve the purpose."

"Listen, Penelope, we need to talk before things get crazy tomorrow," Susan said.

Penelope drained the rest of her drink and slammed the glass loudly on the wooden coffee table. "I don't have anything else to say."

Susan's lips formed a line before she turned to Willa. "Can you give us a few minutes?"

The assistant's face mirrored the disappointment of a grade-schooler being sent to her room while her parents had an interesting conversation.

"Fine." Willa rolled her eyes as she stood, grabbing the binder off the table. "I'm just next door if you need me."

"Is that supposed to comfort me?" Penelope said, adjusting the way her gown fell upon her lap.

Willa and Susan glanced at one another before Willa turned and marched out of the room.

After the sound of the door clicking shut, Susan shook her head and sat on the other end of the couch.

"I just don't get it, Penelope. I've tried. God knows I've tried. But I can't understand why you're being so self-destructive. Why retire when you're at the top of your game?"

"My reasons are my own."

"You might look old enough to retire, but you're only fifty-four."

"I'm fifty-five, and screw you."

"My mistake, fifty-five. I know you, Penelope. You'll be going stir-crazy in less than a year."

"What's the matter, Susan?" Penelope asked, her bottom lip stuck out. "Can't bear to see your cash cow ride off into the sunset?"

Susan recoiled as if she'd been slapped. "Don't be such a conceited bitch. I'll survive—I have plenty of other clients. That's not what this is about."

"Then what, pray tell, is this about?"

"Penelope, we've been together for over thirty years. I'd like to believe that I'm more than just your agent; I'm also a friend."

The lines on Penelope's face softened. "You are a friend."

"Then, for the umpteenth time, please tell me what's going on with you."

Penelope looked away and pulled on her ear. "You're not that kind of friend."

Susan pulled back, absorbing the verbal blow. "Fine, at least tell me why you chose this as your last book. You've solidified your place in the annals of prominent writers by churning out nothing but cozy mysteries. The characters you've created are beloved. You're known in the industry as the queen of the plot twist. So, why on Earth did you switch to non-fiction, and a true crime book at that?"

"You know why." Penelope's attention returned to her hands in her lap.

"No, I don't," Susan said, frustration tinging her voice. "So there were murders that took place in your hometown when you lived here as a kid. Boo-hoo. Sure, it was tragic, and nobody ever caught the perpetrators, but these kinds of books are commonplace. And I've told you this before. Yours is mediocre… at best."

Susan put her hands together, almost as if she meant to pray.

"I'll give you credit for exposing the boy's lie about his alibi, but the rest is nothing more than gossip and a cliché view of how the murders affected your small town. Even the title, Malignant Doubt. The critics are going to have a field day with that. There's nothing truly revealing in the book, no new theories or suspects, nada. So what if the brother manufactured an alibi? It doesn't mean he killed anybody, and the book doesn't provide any fresh evidence to support that assumption. It's no surprise that the pre-orders have been disastrous."

Penelope gave her agent an icy stare. "Why don't you tell me what you really think, Susan?"

"I've never misled you about how I feel about this book. It's a huge mistake. It can only tarnish the sterling reputation you've cultivated over the years. Everyone is already wondering why we haven't sent our customary review copies. Our long-time relationship with Trent and Monolith Publishing is the only reason it's being published."

"That and the seven hundred fifty million books I've sold for them, you mean?"

"Yes, there's that. But Trent is still unhappy."

Penelope snorted. "Trent is never happy. That man was born with something pointy up his ass. I've never liked him ever since he took over the business from his father five years ago. He's a conceited nimrod."

"Is he why you're doing this?"

Penelope shook her head. "He's irrelevant."

"He's not irrelevant. Tell me, why is this book so important that you'd throw everything away? You really want this to be your swan song?"

"You'll understand everything after the launch tomorrow."

"That's another thing. Why did you change the launch location at the last minute and want the event here in Willow's Bane?"

"This is the only place that makes sense."

"I understand the book is set here, but the local bookstore is too small for everyone, and the locals don't seem very friendly. And what's this special reveal you've been talking about during the launch? What are you up to?"

"You'll understand everything tomorrow."

"Christ, will that be your response to everything now?" Susan ran her fingers through her hair, shifting it away from her face. "You'll understand after the launch? What will you say then that you couldn't put in the book? When did you get so secretive?"

Penelope gave her agent an insincere smile. "I'm an open book, Susan, you know that."

"You certainly used to be."

The two women regarded each other, one looking confused, the other resolute.

Susan rose from the couch. "I'm tired of banging my head against the wall, and think I'll turn in. Let me just say one last thing. It's not too late, you know. We can publicize Malignant Doubt, let it run its course, and then go back to writing what you are good at. I'll tell everyone that you were in a rut and needed a change of pace. We can even look for a new publisher if you want. But let's take retirement off the table for now. What do you say?"

"What I say is good night, Susan."

Susan sighed, looking deflated. "Good night, Penelope. Breakfast tomorrow?"

"I'll meet you in the lobby at nine."

"See you then," Susan said as she disappeared around the corner. Immediately after hearing the room door open, a different voice broke the silence.

"Oh … hello … is Miss Highsmith in?" a young female voice asked.

"Penelope, there's someone here for you," Susan called out.

Penelope rose and headed for the door. There she found Susan conversing with a young hotel employee - camel-colored curls bouncing against her shoulder, a single lock caught in her name tag. The new arrival was holding a paperback copy of Penelope's latest mystery.

"One of your fans," Susan said before walking away.

"I'm sorry to bother you, Miss Highsmith," the staff member said tentatively. "You must be terribly busy. I'm the night manager here at the hotel, and… well… I'm a huge… huge fan of yours. I've read all your books, most of them more than once. Never in a million years did I think I'd ever meet you in person, but here you are."

Penelope displayed one of the brightest smiles in her arsenal. "Here I am, indeed. What's your name, darling?"

The woman returned the smile. "Belinda. Belinda Ferguson."

"Well, Belinda, I'm always happy to meet a fellow book lover."

"Oh, that I am, especially yours. My boyfriend regularly complains that my nose is always buried in a book when I should be paying more attention to him."

Penelope frowned. "How long have the two of you been together?"

"Just a couple of months."

"Then take my advice, honey, cut him loose. Any man who's that needy will only bring you trouble down the road. Trust me. Save yourself some heartache and find someone who loves books as much as you do."

Belinda looked concerned. "Oh, I'm sure he was only joking."

"Men have a way of camouflaging their true feelings with humor or witty banter. But it only works on the naïve, so don't be naïve, Belinda. Got it?"

"Yes, ma'am," Belinda replied, although her expression made it clear she wasn't so sure.

"I'm guessing from that book in your hands that you want an autograph?"

"Oh, yes, I won't be able to make your book launch tomorrow because I have to be here, but would it be too much trouble for you to sign my book for me?"

Penelope reached out and took the book from Belinda. "Do you have a pen?"

Belinda appeared stricken. "I forgot to bring one. I'm sorry, I'll run back to the desk—"

Penelope put up her hand. "I have one inside."

The author started back into the room, then paused, turning back to face Belinda.

"I can do you one better. Are you interested in the book I have coming out tomorrow? Malignant Doubt?"

Belinda's eyes narrowed. "It's true crime, right?"

"It is."

"I don't read much true crime. Honestly, I've never read any. But I'll read anything written by you."

Penelope smiled genuinely. "Hang on just a minute then," she said before disappearing into the room. A few minutes later, she returned with the paperback and an additional hardback book.

"I've signed them both. You're only the second person to possess the new book. I hope you enjoy it."

Belinda's smile was beaming. "I'm certain I will. Thank you so much."

"Anything for a fan. You have a good evening, Belinda."

"You, too. Don't hesitate to call the front desk if you need anything. I'll be here all night."

"Nice to know. Good night."

As the door clicked shut, the smile on Penelope's face faded. She put her back against the door, closed her eyes, and drew in a deep breath. When a single tear rolled down her cheek, she pushed herself away from the door and headed straight for the makeshift bar on the kitchen counter. She poured two fingers of gin from the already open bottle, downed it in one swallow. Having poured a refill, she contemplated the glass in her hand for several seconds before consuming the alcohol and placing the glass on the counter. Wandering around the room, moisture covering both cheeks,

Penelope seemed lost. She plodded over to the bathroom, stood before the mirror, and gazed at her reflection. When she reached for the tissue box, her eyes locked onto the prescription medicine beside it. She continued to stare at one particular bottle for a long time.

Another knock at the door interrupted her trance. Penelope plucked a pair of tissues from the box, dried her eyes, then walked to the other room.

She opened the door and regarded the person standing there.

"I was wondering when you were going to make an appearance."

Two

The feeling of something rubbing up against Parker's side interrupted the introspective daze she had fallen into. The snow-white Persian cat wormed between Parker's hip and hand, seeking attention. Parker picked the feline up and placed it in her lap. She was rewarded with some appreciative purring. As she stroked the soft white fur, Parker's attention returned to the cardboard boxes she'd been filling with clothes. The chore was only halfway finished and taking longer than she had planned. If she'd stop taking so many breaks, she might be finished by now, but this was torture. She knew now that she probably should have accepted Kat's offer to do it for her, but Parker was knee-deep in it now, and there was no turning back. Time to put on those big-girl pants and get it done.

Parker set her cat aside and rose from where she had been sitting cross-legged on the bedroom floor. She had just started folding a pair of sweatpants when she heard the front door to the condo open and slam shut.

"Parker!" Kat's yell came from the other room.

"Back here," Parker responded, depositing the sweatpants into the box she'd designated for casual clothes.

Kat burst into the room with a piece of paper clutched in her hand. She came to a sudden stop, her ample bosom heaving from being out of breath. She rested a hand on her stomach.

While Parker was in her mid-thirties with shoulder-length blonde hair, sharp features, a slim build, and dark blue eyes, Kat was at least ten years younger, ten inches shorter, and ten pounds heavier.

Kat surveyed the mess Parker had created.

"Oh… you're finally doing it," Kat observed.

"It was time." Parker pointed to the paper in Kat's hand to change the subject. "What's that?"

Kat handed her the paper. "Read it."

PENELOPE HIGHSMITH FOUND DEAD FROM APPARENT SUICIDE ON DAY OF LATEST BOOK LAUNCH

Penelope Highsmith, the internationally renowned best-selling author of mystery novels, was pronounced dead this morning after being discovered in her hotel room by her literary agent. Preliminary reports by medical authorities stated it appeared Highsmith had ingested a large quantity of her own prescription drug. The death is currently categorized as accidental suicide. Penelope is survived by her only daughter, Lynn Highsmith, who has been estranged from the author for many years.

Penelope Highsmith was in Willow's Bane to celebrate her latest release, Malignant Doubt, a true-crime novel that documented the unsolved deaths of three high school girls in 1986 in the same city. An unknown individual dubbed the Snake River Killer committed the crimes. The book stirred up quite a commotion in the literary world because of its drastic divergence from Highsmith's usual genre of Cozy Mysteries. Her previous books, which have sold seven hundred and fifty million copies across seventy-two countries and fifty-three languages, were light, comedic, and comforting. After the news of Highsmith's passing, the organizers of the book launch that was scheduled for later that same day canceled the event.

Highsmith made headlines earlier this year when she suddenly announced her retirement following the upcoming release of

Malignant Doubt. Only fifty-five years old at the time of her death, her announcement took many by surprise. Highsmith gave no explanation for her decision, upsetting many of her devoted fans.

Penelope Highsmith graduated from Oregon University and married her college sweetheart, Sam Wortham (keeping her maiden name). After working briefly as a medical transcriptionist, Penelope Highsmith wrote three books. None of those books were published, but she did give birth to her daughter Lynn in 1989. Highsmith broke onto the literary scene with her first novel, That's All She Wrote, an Agatha Awards winner and instant best-seller. After that, her career slowly took off. Each of her published books has been a bestseller.

Highsmith has been reputed for her 'larger-than-life' personality in the entertainment industry and a self-proclaimed DIVA of the publishing world. Her past struggles with alcohol and drug abuse have been evidenced by her multiple stays at high-dollar rehabilitation spas. She divorced Sam Wortham (deceased April 2010) in 1993 and never remarried. Over the years, she has been linked romantically to several prominent personalities.

At time of publication no funeral arrangements were available, nor the release of prescription drugs used in the accidental overdose.

Parker sat on the edge of the bed and read the article a second time, her eyes soaking in all the details.

"Are you alright?" Kat asked.

Parker looked at Kat, appearing dazed. "Yeah. I'm numb, I guess. Not sure how I should feel."

"I know, it's a shocker. What about the way it says she died?"

Parker shook her head. "That isn't right. The Penelope I know wouldn't do that."

"I know, right? That's what I thought when I first read it."

Parker's gaze returned to the piece of paper in her hands.

"Do you think they'll want you to organize the funeral or something?" Kat asked.

The gap between Parker's eyebrows narrowed. "Me?"

Kat hunched her shoulders. "I mean…you are related."

Parker shook her head. "Her sister will handle all that, I'm sure."

"Hey, wasn't Penelope supposed to reveal her big secret yesterday?"

Parker was stricken. "You're right, she was. I totally forgot."

Kat shrugged her shoulders. "Yeah, me too, until I came across that article."

Parker briefly put her hand over her mouth, then lowered it to her throat. "How could I have done that? I was supposed to—" Parker left the thought unfinished.

"Suppose to what?" Kat asked when Parker didn't continue.

"It doesn't matter."

"The way you're behaving, I kinda think it does. What gives?"

Parker seemed to snap out of her trance and quickly rose from the bed. "Don't worry about it. Right now, we need to call someone. It says they're classifying this as a suicide, and that means there won't be an investigation."

"Who do we call?" Kat asked.

Parker contemplated her options. "I have a better idea. I'm going out there."

"Where?"

"Willow's Bane. I have to get the police to investigate her death properly and find out what Penelope intended to announce. And fast… before the trail goes cold."

"What if they won't listen to you?" Kat asked.

Parker stooped down and pulled a suitcase out from under the bed. "I'll find a way. It's the least I owe her."

"Then I'm coming with you," Kat said.

Parker put her hands on her hips and regarded her friend. "I'm not sure that's a good idea."

Kat frowned. "Why not?"

"Things could be tricky, and I would feel more at ease on my own."

Kat's expression morphed into a full-fledged pout. "Oh please…please…please. I never get to go anywhere."

Parker stared at Kat's sorrowful face, then slowly smiled. "Okay, but you're only coming along for moral support, got it? I do all the talking."

Kat leaped in the air and clapped. "Whatever you say."

Parker laughed. "Now go get packed while I book our flights. And bring your laptop just in case."

"Willow's Bane, here we come," Kat said as she flew out of the room.

When Kat was gone, Parker reached for her phone. Finding the contact she was looking for, she hit the dial button, then casually moved to the bedroom door and pushed it closed. Her call was picked up on the third ring.

"Parker, to what do I owe the pleasure?" the chipper male voice answered.

"Hey, Chuck. I wanted to call and let you know I was going to be out of town for a couple of days. I knew you'd want to know."

Chuck's voice dropped an octave and turned serious. "Parker, it's less than a week until you're due in court. This isn't the time for last-minute trips."

"I know, but this can't be helped. I promise I'll be back in plenty of time."

"Can you at least tell me where you're going?"

"I'd rather not. It's personal, but I'll be back before the weekend, so there's no need for you to worry."

"Come on, Parker. Don't do this to me. Just tell me where you're—"

"Chuck, I gotta go. I'll call you when I get back," Parker said in a hurry and ended the call. She stared at her phone momentarily, then flipped open the top of her suitcase.

Three

Parker pushed open the door, allowing a blast of cool October air to rush inside ahead of them. She and Kat paused to survey their surroundings.

Words stenciled in big, bold letters on the facing of a drop-down ceiling read:

Willow's Bane
POLICE

On the right side of the small reception area was a waist-high counter with a tall female officer standing at a computer monitor. Someone had affixed a sign to the back of the monitor that read INFORMATION DESK. A metal desk occupied the left side of the room, with a male officer sitting at it. There was just enough room between the two work areas to allow access to a doorway leading into the rear of the building.

Parker approached the information desk. "I need to speak with the sheriff."

"Sheriff Webber is not in at the moment," the tall officer said without taking her eyes from the screen.

"Then, can someone else help me?" Parker asked.

"What is this regarding?"

"Penelope Highsmith."

Both officers stopped typing, and Parker felt herself being appraised.

"Our office has already released an official statement, and we don't do interviews," the officer stated.

"Official statement my ass," Kat said under her breath.

"I do the talking, Kat, remember," Parker said before addressing the officer. "I'm more interested in making sure your people are investigating her death seriously."

"And how are you associated with Miss Highsmith?"

"This is her daughter, Lynn," Kat blurted.

Parker shot Kat a disapproving look. "Kat, please."

"You're Lynn Highsmith?"

Parker shifted her weight and appeared uncomfortable. "My surname is Parker now. I'm married. But yes, Penelope was my mother."

The officer's expression softened. "I'm sorry for your loss."

"That makes one of us. So, who can I talk to about the investigation?"

The officer turned to address her co-worker. "Ask Deputy Tate to come up here."

The male officer promptly picked up the phone.

"Miss Highsmith—"

"It's Mrs. Parker."

"Mrs. Parker—has somebody from this office contacted you about your mother's death?"

"If they had, then you'd be expecting her, wouldn't you?" Kat quipped, drawing a harsh look from the officer.

"Kat, that's enough. No. No one contacted me, and I doubt anyone could. Penelope and I weren't part of each other's lives."

"That's the understatement of the year," Kat muttered.

The officer looked at the short woman for the first time. "And your name is?"

Kat crossed her arms and tilted her head. Her shoulder-length brunette hair was uncombed, and the way she was dressed looked like she had done so in the dark–a mismatch of different styles and colors. "Why do you need to know my name?"

"Because we log the names of all visitors."

Kat's shoulders relaxed. "Oh. It's Kat Anderson."

"She's a friend," Parker added.

"I'm here for moral support."

A uniformed man strode through the doorway, trailed by an older woman. The woman was taller and stockier than the deputy, wearing a vintage aesthetic wool sweater with a large silver cross dangling around her neck. Her brown eyes shined with wariness as she approached.

There was a long pause before anyone spoke.

"Hi, Aunt Trudy," Parker said, forming a timid smile.

Confused, the old woman glanced at the male officer and then squinted at Parker.

"Lynn… is that you?" Trudy asked hesitantly.

When Parker nodded, Trudy moved past the male officer and awkwardly embraced her. A few moments later, Trudy pulled back and studied Parker, taking in everything, including the coffee stain on her sleeve.

"I almost didn't recognize you. It's been so long. You've really blossomed into a wonderful woman, haven't you?"

Parker shrugged, brushing off the compliment, saying, "I've done okay, I guess. You haven't changed much, except maybe the hair."

Trudy brushed the gray strands off her cheek as she laughed. "I grew tired of fighting the inevitable and stopped coloring it."

Parker put her hand on Kat's shoulder. "This is my friend, Kat. Kat, this is my Aunt Trudy."

"Hi, Aunt Trudy," Kat said.

"Where do you call home now, Lynn?" Trudy asked.

"I moved to LA a few years back."

The friendly smile on Trudy's face disappeared. "How did you find out about Penelope?"

"I read the report yesterday. News travels fast these days."

"It makes little sense what they're saying, Lynn. My sister wasn't suicidal. She just wasn't."

"That's why I'm here, Aunt Trudy," Parker said, taking hold of the old woman's hands and then turning her attention to the male officer accompanying her aunt. "Are you the one I need to see to get some answers?"

The deputy in his late twenties walked up to them. The sleeves of his button-up shirt were rolled up, showing his muscular arms. His flat-top haircut complemented his angular face, emphasized by a pencil-thin mustache.

"I'm Deputy Bonner, and I'll have to do until the sheriff returns."

"Isn't there somebody we can talk to with a few more miles on them?" Kat said. "You're kinda young, aren't ya?"

The deputy studied Kat like he would an irritating fly that stayed just out of fly-swatter distance. "I've been on the force for three years. I think I can answer your questions."

Kat snorted and looked down at the ground.

"Lynn, they're finished with me, but I want you to promise you'll come to see me later," Aunt Trudy said wistfully. "Do you have my address?"

"I'm sure I can find you."

"Where are you staying?"

"We'll be at the same place Penelope was staying."

Trudy reached out and touched Parker's elbow. "Mention me when you check-in, and they'll give you a discounted rate. I work there part-time."

"I will. We'll talk soon."

Trudy's hand moved from Parker's elbow to her cheek. "It's so nice to see you again."

Parker squeezed the elderly woman's hand, and then watched as she departed.

"Why don't you follow me back to the conference room," Deputy Bonner said.

Parker and Kat trailed behind the deputy as he turned right through the door. The deputy escorted them through a narrow hallway with lockers labeled Temporary Evidence, past a copy machine, and to a door identified by a placard that read Interviews. The room seemed small because of the dominance of an eight-by-ten table and an abundance of conference chairs. An American flag hung proudly on one wall, and a Willow's Bane Police Department flag on another.

"Take your pick," Deputy Bonner said as they entered the room, gesturing at the multitude of chairs. "Can I get either of you anything to drink?"

"I don't suppose you have sparkling water?" Kat asked as she slid into the chair closest to the door.

"Sorry, just regular bottled water."

"Pass." Looking around the room, Kat remarked, "Quite a bit different from the police stations in LA, huh, Parker?"

"You spend a lot of time in police stations, do you?" the deputy asked, waiting for Parker to take a seat before sitting himself.

"I've seen my share," Kat answered.

"Let's just say Kat is the product of an unfocused youth," Parker said, looking over at her companion, who beamed.

"I noticed she called you Parker?"

"I'm married now, or at least I was. I'm a widower. I told your receptionist upfront that I go by Parker, not Highsmith. Most of my friends just call me Parker."

"I'm sorry for your loss, both of them, but I have to say I'm surprised to see you here in Willow's Bane, Mrs. Parker. Miss Highsmith's agent told us you haven't had contact with your mother in years."

"That is correct. I've been estranged from Penelope and on my own since I turned eighteen."

"Then, if you don't mind me asking, why are you here now?"

Kat slid her feet into an empty chair. "They may have been Splitsville, but she was still her mother, Barney."

"Kat, chill," Parker said.

"I get that. I do. But we only found your mother yesterday morning, and here you are already. You must admit, that's unusual, given your strained relationship."

"I'm here because Penelope Highsmith did not accidentally overdose, nor did she commit suicide. I want to make sure you're doing right by her."

The deputy looked down at his lap and shook his head. "Do you know how many friends and family of suicide victims say the same thing? People just cannot tell what's going on inside another person's head. And you even admitted that you've not had a meaningful relationship with your mother in what, fifteen years?"

"You didn't find a suicide note, right?"

"No, but that means nothing. Statistically, only twenty-five to thirty percent of people who take their own lives leave behind a note," the deputy said.

"You really believe someone who writes for a living wouldn't leave behind a note?" Parker asked.

The deputy took a deep breath. "How can you possibly know what sort of mental state she was in?"

Parker dipped her head and shifted in her chair. "Because Penelope reached out to me eight months ago."

Deputy Bonner looked surprised by that, and sat forward in his chair. "Is that so?"

"Yes. I received a phone call from her one day—out of the blue. I don't know how she got my number, but there she was."

"Can I ask what she wanted?"

"She wanted to repair our relationship. She told me she had a lot of things to make amends for if I would give her a chance."

"And how did you respond to that?"

"I hung up on her."

The deputy sat back and crossed his arms. "Is that so?"

"But she called back the next day, and the day after that, and the day after that. She kept calling until I finally broke down and spoke with her. We ended up having a decent conversation, but I was still leery of opening myself up to her."

"That's understandable."

Parker leaned forward in her seat, growing more intense. "You need to understand something, deputy; I grew up alone with a mother who was both an alcoholic and frequent drug user. She treated me as more of a burden than a daughter. I had a revolving door of people who were supposed to look after me, but they thought they were being hired as Penelope's personal assistant and ended up as glorified nannies instead. Resentment was a common theme between me and them, and some were downright unfriendly about it. Her adoring fans knew Penelope as this witty writer. She behaved like a cross between a female version of Oscar Wilde and Liberace in public, but the person I knew was a complete train wreck. I jumped off those tracks as soon as possible and never looked back."

"I'm sorry to hear that."

"I don't tell you all of that to gain your sympathy. I need you to see why I'm here now. When I finally spoke to Penelope after all those years, she told me she had skeletons in her closet. Secrets that she's been keeping for years about things that happened before I was even born. She said it wasn't an excuse… but keeping those secrets probably drove her to become so messed up, and I paid the price for her failure to deal with them. Penelope told me she was planning to reveal those secrets to the world on the day of her book release to atone for my crappy childhood. That day was yesterday, but I've heard of no revelations… and now she's dead."

"Duh… duh… dum," Kat uttered in an ominous tone.

"Maybe the revelations you speak of were too much for her to face up to in the end?"

"Or somebody killed her to keep those secrets buried," Parker said.

"That's the option I'd pick," Kat added.

"What about her new book? Could she have confessed her secrets in it?"

Parker shook her head. "Penelope emailed me an advanced copy. I almost deleted it, but my curiosity got the better of me. It's an interesting read with a few significant questions raised, but nothing is earth-shattering there."

"Can you give me the Cliffs notes version? The only thing I know about the book is it's about the murders that happened here in Willow's Bane back in the eighties."

Parker nodded. "Nineteen eighty-six, to be exact. Three girls. All high schoolers who disappeared into thin air before being found a few days after they each disappeared, floating in the Snake River. They were Penelope's classmates. It all happened over the course of a couple of months."

"They were all found naked and beaten to death," Kat added.

"Because the bodies were in the river, they couldn't determine if there was any sexual assault. Even though Penelope was in the same grade as those girls, she wasn't particularly close to any of them. They never made an arrest and only had one real suspect, the high school soccer coach. Two of the three girls were on his team. The first girl murdered, Mikayla Jamesison, had an older brother who the police talked to, but he had an alibi. He was supposedly working for a local farmer that day, who vouched for him, but Penelope destroyed that alibi in her book. Initially there was some speculation the deaths could have been related to other unsolved murders that took place a year earlier in Lewiston, which I understand isn't too far from here, but in the end, there were too many dissimilar factors. According to Penelope's book, the city of Willow's Bane fell apart afterward."

"How is that?"

"They didn't catch anyone, and people felt nervous, suspicious, and distrustful. Parents kept their kids home at night. Someone was always pointing the finger at somebody else. A lot of what Penelope writes about in the book is how the moral fiber of Willow's Bane deteriorated and has never fully recovered."

Deputy Bonner considered this for a moment. "Thanks for the synopsis, but I still don't know what to tell you, Miss Parker. Her agent became concerned when Penelope didn't turn up for breakfast and she talked the hotel manager into checking her room. They discovered your mother lying peacefully on the bed, an empty bottle of her antidepressant medication clutched in her hand and an empty bottle of gin on the bedside table. There was no evidence of foul play. Seems pretty straightforward to me."

"It's kind of ironic, don't you think, that somebody would use antidepressants to commit the ultimate act of depression," Kat pointed out.

"Have you looked at the hotel's CCTV footage?" Parker asked.

"There was no need. This is about as open and shut as they come."

"Said every dim-witted, close-minded policeman on every cop show I've ever watched," Kat said.

"Deputy, think about it. It all feels too staged."

"Like who kills themselves then lays down like Sleeping Beauty?" Kat interjected.

"And why hold on to the pill bottle? The answer is they wouldn't. Somebody put that bottle in her hand to point you toward suicide. If you ask me, they're succeeding."

"Miss Parker, you are thinking about this rationally."

"Duh," Kat commented.

The deputy closed his eyes and drew in a deep breath. When his eyes opened again, they were focused on Parker. "What I'm saying is your mother was suicidal, and that's not a rational frame of mind. Holding onto the pill bottle delivering your chosen fate might seem logical to a person in that state."

Parker tossed her head back and stared at the ceiling, frustrated. A moment later, it snapped back. "But you even have her sister telling you she wasn't suicidal."

The deputy shook his head. "Your Aunt Trudy admitted she hadn't communicated regularly with her sister in quite some time."

"What about other people who knew her? She has an agent, right?" Parker asked.

"Her agent, publisher, and personal assistant all say that she has been acting strange recently, doing things that were out of character. However, they all also said she was looking forward to the book launch."

"Because I'm telling you she was going to drop a bombshell. Somebody silenced her before she could do that. It's why Kat and I came out here as quickly as we did. The first couple days of any investigation are crucial."

"Can I ask how you know that?"

Parker made a face. "I've read stacks of crime books and seen enough TV shows. Everyone knows that."

"We prefer British mysteries on the BBC. Line of Duty is my favorite," Kat said.

The deputy rose to his feet. "I'll admit, there are some unanswered questions, but I'm not sure it's enough to warrant a full-scale investigation. That's the sheriff's call, and he won't be back for a while. Best I can do is have him find you when he gets back, and you can make your case to him."

Parker and Kat looked at one another, and then got up from their seats.

"You owe me ten bucks," Kat said to Parker.

"Ten bucks?" Deputy Bonner asked.

"I told her that coming here would be a waste of time, and she bet me ten dollars that she could convince you to see things her way. I won," Kat explained.

The deputy looked at Parker. "Sorry."

"Oh, don't worry. I'm not paying up yet," she said before leaving the room.

Four

As the two women returned to their rental car, Parker considered what they had accomplished with the local authorities. It wasn't much. Despite her optimistic bet with Kat, she wasn't completely surprised with how little they'd achieved. So much depended on the attitude of the people who were in charge, and not being able to talk with the sheriff directly left things up in the air. Cooperation would be nice, but her strategy wouldn't change regardless: find out who silenced Penelope and why. What was the big revelation that nobody got to hear?

At least they'd passed one major hurdle.

"How far is it to the hotel?" Kat asked as she climbed behind the wheel of their compact car.

Parker checked the GPS on her phone. "Looks like ten minutes, but in a town this size, I think everything is ten minutes away."

"True dat," Kat said as she pulled out of the parking lot.

"Go back to the main road we came in on and turn left."

"Ten-Four," Kat replied as she aggressively maneuvered the car on the quiet roads.

Parker looked out of the passenger window, taking in the small city of Willow's Bane. From Penelope's book, Parker learned the city was the county seat and had a population of just under twenty-five thousand. The town incorporated in 1862 and quickly expanded to three hundred percent of its original size over the next decade. But it gradually fell behind other cities in the area after the transcontinental rail lines bypassed it. After the gold rush died out, the city developed into an agricultural hot spot; a popular source of onions, apples, peas, and wine. Primarily a farming town, wheat was the main crop nowadays, though wineries were gaining ground. The daily mean temperature was 54.3 degrees, and the average age of its residents was thirty-four. The crime rate was almost non-existent.

Almost.

But it was the way everything appeared so normal that surprised Parker. The details Penelope used to describe Willow's Bane in her book, using dry, de-personalized prose, was a departure from her usual flamboyant style and painted a different picture in Parker's mind. She didn't know why, but she'd expected to see shuttered buildings, streets covered with potholes, dilapidated facades, weeds everywhere, streets empty of cars and pedestrians, and a general sense of gloom pervading every direction you looked. But Willow's Bane looked like every other small-town Parker had ever encountered. Penelope had done a fantastic job of taking the dread fostered by the unsettling murders and the search for a ruthless killer and superimposed it against the backdrop of the city. It was a talented bit of writing, one that Parker begrudgingly had to tip her cap to.

"Are you sure you want to stay in the same hotel Penelope died in?" Kat questioned tentatively.

"The deputy said Penelope's agent and publisher were staying there, so yes, that's where we'll stay as well."

They rode in silence until Kat sped through a yellow light that turned red as they entered the intersection. Their car swerved onto the principal thoroughfare, and Kat blew her horn at a gray pickup moving at a reasonable speed, forcing her to brake.

"You should probably lay off the horn. People around here don't respond to being honked at like they do in LA."

"He cut me off. Besides, how would you know? You've lived in LA almost as long as I have."

"I've traveled a lot and driven in areas like this before. You've never been out of LA."

Kat blew a raspberry. "Driving is driving wherever you go."

"But people aren't people. Drivers in LA have become desensitized to horns. It's like background noise. But here, they take it personally, and you could get us in a jam quickly. We need to keep a low profile. No horn."

"Fine," Kat replied, taking one of her hands off the wheel and letting it drop to her lap.

Not for the first time, Parker had second thoughts about bringing Kat along on this trip. She had mulled the decision before they got on the plane, began to regret it when Kat argued with the car rental agent about the necessity of insurance, and again at the police station when she irritated the very people they needed help from the most. She was continually demonstrating how much of a fish out of water she was. Kat was a hard-core LA girl, but that wasn't what concerned Parker most. It was her friend's unfortunate lack of social skills.

Kat had grown up in the foster care system, which was not a simple path through life for sure, but somehow, the girl managed to come out of it in one piece. To her credit, she'd even become an impressive computer nerd. Sadly, the computer skills she learned weren't the springboard to success everyone hoped they would be. As a teenager, she spent years performing court-ordered community service because of the illegal activities she was caught doing with her laptop. It wasn't easy, but with a bit of help, she eventually turned things around and became the youngest software engineer for an LA-based advertising company despite her free-wheeling mouth.

There was no denying that Kat was an acquired taste. She could be headstrong and impulsive, and her brashness over-compensated for her feelings of inferiority. But once you got past all the noise and got to know the woman underneath, she could be fiercely loyal, unselfish, and deeply emotional. Many of the people who knew Parker wondered why she spent so much time with the ex-juvenile delinquent. She let them keep wondering. Despite the age difference between them, Parker considered Kat her closest friend. The fact that Parker treasured the relationship so intensely said more about her than it did Kat.

However, this trip had landmines everywhere, and Kat's behavior could become problematic. What kept Parker from sending Kat home was that she was equally as convinced they were doing the right thing by coming to Willow's Bane. Parker needed as many people on her side as possible, which meant making some allowances and cutting Kat some slack.

"I'm not sure we're doing the right thing," Kat suddenly said, looking straight ahead.

Parker gawked at Kat. "What do you mean?"

"I mean, Penelope was a massive C U Next Tuesday."

"Don't I know it! And?"

"I'm just thinking of you."

Parker embellished the way she let her jaw drop open.

"I know, shocker, I'm considering someone's feelings other than mine," Kat said. "But I remember you saying not too long ago that you didn't want to get pulled into the whole Penelope drama. I'm just worried for you."

"Back in LA, I couldn't talk you out of coming. Now you're saying we shouldn't be here at all?"

"All I'm saying is, we're taking a chance, and it could backfire on you, big time. I couldn't stand to see you get all depressed again."

"I'm doing what is right, despite how I feel about Penelope. End of story. Now, the hotel is about five miles ahead on the right."

Parker didn't want to say it out loud, but she agreed with her friend. She was worried about what she was getting herself into. Still, she had already accepted the risk of being in Willow's Bane despite the professional and personal gamble, and she had to follow through. Her torn emotions about Penelope aside, the spotlight was one thing Parker needed to avoid at all costs. Running around yelling murder wasn't exactly the way to do that.

"I told you it'd be a waste of time going to the local Po Po's," Kat said.

Parker turned away from the passing sights and stared at Kat. "You understand we will need their help if we hope to see this investigated properly, right?"

"I say the only people we can count on are me and thee, Parker. Together, we can figure this out."

"You've seen too many episodes of Miss Marple."

"I'm telling you that in one of my past lives, I was a detective or something like that."

"I can believe the or *something* part."

"And I already have our first clue."

"You do? Pray tell."

"The news article about Penelope's death said her agent discovered the body when Penelope didn't come down for breakfast."

"Yeah, so?"

"Why make plans to meet for breakfast if you intend on killing yourself that night? Explain that."

"I agree it's suspicious, but not proof. We both know how quickly people can spiral under the right circumstances. Penelope could have been fine when she made those breakfast plans, but then something happened that turned the tables."

"Now you're sounding like that deputy."

"I'm not saying I believe that's what happened, only that we will need more to convince them." Parker pointed to something up ahead. "There's the hotel."

Kat directed the car into the Knights Lodge parking lot. Adjoining the four-story hotel was the Knights Pub, a combination bar and restaurant. With their car parked under the alcove in front of the main entrance, the two women strolled through the automatic doors into the spacious hotel lobby. A young man standing at the reception desk looked up and displayed a well-rehearsed, toothy smile.

"Welcome to Knights Lodge," the man said. "Checking in?"

Parker glanced around the lobby before responding. She saw a modern layout with updated furniture and decor, a sitting area with four plush chairs, a long-elevated table in front of a large LCD screen, and a logically arranged breakfast area. The only people occupying the space, other than the man at the front desk, were a man and woman sitting in two of the plush chairs conversing and a young woman sitting alone in a chair against the wall.

Parker turned towards the hotel employee. "Yes, we are. We'd like a single room with two queen beds."

"Do you have a reservation?"

"We do not."

"No problem, let me see what we have," the man said, typing on his keyboard.

"Oh … I'm supposed to mention that my aunt works here. Trudy Highsmith?"

The man grinned. "Trudy is a sweetheart. That shouldn't be a problem."

Parker rested her forearms on the counter and leaned forward. "While you're doing that, can you please tell me if Susan Reynolds is still staying here?"

She watched the desk manager lift his head, and his eyes quickly cut to the man and woman sitting in the lobby.

"I'm sorry, but we can't give out that sort of information," he answered with a smile.

Parker returned the smile, pulled her cell phone from her back pocket, and extracted a credit card from a sleeve.

"Finish checking us in," she said as she handed the card to Kat. "I'll be right back."

Leaving Kat with her mouth hanging open, Parker strolled over to the couple sitting in the plush chairs.

"Excuse me," Parker said as she approached the man and the woman. They both looked up, the man with an expression of obvious irritation. Parker immediately disliked him.

"Can I help you?" the middle-aged woman responded. The bags underneath her blue eyes made her appear tired.

"I think so. Are you Susan Reynolds? Penelope Highsmith's agent?"

"Are you a reporter?" the man barked. He was much younger than the woman, sharply dressed in a suit and tie, with a haircut that Parker imagined cost more than their room would at this hotel.

"Miss Reynolds?" Parker continued, ignoring the man's question.

"I asked you a question, lady," the man said.

"And I asked one first," Parker said, refusing to take her eyes off the woman.

"Listen, bit—"

"Yes, I'm Susan Reynolds," the female literary agent interjected. "Who might you be?"

"You don't recognize me, do you? I'm Penelope's daughter."

Susan Reynolds's jaw dropped, and all the color drained from her male companion's face. Susan scrutinized Parker from head to toe as she rose from her chair.

"My god. Lynn? I haven't seen you since you barely came up to my waist. I hardly recognize you."

"It's been a few years."

The man cleared his throat as he rose and stuck out his hand. "I'm sorry, we got off on the wrong foot. I'm Trent Carson, Penelope's publisher."

Parker hesitated before finally grasping the offered hand.

"I am so sorry, Lynn," Susan said as she gave Parker a cordial hug.

"Yes, my condolences as well," Trent said.

"I'm so happy to see you, but what are you doing here?" Susan asked.

"Believe me, I don't want to be. I left this circus behind a long time ago and never looked back, but I had to make sure the police investigated Penelope's death properly. She did not commit suicide."

"Oh, honey," Susan said, her face looking forlorn. "I was there when they found her. She looked at peace. I don't see how it could be anything else."

Kat walked up and put her hands on her hips. "What did I miss?"

Parker put her arm around Kat's shoulders. "Susan, Mr. Carson, this is my friend Kat."

"Please, call me Trent," the publisher said.

"Sharp suit," Kat responded. "So, who's our prime suspect?"

"They think Penelope committed suicide," Parker said, drawing a frown from Kat.

"Is everybody drinking from the same well of denial in this town?" Kat asked. "I don't know if you noticed, but that woman sitting in the corner over there has been extremely interested in what you guys have been saying."

Parker glanced at the eavesdropper, and the thin and pale woman quickly diverted her eyes away from their group.

"That's Samantha Trimble," Susan commented without looking at the woman. "An up-and-coming Zoomer who hosts a true-crime podcast about the Lewiston murders—the deaths that took place a year before the murders here in Willow's Bane."

"The way she was staring at you, she might perform some true crime on you," Kat observed.

"What is she doing in Willow's Bane?" Parker asked.

"Why don't you sit," Susan said, gesturing to the chairs beside them. She sighed deeply after everyone took their seats. "Samantha is an angry young woman. She has been researching the Lewiston murders for over two years and hosting a podcast for the last few months. The show has a small following, maybe a hundred subscribers, if that. I've listened to a couple of episodes. They're not bad, a bit amateurish for my taste. After Penelope came along with her massive book deal about the murders in Willow's Bane, it sucked all the air out of what Samantha had been struggling to do in Lewiston. It didn't matter that it was unrelated. In Samantha's mind, Penelope stole her thunder. She's resentful… but harmless."

Parker stole another glimpse at the podcaster. She couldn't help but feel sorry for her. Penelope had a long history of pushing people out of the way on her way to the limelight, so Parker could relate to her situation.

Turning her attention back to Susan, Parker asked, "What makes you think Penelope took her own life?"

Susan reached out and took hold of Parker's hands.

"For the past several months, your mother has been acting erratically. Not like herself at all. She was turning down invitations to events she normally would look forward to. She'd let a week or two go by without returning my calls—and we would normally talk daily. She even stopped responding to her fan mail. And that's not even addressing the whole retirement thing and the other mess."

Parker pulled her hands back. "You mean her book?"

"I don't mean to speak ill of the dead," Trent said in such a way Parker believed he was perfectly comfortable doing just that. "But *Malignant Doubt* was a mistake. For the life of me, I can't fathom what Penelope was thinking when she wrote it. Even though it was miles ahead of what that poor woman over there is doing with her podcast, it's still a low-rent attempt at something like *In Cold Blood* by Truman Capote, lacking the elegant prose or breathtaking insight. It wasn't what she promised us."

"And yet you published it," Kat pointed out.

"Of course, I was going to publish it. Even a book like that written by someone of her stature in the industry would sell plenty of copies."

"Leach, much?" Kat said with no attempt at concealing her eye roll.

"Kat, please," Parker said, then locked eyes with Trent. "I thought it was an interesting read. Definitely not as bad as you make it sound."

"It only came out yesterday. You read the whole thing already?" Susan asked, confused.

Parker shook her head. "Penelope sent me an advanced copy."

Susan and Trent exchanged perplexed looks.

"We didn't send out advanced copies of the book," Trent said. "Penelope insisted."

"This wasn't an actual bound book. It was a Word document."

This time, the look Susan and Trent exchanged was more intense.

"How many chapters did the version you read have?" Susan asked.

Parker considered the question. "I don't remember. It's been a while since I read it. Why is that important?"

"Penelope was late delivering the book, so much so it threatened to delay our publication date. She told us her reasons for the delay were that she was struggling with chapter fifty, the last chapter, and she needed to get it right. When she finally gave us the book, there were only forty-nine chapters. When we asked about the missing chapter, she told us she cut it, which mystified us. Said it was extraneous. I thought it was unprofessional of her," Trent explained.

"Both Trent and I believe that chapter contained something that would blow the lid off the whole Snake River murders investigation, something that would totally justify the book's existence, but for some reason, Penelope decided not to include it," Susan added.

"Why would she do that?" Kat asked.

"Not a clue. Maybe there were some legal considerations she was concerned about that she never mentioned. I'm not sure, but she never said. She told me the chapter was just a bunch of crime statistics and such, that the book stood on its own without it. I didn't believe her," Susan said.

"What I read had nothing like that in the last chapter. It focused mainly on life in Willow's Bane today and how the murders left a permanent stain on the city. Her words, not mine."

"Susan told me she believes Penelope had plans to reveal whatever was in that last chapter at her book launch yesterday," Trent said.

"It was her idea to move the launch here to Willow's Bane, and she wanted to have as much press present as possible. She had something up her sleeve, but she wouldn't talk about it," Susan added.

"And yet you still think she committed suicide?" Kat asked, crossing her arms.

"That's the only thing that gives me pause. She was really looking forward to the launch," Susan admitted. "Willa said the same thing."

"Who's Willa?" Parker asked.

"Willa is... sorry... was... Penelope's personal assistant," Susan answered.

"Is she still here?" Parker asked. "Can I speak with her?"

"She is, and you're more than welcome to do that. Though I don't know how much she can tell you."

"I don't understand. She was Penelope's assistant; she should have quite a lot to say."

"When she was hired, Penelope required her to sign a non-disclosure agreement that prevents her from disclosing anything about her personal life."

"But the woman's dead," Kat pointed out.

"The NDA has no termination clause, which means it is binding even if Penelope dies. Your mom was adamant about keeping her private life private." Susan looked directly at Parker. "That's something I think you might understand."

"Unfortunately, I do. Will Willa talk to me?"

"You can try, but I wouldn't hold out much hope. Penelope's lawyers are a vicious lot, and Willa knows it."

"What room is she in?" Parker asked.

A noisy group entering the lobby from outdoors interrupted the answer. Parker watched as the gathering composed of a dozen individuals, most of them past retirement age, made their way to the front desk. None of them looked happy. A woman who trailed at the back of the pact noticed Parker's group and pointed them out to the others, resulting in the band moving in their direction.

A woman wearing a plaid shirt and jeans stepped to the forefront.

"Which one of you is Penelope Highsmith's agent?" the woman asked, her voice low and throaty.

"That would be me. I'm Susan Reynolds."

"We heard a rumor that you're considering rescheduling the book launch for tomorrow. Is that true?"

Susan glanced at Trent, then back to the woman. "It was something we were still discussing as a possibility."

A hushed murmur rippled through the people gathered.

"May I ask why you're interested?" Susan asked.

"My name is Trisha Jamesison."

Parker recognized the name at once. The woman's daughter was one of the girls killed by the Snake River killer, and Penelope had exposed her son's fake alibi in her book.

"We're all here to ensure that book launch doesn't happen," Trisha said.

Five

From the expression Parker observed on Susan Reynold's face, the agent also recognized the name Trisha Jamesison. Susan blinked once, then adopted a gracious smile.

"Mrs. Jamesison, as I said, we are still only considering going forward with the launch, and we'd certainly welcome your input on the matter." It was evident to Parker that the agent was well-practiced in handling challenging conversations. "May I ask who you've brought with you?"

Trisha Jamesison had obviously come to the hotel geared up for a confrontation. Susan's affable manner seemed to perplex Trisha, who demonstrated this with fluttered blinks and a small step back. She quickly recovered.

"Uh… this is Greg Pool, Mary and Dan Emerson, and Poppy Jackson. Everyone else is from our church." As Mrs. Jamesison introduced her companions, Parker mentally checked off the names against those she remembered from Penelope's book.

Mikayla Jamesison was Trisha Jamesison's daughter and the first murder victim back in 1986, and Hutch Jamesison was her older brother. Trisha looked like a woman who worked on a ranch or farm for years, a hard life made even more challenging by the loss of a child and the glare of suspicion on another.

Greg Pool was the father of the second victim, Deidre Pool, and unlike Trisha, he dressed professionally in a sports coat, button-down shirt, and slacks. He was a doctor, or at least had been back then. He was the tallest of the group, with a large nose supporting black spectacles.

The Emersons, Mary and Dan, were the parents of the last victim, Maddy Emerson. As a couple, they lent credence to the notion that opposites attract. He was tall, slim, and bald, while she was short, plump, and had hair that went to the small of her back.

Parker found it odd that the group's last member, Poppy Jackson, was with the entourage. She was the wife of Matt Jackson, the soccer coach who had been the primary suspect in the investigation. Although the woman must have been in her mid-seventies, she had the look of someone much younger. Her face was immune to wrinkles, and her body was fit and tight, no doubt due to countless hours spent in a local gym. She had an intensity coming off her that Parker felt more than the others. Still, how had she come to be accepted by this group?

"I recognize all your names, and must admit I'm a bit surprised that you're against going forward with the book launch," Susan said.

"I would have thought you would welcome the publicity to shine a light on the murders, much as Penelope's book does, to urge further investigations," Trent added.

"If we thought that would happen, of course we would," Trisha said, gesturing to everyone behind her. "When Penelope first started calling people for interviews and doing her research, we had high hopes something like that might happen. But it's turned into this sideshow like something you'd see from TMZ, and now I understand that bitch tried to implicate my son in her trash book. The hell we've lived through every day and what we experienced all those years ago is being used now as entertainment. Once again, Penelope has made it all about her, and we're left dealing with the fallout."

"It's not right," a man from the back of the group shouted. The body language among the gathering was stiff, with pinched or disgusted facial expressions on more than a few faces.

"Sometimes, these things take time before you see real action. The book only came out yesterday," Trent said.

"Who are you?" Greg Pool asked.

"I'm Trent Carson. I run the publishing company that published the book."

"What about you?" Poppy directed at Parker.

Before Parker could answer, Susan spoke up. "This is Penelope's daughter."

The entire coalition stared at Parker as if they had just won a jackpot via a scratch-off lottery ticket. Parker gave the group a weak smile, but inside, her heart was racing. She stared at their curious faces and wanted to hide. A stab of panic constricted her chest, and her stomach churned. She could feel her face burn as the flush spread down her neck. Susan's revelation of her identity was precisely what she didn't want to happen.

"Well then, maybe we can appeal to you to end this sideshow," Trisha said, directing her remark at Parker.

"I'm not really part of all that," Parker offered, waving her hands back and forth in front of her waist.

"Surely you have a say in the decision?" Greg Pool said.

"Not rea—" Parker mumbled.

"Sure, she does. Everyone here does," Susan interrupted. "We welcome everyone's input. We're trying to do what's right for Penelope and the book. She worked extremely hard on writing it, and I feel we would be letting her down if we did not allow it to inform this new generation about the tragic events that happened in this town."

"From what Van says at the bookstore, the book needs no more publicity. Since the news of Penelope's suicide, the book has been flying off the shelf," Trisha said.

Parker thought she spotted the hint of a smile on Trent's face.

Poppy Jackson spoke up for the first time. "I don't have a clue why Penelope wrote this book. I've read her other novels, and I've always enjoyed them, but this book… it's just wrong."

Poppy ran her hands up and down her thighs. Mary and Dan Emerson seemed content to be there for moral support only.

"We've been against this launch since we first learned about Penelope's plan to have it here in Willow's Bane," Poppy continued. "We've written letters and emailed everyone we could think of trying to head this off, pleaded with Van until we were blue in the face not to host it, and still, the plans moved forward. Now Penelope's dead, and it still might happen. When is this nightmare going to end?"

"I remember your letter, Mrs. Jackson. You were quite passionate about your opposition to the event," Susan said. "But we had to consider all points of view."

Poppy turned her attention to Parker. "You're just interested in selling books, and we're left to relive the whole thing again. It's unimaginable."

"I couldn't care less if the book sells a single copy."

"I don't believe you," Poppy snapped back.

"Whatever. Believe what you want but I'm not here for any of that," Parker reiterated.

"Have any of you read the book?" Susan asked the group.

No one responded in the affirmative. Parker wasn't surprised, not because nobody claimed to have read the book - she was positive some of them had - but because the book had revealed that Trisha Jamesison, mother of victim number one, had been having an affair at the time of the murders with Dan Emerson, father of victim number three. Parker imagined that if either of them admitted publicly they had read the book, it would dispel the illusion of ignorance they were attempting to maintain. She doubted the two of them would be caught anywhere near one another once more people had time to read the book. Surely, someone in Willow's Bane would let it slip soon enough.

Then there was also the revelation that Hutch Jamesison's alibi was faked, which would no doubt be terrible for his mother but great news for the soccer coach, seeing that there was now another suspect.

"I can appreciate your position, all of you, but plenty of people here in Willow's Bane were excited about this launch and quite hopeful that we will reschedule it."

"We can file for an injunction to stop it," Greg Pool spat out. It did not surprise Parker to see he'd be the one to go the judicial route, given what she'd read about his legal issues in the book.

A disappointed frown appeared on Susan's face. "On what grounds, Mr. Pool? This is a public event. The bookshop invited us. What harm would it be doing?"

"It could damage more than a few reputations from the publicity. We could sue all of you. The book reveals closely guarded and humiliating secrets. We could claim emotional damages or pain/suffering, not to mention slander."

Parker was now positive that Greg Pool had read the book. Penelope had revealed in it that the man had numerous malpractice suits filed against him.

"Look, we're not against holding some sort of event to celebrate Penelope's book launch," Trisha stepped in, seeking calmer waters. "Please, just don't do it here in Willow's Bane. Now that Penelope's gone, there's no point. Surely you can see that."

Susan seemed to relent, but instead of saying anything, she looked at Trent.

"You make some good points. Listen, we won't decide this tonight and not until we speak to a few more people, but I promise we will keep your concerns at the forefront of our consideration," Trent said.

And if you buy that, I have a timeshare to sell you, Parker thought.

"Thank you for listening to us," Trisha said, then turned with everyone else to leave.

Poppy Jackson had taken a few steps to leave, then turned and pointed at Parker. "You should be ashamed of your mother."

"Get lost, KAREN," Kat snapped, springing up from her chair.

Poppy gave Kat a once-over and said, "Why don't you eat a salad once in a while?"

"Shut your mouth before I take a bite out of you, ol' hag," Kat replied, snapping her teeth.

Poppy's face turned red before she stormed off to catch up with the others.

When the group had gone, Parker gave Kat a stern look. Her friend just shrugged.

"As you can see, not everyone in Willow's Bane was thrilled about your mom's book," Susan said.

"I can see that, but I didn't appreciate how you pulled me into your disagreement and told them who I was. I've spent years distancing myself from Penelope, so I'd appreciate it if you would leave me out of it."

"You're right. I'm sorry. I wasn't thinking." Parker could see the sincerity in her eyes.

"I was surprised to see Poppy Jackson among the group. I would have thought she'd be shunned," Parker said.

Susan shrugged her shoulders. "United for a common goal, I guess, in stopping the book launch. Then again, not everyone in Willow's Bane believed her husband had anything to do with the murders."

"I guess so. You were going to point me in Willa's direction?"

"Right. Let me call her," Susan said.

Susan stepped away and left Parker and Kat in an uncomfortable silence with Trent.

"Do you publish any Anime?" Kat asked.

"Anime?"

"Yeah, Anime or Manga. *Chainsaw Man, Demon Slayer, Tokyo Ghoul,* that sort of stuff?"

Trent made a face like he had just smelled a fart. "No."

"You're missing out. Great stuff."

"What's great stuff?" Susan asked, having rejoined the group.

"You don't want to know," Trent answered.

"Well, Willa has agreed to meet with you. She is in room 128, down this hall on the left-hand side," Susan said.

"Thank you. I'm sure we'll talk again before we leave."

"That would be nice. I'm sorry again, but it's good to see you despite the circumstances."

As the two women walked away, Parker glanced at Samantha Trimble. The Podcaster was pretending to read an upside-down book.

Making their way down the hallway the agent had directed them towards, Kat started fidgeting with her phone.

"What are you doing?" Parker asked.

"It's something one of those people said," Kat replied, continuing to interact with something on her device.

"What?"

"Got it. Yep. Sure enough."

"Kat?"

"Malignant Doubt is trending on Amazon right now."

"Why is that surprising? Most of Penelope's books were best sellers."

"You remember Tanya, my writer friend? She told me that true crime doesn't sell. Also, there were no advance reviews, and no advance copies sent out, and it's a genre Penelope is not known for. Makes you wonder if it's her reputation driving all those sales or the fact that she committed suicide?"

Parker didn't have an answer, and it was just as well as the two of them stopped in front of room 128. The door was already partially ajar, kept in place by the latch on the inside that had been engaged while the door was open.

"Hello?" Parker called through the open space in the door.

"Come on in," a voice from inside the room replied. "Susan said you were coming."

The two women stepped inside, closing the latch and allowing the door to close fully behind them. Sitting at a mid-size desk typing on a laptop was a young woman in her late twenties or early thirties wearing an oversized purple LSU sweatshirt and very little else. The sweatshirt perfectly matched the purple highlights in her hair.

"Willa?" Parker asked.

"Let me just finish this thought," Willa said, still focused on whatever she was typing. Moments later, she closed the lid and turned to face them. "Hi, yes, I'm Willa. You must be Lynn?"

"I am, but you can call me Parker. This is my friend Kat."

Willa nodded at both of them, but Parker could have sworn the woman's eyes lingered longer on Kat.

"Have a seat," Willa motioned to the couch next to the desk. "Can I get either of you something to drink or a snack? Penelope always had me bring a wide variety of everything for her guests, so whatever you want, I probably have."

"No thanks," Parker replied. She half-expected Kat to request some sparkling water, but her friend remained silent as they both took a seat.

"I have to say that today has been nuts. After we found Penelope yesterday morning, it has been non-stop phone calls, texts, emails, instant messages, everything. And I'm sure Susan told you about the NDA, so I can't say anything to anyone other than to confirm it's true. Penelope Highsmith is gone."

"You were there when they found her?" Parker asked.

"Oh, sorry, no, figure of speech. It was Susan and the hotel manager who found her."

"And were you surprised? I mean, about them saying she committed suicide?"

"I hope you understand, but I must be careful with what I say, even to you. Your mom was dead-serious… oh, sorry, poor choice of words. She took her private life very seriously. If I told you something that somehow made it into the papers or magazines, or worse, online, her lawyers would come after me, not you."

"We wouldn't say anything to anyone," Parker said.

"I'm sure you wouldn't, but I can't control where the information goes once it leaves my mouth, so it's safer for me to say very little."

"I get it, but surely you can tell me if you were surprised."

Willa appeared to be considering her answer. "Yes… and no. Ever since she announced her retirement, she hadn't really been herself. She'd been relying less and less on me. Doing things by herself, which was unusual. Penelope was spending an increased amount of time on her own. I know she was keeping things from me, which never happened before. In that respect, that's why I said I wasn't surprised."

"On the other hand," Willa continued. "I know she was really looking forward to today and launching her new book, so the timing seems odd."

"Did you know she had been in touch with me recently?" Parker asked.

Willa displayed an embarrassed smile. "To be honest, I had forgotten she even had a daughter. She mentioned you once when I started working for her, but there has been nothing else since then. That's exactly what I was saying before. She was doing things and keeping them from me."

"Can you tell me what prompted her decision to retire?"

Shaking her head, Willa said, "I was as shocked as everyone. She didn't even tell me. I found out by reading it online. When I approached her about it, she said I shouldn't worry; my job was secure regardless."

The three of them sat silently for a brief moment, contemplating.

"Would you like to see her room?" Willa suddenly offered. "I guess technically everything in there is yours now, anyway. I mean, I have no idea what's laid out in her will, but you're her only heir, right?"

Parker straightened her back. "She has a sister, but I want nothing of hers, will or otherwise. Technically, no one should touch anything of hers until they read the will. I would like to see her room, though, if you don't mind."

"Sure," Willa said as she rose. "Let me slip on some sweatpants."

"We'll wait for you in the hall," Parker told her, then led Kat out the door.

A few seconds later Willa emerged from the room wearing a pair of grey sweatpants, holding a room security card in her hand. "It's a couple of rooms down the hall."

Parker and Kat followed the personal assistant to another room two doors away. After opening the lock, she stepped aside to allow Parker and Kat to enter first.

The room they walked into was vastly larger than Willa's, with a distinctly different format. A small hallway opened into a guest reception area with a small kitchen, a full tan couch with blue throw pillows, and two matching tan chairs in the front room of the suite. A couple of expensive bottles of alcohol and an ice bucket rested on the kitchen counter. A dark wooden desk and frost glass panels separated that room from the sleeping area containing a king-size bed with a navy duvet and two dark wood dressers, one of which had a wide-screen TV resting upon it. Four large suitcases still sat unopened next to the bed.

Parker noticed a stack of hardback books on the corner of the desk. She walked over and saw that they were copies of Malignant Doubt.

"She hadn't even unpacked," Parker observed.

Willa looked pained. "I usually did that for her. I planned on doing it yesterday morning while she was at breakfast."

Parker nodded. "Is anything missing?"

"The police confiscated all of her prescription medication, but other than that, it's as I remember it."

Parker picked up a book. On the cover was a picture of a small town taken from a high altitude, with a dark mass superimposed on top of the city, black veins, and blood vessels extending outward. It was a grim image. This was her first time seeing a physical copy of the book. She flipped a couple of pages and came across an illustrated representation of the actual city of Willow's Bane. It was a map of the town and surrounding areas detailing key sites linked to the murder investigation. As she studied the map, something felt wrong, or different, from what she remembered reading in the book.

"Do you mind if I take this?"

"I don't think one book would break any rules. Go ahead."

"Let me ask you something," Parker said. "Susan and the publisher referred to a chapter that was left out of this book. They said Penelope pulled it at the last minute. Do you know anything about that, or where it might be?"

Willa shook her head. "I had very little to do with anything involved with her writing. It might be on her laptop, but that's back home in her office."

"She didn't bring it with her?"

"Nope. There was no need. She wasn't writing any more books."

After taking one last look around the room, Parker led everyone back into the hallway. Once there, she turned to face Willa. "We're staying at this hotel until we figure out what really happened to Penelope, so if you think of anything that might be useful, please call me at this number?"

After typing Parker's cellphone number into her phone, Willa gave her a sober look.

"You don't think Penelope committed suicide, do you?"

"No, I don't."

"Shit. You're the first person I've heard say that out loud," Willa said, turning to gaze off into the distance.

"Hopefully, I'm not the last. Thank you for letting us see her room."

After Willa disappeared into her own room, Parker and Kat headed back towards the lobby.

"What room are we in?" Parker asked.

"330," Kat answered.

While walking to their car to retrieve their bags, a thought kept swirling around in Parker's head, and it bothered her.

Why didn't Kat didn't say a single word the entire time they were talking with Willa?

Six

"I call dibs on the bed by the window," Kat announced as they opened the door to their room. The layout was similar to the room Willa occupied on the first floor, but with double queen beds instead of a single King. Kat made a beeline for the far bed, and splayed-out spread eagle on top of it.

"What does it matter?" Parker asked, setting her travel bag on the first bed.

"I need the fresh air when I sleep," Kat's muffled voice said into the bedcovers.

"You know you can't open that window, right? It's sealed."

Kat bounced up from the bed and went to the window. After a careful examination, she said, "This is going to be a problem."

A realization struck Parker. "Is this your first time staying in a hotel?"

"I spent a night in lockup once. Does that count?"

"Oh, jeez. You've slept at my place plenty of times and never had a problem there."

"That's because you keep the windows open all the time."

"Just don't go all claustrophobic on me."

"Don't worry about me." Kat sat back on the bed, still facing the window. "So, what do you think? Did we come out here for nothing?"

Parker moved her bag aside, then sat on the bed facing Kat. "No. I'm more convinced than ever. Somebody murdered Penelope."

Kat pivoted and leaped over the bed so she could sit facing Parker. "What's convinced you?"

"Most people who experience suicidal thoughts feel lost, hopeless, overwhelmed by negative thoughts," Parker said, punctuating each word with a pointed finger. "They feel like they have nothing to look forward to. No reason to go on living. Almost everyone we've talked to mentioned how much Penelope looked forward to this launch. It makes no sense that she would deny herself that. Combine that with the assumption she planned to reveal something at the launch, and she no longer has that opportunity; being silenced is the only thing that makes sense."

"You've convinced me. But silenced by who?"

"That's the million-dollar question. And it doesn't look like the local cops will be much help, so we'll have to do this ourselves. So, who are our suspects, miss *I was a detective in my past life?*"

Kat grinned widely. "Well, her daughter, naturally, as she'll probably inherit everything."

Parker returned a fake smile. "She has an airtight alibi. Next?"

"Both Susan and that Trent guy have financial motives. The book sales have shot through the roof with Penelope's death."

"That's weak. Killing the author to goose sales is a stretch."

"Yeah, but remember, this was supposedly her last book. All of her other books will likely sell like hotcakes as well."

"True, money is a huge motivator, but I don't know. Next option."

"How about Willa?"

Parker's ears perked up. Maybe Kat would explain her behavior towards the personal assistant. "Okay. Make your case."

"We don't know how well the two of them got along, but she made it sound like Penelope wasn't easy."

"I can vouch for that."

"Maybe there was something Penelope did that sent Willa over the edge. We only have Willa's word that she would still have a job after Penelope hung up her typewriter, so maybe this was payback for how she was treated and then being kicked to the curb?"

"I can buy that more than the agent or publisher." Then, after a pause, "You didn't have much to say when we were talking with her. And she seemed to take a special interest in you."

Kat's expression remained unchanged. "How do you mean?"

"She seemed to eyeball you a lot. Maybe it was my imagination?"

"Hey, you don't think I'm worth eyeballing?" Kat asked, feigning shock.

"Totally."

"That's more like it. So, what about the group we met down in the lobby? The ones upset about the launch being here in Willow's Bane. Maybe one of them? They were pretty upset."

It was plain to see that Kat was purposefully re-directing the conversation, but Parker decided not to push it. She contemplated her response to Kat's observation. "They were, but I'm not sure."

"I can totally see Miss Tight Butt going Lizzie Borden under the right circumstances."

Parker chuckled. "Poppy Jackson? You just don't like her."

"That's true, but that doesn't mean she didn't do it. How about the podcaster? Penelope stomped all over her podcast. Resentment is a pretty good motive."

"It can be, and she seems to have a lot of anger. Anyone else?"

"Only the most obvious… the Snake River killer himself. They never caught him. It could be Hutch Jamesison. Penelope trashed his alibi, so maybe he did his sister and the others," Kat offered.

"That's a definite maybe, but why would he kill Penelope if the damage was already done? She'd already blown his alibi in the book."

"Revenge?"

"Possibly, but nobody has seen him for years, and I don't see her opening her door to a stranger."

"Good point," Kat said. "Maybe Penelope knew something about the killer she was about to reveal, something big that she didn't want to put in the book. Maybe even his identity. It can't be a coincidence she was making a huge deal about disclosing something during the book's launch. You don't need to be Sherlock Holmes to deduce those clues. As you said, somebody stopped that from happening. And then there's the whole missing chapter puzzle. I would love to get my hands on that."

"You think the killer still lives here, thirty-eight years later? If so, why did he stop after killing three girls?"

"He doesn't have to live here. It was widely publicized Penelope's launch was going to have a special reveal, so the killer may have traveled here to Willow's Bane fearing his identity was going to be revealed. Snakey could be doing his serial-killing somewhere else now? Or it could still be that Hutch dude."

"Maybe." Parker put her hands against her temple and fell backward on the bed. "Hell, it's all possible. I don't know where to begin."

Kat followed suit and fell back on her own bed. "I know where I'll start. I'll get online and start stalking social media, do a deep dive on backgrounds, the normal stuff. See if anybody is hiding a dirty little secret."

"I also want you to get into Penelope's laptop. Willa said they left it in her home office. Hopefully, she left it on and plugged in, and you can get into it. I want to find that missing chapter. Oh… and don't forget to include the sheriff on your list. Lou Webber. He was just a deputy on the force when the murders took place."

"Ten-Four."

The two of them lay there staring at the ceiling, lost in their thoughts.

"How are you holding up?" Kat asked while staring at the smoke detector.

"I'm okay."

"You sure? It was kind of rude, Susan outing you in front of all those folks."

"Yeah, that wasn't ideal. Hopefully, it won't mess anything up."

"You think anyone knows?"

"No. Penelope wouldn't have said anything. Besides, we would have heard something by now."

"I hope you're right."

The room went silent again as Parker became lost in her thoughts.

Then, after a brief pause, Kat turned her head towards Parker. "I told you what I would do. What about you?"

"I think I'll swing by the bookstore where the launch was supposed to be held in the morning and talk to the owner. I got the sense from Susan that there was more than just a professional relationship between Penelope and the owner."

"Sounds like a plan."

Another round of pondering silence passed.

"How hard would it be to cut a hole in this window?"

Parker chuckled. "Just take a couple of deep breaths and relax. You'll be fine."

Kat popped up from the bed and headed for the door. "I'm going to take a walk and get some fresh air. Wanna come?"

Parker tucked her hands underneath her head. "I'm good. Don't wander off too far."

"Transmission received," Parker heard Kat respond as the door opened. When the door didn't immediately close, Parker rose onto her elbows.

"Change your mind?" Parker called out.

Kat strolled back into the room, scrutinizing a piece of paper she was holding in her hands.

"This was pushed under the door," Kat muttered, handing the paper to Parker.

Parker took the paper and read what was written on it.

I know your secret. Go home... or so will everybody else.

Seven

Parker awoke the following morning to her cellphone's obnoxious ringtone, the unmistakable power chords of her mother's favorite song–Survivor's *Eye of the Tiger*. Looking at the time before she answered the call, the screen displayed 7:05am.

"Hello?" she said groggily.

"Lynn Highsmith?" a deep, gruff voice asked.

"It's Parker, actually, but yes. Who is this?"

"This is Sheriff Webber. I'm down in the lobby. Can you meet me?"

"Now?" Parker glanced at the window. Although she had drawn the inside curtain, Parker could see dim light peeking through. Kat groaned in the bed next to her, then rolled over to face away from Parker.

"You wanted to talk? This is the time I have. Take it or leave it."

"Give me five minutes," she replied, swinging her legs onto the floor.

Ten minutes later, she stepped out of the elevator wearing jeans, a long-sleeved T-shirt, and cross-trainers. Scanning the lobby, she spotted a man in uniform in the vestibule between the two sliding doors talking on a cell phone. As she approached the doors, the sheriff abruptly ended the call.

Sheriff Lou Webber reminded Parker of pictures she'd seen in history books of Teddy Roosevelt. He had that signature sandy brown bushy mustache that seemed to dominate his face with thick eyebrows to match. Dark sunglasses occupied the space between the two hair masses. A round belly protruded from his open jacket, and his cowboy hat sat back on his head to round out the look.

"Good morning, Sheriff Webber," Parker said when the door slid open.

"Come with me, Miss Highsmith," the sheriff said before exiting outside.

"I told you it's Parker, and where are we going?" Parker said as she trailed the man leading her towards the Ford SUV patrol car still running underneath the alcove.

"We're going for a little ride," the man said over the top of the car's hood before climbing behind the wheel.

Parker hesitated after opening the door. Despite the man being a sheriff, she recalled a true crime podcast she listened to about members of law enforcement who used their position to assault vulnerable women, and accusations of any kind against them were routinely dismissed. Although she wouldn't consider herself particularly vulnerable, the thought made her pause. No one was at the front desk, and she hadn't bothered to wake Kat and tell her where she was going. If she disappeared, nobody would know where she'd gone or who she had gone with.

"I'm not sure I'm comfortable with this."

"With what?"

"Riding off alone with you," Parker said.

The sheriff draped his arms across the steering wheel. "Lady, there is no safer place to be in this town. Now, I'm a busy man, and this is the time I have for you, so get in, or you'll have to take your chances that I might have some time later."

Parker felt a cool morning breeze on her cheeks, tossing her hair around. "Maybe I should get something warmer to wear?"

"You won't need it," the sheriff responded, starting the engine.

The patrol car was heated, and they probably wouldn't be taking long walks at this time of the morning, so she climbed into the passenger seat. As soon as she pulled her door shut, the car lurched forward.

They rode along in silence for several minutes.

"Where are you taking me?" Parker asked.

There was a long pause before the man answered. "My deputy tells me you came by our office yesterday looking for me?"

"I did. I wanted to know the status of your investigation."

The sheriff stole a quick glance at Parker. "My investigation?"

"Yes, of Penelope Highsmith's death."

"My deputy told you her death was ruled as a suicide by the coroner, didn't he? There is no investigation."

Outside the passenger window, Parker watched as the buildings became fewer and fewer, and they headed into the countryside.

"He did, but I believe that the ruling was premature. There are facts you didn't have at the time."

"Really? Such as?"

"Penelope contacted me weeks ago and told me there was important information she was going to disclose during her book launch this week that would answer a lot of questions about her past. I believe somebody killed her and made it look like a suicide so it would never come out."

"Did she tell you what the nature of this information might be?"

"Unfortunately, no. She wasn't very specific, but she made it sound like it would be dramatic."

The sheriff yanked the SUV to the left without slowing, slamming Parker up against her door. The patrol car veered off the main road and onto a side road.

"Let me understand this. You want me to re-classify your mother's death as a murder based upon vague facts that she may or may not have been in possession of about an incident you have no clue about. Do I have that straight?"

Parker glanced at the sheriff, seeing his clenched jaw and hands tightly gripping the steering wheel. She could feel the temperature of the car's interior rising. The air in the car felt thin, like the sheriff and his accusations were somehow taking up all the oxygen. Parker took a shaky breath and swallowed hard. She would not be intimidated.

"You're minimizing what I'm saying. For her to reach out to me in the first place was miraculous. We hadn't spoken in years. She tells me she's going to tell the world a secret and wants me to know this because whatever it is will explain why she treated me like crap my whole life. Somehow, this secret is connected to a book that nobody understands why she wrote— about murders that happened during her youth here in Willow's Bane three decades ago. No, I can't give you specifics, but I know she didn't take her own life before telling somebody about this mysterious revelation. It's not possible."

The patrol car tires made a loud thumping sound as they passed through a narrow wooden bridge over a large body of water. When they emerged on the other side, the sheriff pulled over to the narrow shoulder and suddenly came to a halt.

"Get out," the sheriff instructed, exiting himself.

"Wow, okay, I need a second," Parker said, as she rubbed her neck.

Parker looked out the window at the surroundings. They had stopped alongside a dirt road in the countryside. No buildings or structures were in sight other than the bridge they had just passed over. She climbed onto high grass and peered down the bank twenty feet to the water's edge. Large rocks and boulders lined the bank up and down the shore. Beams of sunlight were still low on the horizon, and the only sound was that of the running river. The water was calm and in the cool morning dew—uninviting.

The sheriff came up beside Parker, giving her chill bumps as his shadow in the early morning light consumed her. She had put herself in a strange place with a strange man, something that all women are taught not to do—case in point… three murdered girls. Parker casually moved her hand to the rear pocket of her jeans, confirming that her cell phone was still close by.

The sheriff followed Parker's gaze across the body of water. He inhaled deeply, then let the air slowly escape through his nostrils.

"This is the Snake River," he said solemnly. "It's the largest North American river that empties into the Pacific Ocean and the thirteenth longest river in the United States. It rises in western Wyoming, then flows through the Snake River Plain of southern Idaho, the rugged Hells Canyon on the Oregon–Idaho border, and the rolling Palouse Hills of Washington, emptying into the Columbia River at the Tri-Cities in the Columbia Basin of Eastern Washington."

The sheriff pointed to a spot near the base of a support for the bridge. "Right there is where we found Mikayla Jamesison. The farmer who uses this road a lot is the one who found her and called us. I was unlucky enough to arrive first. Her body had gotten hung up on a tree branch, and all you could see at first was her arm. Didn't have a stitch of clothes on her. She had been missing three days before that, and the whole town had been out looking for her. In truth, we thought she'd run off because she had a reputation for being rambunctious. But sadly, no. Her face was so badly beaten that we could only identify her by a birthmark on her upper arm. It was morning when we found her, and I lost my breakfast right where you're standing. Scrambled eggs, turkey sausage, hash browns, and two cups of coffee. Afterward, I rode with Sheriff Crane to notify her parents. That day, the course of history for Willow's Bane changed forever. April thirteenth, nineteen eighty-six."

Parker's mouth had gone dry and without knowing why, her eyes had teared up.

"We pulled two more dead girls out of this river before it was all said and done. All of them were young, starry-eyed, and innocent. Then, the killings stopped. No one knows why, but no one was complaining either, except for the parents of those girls. We didn't have any answers for them, which still eats at my gut every day. Somebody preyed upon and terrorized our peaceful little town, then faded into the ether."

"I... I don't know what to say, Sheriff."

The sheriff turned and looked directly at Parker. "Your mother's book ain't helping anything around here. Understand? All it's doing is causing more misery. It's like thawing out frozen meat that has already gone rancid. The worst period in this town's history is now plastered all over the best-seller list, and everyone is reading about it. Whoever said there's no such thing as bad publicity is full of horseshit because there certainly is."

"I get it, Sheriff, I really do. But let me ask you something. Why do you think Penelope wrote this book? And why now? I've read that she wasn't even tangentially involved in the original investigation. Nor was she friends with any of those girls."

"I didn't know your mother very well, but from what I've gathered, she was an attention-whore who got off on the limelight. The book is nothing but an embarrassing attempt to use tragic events and turn them into some kind of bloody soap opera. And now you're helping her do it."

"You spoke to her when she was researching the book, did you not? You're quoted several times in it."

The sheriff nodded. "We talked."

"Have you read any of it?"

"Why would I? I lived it. Still am."

"Then you're probably not aware that she was openly critical of the investigation that took place. She described it as sloppy, disjointed, amateurish. I mean, look how she took apart Hutch Jamesison's alibi."

The bushy mustache on the sheriff's face rose as he pursed his lips. Even though he was wearing dark sunglasses, Parker could feel the heat coming from behind his eyes.

"Are you trying to piss me off, Miss Highsmith?"

"Not any more than you are by purposefully calling me by a name you know I don't use, Sheriff. I didn't write any of that. I'm just trying to understand why Penelope did."

The sheriff's gaze returned to the river. "Yeah, well, plenty of people felt that way back then. We were out of our depth. Sheriff Crane was a good man but wasn't suited for something like that. And don't get me started on the FBI. Useless as a red light at three AM. We knew that Hutch had a volatile relationship with his sister, but his alibi seemed solid. How could we know the farmer he worked for would lie for him?"

Parker decided to take a different tact. "Is Abner Crane still living in Willow's Bane?"

"If you could call it that. He has a bad case of dementia and doesn't know which way is up some days."

"That's awful. I met the parents of the murdered girls yesterday. They weren't too keen on Penelope's book either, or the launch."

"They've been pestering me to stop it. Can't blame them."

"Seeing how many of them still lived here surprised me."

"Why? This town is settled. Despite what happened, we don't have many folks moving in or away. The people of Willow's Bane have deep roots. At least it's true for the older folks. Don't get me started on this younger generation."

"Penelope never returned to Willow's Bane after she graduated from high school. Don't you find that odd, especially since she has a sister still living here?"

"Odd is the new normal. Isn't that one of your generation's sayings? Obviously, the murders bothered her more than others because she wrote about them years later. Some people are just more sensitive than others."

Parker could use a lot of words to describe Penelope, but sensitive definitely wasn't one of them.

"We'll be releasing your mother's body later today, so I expect you to make the proper arrangements and leave Willow's Bane as soon as possible. Comprende?"

"Are you sure you want to do that, Sheriff? Her body is evidence. And I haven't changed my mind about her death. There are still a lot of unanswered questions."

"You really think we have a murderer in Willow's Bane, missy? Again? Do you know the last time we had a murder here? I'm not talking about manslaughter or anything like that. I'm talking about one person deliberately ending the life of another. Nineteen Eighty-Six, when those three girls died."

"Maybe this time you'll have better luck catching him."

The intensity behind Sheriff Weber's glare made Parker rethink her choice of the last remark.

The sheriff abruptly did an about-face and started walking toward the cruiser. Parker took one last look at the spot where Mikayla Jamesison was found, sending a shiver up her spine, then she turned and headed towards the road as well.

By the time Parker reached the police cruiser, the sheriff was already behind the wheel, and the engine roared to life. She pulled up on the door handle, but nothing happened.

The driver-side window lowered a few inches.

"Get things sorted and get out of town," the sheriff said before driving off, leaving Parker standing next to the road, staring after the disappearing vehicle.

Eight

"Tell me again because it's early, and I'm having a hard time understanding," Kat said as she turned up the heater in their rental car after noticing Parker shivering. "The sheriff drove you out to the middle of nowhere to lecture you about the bad juju Penelope's book was infecting the town with, and then he simply drove off and left you?"

Parker nodded as she took a gulp of the hot coffee Kat had grabbed from the hotel. "It was like something straight out of an old-time western. You know where the sheriff threatens the hero and tells them to get out of town or else? Just my luck that this is the West Coast during the late fall instead of Texas in the summer."

"That kind of stuff really happens? That's surreal. But why out here?"

"Where you picked me up was the spot where they found the body of the first murdered girl."

Kat shook her shoulders. "Ewwww. That sent shivers down my spine."

"Tell me about it."

"So, what are we going to do?"

Parker took another sip of coffee trying to warm herself from the inside out. Her time with the sheriff had shaken her, but it had an effect the man had not probably intended. When she arrived in

Willow's Bane, she was curious, inquisitive, and determined. Now, she was angry as well.

"Same as we had already planned. You do your computer wizardry, and I'm heading to the bookstore, but not before I take a shower that will probably drain all the hot water from the hotel. I'm not letting some backwater sheriff scare me that easily."

"That's my Parker."

Ninety minutes later, following a long shower and a call to Willa to confirm she could handle arrangements for moving Penelope's body, Parker was back in the car heading for Willow's Bane city square.

Parker was slowly discovering that her initial impressions of Willow's Bane might have been too hastily formed. A passer-by might think of the city as a sleepy, trade-oriented collection of businesses with little or no personality, a convenient rest stop on the way to somewhere more exciting. But what she observed during her drive to the city's center struck her as more of a laid-back, artsy downtown—serenely bisected by the mighty Snake River—giving off an immaculate small-town warmth. Fresh air, tree-lined streets, plenty of opportunities to use the word "quaint"—with enough culture, bars, and restaurants to keep up with the big boys. Willow's Bane had plenty to offer if you could adjust to the slower pace and were willing to explore.

Reading about the Book Ends store from its Facebook page, Parker learned it was an independent bookstore that held around 90,000 new and used books. The store had been in business for over twenty-five years, though its ownership had changed many times with it currently being run by Vanessa Sanders.

There was only parallel parking on the street where the bookshop was located, but luckily, Parker found an open spot half a block away and surprised herself by expertly executing the difficult maneuver.

Taking her time before entering, it amazed Parker that the shop, situated between a pizza place and a bank, could hold as many books as they advertised. Although she couldn't tell how deep the store went, it was only twenty-five or thirty feet wide, which, to her thinking, was very narrow. Copies of Malignant Doubt filled a display behind one of the plate-glass windows facing the street, along with an enormous sign announcing the launch event that was supposed to have taken place yesterday. Somebody taped a piece of regular notebook paper with the handwritten words TO BE RESCHEDULED on the corner.

Parker pulled open the entrance door, and a small bell rang to announce her arrival. Once inside, she immediately changed her mind about the store's capacity because the shop seemed to go back forever, and there were books and knick-knacks EVERYWHERE. There was a central aisle that seemed endless, with overflowing shelves of books on either side. Novels and paperbacks were stacked on the floor as well. The shelves appeared to be made up of a collection of different styles and designs, with no apparent decorative flow, indicating that they had been pieced together over time.

Book Ends looked as if it had been struck by a literary cyclone—and a book lover's dream.

Parker had only taken one step inside the entryway when a head peeked out from behind the stacks. The middle-aged woman looked over the top of the glasses she had perched on the end of her nose.

"Can I help you?" she asked in a high-pitched voice.

"I was hoping to talk with the owner. I'm Lynn Parker, Penelope Highsmith's daughter."

The woman's eyes grew wide, and with a tilt of her head, the glasses on her nose fell, held in suspension by a thin chain around her neck. When she stepped into the aisle, Parker could see she was tall and in excellent shape, and she wore an apron with BOOK ENDS scrolled across the front over a light blue sweater.

Before moving, the woman grabbed a walking cane leaning against the shelf and used it as she made her way to the front of the store with a noticeable limp.

"I heard you were in town and hoped you might stop by," the woman said. "I'm Vanessa Sanders, but please call me Van."

"Pleased to meet you, Van. This is quite a bookstore you have here. You should be proud."

Van glanced behind her. "I am. It's my home away from home. Once upon a time, I aspired to become an author like Penelope, but sadly, I didn't have what it took. I turned to the next best thing."

"You've succeeded in that regard. It's hard to imagine holding a book launch here, though. Could make things a bit cramped."

"Oh… there's a large open area in the back where Penelope would have been set up, and we have chairs for guests and visitors. Her agent and publisher are still considering rescheduling the whole thing." The smile that had been on Van's face disappeared. "I can't tell you how sorry I was to hear about your mom. Unfathomable."

"It truly is. How well did you know her?"

The smile returned to the bookstore owner. "Penelope and I grew up together. We were besties, you could say. But we grew apart after she moved away, and it had been some time since we talked. My dentures almost fell out of my mouth when she called and told me she wanted to hold her book launch here."

"When did you last speak to her?"

"The day she arrived. She and her personal assistant dropped in here to check the place out before they headed to the hotel. It was as if she had never left. We were finishing each other's sentences by the time she headed to the hotel."

"Did you get any sense of her frame of mind? Was she depressed?"

"No, not at all. She was her flamboyant self. That's why it's so mystifying to me. She was excited about the launch. Making last-minute adjustments and worrying over the tiniest of details."

"I imagine. I wanted to ask you, were you surprised when you found out what Malignant Doubt was about?"

"I was," Van said with a nod. "Like everyone else. I tried to get Penelope to spill the beans and tell me why she wrote it, but she wouldn't budge. Kept saying it was personal, which is surprising because I feel it's the least personal thing she's written."

"You've read it?"

Van smiled. "I've read everything of hers."

"What's your opinion?"

The expression Van adopted was something Parker would expect to see on a husband's face when his wife asks him how an unflattering dress looks on her.

"It was… different. Revealing in some respects. Gratuitous in others. There were a few perceptive observations about what life was like going through all of that back then. Overall… a solid read."

Parker frowned. "Spoken like a true critic."

Van grinned. "Fine, it wasn't my cup of tea. Are you happy?"

Parker smiled back. "I am. Penelope did unearth something interesting when she dismantled Hutch Jamesison's alibi."

Van shook her head. "I don't think Hutch did it."

"You knew him?"

"Vaguely. Mostly by reputation. He was two years older than most of us. He dropped out of school his senior year and went to work as a laborer. But he was mostly into drugs, which is why his sister, Mikayla, couldn't stand him. I can't see him beating his sister to death, much less two other girls, and leaving them all naked in the river."

"What happened to him?"

Van shrugged her shoulders. "Who knows? He left town about a couple years after the murders, and nobody has seen him since."

"When you said gratuitous before, I assume you're referring to the name-dropping of who was sleeping with whom."

"Yes. It made me feel like a peeping tom reading it. It was unneeded."

"But you went through it all with Penelope back then. Didn't you already know about those relationships since you were close with one another?"

"We were close, and some of it I knew and had just forgotten. But we didn't share everything. We both had gossip we kept to ourselves if you know what I mean. But that's my whole point. It was just gossip, and even though it was true, it didn't mean it needed to come out in Penelope's book."

Van started hobbling towards a stool behind the register. "You'll have to excuse me. I can only stand to be on my feet for so long. An old car accident that didn't heal correctly. We have chairs in the back, but I need to watch the front of the store. I could get one for you if you'd like."

"No, I'm fine. Thank you though."

"Let me know if you change your mind."

"I will. I have to say I was slightly surprised when I first arrived," Parker stated, leaning back against the counter. "The way Penelope talked about Willow's Bane in her book, you get the impression that the city has been on life support ever since the murders took place. I don't see that when I look around."

Van shook her head. "Don't be fooled. Penelope hit that one on the head. If a city can have a collective personality, a soul if you will, then Willow's Bane had theirs ripped to shreds and left cowering in the dark. Anyone who's been around since the murders would tell you the city has never recovered. If we had a billboard, it would read – Willow's Bane – Nothing to See Here. The elderly folk in town talk in terms of before SRK and after SRK."

"SRK?" Parker asked.

"Snake River killer."

"Oh. And the younger crowd?".

"Hard to explain. You would think they'd largely be unaffected by the SRK, but in some ways, the dread and shame from that period has seeped into their psyche."

"I understand that some of your fellow residents didn't care for the fact that you were hosting the book launch."

Van scrunched up her face. "There were a few detractors, but I mostly heard positive things. This is a small town, Lynn. Off the beaten path and very set in its ways. Now don't get me wrong, I understand the painful memories the book revived for those families who lost their children and that it might not be easy for them, but their discomfort shouldn't be allowed to hold a whole town hostage."

"Sheriff Webber is one of them. He wasn't a Penelope fan, or a fan of me for that matter."

"The man's a relic. Pay him no mind. But I'm curious about your situation. I understood that you and your mom weren't on the best of terms."

"That's putting it mildly."

"And yet, here you are."

Parker grinned awkwardly. "I can't believe Penelope took her own life, and I'm going to prove it."

"That's what all these questions are about? You think there's a murderer in Willow's Bane? Again?"

"That's funny, the sheriff said almost the same thing. Did Penelope talk to you about what she would say at her book launch?"

"No, sorry." She shook her head, her hair swaying with the motion. "I figured it would be less about the book and more about her retirement. A sappy farewell speech, that type of thing."

"Penelope told me she was going to reveal a secret at that launch that she'd been keeping for years, and it was going to be staggering. I'm convinced somebody made sure that didn't happen."

Van's eyes grew wide. "My god, Lynn. Have you told Sheriff Webber about this?"

Parker chuckled. "I did. He wasn't interested."

"Maybe you could try the State Pol—"

A deafening crash of shattering glass startled both women. Van cried out and her hand went to her chest. Parker's reflexes caused her to pivot towards the noise, just in time to see the last piece of a front window collapse to the ground. It was the window where the Malignant Doubt book display had been set up. As she cautiously approached the mayhem, her breathing slowly returning to normal, she could make out a red brick with the word LIAR printed in white paint lying among the windows' ruins.

Realizing what had happened, Parker sprinted out the front door and looked up and down the street, but no one was there.

When she returned inside, Van was staring disbelievingly at her damaged window.

"A few detractors, huh?" Parker said.

Nine

"This town is too much," Kat said, sitting cross-legged in the middle of her bed. "First, the sheriff leaves you to die in the middle of nowhere, and now someone tries to kill you with a brick. And they say LA is going to hell."

"I don't believe my life was in danger either of those times," Parker replied, sitting at the desk, using her phone to search for retirement homes.

"But it could be," Kat pointed out. "We're searching for a murderer. Who's to say he won't come after you?"

Parker didn't bother to look up from her phone. "Not going to happen."

"You only say that because you're an optimist. You're a glass-half-full type of girl and refuse to look at anything negatively."

"Yeah, and what are you?"

"I'm a Neoist."

Parker paused, her attention piqued, and looked at Kat. "A what?"

"A Neoist. There is no spoon. You know, from The Matrix."

Parker shook her head and returned to her scrolling.

"What's your next move?" Kat asked.

"I'm trying to find out where the old sheriff is staying so I can talk to him. It's a long shot, but maybe he'll remember something useful about the murders. Penelope didn't quote him as a source in her book."

"The guy who has dementia, according to the current sheriff?"

"That's the one."

"That's not a long shot. That's a hope and a prayer, and you're not religious."

"But I am an optimist, remember? I'm going to text Van. Maybe she knows."

"What did you think of Van, by the way?"

"She was nice. Resilient. She didn't bat an eye after her window was smashed. Just picked up the phone and called someone to come seal it until they could replace it. I'd still add her to the list of people you're doing background checks on. She was tight with Penelope once upon a time and there might be more she's not saying."

"Ten-Four," Kat said, laying back on the bed.

"How are you coming on those background checks, anyway?"

"Oh… I'm about to start."

Parker turned her attention towards her friend. "What have you been doing while I was gone?"

"I fell back to sleep. I gotta get my nine hours, and you interrupted that this morning with your rescue call."

"Okay, but please jump on that right away. It could lead me—
"

The ringing of the hotel room phone startled both women, interrupting their conversation. Parker glanced at Kat, who shrugged her shoulders.

"Hello?" Parker asked after picking up the handset.

"Is this Penelope Highsmith's daughter?" a young female voice asked.

"Who is this?"

"My name is Samantha Trimble. I host a true-crime podcast investigating the unsolved murders in Lewiston."

Parker remembered the young woman who paid particular attention to them in the lobby when they arrived. Though the woman's voice was youthful, Parker thought she detected an abrasive edge in the tone. "I've heard of it. What can I do for you, Samantha?"

"I was wondering if we could talk?"

"What is it you think we would have to talk about?" Parker said.

"For one thing, there were details your mother left out of her book. Wouldn't you like to know what they were?"

"I'm confused. I thought your investigation centered on the murders in Lewiston, not Willow's Bane."

"The murders were linked."

"Not according to the police reports."

"Listen, do you want to talk or not?" Samantha replied, sounding impatient.

Parker hesitated before answering. On the one hand, she didn't have time to waste with an attention-seeking podcaster with a poor attitude, but if the woman really did have information that could shed new light on things, it would be foolish to pass that by.

"Okay, sure. Where at?"

"Do you know where the Willow's Bane library is?"

"I can find it."

"Meet me there in the parking lot in fifteen minutes. I'll be in a blue Honda Civic."

The line went dead, leaving Parker to stare at the handset. "Looks like I'm going to meet the angry podcaster."

"Want me to come with you?" Kat asked.

"No, just get going on those background checks."

Kat pouted and groaned. "Ugh. Ten-Four."

Parker pulled her jacket off the back of the chair and slipped it on. "I'll text you when I'm finished. It's getting close to lunchtime. We can figure out somewhere to grab a bite."

"Sounds like a plan."

Fifteen minutes later, with the help of her phone's GPS, Parker pulled into the small parking lot of Willow's Bane Public Library. The lot contained only four cars, one of which was a blue

Honda Civic parked in the handicap spot near the front of the building. Parker noted the Honda did indeed have a handicapped license plate.

Parker pulled into the spot next to the podcaster's. A stiff burst of chilly wind met her as she exited her car, briefly taking her breath away. All the trees that outlined the lot swayed with the rushing air. The gust swirled Parker's hair around, and blocked her view of the car for a second before she pushed it out of her face. She could feel her cheeks flushing as she opened the Honda's passenger door and slipped inside.

Seeing Samantha Trimble up close caused Parker to update her earlier impression of the woman. Although she was more slender and more ashen than she first thought, what stood out now were the dramatically thick eyeglasses she was wearing. The glasses exaggerated her hazel eyes, making them look four times bigger than they were, and dominated her mousy face. Samantha sat hunched over the steering wheel as she eyed Parker.

"I have 20/200 vision. It's on the border of still being able to drive but bad enough to qualify for a handicap license. Some people call that a perk, but I don't. Just thought I'd get that out of the way."

"Is it progressive?"

"Yes. The doctors predict I'll be totally blind in another five to six years."

Parker winced with sympathy. "I'm sorry."

Samantha shrugged. "It is what it is. I made peace with it a long time ago."

"Is that why you've chosen podcasting as the medium to tell your stories?"

"In a way. I believe podcasting can be much more than discussing a particular topic or current event. I like to think that mine is different. I have a partner who maintains a website for me with links and notes, guest biographies, transcripts, additional resources, and allows for listener commentary."

"That's impressive. You're not recording me now, are you?"

Samantha scowled. "I'm not some low-rent hack who'd resort to doing things like that. I have standards. If I wanted to record you, I'd ask your permission first."

"Sorry, just being careful. So, why am I here?"

"That's a good question. Why ARE YOU here? Here in Willow's Bane, I mean. I've done my research. You haven't been in the same location as your mother for over eighteen years. I realize she's dead and all that, but why come to Willow's Bane?"

Parker frowned. "I didn't come out here to educate you about the complicated relationship I have… or had… with Penelope. You said on the phone that there is a connection between the Snake River murders and the killings in Lewiston. How? And why are you the only one saying that?"

Samantha dipped her head and shook it from side to side, her brown hair swaying and obscuring her face. "They never gave the deaths in Lewiston a cool moniker… you know… like the Snake River murders. I guess our newspaper wasn't ingenious enough to come up with something clever, or maybe they felt names like that were cheap stunts that proper journalists avoided like the plague. Better yet, maybe nobody cared enough to give them a name. Ambivalence on display. But not here in Willow's Bane. Oh no, they cared so much that the whole town fell apart. At least that's if you believe what Penelope wrote in her book. What utter bullshit."

Parker was sensing more of the pent-up anger the young woman was carrying inside. Her words were coming in rapid-fire succession while she stared out the windshield. Her hands gripped each other in her lap. Parker would have to tread carefully if she hoped to get anything other than bitter assertions from her.

"Why the Lewiston murders?" Parker asked.

Samantha looked surprised by the question.

"Why not a podcast about the Snake River killer?" Parker continued. "I've been told you've been at this for much longer than Penelope, so why did you focus on what happened in Lewiston instead of Willow's Bane?"

"How much do you know about what happened in Lewiston?"

"Only what I read in Penelope's book. The first murder was in early 1984, a young man whose body they found dismembered in trash bags, left in a public dump. The next was a woman, also young. The police discovered her body in a ditch just outside of town. She had been stabbed. She had gone missing after seeing a movie with her friends and walked home alone. They found the last victim the following year, in March. A twenty-one-year-old married woman who had been strangled. They found her body floating in a lake."

"There were also two other disappearances in that time span, one man and one woman, both never officially tied to the other murders, but they were never located and it's a fair bet they were also victims," Samantha added.

"I remember. But all those victims, including the disappearances, were twenty-one-year-old adults or older, of different sexes, killed in three different ways, and almost eighteen months before the Willow's Bane murders. The police and FBI couldn't even say for sure that the Lewiston murders were all committed by the same person, so it was easy to see how they determined that the Snake River killer was someone different. I think it's time you answered my question. Why your fascination with the Lewiston murders?"

Samantha's expression hardened. "The last victim, the one found in the lake, was Lisa Keller. She was my grandmother."

That took Parker by surprise. "Your grandmother?"

Samantha nodded. "When Lisa was killed, she had a three-year-old daughter at home, Becky, my mother. My grandfather took my mother and moved to Portland afterward, where she's been ever since. Last year, following my graduation from college, my mother finally told me about our family history. I had never been curious before that. After she told me what happened, I decided to use the podcast I developed as a hobby in school to find out what really happened to my grandmother. And I was slowly making progress too, that is until hurricane Penelope came along."

"How did Penelope's book interfere with your podcast?"

"Because nobody would talk to me anymore. They only wanted to talk to the famous author and didn't have time for my piddly podcast."

Despite Samantha's prickly manner, Parker now felt bad for the woman. Not only had she been deprived of the opportunity of experiencing the love of a close relative, but Penelope had come along and sucked all the air away from the fire she was trying to light beneath the stagnant investigation.

"Listen, I'm sorry for that, but I'm not sure what you want me to say or do. If you've really done your research, you'd already know I had nothing to do with Penelope or her book. But that's why you wanted to talk with me, isn't it? You wanted to know if I came to Willow's Bane to pick up where Penelope left off, help promote the book, and continue pulling interest away from your investigation. That's why you called me."

Samantha raised her chin. "And you came, didn't you? I dangled a few mysterious facts, and here you are."

"But not for the reason you think."

"Really? Then why are you here?"

Parker considered her answer, chewing on the inside of her cheek. Now that she better understood Sam's podcast motivation, that it was personal and not some pathetic attention-grabbing publicity stunt, being more open and truthful seemed like less of a risk.

"I'm here because I don't believe Penelope killed herself." Parker paused before continuing, watching Samantha for her reaction. "I want to make sure someone in this town is asking the right questions."

Samantha's eyebrows rose beyond the top of her eyeglasses.

"My turn," Parker stated. "Why are you here in Willow's Bane, and what details were left out of Penelope's book?"

Samantha's demeanor appeared to soften. "I came to hear what Penelope was going to say at her book launch. Big revelations are what I was told to expect, and I hoped that might include something about Lewiston. I thought maybe what she had to say would help uncover the link between the two cases or at least provide fresh evidence."

"What makes you think they're linked?"

"Why do you care, if you have nothing to do with Penelope's book?"

"Because I think her book is the reason she's dead, and the more I know about it, or anything to do with it, the better chances I have of figuring out who killed her. You said you had something to tell me, so let's hear it."

Samantha remained silent for several seconds before responding. "There are two things I've uncovered that I've yet to broadcast on my podcast, both of which never made it into the papers and I'm certain were never passed along to the Willow's Bane investigators. They also were not in Malignant Doubt. The first was that when my grandmother's body was found in that lake, she had no clothes on."

That detail piqued Parker's interest. The Snake River Killer left all three of his victims bare. Parker mulled over this new piece of information. Could this have something to do with Penelope's announcement?

"And the second, the Lewiston police had a suspect they talked to who had connections to Willow's Bane."

Samantha sat back and crossed her arms, a smirk slowly spreading across her face.

"But they obviously never charged him," Parker said.

The gloat on Samantha's face faded. "No, but much like the soccer coach here in Willow's Bane, he was never completely cleared."

"What's his name?"

"I'm not going to tell you that."

"Why not?"

"Because it's true that I asked you to meet with me because I wanted to find out what your role was in Penelope's sideshow and see if you knew anything about what she was going to announce. You don't, so there's no upside in telling you his name. He's long dead now, anyway. He couldn't have hurt Penelope."

Parker briefly considered offering to work together with the podcaster to investigate both sets of murders but quickly quashed that thought. It was a complication she didn't need. Their task was already complicated enough.

"That's fair," Parker said, opening her car door. "Thanks for the info, and best of luck with your podcast, Samantha."

"You can call me Sam," she said as Parker exited the car. "Can I give you a bit of advice?"

Lowering her head to peer back in the car, Parker said, "Sure."

"I'd avoid the sheriff here in Willow's Bane if you can. He's a piece of work."

Now she tells me, Parker thought as she pushed the door shut.

TWIST

Ten

When Parker checked her phone upon returning to her car, she found that the bookshop owner, Van, had texted the address where retired sheriff Abner Crane was residing. After sending Kat an update informing her of where she was heading next, she loaded the address into her phone's GPS.

Fifteen minutes later, Parker arrived in front of Tranquility Assisted Living. The main parking lot in front of the facility appeared to be full, but there were a few open spots in the overflow lot across the street. Parker thought the assisted living business must be booming in Willow's Bane. She parked the rental car and made her way across the walkway to the main entrance.

The outer building appeared modern. Glancing at a map of the property just inside the entrance, Parker could see that several detached buildings were used for numerous activities, along with senior apartments scattered across the multi-acre spread. Off to the left of the reception lobby was an area that looked like a combination of a visitor's lounge and activity center. The room was filled with a multitude of people, both young and old, who conversed animatedly and busied themselves with craftwork.

Parker stepped up to the reception desk and was greeted by a smiling woman in a white nurse's outfit. Parker thought how the look seemed dated, considering medical scrubs was usually the preferred way to dress nowadays.

"Can I help you?"

"Yes, I'm here to visit Abner Crane, if that's possible?"

The woman keyed the name into her computer. "It looks like Mr. Crane is in our Memory Care unit. Have you visited with him before?"

"I have not."

"Are you a relative?"

"No. Is that a problem?"

"Not at all. They cleared Mr. Crane for all visitors. We just like to record these things. It shows that Mr. Crane is due for his lunch in thirty minutes. Will that be enough time? Otherwise, you'll have to come back after he's eaten."

"Thirty minutes will be plenty."

"Perfect. Your name?"

"Lynn Parker."

The woman logged Parker's name into the computer. "All set. If you follow this hallway behind me and take the first right you come to, it will be room 1515. You'll hear three tones when lunch is about to be served, which will be your cue to exit. Please be prompt. Got it?"

"Got it. Thank you."

"My pleasure."

Following the receptionist's directions, Parker made her way down the noticeably clean hallway. She smiled at everyone she passed, and they smiled back at her. She had been told several horror stories about nursing homes by friends, but this one seemed to be on the other end of the spectrum.

Stopping in front of the door with a plaque reading 1515, she hesitated. Taking one deep breath, she knocked.

"It's open," a soft, raspy voice informed her.

The door opened into a clutter-free living area with a leather couch, a cloth recliner, a coffee table, and a big-screen television. A talk show was being displayed on the television, but the sound was muted. The recliner was laid back, facing away from the door, and Parker could see a man's loafers on the footrest.

"You'll have to come on in so I can see you," the raspy voice said. "I'm too lazy to get up."

Parker entered the room and took a spot in front of the couch. In the recliner was an old man weighing no more than a hundred pounds, his clothes draped like they'd been made for a much larger person.

"Do I know you?" the man asked, his blue eyes searching her face.

"No, sir. My name is Parker."

The man frowned. "Is that a first name or last name?"

"It's my last name, but everybody just calls me that."

"Don't recall any Parker's, but I don't remember much of anything these days. My name is Abner. You sure are pretty." A flirtatious grin spread across his face.

Parker's cheeks flushed at his compliment. "Thank you."

"Take a load off. I apologize in advance if I drift off while we're talking. I assure you it won't be because the conversation isn't interesting, though that remains to be seen. It's just that my batteries don't hold a charge for very long these days."

Parker smiled as she lowered herself onto the couch.

"What did you say your name was again?"

"Parker."

"Don't know any Parker's, I think, but I don't recall much of anything these days. Have I told you how pretty you are yet?"

Parker laughed. "Yes, sir, you have."

"Well, you're pretty enough to hear it twice." Abner winked. "What were we talking about?"

"I just arrived. I was hoping you might answer some questions about your time serving as Willow's Bane sheriff?"

"I was the sheriff?"

Parker's shoulders sagged.

The retired sheriff broke out with a wide smile. "I'm just joshing ya. I can't remember what I had for breakfast, but give me a case number, and I can recite the facts backward and forward. What do you want to know about?"

"The Snake River murders."

Abner's smile evaporated. "That's one I really wish I could forget. Wouldn't you rather hear about the time I arrested a streaker who had no arms? Wanna know how I handcuffed him?"

"Sir, I really need to know everything you can remember about those three murders. It's important."

Abner went silent and seemed to shrink in his chair.

"Why would a pretty thing like you want to know about something so ugly as that?"

"I'm writing a book about it." Parker took comfort in the fact that it was partially true.

"That was a dark time." The retired sheriff turned his head away. "I never felt so helpless. Those poor families."

"Is there anything you can recall about that time that never made it into the official reports? Anything at all, no matter how small."

Abner remained silent and continued looking towards the other side of the room, unwilling to look at his visitor. His obvious discomfort brought a twinge of guilt to her stomach.

"I know this isn't pleasant to think about, but I —"

"We found the bodies, but we never found where they were killed," Abner suddenly said. "That bothered me."

"Was there anyone you suspected? Maybe it was a gut feeling, but you had nothing to justify questioning that person formally?"

The ex-sheriff seemed to focus on the muted television.

"What was your impression of Hutch Jamesison?"

That brought Abner back from where his mind had wandered off to. "Hutch? Dealt drugs, but harmless otherwise. Galled me, the way he was always with younger girls. But he was pretty broken up when his sister went missing. He's not what bothered me, though. It was something else." Then, after a pause. "I can't stand daytime television, but I leave the TV on without the sound because it makes me feel like things are happening around me. I worry it's running up the electric bill, but the nurse told me these newfangled TVs hardly use any juice."

"That's true. You were telling me about the one thing that bothered you about your time working on the Snake River murders."

"I was?"

"Yes, sir."

Abner shook his head slowly, but then his eyebrows rose. "There was something."

Parker looked at her phone. Time for the lunch bell was approaching. Looking back at Abner, she saw that his eyes had closed, and he was breathing heavier.

"Shit," she whispered. Should she wake him up? Was she so desperate that she would disturb a dementia patient's badly needed rest?

After a couple of agonizing minutes, Abner's eyes popped open.

"Hello," Abner said.

"Hi."

"Do I know you?"

"My name is Parker, and we were talking about your time as sheriff and the Snake River murders."

"Don't recall any Parker's, but I don't remember much of anything these days."

Three tones sounded over the internal speaker system.

Parker began talking faster. "You were telling me there was something about the murders that stood out to you. Do you remember what that is?"

"I fell asleep while we were talking, didn't I?"

"Yes, sir, but that's okay. I really need to know what you remembered about the murders."

A knock came at the door just before it swung open to reveal a different nurse. She gave Parker a stern look.

"I believe you were told at the front desk you needed to depart when the lunch tones sounded?"

Parker held up her index finger. "I just need a couple more minutes."

The nurse crossed her arms. "We run on a tight schedule here. It's best for our residents. Structure and consistency."

Parker opened her mouth to protest further, then thought better of it. She nodded her head as she stood up. "I understand. I'm sorry. I'm going now." She looked down at Abner and smiled. "It was nice talking to you, Mr. Crane."

"You as well. I'm sorry, I don't recall your name."

"It's Parker," she said, then headed for the door. She offered the perturbed nurse an awkward smile and was almost in the hallway when Abner called out to her.

"Parker?" came his strained, raspy voice.

Parker darted back to Abner's side, drawing a loud huff from the nurse.

"What is it, Mr. Crane?"

Abner looked deep into Parker's eyes. "There was a fourth. But it was different somehow. But I think... maybe... I'm not supposed to be telling anyone that."

"Who told you to keep that a secret?"

Abner narrowed his eyes, then looked at the nurse. "I'm hungry, Stella."

"We're headed to the cafeteria right now," the nurse replied, giving Parker another look.

"Thank you, Abner," Parker said, then strolled confidently out of the room and down the hall.

When she was back outside, squinting against the midday sun, she pulled out her phone and dialed Kat.

"What up, Parker?" Kat answered.

"I think I got us our first real clue, though I'm unsure what to do with it."

"Spill girl."

"Mr. Crane told me he remembers feeling that there was a fourth murder, but it differed from the others, but he doesn't remember how or why. There was nothing like that in Penelope's book. He also let slip that he was supposed to keep it a secret."

"Ohhhhhh... mysterious."

"He said I was pretty. Twice."

"So, he obviously hasn't lost any of his observational skills."

Parker rolled her eyes. "Obviously."

"So, where are we going to eat? I'm starving."

Parker began walking. "You want fast food or sit down?"

"Definitely sit down. I want to be spoiled. I found out some interesting stuff myself."

Parker paused at the crosswalk, looked in both directions, then kept walking.

"Tell me."

"Not until I see a thick, juicy T-Bone in front of me."

"You realize we don't have unlimited funds to waste—"

Screeching tires in close proximity froze Parker in her place. In that split second she worried she hadn't checked the traffic before stepping onto the road, but she was positive she had. She perceived a flash of blue out of the corner of her eye, rushing at her. Before she had time to process what was happening, her instincts took over and she dove forward and rolled. The dark blue Econoline van missed her by mere inches, continuing down the street without slowing, then disappearing around a corner, tires squealing yet again.

Kat's voice echoed from the phone lying in the middle of the road.

"Parker? Parker? What's happening? PARKER!"

Eleven

Parker sat perched on the curb while one of the kind nurses from Tranquility tended to the scrape above her right eye. The nurse was about to apply a band-aid when a gray Kia came racing down the street and screeched to a halt in front of them. Parker was surprised to see Kat leap out of the car, leaving it running in the middle of the road. Her friend rushed up to her, panicked.

"Oh god, Parker, are you alright? What happened?" Kat gasped.

"Some nut job almost ran me over," Parker answered, flinching when the nurse pressed the band-aid into place. "A blue van. I'm pretty sure it was deliberate. I barely got out of its way."

"Our town has some pretty reckless drivers," the nurse said as she closed her first aid kit. "You're good to go, but if you feel a headache coming on, you should probably go to the hospital to have yourself thoroughly checked."

"Thank you," Parker said, smiling.

After the nurse walked away, Kat plopped down next to Parker and put her face in her hands. "I freaked out when you didn't answer me. I broke out in a cold sweat and started shaking on the way here. Please, don't do that to me again."

"I promise," Parker said, then looked at the Kia still running on the road. "Whose car is that?"

"Did you know this friggin' town doesn't have Uber or Lyft or anything like that? It's like we're back in the ice age."

"Kat, whose car is that?"

Kat glanced uncomfortably at the car with a shamefaced expression. "I'm not really sure."

Parker glanced around to make sure no one was within hearing distance. A pair of bystanders still lingered in front of the Assisted Living center, talking amongst themselves but well out of earshot.

"Did you steal it?"

Kat refused to meet Parker's unbelieving stare. "I borrowed it."

"Did you have permission to **borrow it**?"

"Not technically," Kat responded, then looked at Parker pleadingly. "But how else was I gonna get here? It was an emergency."

"So, you've graduated from cybercrime to car theft now?"

"I've already said it was an emergency, and besides, that car deserves to get stolen. Kia made that model ridiculously easy to boost."

"Oh, Kat. You can't be doing this. Not here, not now." Parker slowly rose from the curb, her body still aching from her brush with death. "We are going to return it right now and pray that the owner hasn't noticed it was missing. Where's my phone?"

The two women scanned the surrounding area.

"Uh-oh," Kat whispered.

Parker followed Kat's gaze to the ground beneath the Kia and spotted her crushed phone.

"Perfect."

"Didn't you say that you were ready for an upgrade? I'll buy you a new phone," Kat offered.

"With what money?"

"Can you loan me some until we get back to LA?"

Parker turned to face Kat straight on. The expression as she spoke left no doubt about her mood.

"You will climb into that car and follow me back to the hotel. You will not exceed the speed limit. You will not change lanes unless I do. When we get there, you will put the car back where you found it, walk away calmly, and climb in with me. Do you understand me?"

"I was worried about you, Parker."

"Do you understand?"

Kat nodded her understanding.

Parker marched over to the Kia, scooped up her damaged phone, then reversed direction and walked past Kat without looking at her.

"Let's go."

The return to the hotel turned out to be uneventful. Once they arrived, Parker chewed on her cheek as she watched Kat pull the Kia into a vacant spot at the rear of the building, nonchalantly exit the car, then climb into their rental car. Parker squeezed the steering wheel as she resisted the urge to look around to see if they were spotted as she drove off.

The two remained silent while they traveled south for two blocks and pulled into the parking lot of a popular steakhouse chain. Parker entered the restaurant and flashed the greeter a signal showing they desired seating for two, and the greeter immediately ushered them to a booth near the rear of a semi-dark room. The lunchtime crowd was sparse, and their waitress appeared next to their table almost at once.

"Can we have a couple of waters? And we'll need a few minutes before we order," Parker told the young waitress, ignoring the menu altogether.

When the waitress disappeared, Parker leveled her gaze at Kat seated across from her.

"Listen, I get it. I really do. You were worried about me, and I really appreciate that concern, but we're walking on eggshells here and can't afford to draw attention to ourselves. You need to really think about the things you do and say. I know that's not always easy for you."

"Do you want me to go back to LA?" Kat asked, drawing circles on the table with her finger.

"No," Parker answered, surprising herself. "We're in this together, and I need your help. Just be more careful, please."

Kat's youthful smile returned. "I can do that. What did the podcaster have to say?"

"Not a lot. Turns out she's related to one of the victims in Lewiston. She told me that the Lewiston police had a suspect with ties to Willow's Bane, so at some point, I'll probably need to visit Lewiston."

"How far is that from here?"

"I think the drive is a touch under two hours."

"Cool. Do you want to hear what I found now?"

Parker gestured at their waitress, who was standing at a nearby vestibule. "Not until after we order. I'm starving. Almost getting killed really amps up the appetite."

After the waitress took their orders, which at one point drew a grin from Parker when she heard her friend request a side salad—something she never did, Kat pulled out her phone and accessed the notes app.

"This is the dirt I've dug up so far. I'll start with Penelope's agent, Susan Reynolds. She's got some serious money probs. Maybe she's a wonderful agent, but she's a dweeb when it comes to investing. Her portfolio took a bath last year. I'm talking about a Chernobyl-level meltdown. She put her money into a high-yield, high-risk merger that went south. She's divorced and on her own, so there's no knight in shining armor coming to bail her out. It's my guess that she'll probably lose her house in a couple of months if she doesn't find a golden spoon, and the book sales from Penelope's book might fit the bill."

"That's interesting, and it makes your theory about her killing Penelope to boost book sales more believable. Desperation is a powerful motivator that can lead to rash behavior."

"I know, right? I could probably pitch a series to Netflix or Prime Video based on my life. We could call it The Reincarnated Detective," Kat said flippantly.

Parker laughed, shaking her head. "How about we just concentrate on finding out who killed Penelope first, okay?"

"Oh, sure."

"Anything else?"

"Loads." Kat returned to her phone. "The publisher, Trent Carson, wasn't as willing to publish Penelope's book as he let on. In fact, she had to blackmail him into it."

"What?"

"I found communications between Susan Reynolds and Trent, and he turned down the book several times. Then I unearthed a deleted email on the Monolith Publishing server sent to Trent directly from Penelope, and in it she threatened to expose a sexual harassment complaint that was put into Anne Frank mode if he didn't agree to publish Malignant Doubt."

"What mode?" Parker said, puzzled.

"He swept it under the rug," Kat said, making a sweeping motion with her hand. "Hid it from everyone. Of course, I found it. Apparently, he came on too strong with one of his assistants, and when she pushed back, he threatened her paycheck. Total scum bucket material. Paid her a boatload of money to make it go away."

"That could be really damaging for him, especially in this day and age. But I don't see how that's a motive for murder. Especially since he went ahead and published the book," Parker sighed.

"Check it. What if Trent's harassment complaint was the thing Penelope was going to reveal at the launch? A MeToo moment. Maybe Trent wasn't willing to take the chance?"

"It's a stretch but keep going. Anything else?"

Kat hesitated, her lips drawn in tight, but when she opened her mouth to speak, the waitress appeared with their food. After the waitress distributed all the plates and retreated, Parker twisted her fork to ensnare some pasta noodles and looked at Kat.

"You were going to say something else?"

Kat paused as she was cutting into her steak. "Oh, yeah. I found out something about Penelope's assistant as well."

Parker's ears perked up. "Do tell."

Kat moaned after she put the cut of meat into her mouth. "Willa has been in contact with a lawyer. Someone from down in our area, LA. They started emailing back and forth about the same time Penelope made her early-retirement announcement. I'm thinking she's looking for a way out of her NDA. And that's not all. She's also been in touch with a Hollywood agent who represents people in the movie biz."

"She wants to pitch them a tell-all script about Penelope's life." Parker leaned back in her chair, mulling over this latest bit of information.

Kat tapped her forefinger to her nose.

"And ending that movie with a tearful suicide instead of Penelope living her life out in relative obscurity would definitely be more appealing, and time efficient."

"Definitely."

"Let's not forget that she's also the suspect with the best opportunity to make it happen."

Kat swallowed a mouthful of mashed potatoes. "When do we cuff her?"

"Slow down, Columbo. We're a long way from having any actual proof."

"I wonder if the hotel keeps track of key card swipes? If she used her key to get into Penelope's room late at night, that could be proof."

"Hotels usually assign and track key cards to rooms, not people. Besides, Willa could have knocked and Penelope let her in. Same could be true for Susan, Trent, or just about anyone. The CCTV footage would help."

"They will not give it to us schmoes. And before you ask, I checked. They didn't network their closed-circuit system, so I couldn't hack it."

"Damn it."

The two of them ate in silence for a while until Kat noisily dropped her knife and fork on her plate. She rubbed her belly.

"Are we seriously not going to talk about the fact that someone legitimately tried to kill you?"

"I'm trying not to think about it," Parker said. She couldn't allow her brain to drift in that direction. She needed to focus.

"I can tell. I told you something like this would happen. Doesn't it give you the heebie-jeebies, knowing that I could be planning two funerals right now?"

"Like you could even plan one funeral."

Kat tilted her head to the side and scowled.

"Listen, I'm fine," Parker said. That was a lie, but she had to push that aside right now to stay focused on what they were there for. She could curl up in bed with a pillow later. "In fact, I'm more determined than ever now. You know why?"

Kat shook her head, confused.

"It means that we were right about coming here and about somebody murdering Penelope. I'm making that person nervous."

"They're not the only ones. I don't want you to get hurt."

Parker wrinkled her brow. "We're doing this for her."

"I know. But would she want you to get yourself killed trying to force out the truth?"

"Nobody is getting killed."

"I hope so because in stories like this, it's always the sidekick who gets taken out." Kat's eyes suddenly grew big, and she looked down at the sweat-shirt she was wearing. "Oh shit, I'm wearing red."

"So?"

"It's always the crew members wearing red uniforms in Star Trek who bite the dust. I'm doomed."

Parker chuckled. "Finish your food. We got things to do."

"Such as?"

"Well, you've got to get back in front of your laptop and do more digging, and I also want you to go back through Penelope's book, specifically the part concerning the forensic evidence. Maybe it can tell us something about what Abner Crane was talking about."

Kat scrunched up her face as if she had bitten into a lemon. "Ugh. You know, I don't enjoy reading about that type of stuff.

Blood splatter patterns, puncture wound depth, lividity, bodily fluids. All that stuff gives me the creeps."

"How can you ever become the *Reincarnated Detective* if you can't stomach analyzing evidence? It's like crime investigation 101."

Kat seemed to consider this. Nodding, she said, "I guess you're right. Transmission accepted. What about you?"

"I think I'll pay a visit to Matt Jackson."

"Who's Matt Jackson?"

"He was the high school soccer coach in 1986."

"Why him?"

"If I'm going to re-investigate the murders, then there's no better starting place than the prime suspect."

Twelve

Matt Jackson and his wife, Poppy, lived on the outskirts of the city in a closed subdivision. Their medium-sized home, like many others in the area, was on a small lot with a compact lawn in front and back. What set the Jackson's house apart was the lack of anything to enhance the curb appeal, such as decorative adornments, trimmed bushes, colorful flowers, or other landscaping methods. The front of the house was as nondescript and uninviting as they come. If it weren't for the Toyota in the drive, it might even seem uninhabited. To Parker, the Jackson's home accomplished exactly what she was trying to do herself, not attract attention.

From Penelope's book, Parker knew Matt was no longer a teacher and had turned to day-trading stocks, working from an office in his home. Even though the school district stood behind him during the murder investigations, they mutually agreed before the start of the following school year that it would be in everyone's best interest to part ways. That left Matt searching for alternate ways to earn a living, even though Poppy's job as the HR manager at one of the local plants brought home a decent salary. Matt fell back on his mathematics degree and part-time hobby of buying and selling stocks to become a day trader, eventually hooking up with a large hedge fund that gave him access to lucrative amounts of capital and leverage.

The Jacksons never had any children. They didn't take part in any community groups, local activities, nor were they registered to vote. Parker had to give Penelope credit; the woman knew how to do her research.

Parker brought her car to a halt next to the Toyota and, after exiting, looked to the south. Dark clouds were gathering on the horizon, and she could tell from the smell in the air that rain was heading her way.

In a few hurried steps, she stood at the landing just as drops fell around her. She was about to push the button on the video doorbell when her phone rang. When she saw the name on the caller ID she stepped away from the door and answered the call.

"What's up, Chuck," Parker said.

"You know what's up Parker and why I'm calling. Tell me you're on your way back here," Chucks replied, his voice less than friendly.

Parker made an awkward face. "Can't really say that."

After a couple seconds of silence Parker looked at the screen to make sure the call was still active.

"You can't mess around here, Parker," Chuck finally said. "This trial is important, and you're going to be the first witness called."

"I'm aware, and I promise I'll be back in time. Trust me." Parker looked up at the threatening sky. "Look, I'm about to get rained on so I gotta go."

"Parker, I know how you get, and these people you're testifying against are—"

"Bye Chuck," Parker said without letting him finish, then ended the call. She hated shutting him down like that, but she knew he would keep insisting that she return immediately. The back and forth might eventually end with threats, and she really hoped to avoid that.

Stepping back up to the door Parker jabbed the doorbell. When there was no reply, she reached out to push the button again just as a man's voice emanated from the device, startling her.

"We're not interested. Whatever you're pushing." the disconnected voice said.

"Is this the Jackson residence?" Parker asked, even though she was pretty sure it was.

"Congratulations, you know how to read a mailbox. Like I said, we're not interested."

"Mr. Jackson, my name is Lynn Parker. My mother was Penelope Highsmith. I was hoping I could speak with you for a few minutes. I promise not to take too much of your time."

Parker stared at the doorbell, waiting for a response, but nothing was forthcoming.

"Mr. Jackson?"

"What do you want with me?"

"Only to ask you a few questions."

"And why should I answer your questions?"

Parker thought for a moment. "Because I believe Penelope might have been murdered by someone who was afraid of questions."

The sound of rain on pavement filled the silence until finally he replied, "Give me a minute."

Parker wondered if Matt Jackson was one of those work-from-home types who stayed in their sweats throughout the day, and now he was scurrying to dress for a visitor. Her answer came a few moments later when the front door opened to reveal a man in his early sixties who was tucking the shirttail of a bright red polo into his slacks.

"Come in," the man instructed, stepping to one side to let her pass. He had scraggly salt and pepper hair, with stubble covering his face from a lack of shaving. Apart from that, he appeared to be healthy and in good shape, though from what Parker could smell, he could use a shower.

"Thank you for seeing me, Mr. Jackson."

"It's Matt. Please, have a seat."

Parker stepped down from the entrance hall into a nicely furnished living room and sat in a gray velvet accent chair close to the door. Matt walked to a corner-blocked sofa with roll arms and nailhead trim.

"Can I get you anything? Coffee, water?" he asked before sitting.

"I'm fine, thank you. Is your wife home?"

Matt leaned forward on the sofa and put his hands between his knees. "She's at work. You mentioned that someone murdered your mother. That's the first I'm hearing of that."

"That's my belief. The sheriff's office is still calling it a suicide, but I'm trying to convince them otherwise."

"What makes you think that?"

"Penelope conveyed to me she intended to disclose some damaging information at her book launch, and I feel somebody killed her and made it look like suicide to stop that from happening."

"What was she going to say?"

"She didn't tell me that. She told no one. I suspect it was connected somehow with her book and the murders that occurred in 1986, something I know you're intimately familiar with."

Matt Jackson frowned. "Odd choice of words… intimately. Not one I would have chosen."

"Have you read Penelope's book?"

Matt shook his head. "I'm not interested. But I've been told by others some of the lies in it."

The man's comment made Parker think about the red brick that destroyed the pane of glass window at Book Ends shop.

"I'm assuming Penelope contacted you when she was researching the book?"

"She did. And now here you are, her daughter, doing the same. There's irony in that somehow, don't you think? Are you going to fabricate fairy tales about me as well?"

"I'm only here to find out who murdered Penelope. Do you mind talking about the time during the murders?"

"I just as soon not, but then again, I didn't want a book written about any of it either, so I guess you can get it over with."

"The police and FBI seemed to focus their investigation on you because two of the murdered girls were on the soccer team you coached, and you had no alibi for the time surrounding all three disappearances."

Matt Jackson took a deep breath and appeared tired before he even answered. "Mikayla Jamesison disappeared while walking home from school. She had stayed late to work on a science project with her partner, Carmen Ruiz. At the time Mikayla was walking home, I was here, alone, grading papers. I taught history as well as being the school's soccer coach. Poppy was out of town at a work conference in Bend. I last saw Deidre Pool after practice a week later. She told me she was catching a ride home with Candice Bower, another one of my players, so I left the two of them at the field and drove off. We later found out that Candice had no such arrangement with Deidre, even though Deidre had told her parents she would ride home with her. Candice took off shortly after I did, leaving Deidre alone waiting for someone. If I knew Deidre wasn't riding with Candice, I would have never left her by herself."

"You drove to Dyerson after practice, about forty-five minutes from here one-way?"

Matt Jackson nodded. "I build my own computers and had ordered a motherboard from a computer shop I favor in Dyerson, but I got there too late. The shop was already closed. The FBI claimed I had two hours of unaccounted-for time."

"And Maddy Emerson?"

"She disappeared two and a half weeks later. She told her mother she was going to the library after dinner to do some research for a paper she was writing. They found her car in the library parking lot, but nobody had seen her enter. I was doing a lot of running back then. Long distance stuff, working my way up to trying a marathon. When Maddy disappeared, I was running Highway 41 and other back roads. Nobody saw me."

Parker considered what she said next carefully. "You must admit, it's suspicious that you were missing for all three disappearances."

Matt Jackson's face turned red. "God… I wasn't missing. I was exactly where I said I was. There are such things as coincidences, you know, despite what people in law enforcement believe. But since nobody could confirm my whereabouts, the FBI turned me into public enemy number one in this town and it almost ruined me."

"Penelope claimed in her book that—"

"I can only imagine what she *claimed*, and it's an absolute lie," the man barked as he rose from the couch and stalked over to a bookcase holding volumes of books about financial markets and technical analysis. "I did not hit on any of the girls on my teams, period. The sheriff and the FBI spoke to all of the girls on the team, as well as the girls who took my history class, and not one of them said anything about me coming on to them. Suddenly, years later, anonymous girls who are now women insist my touchy-feely manner gave them the creeps back then. It is nothing but a blatant attempt by Penelope to raise suspicion… and sell books."

Knowing what she did about Penelope, Parker could see her doing something like that, but not for the reason Matt Jackson thought. Parker couldn't accept the idea that book sales drove any of Penelope's actions. No, there had to be another reason for throwing mud at Matt Jackson. Parker just had to figure out what that was. First, she had to calm the man down or else she risked being thrown out on her ass.

"I didn't mean to upset you, Matt. I'm on your side, truly. I hope you see that."

Matt turned away from the bookcase, the intensity in his eyes gone.

"I'd like to believe that. There have been so few."

"Tell me about the two girls who were on the team. Deidre Pool and Maddy Emerson. What were they like?"

Matt retook his seat on the sofa. "Deidre was my sweeper. Incredible speed and good instincts. She was outgoing, full of energy, and probably had an undiagnosed ADD. She was my most vocal player, and that wasn't always a positive thing because she could be challenging. That girl had a short fuse and a nasty temper."

"Maddy was the opposite of Deidre in every way. She was my goalie and team captain. Quick, but not terribly fast. I would describe her as reserved, thoughtful, and a tad insecure."

"Penelope was on the team as well, right?"

Matt's expression had been good-natured as he talked about Deidre and Maddy, but that changed with Penelope's mention.

"She was, but she rode the bench most of the time. She was one of those girls who was more interested in the social aspect of being on a team than the sport itself. It was hard to get her to be quiet."

"How did the three of them get along?"

"To be honest, they didn't. Not that they disliked one another, it's just that they seemed to run in different circles."

"I got that same impression from the book. But the first victim, Mikayla Jamesison, was close to Deidre Pool, although Mikayla didn't play soccer for you."

"That's right. I didn't know Mikayla at all."

"Did you know Mikayla's older brother, Hutch?"

"I had him in my class when he was younger. Not the brightest of bulbs. I think he rode a motorcycle."

"Do you know if Deidre or Maddy knew him?"

Matt made a face. "No clue. Why are you asking about Hutch?"

"Just curious. Mikayla played soccer for a classic travel team during the summer from a neighboring town, just not for Willow's Bane's team. Do you have any idea why that was?"

Matt Jackson's face had turned expressionless. "Probably because the competition level for classic teams in this area far exceeds that in the school system. We were always losing players to them."

"Did you ever approach Mikayla about playing for the Willow's Bane team?"

"I —"

The sound of the front door flying open behind Parker prompted her to twist around to see who had entered. The wet and wild-eyed face of Poppy Jackson stared angrily back at her.

"What the hell are you doing in my home?" the woman seethed at Parker.

"Mrs. Jackson, I'm just trying—"

Poppy turned her wrath toward her husband. "And why did you let her in? You know who she is, right? Penelope Highsmith's daughter. She's picking up right where her mother left off."

"Poppy, don't be insensitive. She did just lose her mother."

"Oh, please… a mother she hasn't seen or talked to for eighteen years, so forgive me if I lack compassion."

"How did you know I was here?" Parker asked.

Poppy raised her arm, a cell phone still clutched in her hand. "Our doorbell sends me a notification when it's activated, along with a screenshot of who's on our doorstep."

"She was just asking me a few questions, darling. Nothing I haven't answered a million times before."

Poppy moved to the couch and sat next to her husband, taking his hands in hers. Parker thought she detected genuine concern in the woman's eyes.

"Honey, we can't get drawn into this again. Things were good before that contemptuous book came out, and it will be again if we just keep our heads down and let this blow over. People like this woman won't let us do that."

"I'm not here to —"

Poppy's head snapped in Parker's direction. "We're not interested in anything you have to say, good intentions or not. You do not know the damage people like you do. Others see you here, questioning my husband, like they did years ago, and you know what they think? Where there's smoke, there must be fire. Cute little idiom, isn't it? But even smoke leaves damage. Smoke goes everywhere. It permeates surfaces, violates crevices, and eats away at everything. It's toxic. It becomes an irritant, sometimes a deadly one, and it enveloped us."

Parker could see that any efforts to continue her conversation with Poppy's husband would be fruitless, so it was time to cut and run. She rose from her seat.

"Matt, I meant what I said earlier. Please remember that," Parker said, then left the way she came in.

TWIST

Thirteen

"I'm heading over to the Jamesison house now," Parker said to the empty passenger seat where her replacement cell phone rested, speakerphone engaged. "Maybe it will be more informative than my trip to the Jacksons."

"Are we liking him any better for the murders now that you've met him face to face?"

"No, but I'm not ruling him out either. There was something about him. He felt… off. I don't know how to describe it. How are things going on your end?"

"Bupkis. I've been trying to break into Penelope's laptop since you dropped me off, and the chick has military-grade encryption on that thing. It's gonna take me a while. I'm taking a break and moving on to some of our other suspects instead."

"First on your list should be—"

A loud bawling yelp sound caught Parker's attention at the same time flashing blue lights appeared in her rear-view mirror.

"Uh oh, I'm getting pulled over," she said, looking ahead for a place to turn off the road.

"That sounds like something I would say. Start working up some tears now, and you'll get off with a warning."

"I'll call you back. And for the record, I haven't done anything."

"Story of my life. Later gator."

Parker directed her car into the lot of an auto repair store and the sheriff's cruiser followed suit. She thought about getting out her driver's license and retrieving the rental agreement from the glove department but decided not to. If this was just the sheriff here to give her more grief about leaving town, why bother?

A soft tapping triggered her to roll down the window and look up, steeling herself for the confrontation to come.

Instead, she found Deputy Tate Bonner peering down at her, smiling. "Good afternoon, Miss Parker."

"Oh… deputy… I was expecting your boss," Parker said, relieved.

"Sorry to disappoint you. He said that the two of you had spoken."

"Is that all he said he did?"

"I don't catch your drift."

"Never mind. How can I help you? I don't think I was breaking any traffic laws."

"I understand you were involved in a serious incident this morning. A car almost ran you down?"

"Wow… small towns… news certainly travels fast here."

The deputy grinned. "My wife is the one who gave you that bandage on your forehead."

Parker touched the bandage and smiled. "Very nice woman. You're a lucky man."

Deputy Bonner's grin faded. "Why didn't you call our office and report it?"

"So you can accuse me of rigging the whole thing just so you'll start taking what I say seriously?"

"Give us a little more credit than that."

"You forget deputy, I've met your sheriff."

The deputy stared over the top of the car for a moment, then looked back. "What kind of car was it?"

"A blue van. Ford, I think. Things were hectic. Look, maybe it was just an accident, and the driver panicked."

"But you don't think so."

"No. I don't. That son of a bitch tried to splatter me all over the road."

"Okay. I'll keep an eye out for the van. Like you say, small town. I don't suppose you caught a look at the driver?"

Parker chuckled. "I was too busy trying to avoid becoming roadkill."

"Right. I knew it was a long shot. Where are you heading now?"

"I'm continuing to do what your department won't… investigate Penelope's death."

The deputy's expression hardened. "Listen to me Miss Parker, I may not agree with the sheriff's decision not to look into your mother's death, but you cannot go around Willow's Bane bothering our citizens and stirring things up. You have no legal authority to do so. This is a quiet little town, and we'd like to keep it that way."

Parker felt her temper rising. "Yeah, well, this quiet little town has seen both a murder and an attempted murder in the past thirty-six hours. If you'd get your head out of your ass, you'd realize that."

The deputy's eyes narrowed. He took a step back, placing his hands on his hips.

"Can I go now?" Parker sneered, glaring straight ahead.

"Have a nice day, and—" the deputy deadpanned, "—watch yourself."

Parker stomped on the gas, kicking up loose stones from her spinning rear tires until finally gaining traction. Her car sped out of the parking lot and onto the main road. Thankfully, traffic was light, allowing her to merge without incident or ruin her vehicular theatrics.

Her anger continued to simmer as she drove down the street, but she forced herself to decelerate until her car fell in line with the others. She didn't know why it bothered her so much that nobody was taking her seriously. She'd known it was going to be an uphill climb when she came. Maybe it was because the deputy seemed intelligent and open-minded, to a point, but still wasn't willing to go up against the sheriff. Or maybe it was the way time was quickly becoming her enemy. The longer the determination of suicide was used to label Penelope's death, the harder it would be to get anybody to think otherwise. Whatever the case, she acknowledged the fact she had to rein in her emotions and remain logical, assemble the clues like Kat did with the Lego sets she loved building, until the entire framework reveals itself. A tirade like the one she just had certainly wouldn't help their cause, and besides, acting like a spoiled brat was Kat's job.

Leaving the city limits, Parker drove ten more miles before turning onto a long driveway that led up to a large house on a hill. As Parker drew closer, she could see a barn farther back from the main road on the opposite side of the drive from the house. Both buildings were old and dilapidated.

As soon as Parker put the car in park, a trio of large dogs, all different breeds, came bounding from the back of the house, barking loudly. She considered herself a dog person, but three country canines who were probably unaccustomed to strangers was something different. She sat listening to them bellow, trying to think of a way to distract the pack until she could reach the house, when a female voice called out a single command. Each of the dogs stopped where they were and sat down, tongues hanging out of their panting mouths, their attention focused on a woman who was standing on the rickety porch.

Trisha Jamesison, standing with her arms crossed, glared at Parker from the deck. She was wearing the same style of plaid shirt and jeans as when they first met, though the shirt was a different color now, and Parker now noticed her well-worn brown boots.

Opening the car door cautiously, Parker slowly climbed out of the car.

"They won't bother you now," Trisha called to her. "Unless I tell them to."

"I guess I should stay on your good side then," Parker said, half-smiling.

"You have to get there before you can stay there," the woman replied flatly.

Parker glanced at the closest dog again, waiting to be invited in.

"Why are you here?" Trisha asked.

"I was hoping we could talk."

"Talk? I said everything I had to say at the hotel. What's the point?"

"Does there have to be a point?" Parker replied, smiled again.

The old woman regarded Parker for a moment before finally said, "I guess you can come in since you're already here."

Trisha turned and entered the house, a screen door banging close behind her. As soon as she was out of sight, the heads of the dogs turned towards Parker.

"Ummmm… just so you guys know, I'm a dog lover. I also donate regularly to the humane society."

The dog closest to her, a black Labrador, licked its chops.

"Good talk." Parker stepped around the hounds, three sets of eyes not leaving her as she made her way, then she picked up the pace heading for the porch stairs. Just as she reached the steps, she noticed a tarp covering something fairly big near the house.

Even though the temperature outside was somewhere in the mid-fifties, a screen door was the only barrier to the interior of the Jamesison home. Parker paused momentarily before entering the house, collecting her thoughts.

The temperature inside the house was only a few degrees warmer than outside, which Parker surmised was because of the fire she could hear popping from another room. Swerving from the foyer into a living area, the interior was faintly lit. All the shades were pulled down, and the only light source was the fireplace she had already heard. What she could see told her that nobody had taken a serious cleaning to this home in a sometime. Dust covered everything, and a cobweb draped a floor lamp in the corner.

Trisha had taken a seat in a rocking chair next to the fireplace and was swaying back and forth. She had lit a cigarette, which was now dangling from her fingers. The smell was pungent. Definitely not a filtered brand. The woman was staring blankly at Parker.

"I still don't know why you came out here?" Trisha asked.

Parker looked around for a place to sit. A pile of unfolded linen took up most of the leather couch with cracks on the arms, so she sat on the edge of a much-used recliner.

"I wanted to ask you some more questions about your daughter and her relationship with Penelope in high school."

Trisha took a long drag on her cigarette and blew the smoke out through her nose. "What for? It's all in Penelope's book."

"I'd like to hear it from you if you don't mind. I know what's in the book, but I'm interested in what's not in the book. Things Penelope might have purposefully omitted."

"Why?"

"Mrs. Jamesison, I don't believe Penelope killed herself. I think someone killed her to keep a secret buried."

"It's Gaither now. Been divorced for years, and I took my old name back. Why do you want to know this stuff, anyway? I won't have any answers that will help you, even if what you're saying is true."

"Maybe not, but I'd still like to hear it, anyway. I understand your daughter and Penelope weren't really friends in school."

Trisha shook her head. "I never heard Mikayla mention Penelope once."

"Did you know Penelope's parents?"

At that moment the sound of a creaking board came from overhead. Parker glanced up at the ceiling. When her attention returned to her host, she was still staring straight-ahead.

"This is an old house," Trisha remarked. "And just like me, it tends to groan from time to time."

Parker smiled awkwardly. "Penelope's parents, did you know them?"

"No. The father, Larry, I think his name was, was a car salesman at one of the dealerships. My husband might have bought a car from him once, maybe, but that's it. I didn't know the mother at all."

"Did your daughter have many friends?"

"The same number as most girls, I guess. She was closest to Deidre, obviously."

"I understand she played soccer for a traveling team and chose not to play for the high school team. Can you tell me why that was?"

For the first time the semblance of a smile appeared on the older woman's lips.

"She loved soccer, but she struggled with her grades at school. Her father and I told her that if she hoped to get into a decent college, she needed to keep her grades up and that would not happen if she played for the Badgers."

"The Badgers are the high school team?"

Trisha nodded. "We compromised by letting her play for the classic team in Dyerson during the summer, even though it was a ninety-minute commute, three days a week for practices."

"So, the reason she didn't play for the Badgers wasn't because she heard rumors about coach Jackson?"

Trisha scrunched up her face. "No. Of course not. Who told you that?"

"No one. It's just that in Penelope's book, she mentioned some girls had uncomfortable experiences with him."

"Right, the anonymous girls you mean. Bullshit is what that is. It never happened."

"How can you be so sure?"

"Because I know the man. Been friends with him and his wife forever. We all grew up in this town together, so you can stop spreading those rumors right now."

"I'm simply asking questions, not making accusations."

"That's what people like you don't understand. Sometimes asking the question is as good as an accusation."

Parker could see the truth in that statement.

"Fair enough. What was Mikayla's relationship with her brother like? Hutch, right?"

Trisha's hardened expression turned into a scowl. "My boy did not kill his sister, or any of them girls. Your mother had her facts wrong with what she wrote in that book."

Parker could see that she struck a nerve. Time to tread carefully.

"Okay. Just to be completely transparent, I don't believe, or not believe, what Penelope wrote. I'm only trying to get to the bottom of her death. Do you know where he's been the last several years?"

"No. I just know he's not here. He left this town and never looked back. Can't say I blame him."

"You don't keep in touch?"

"Are you almost finished with these questions?"

"Just a couple more. Another thing that came up in Penelope's book was your affair with Dan Emerson."

Trisha's face hardened again and she took another drag. "What about it?"

"I'm curious. Was your relationship with Dan ever brought up during the initial investigation?"

"No, and why should it? Our affair had absolutely nothing to do with any of that. It ended the day Mikayla disappeared."

"Did anybody ever know about the affair before it came out in Penelope's book?"

"No. The fact Penelope included it in the book tells me she was nothing but a money-hungry, attention-seeking bitch."

"But somebody had to know about it. It was in the book. Is it possible Mikayla suspected and told somebody else? Hutch maybe?"

That made Trisha stop and think. "I… I don't know how. We were very careful."

"What about Penelope's assertion that Dan was actually having multiple affairs with different women at the same time?"

"That didn't happen. I would have known. The book didn't name names apart from mine."

"Have you spoken to Dan about any of this since it became public?"

"No, and I don't intend to. We don't speak to one another anymore."

"But you were with him at my hotel yesterday."

"That was for a common purpose, nothing more."

"What about Mary Emerson?"

"What about her?"

"Have the two of you talked?"

"About the affair?"

"Yes."

Trisha looked at Parker as if she had just belched at a formal event. "No. Why would I?"

"But she's aware?"

"Everyone is, or at least they will be, thanks to your mother. It happened a long time ago. There's nothing to talk about."

Parker contemplated her next question.

"You weren't by chance with Dan when Mikayla disappeared, were you?"

Trisha became stoneface. She flicked the half-smoke cigarette across the room, still lit. "I think it's time for you to leave."

"Surely the sheriff questioned you about—"

"You have thirty seconds to get to your car. After that, I'm giving my dogs another command."

Parker swallowed hard.

"And it's not one you're going to like," Trisha growled.

Fourteen

Walking through the Knights Lodge lobby, it surprised Parker to see Kat occupying one of the tables. She was sitting with her back to a partition, her laptop open in front of her, a coffee mug off to the side, earbuds inserted, and her backpack laying in one of the three other chairs. The hotel breakfast area bustled with activity. Most of the other tables were occupied. Susan Reynolds was there as well, sitting in a lounge chair talking on her cell phone.

Parker made her way to Kat's table and stood opposite her, waiting to be noticed. It was several seconds before her friend glanced up and spotted Parker, jumping when she did. She removed the earbuds and smiled.

"How long have you been standing there?"

"I just walked up. What are you doing down here?"

"I was getting antsy cooped up in that room, so I came down for a change of scenery."

Parker slid into a chair. "Making any progress?"

"Hit and miss. Still no luck with Penelope's laptop. I might have to ask someone I know for help with that. Don't see that level of security every day, and I'm surprised to find it on her laptop."

"I understand most writers are security conscious, afraid to have their work stolen and all that."

"Maybe, but this is next level shit, not something you can download off the internet. Somebody had to install it for her."

"Keep plugging away at it. If we can find that missing chapter, it might answer a lot of questions. Have you looked at that forensic stuff from the book yet?"

Kat winced. "I've been putting that off. Not something I'm really looking forward to."

"Maybe I can tackle it instead. I was going to visit Deidre Pool's father next, but I can put that off until tomorrow."

"That would be awesome. How'd it go with the Jamesison woman?"

Parker decided to not mention anything about the dogs. Kat was more of a cat person.

"She lives all by herself in this run-down house out in the middle of nowhere. It's like she's given up on everything, just waiting around to die. It was depressing."

"I bet."

"She told me Mikayla didn't play for the high school soccer team because of academics. Struggled to maintain her grades. She also defended Matt Jackson when I asked her about him. She's been friends with him and his wife Poppy for years. They grew up here together. Said Penelope was lying when she wrote Matt was drooling over high school girls. She wouldn't talk about her son Hutch at all."

"Do you think Penelope was a poop shooter? Making a stink just to muddy the waters?"

"Don't know. She was spot on about Trisha's affair with Dan Emerson, though. The woman didn't bother to deny it."

"Could that be important? Two of the parents of the murdered girls were having an affair with one another?"

"Unclear, but there was something else. I think somebody might have been there listening to our conversation."

"Who?"

"Could have been her son, Hutch. There was a tarp covering something in front of the house, maybe it was a motorcycle. He used to ride one when he still lived here."

"Shit, Parker. Do you think it was him who tried to run you down?"

"You don't think I can tell the difference between a motorcycle and a van."

"He could have boosted it."

"Maybe. It got me thinking, though. Why did the killer select these three girls? And even more specific than that, why was Mikayla Jamesison targeted first?"

Kat shook her head. "I know where you're heading, but I think it was opportunity, pure and simple. I can't tell you how many lectures I've sat through at the youth center growing up that yammered on about how that was the number one reason for becoming a victim. I can still recite the rule book for you. Stay in lighted areas or with other people. Don't hitchhike or accept a car ride from a stranger. Be aware of your surroundings. Don't talk to strangers. Walk facing traffic, it's harder to be forced into a car. Want to hear more?" Kat said, using her fingers to count off each point.

"You think it's really that simple?"

Kat's expression went blank, and she turned her gaze to the windows. "It was for me. Probably should have paid closer attention to those lectures when I was younger."

Parker was aware Kat had a terrible experience when she was younger, an incident that she still refused to discuss, and she respected her friends' boundaries. But a part of her secretly ached to know more.

Kat shook her head and met Parker's eyes again. "Mikayla was walking home alone in the dark. Opportunity, that's all."

"And maybe she caught a ride with her brother?"

"Not everything is something out of a James Patterson novel," Kat replied.

"Even if it wasn't him, that still means someone was watching her."

Kat shook her head. "Not necessarily. Pervs like this are constantly trolling, like sharks. It could have been pure luck he came across her. An opportunity."

"Now I'm even more depressed than I was when I walked in. Thanks," Parker sighed, rolling her eyes.

"Then I'm not sure if this will help or not," Kat said as she used her mouse to navigate on her laptop, then she turned it around so Parker could see the screen.

On the screen was a PDF picture showing headshots of multiple teenagers, arranged in rows, with names printed on the left side of the page. Parker scanned the list until she found a name she recognized in the middle of the page. Mikayla Jamesison. Finding the picture that matched the order placement of the name, she recognized the young girl immediately.

"That's the picture that was used in Penelope's book," Parker said, peering closer.

"It's the high school yearbook from that year. They took the pictures in the fall and printed the book before the murders began."

To Parker's eyes, Mikayla was cute, but not Prom Queen material. She had dirty-blonde hair grazing her shoulders, azure eyes, luscious lips, and a beaming smile. She was wearing a red V-neck sweater in the picture. Parker couldn't help but contemplate as she stared at the girl's sweet and innocent smile, about the horrors she would soon face. A shudder ran through her.

"Show me the others."

Kat slid her chair around until she was next to Parker, then used her mouse to scroll down. After a couple of clicks, Deidre Pool's picture was on the screen. Deidre had straight blonde hair, brown eyes, a snub nose, and a tiny gap between her two front teeth. Her easy grin showed off the sass she was known for.

"Now Maddy Emerson," Parker requested.

More clicks on Kat's mouse flashed the young girl's picture onto the screen. Maddy's hair was the longest of the three and black. She also had blue eyes, a small mouth displaying the tiniest of smiles, and high cheekbones.

"What about Penelope? Is her picture there?"

Kat nodded as she manipulated the file again. "There she is."

Penelope's picture stood out from the other three. She had bundled her hair on the side, arranged in such a way that she resembled Princess Leia from Star Wars. She also had a red ribbon weaved through her hair on one side. Her face was full, cheeks red from an overuse of blush, with plenty of eye makeup. Parker could see glimpses of the future Penelope in that tiny picture.

"I bet she grew up regretting that style choice," Kat commented not even attempting to hide her snarky side.

"Did you go through the whole thing to see if there are other photos of the girls?"

"I didn't have to. There's a legend at the back that details every student and the page number corresponding to a picture they're in or referenced in some other way."

"Show me," Parker said.

Using the page numbers she had previously written on a notepad, Kat began jumping to specific spots in the file. There were pictures of Maddy Emerson with the Drama Club, Deidre Pool standing next to a Spanish teacher, Mikayla Jamesison with the Cross-Country team, Maddy Emerson again as part of the Student Council, Deidre and Maddy together in a random soccer photo celebrating something that was taking place out of frame.

"Hold up," Parker said, pointing to something on the screen. "Isn't that Penelope in the background?"

Both women leaned in to get a closer look at the soccer pic. Kat clicked on a button on the screen and the picture enlarged. The picture showed Deidre and Maddy embracing, mid-jump, with other girls from the team also frozen in various forms of glee. In contrast, a lone girl, Penelope, remained sitting on a white wooden bench behind everyone, wrapped in a blanket, directing an ireful stare at Deidre and Maddy.

"It could be," Kat said, unsure.

"If it is her, she's pissed at one or both of them. Soccer is a fall sport, which means they took this picture months before the murders began."

"Or it could be perfectly innocent and not have anything to do with anything. You're doing that thing again where you interpret signals in a way that matches your assumptions."

"That's not a thing I do."

Kat blew a raspberry with her lips. "That is totally a thing. You did it with me when we first met. They convinced you I was some kind of low-life intending to steal you blind."

"I was right about that. You are a low-life and constantly stealing my Starbuck points."

"Screw you, and that's the last time I make a coffee run for you."

"Hey, can you find a picture of Hutch Jamesison in there? He was a couple years ahead of the girls, but he dropped out his senior year. Maybe there will be one in his junior yearbook?"

Kat attacked her keyboard with an occasional side-step to her trackpad, and a few minutes later she sat back and said, "Wallah."

Parker leaned over and looked at the picture on Kat's screen. The boy she saw had long, uncombed hair down to his shoulders, long sideburns, an oversized Adam's apple. By the expression on his face, he also had a distinctly sour attitude.

"Can easily see dealing drugs in that boy's future," Parker said.

"Good afternoon, ladies," Susan Reynolds greeted as she approached their table.

"Hey, Susan," Parker replied, discreetly closing the lid of Kat's laptop.

"I wanted to let you know that we've decided to hold the book launch for Penelope's book tomorrow at the bookstore. We'll be making some remarks at three o'clock in case you want to drop by," Susan said, a sweet smile plastered on her face.

"You did hear that somebody threw a brick through the bookstore's front window, right?" Parker asked, raising an eyebrow.

"I did. Van has informed me they will replace the window in time, and it shouldn't be an issue."

"I was thinking more about the overall mood of the city. The folks that were here yesterday won't be too thrilled, for instance."

Susan nodded. "Yes, indeed. What you must understand is we are trying to balance those feelings against others who are more open to the event. Most of the media representatives who were here Tuesday for the original launch are still here and Monolith publishing would be negligent if they didn't take advantage of that fact to maximize the book's exposure. We are also trying to be respectful of Penelope's passing, but we are in the bookselling business."

"Once again, the almighty dollar wins out," Kat commented.

For the first time, Parker thought Susan appeared uncomfortable. The agent shuffled her feet as she stared at Kat.

"Yes, well, I guess you're right. I'm sorry for whatever discomfort this may cause you, Parker."

"Oh, it's no skin off my nose. I'm Switzerland as far as all that goes. I'm here to find out who killed Penelope." Parker smiled at Susan, but the smile did not reach her eyes.

Susan scrutinized Parker carefully. "You still feel that way?"

"More than ever. I also met that podcaster, Samantha. Did you know about her relation to one of the murder victims in Lewiston?"

"I did not. I guess that would explain her passion and why she'd get so upset about Penelope's book."

Parker's distinctive ringtone interrupted the conversation. "Hello?"

"Am I speaking with Lynn Highsmith?" a male voice asked.

"I'm Lynn Parker now, but yes, and you are?"

"Miss Parker, my name is Rockford Wells. I'm the mayor of Willow's Bane. Penelope Highsmith's assistant, Willa, gave me your number. I was wondering if we could talk? Maybe over dinner?"

Parker's eyebrows rose and she glanced at Kat. "Uh… sure… I guess."

"My car is pulling up to your hotel right now. Can you meet me out front?"

"Okay… we'll be out in a couple minutes." Parker disconnected the call and looked at Kat. "Quick, pick up your stuff. We have a dinner date with the mayor."

Kat made a long face and started packing her stuff into her backpack. "Yeah? Slick."

Parker turned to Susan. The agent's brows furrowed and her eyes shone with concern. "Watch yourself with Mayor Wells, Lynn. He's not one of your mom's biggest fans."

"Thanks for the heads up," Parker said. "We'll see you at the bookstore tomorrow."

Kat followed Parker out of the hotel entrance, where they found a black Cadillac Escalade waiting for them with the back seat door wide open.

"Climb in," a voice from inside the car called out. Once inside, Parker sank back into the plush leather seats as her eyes scanned the interior of the car. Kat slid in next to her and closed the door, triggering the vehicle to move.

"Rockford Wells," the man behind the wheel said. From where she was sitting, Parker could only make out that he was middle-aged, tall, with a full head of black hair. "Pleased to make your acquaintance. This is Gwen Elliott up here with me."

"Good evening," a woman's voice said. Parker could not see the person through the bucket seats.

"I bet you're wondering what my purpose is for kidnapping you on such short notice," he said, and laughed at his own joke. "So let me get to the meat of things. You'll find that out about me. I have little use for bullshit or time wasters. It twists my jewels in knots, if you'll pardon my French, listening to people who love to hear themselves talk. Life is too short to squander it on inconsequential matters or trivial distractions. I won the election twice by campaigning on a promise to reduce bureaucracy and take decisive action, and toe-tapping won't help you achieve that.

"For someone who hates wasting time, you sure are taking a lot of it to make your point," Kat remarked dryly.

"Pardon my friend," Parker said as she glared at Kat. "She has a broken filter between her brain and mouth."

The mayor chuckled. "I can respect that."

"You were saying?"

"Yes. It's come to my attention from the sheriff and some others in town that there might be some confusion about your mother's death."

"Confusion?"

Talking to Parker as if she were a child, the mayor sympathetically said, "You have been spreading the rumor that your mother was murdered."

"It's not a rumor. She was murdered."

"But our county coroner ruled her death as a suicide. It's all there in black and white."

"He or she, whichever it is, is mistaken."

"Oh… you have a degree in forensic pathology, do you?"

"No."

"You have some experience in these matters, then? What is it you do, over where you come from?" he drawled.

Parker paused before answering. "I'm a social worker."

"Oh… I see. Well, I have to tell you the confusion you are spreading is drawing attention to my city, and not in a good way. You and that book launch, which I thought was canceled but now I'm hearing that they have rescheduled it for tomorrow, are becoming a bother," he sneered.

"You'll have to talk to Penelope's agent and publisher about the book launch. It has nothing to do with me."

"She's next on my list, but first I was hoping we could find common ground and a way to convince you to lay things to rest, as they should be. What can I do to make things easier for you?"

"I don't suppose you have the name of Penelope's killer in your pocket, do you?"

Mayor Wells went silent for a moment. "You're a chip off the old block, aren't you? Your mother wouldn't listen to reason either when I tried to talk her out of holding her shenanigans in my city."

"I am NOTHING like my mother."

"Your relationship with your mother was a strained one, isn't that true?" the woman next to the mayor spoke up.

"So?" Kat growled.

"I imagine that this time must be difficult for you, attempting to resolve your deep-seated issues with such a painful loss, and despite what you might say, I'm sure it is painful."

"I'm sorry. What do you have to do with any of this?"

"Gwen is my psychiatrist," the mayor said.

"What?"

"I brought her along because I was interested to hear her take on whether your emotional stability was a factor in your denial of the coroner's ruling."

"Un-friggin-believable," Kat said, rolling her eyes.

"Could you please take us back to our hotel?" Parker stated, her eyes ice cold.

"But we're almost there. This is one of the finest restaurants Willow's Bane has to offer. Their veal is to die for," the mayor pointed out, smacking his lips together for emphasis.

"If you won't take us back, please pull over and we'll get our own ride back."

"But what about dinner?"

"I've lost my appetite."

Fifteen

After the mayor's black Escalade dropped Parker and Kat back at the Knights Lodge following a conversation-free return, the two women remained standing in the chilly night air. The cold air felt refreshing with the fiery anger brewing inside Parker.

"What a douche," Kat commented, adjusting her backpack on her shoulder as she watched the SUV pull away.

"Yeah. Him and the sheriff are a match made in heaven."

"Beavis and Butt-head."

"I feel bad, though. I did lie to him."

Kat looked at her friend. "About what?"

"I'm starving."

"Totally. Me too. But did you hear that tool bag talk about loving veal? Who can do that… eat the meat from a day-old calf? It's disgusting."

"Try not to think about it. We can go over to the pub and get something, or order room service. They also have food delivery services here in Willow's Bane. I checked, so we can go up to our room and order something to be delivered. Or we can just get a pizza. Lots of options. What do you feel like?"

"I wanna eat with my shoes off, so I'm leaning towards the pizza in the room plan."

"Let's do it, then."

Entering the deserted lobby, the two women had just steered towards the elevators when a female employee with curly hair came down the hallway approaching them. The young woman was walking hurriedly, paying no mind to Parker or Kat, a troubled look on her face. Parker quickly recognized the reason for the employee's anxiety when a man rushed up from behind and grabbed her arm, spinning her around.

The man was medium height and built solidly, evidenced by the tattooed muscled arms and legs protruding from his sleeveless sweatshirt and shorts.

"Don't walk away from me, Belinda," Parker heard the greasy hair man say.

"Whoa buddy," Kat called out, picking up her pace and worrying Parker. One of the hard to shake habits Kat had adopted from her time in the foster care system was her inclination to respond to confrontational situations aggressively. The kids who were submissive tended to get picked on more and have a rougher time, so learning how to be combative—even when size wasn't on your side—was key.

Both the greasy hair man and the hotel employee looked at Kat.

"Hands off," Kat instructed. She and Parker came to a stop a few feet away from the quarreling couple.

"This is between us and none of your business," the man grunted dismissively.

"Is this guy bothering you—" Parker glanced at the woman's name tag to confirm her name, "—Belinda?"

"I asked him to leave, and he won't listen," Belinda answered, jerking her arm to free herself from the man's grip.

"We still have stuff to talk about," the man said, rubbing the stubble on his chin.

"Do you know this guy, Belinda?"

"He's my EX-boyfriend."

Kat reached into her backpack and pulled out an object that looked like a black steel tube with a thermoplastic grip. She dropped the backpack and flicked the tube downward, causing it to expand into a steel rod.

"Last chance, Rufus," Kat said.

The man released Belinda and turned his attention to Kat. "What are you going to do with that, little girl?"

"Come and find out, Zeke."

"I think what my friend is trying to communicate to you is that your presence here in the hotel is no longer appropriate and you should leave before things get out of hand," Parker said, using a measured tone. "Isn't that right, Belinda?"

Belinda moved alongside Parker. "Just go, Todd."

Todd looked at the three women, thinking about his next move.

"You don't think I'm afraid of some dyke with a pig slapper, do you?" he sneered.

Parker shook her head. "No, I don't think you're smart enough for that. But surely you realize that if you don't walk away right now, you'll be spending the night in jail courtesy of the Willow's Bane sheriff's office, so it's time to decide."

"It's that or the hospital," Kat added.

Todd appeared to be weighing his options. Then he pointed a finger at Belinda.

"We're not finished, Belinda."

"Yes, we are, Todd," Belinda responded.

Todd turned and stormed off the way he had come, and a few seconds later the sound of a slamming door echoed down the hallway.

"I'm so sorry you had to see that, but really appreciate the support."

Kat retracted the baton and slid it back into her bag. "Real winner, that one."

Belinda sighed. "Yeah, not one of my best decisions getting involved with him. I just want to put it behind me now."

Parker put her hand on the hotel employee's shoulder. "Please make sure you don't get caught alone with him again. I'm not sure he's gotten the message yet."

"Don't worry, I won't."

Parker and Kat moved towards the elevators when they heard, "Excuse me," from behind them.

Parker and Kat turned to see Belinda looking at them, wringing her hands.

"I don't want to be more of a bother to you and I apologize if I'm interrupting anything," the employee said.

"You're coming between me and half-a-dozen slices of pepperoni pizza," Kat said.

Belinda's face turned red. "I'm so sorry, I'll let you—"

"Ignore her," Parker interjected, smiled. "How can we help you?"

"If you're sure?"

"Positive."

"You're Penelope Highsmith's daughter, aren't you?"

"You gotta love small towns," Parker said to Kat. "I am, but it's not something I like to advertise."

"Oh, I get it. I won't tell anyone. It's just that I'm one of your mother's biggest fans, and I wanted to express my condolences. Her books meant a lot to me."

"Thank you for saying that. She impacted many people's lives." Not always for the better, Parker wanted to add, but decided to keep that to herself.

"I met her that night... the night she... well, you know. She signed her new book for me."

"When was that?" Parker asked, her interest piqued.

Belinda scrunched her brows and tilted her head up. "I guess it was around 9-9:30."

"How did she seem to you?"

"Fine. Upbeat. She even took the time to give me some relationship advice. That's why I was so shocked when I heard what happened the next day."

"Did anyone with the sheriff's office speak with you?"

Belinda shook her head. "My shift ended at six AM, and her body wasn't discovered until hours later. Why would they need to talk to me?"

Kat chortled. "That's the sheriff's line."

"You work the front desk at night? Did you see anyone come in that night who didn't have a room booked? Maybe somebody local?"

"It was busy for a Monday night. We had a lot of rooms booked for people who were here for the book launch, but I don't recall anyone like you're describing. I'm not at the desk all the time, though."

"But you have CCTV cameras, right?"

Belinda nodded. "For the lobby and all the entrances, but not the hallways. They're supposed to be upgrading to add them next year."

"I don't suppose you'd let us look at the footage from that night?"

Belinda's expression turned serious. "I'm sorry, I'd really like to, especially after what you've done for me, but I can't. I would need a warrant from the sheriff's office."

"You could let me into the room where they keep the equipment, and I can do the rest. I just need fifteen minutes," Kat said.

"Sorry, I can't."

Parker could tell by the woman's tight lips that she would not budge. She was about to suggest to Kat that they return to their room and order the food they were craving until she spotted a uniform officer entering the hotel. It was Deputy Bonner. He noticed the three women standing near the elevators and moved in their direction.

"Just who I was coming to see," he said to Parker, then nodded at Belinda. "Hi B."

"Hey Tate. Did somebody call you?"

"No, I was just stopping by. Why? Should they have?"

"Todd was here making a nuisance of himself, but these ladies ran him off."

"I'm guessing the two of you know one another?" Parker asked.

"We dated in high school," Belinda replied.

"When are you going to cut that guy loose, B? He's bad news," the deputy said.

"I'll say," Kat added.

"He's history. Just having trouble getting him to accept it."

"Glad to hear it."

"You find that blue van?" Parker asked.

"I gotta get back to the desk," Belinda remarked, smiled at Parker. "It was nice meeting you, and thanks again for everything."

"Hang on Belinda, this might concern you," the deputy said, then directed his attention back at Parker. "No luck on the blue van, but I've been thinking since we last spoke, and I think you have a right to see the CCTV footage from that night."

Parker's eyes grew large. "Really? What changed your mind?"

"Let's just say I extracted my head from a very uncomfortable spot."

"Does the sheriff know what you're doing?" Parker asked with a raised eyebrow.

"Only if you tell him," answered the deputy. Then turning to Belinda, "What about it, B? Can you let us see the tape?"

Belinda crossed her arms. "You don't have a warrant, do you?"

"No, I don't. But you know I wouldn't be doing this if I didn't feel it was right."

Belinda tilted her head to one side. "You'll take the heat if this hits the fan? I can't afford to lose my job."

"No problem. I won't let anything blow back on you."

"That's good enough for me. It's this way."

Everyone followed Belinda down the hallway, past the front desk, and to a door leading to a room behind the reception area. Using a key on a ring pulled from her pocket, she unlocked the door which opened into a dark room dimly lit by two LCD screens on a desk. One screen was divided into four squares, each segment displaying a different camera feed. A screen saver of fish swimming leisurely across the panel was on the other LCD.

Taking a seat at the desk, the fish disappeared from the screen, replaced by the login screen for the in-house security software. After entering her user ID and password, Belinda looked up at deputy Bonner.

"What time do you want me to start at?"

"You said you spoke to Penelope between nine or nine-thirty," Parker answered, not giving the deputy time to speak.

"You did?" the deputy said.

"See the things you learn when you actually do some investigating?" Kat said.

"Let's start there," Parker said.

Belinda typed some information into the terminal, and the second screen with the camera feeds went blank. Moments later, the pictures returned, still framed. Three of the feeds originated from cameras outside the ancillary entrances pointing towards the doors, and the fourth feed showed the breakfast area with the reception desk in the background. The time in the corner of all four feeds read 9:15PM.

"You can see that no one is at the front desk, which means I'm still talking with Penelope," Belinda pointed out.

"Can you fast forward it until a few minutes before you return? You know, in case you happened to pass them in the hallway."

With a click from Belinda, the video on all four feeds started moving quickly. To Parker, the fast-forwarded video looked like a 1950s Buster Keaton movie. Several guests sped through the lobby in both directions, and it wasn't long until Belinda appeared on the screen wearing her hotel polo shirt.

"Freeze it," Parker instructed.

The four feeds were frozen again, with the time showing 9:29PM.

"Okay, now we need you to fast-forward again, but pause it whenever you see anybody entering the hotel from any of the entrances so we can get a good look at them."

"Got it."

No sooner had the playback started when the Belinda on the screen disappeared down the hall to her right.

"I had to use the bathroom."

Seconds later, a figure entered from outside and moved confidently towards the hallway leading to Penelope's room. Belinda paused the playback.

"I'd recognize that strut anywhere," Kat said. "That's the hag who said you should be ashamed of your mom."

"Poppy Jackson. You're right, it is," Parker said. She made a mental note of the time on the screen. 9:34PM.

"I'll be damned," Deputy Bonner remarked.

"Let it play so we can see what time she leaves."

Playback resumed for several minutes until Poppy reappeared. The time was 9:50PM. The Belinda on the screen was talking to another guest.

"I can't notice everyone. Like I said, it was busy that night."

"We understand. Let's keep going, there might be others," Parker urged.

Following several minutes of stops and starts, Parker shook her head. "It's next to impossible to identify anyone coming through those other doors. It was cold that night, so everyone is bundled up, and those cameras don't provide the best angles."

"Do you want me to keep going?" Belinda asked.

"Yeah. Maybe we'll get lucky."

After ten more minutes of watching the video, Kat pointed to the segment of the screen displaying the breakfast area.

"There's a blind spot with that camera."

"What do you see?" Parker asked.

"The camera covers most of the breakfast area all the way back to the front desk, but you can't actually see the front entrance door."

Parker leaned in closer and realized what Kat was said was true. She narrowed her eyes, staring at the screen, recognizing how easy it was to remain invisible to the hotel cameras.

"If someone entered and immediately turned left, staying as close as they could to the wall, they could make their way underneath the camera without being seen and then do the same thing against the other wall until reaching the hallway. The camera would never see them."

"But Belinda would," the deputy pointed out. "A person would look strange taking that approach."

"I'm not so sure, and we've seen how many times she had someone standing in front of her at the desk. It's possible."

"Let's keep going, anyway."

Belinda continued the process of stops and starts throughout the entire night, but they identified no other unexpected visitors. "I don't know. There were several people who entered through the side-entrances that were hard to see, but not much else."

"You would need a key card to get in one of those doors, which means they were probably guests, anyway. And if needed, Belinda could pull up those records," Tanner said.

"It's easy enough to hang out by a door and slip in when somebody comes out," Belinda pointed out.

"But we didn't see that on the tape."

"True."

"I want to watch it again later. Can you make us a copy of that night, Belinda?" Parker asked.

Belinda looked at the deputy, who shook his head.

"Sorry, but allowing you to have a look-see is as far as I'm willing to go. What are you planning to do now?"

"First, Kat and I are going to scarf down a pizza, then I was thinking about paying another visit to the Jackson's to find out what Poppy has to say for herself. Care to come along?"

"I don't suppose I can talk you out of that until I've run this by the sheriff?"

Parker scoffed. "Not a chance. I'm not waiting for your boss to get a clue."

The deputy pulled a business card from his shirt pocket and handed it to Parker. "That has my cell phone number on the back. Call me when you're headed out there, and I'll meet you."

The four of them walked into the hallway and up to the front desk. Parker turned to thank the deputy again when she spotted something laying on the reception desk.

"Is that Malignant Doubt?" Parker asked.

Belinda looked at the book on the desk. "It is. I just started it. It's creepy thinking about how all these things happened right here in our small town."

"That's the copy Penelope signed for you?"

"It is."

"Mind if I have a look?"

Belinda picked up the book and handed it to Parker. She opened the front cover and read the inscription:

To my number one fan ... Best of Luck... Penelope Highsmith.

Parker started to hand the book back when the dust jacket slipped off. She opened the back flap to replace the cover when the blood in her veins froze. On the inside of the back cover, written in Penelope's handwriting, were two words.

Forgive Me.

Sixteen

"Do we have this all wrong?" Parker asked.

She and Kat were in their car heading to the Jackson's residence after filling up on stuff-crust pizza from a local restaurant. She had been purposefully quiet while they ate, but Kat didn't seem to notice because she had been occupied on her laptop. Parker hadn't told the others about the words she found in the back of Belinda's book, mostly because she wasn't sure what they meant. Or did she?

"What do you mean all wrong?" Kat asked.

"I mean, maybe Penelope committed suicide and we're just letting our over-active imaginations run wild?"

"Speak for yourself. My imagination is the right amount of active. What I want to know is why are you suddenly turning into a Doubting Thomas?"

Parker debated telling Kat about what she had seen in Belinda's book. "I'm just trying to keep an open mind."

"It's because you have an open mind that we're here to begin with. Everyone else is saying that she killed herself, and we're not. At least we were both saying that. Something must have happened to make you wobble. Spill."

Parker hesitated before answering. "Penelope wrote something in the back of the book she gave Belinda. What she wrote confuses me."

"Well… don't make me pull it out of you."

Before Parker could answer, her cell phone rang. She glanced at the caller ID, then declined the call.

"Who was that?" Kat asked.

"Just Chuck. I'll call him back later."

"So… what did Penelope write in Belinda's book?"

"She wrote… forgive me."

Kat went silent for a moment. "Hmmmm. I'll admit that is odd. What do you think she meant?"

"Isn't it obvious? That was the last thing she wrote before swallowing a bottle of pills. It could be an impromptu suicide note."

Kat considered that, then shook her head. "I'm not buying it. I think she was asking forgiveness for something else."

"But what?"

"Maybe how bad the book was? How should I know? You're the brains of this outfit. Put that overactive imagination to work. All I know is that I'm still not buying that she offed herself."

They drove in silence the rest of the way to the Jackson home and parked on the street when they arrived. It was only a few minutes later that a patrol car pulled up. Deputy Bonner stepped out of the car, dressed casually in jeans and a sweatshirt.

"I'm going to let you do most of the talking, since I'm technically not supposed to be here," the deputy said as the three of them walked to the front step.

Parker depressed the video doorbell button and a minute later, Matt Jackson opened the door. His face fell when he recognized who was standing there.

"Haven't we answered enough of your questions?" the man asked, exasperated.

"There is some new information that has come to light, Matt. We just want to clear it up," Deputy Bonner said. "It won't take long."

"The sheriff's office is part of this witch-hunt now?"

"There is no witch-hunt, Matt, and I'm here strictly informally. But we really need to talk to you and Poppy," Deputy Bonner reassured.

For a second Parker thought the man was going to shut the door in their faces, but then he seemed to relent and opened the door wider. When the three of them stepped into the foyer, the warmth of the home hit her as she entered. Her hands tingled as they warmed up. Poppy emerged from the kitchen, wiping her hands on a hand towel.

"Is there no end to this?" Poppy exclaimed, tossing the towel over her shoulder. "And now there are more of you."

"They say they need to ask just a few more questions, hon. Let's just get it over with," Matt dejectedly sighed.

Poppy stared at her guests, chewing on her lip. "Fine. I guess the polite thing to do is to ask everyone to have a seat."

Once seated, Parker immediately began. "We've had a look at the hotel security footage from the night Penelope supposedly killed herself."

Poppy blinked several times, but her face remained neutral. She adjusted her gaze so that it fell on deputy Bonner. "You're looking at security footage now?"

"It shouldn't be a surprise that you were on that footage, would it, Mrs. Jackson?" the deputy replied.

Matt Jackson's head whipped around, staring at his wife. "What?"

"Can you tell us why you were at the Knights Lodge that night?" Parker continued.

"What are they talking about, Poppy?" Matt asked.

Poppy shifted in her seat and cleared her throat. "I was there to see Penelope. I've never tried to hide that fact."

"But you didn't come forward with that information either," Parker countered.

"Why did you go there, Pop? What did you think would happen?"

Poppy's expression softened when she looked at her husband. "I wanted to reason with her so she would cancel that ludicrous sideshow of a book launch. We couldn't stop the book, but maybe she'd consider canceling the launch. I had to try."

"Did you talk to her?" Parker asked.

Poppy addressed Parker again, visibly irritated that her attention was being pulled away from her husband. "I did, and to answer your next question, she was in perfect health when I left."

"How did your conversation go?"

"She was expecting me, actually. All my letters and phone calls had gone unanswered, but she knew about them and assumed I would try something in person once she arrived in Willow's Bane. It was useless, though. She kept insisting that the book launch would solve all our problems, as if a spell would magically be lifted. She was totally uncooperative."

"What was her state of mind when you spoke?"

"She wasn't wearing a mood ring. Like I said, uncooperative."

"Did she seem depressed at any point? Melancholy?"

"No."

"Was there anything you observed that was odd or strange?"

"I found it odd that she asked how Matt was doing. Concerned, even. I told her if she cared so much about him, she should call off the stupid launch of hers, and she laughed in my face."

"You shouldn't have gone there, Poppy. I can fight my own battles."

Poppy put her hands on top of her husband's. "Honey, they're our battles. I'm surprised you don't realize that."

"When you left, did you see anyone else you recognized in the lobby?"

"No, but I wasn't paying much attention. I was pissed."

Parker rose from her seat. "Thank you for answering our questions. I'm sorry for bothering your evening." Then addressing Kat and the deputy, "We should go."

Kat and the deputy stood. "Thank you for taking the time to do this, Matt and Poppy," the deputy said.

"I'd like to believe that was the last of it, but I know better," Matt replied.

Matt walked the three of them to the door, but before exiting, Parker turned and addressed Poppy.

"I don't speak for my mother, but I'm sorry for the grief her book has caused you."

For the first time that Parker could recall, a weak smile appeared on Poppy Jackson's lips. "Thank you for saying that."

Gathering back at their vehicles, Deputy Bonner put his hands on his hips. "Satisfied?"

"Of what?" Parker asked.

The deputy appeared confused. "That Penelope's death was just a suicide."

"No," both Parker and Kat answered in unison.

"I don't understand. Poppy has explained what she was doing there."

"Jeez, they grow them dense out here in the country," Kat said.

"Deputy, all we have is her word about what happened in that room. She could have just as easily forced Penelope to swallow those pills during that time."

"But she didn't even try to avoid being caught by the security camera?"

"She might not have known they were there. This isn't some master criminal we're talking about."

The deputy shook his head. "I don't buy it. If she forced Penelope to take those pills, there would have been marks on her body, and there weren't any."

"Pointing a gun at someone can be pretty persuasive," Kat pointed out. "And no marks."

"I'm not ready to rule her out as a suspect, is all I'm saying," Parker stated.

"Fair enough. What's your next move?" the deputy asked.

"I'm going to talk to the other parents of the original murders in the morning, and then there's the rescheduled book launch in the afternoon. That could be interesting."

"That's what I'm afraid of," the deputy groaned.

Seventeen

Friday morning, Kat was still sleeping soundly when Parker snuck out of the room. The previous night she had arranged a meeting at a local coffee shop with Mary and Dan Emerson, the parents of Snake River murder victim number two. They would only agree to the meeting under the condition that anything they discussed with Parker would be in the strictest confidence and wouldn't end up in a news story, or even worse, another book.

The coffee shop they suggested meeting at was a spot a couple of blocks from the downtown area. Morning Jolt was a quaint little establishment based in a mid-twentieth century house that retained its original ambiance. Parker quickly discovered that the seemingly small parking area outside didn't reflect the considerable space inside, filled with two or four person tables, couches, easy chairs, bench seats, and stools that lined one of the outer walls underneath a ledge. Crackling flames from a brick fireplace added to the cozy atmosphere.

Parker looked over the handwritten menu on a suspended chalkboard above the serving area before ordering an espresso from the smiling employee, then stood to the side waiting for it to be ready. There were lots of people, young and old, in the coffeehouse that morning, but it neither felt overcrowded nor rushed. The four workers behind the bar moved in sync with one another, coordinating their actions, a perfect example of teamwork. Parker reflected that there were some nationwide coffee chains that could learn from this small shop.

Parker accepted her espresso in a much shorter time than she was accustomed to back in the hustle and bustle of Los Angeles, and then she took a seat at a four-person table. It required only one sip for her to decide that she would certainly visit the Morning Jolt again before they left.

A woman sitting opposite another woman at a nearby table kept looking in Parker's direction. *Please don't… please don't,* Parker whispered to herself, making sure not to make eye contact, but to no avail. The woman got up from her seat and approached.

"I'm sorry, but might you be Penelope Highsmith's daughter?"

Parker put on her best fake smile. "That I am."

"I knew it." The woman looked back at her companion. "She is, Marge. I told you."

"What gave me away?"

"I'm friends with Van Sanders. She owns the bookstore here in town. She described you to me, right down to the fleece jacket. I just wanted to say how sorry I was to hear about your mother."

"Thank you."

"I've read all her books, but I can never work out the twists. Left me with my mouth open every time. I'm going to miss looking forward to the next one."

Parker spotted Dan and Mary Emerson walking through the door, accompanied by another couple.

"I really appreciate hearing that. I'm sorry, I'm meeting someone, and they've just arrived."

"Oh, I'm sorry. My condolences once again," the woman said and returned to her seat.

As the group approached, Parker remembered Greg Pool from their encounter in the hotel lobby, but the woman with him was unfamiliar. She was younger than the rest, and Parker didn't think she could be Greg Pool's wife.

Parker stood as they walked up.

"Mr. and Mrs. Emerson, thank you for agreeing to talk with me this morning. I'm afraid I don't know your companion, Mr. Pool."

"This is my daughter, Tina."

Parker smiled and shook their hands. She was a little thrown not having known that Deidre Pool, the second Snake River murder victim had a sister. Tina had to be in her mid-fifties but looked much younger. Her short blonde hair swayed around her chin as she sat down. Her upturned nose reminded Parker of pictures she'd seen of her sister. Her wide set blue eyes smiled at Parker, matching the engaging grin on her lips.

Parker hadn't been expecting anyone but the Emersons and wasn't sure if it was wise to talk to them as a group, preferring to do it individually. But they were here now, and she had to make the most of it.

"Can I get anyone a coffee?" Parker offered.

"Tina can get it for us. I'll have Black Bear, honey."

"Dan? Mary?" Tina asked.

"Nothing for me, thank you," Mary Emerson replied.

"I'll have a large coffee, black, if you don't mind," Dan Emerson said.

"Not a problem," Tina said, then headed to the bar.

"Why don't we all take a seat," Parker suggested.

Mary Emerson nabbed the seat to Parker's left, her husband directly across, and Greg Pool to Parker's right. Once everyone took their seats, Greg Pool borrowed a chair from an unoccupied table and placed it between himself and Dan Emerson.

"I have to say I wasn't expecting you and your daughter this morning, Mr. Pool."

Greg Pool was wearing a different sports coat this morning and, up close, seemed even taller than Parker first thought. He removed his black spectacles and started cleaning them with a napkin from the table.

"I heard you spoke with Trisha the other day, and when Dan told me you made arrangements with him and Mary to speak this morning, I wanted to be part of it. I'm curious to see what you're after."

"Why do you think I'm after anything?"

"Aren't you? I'm not an idiot. I know that you and your mother haven't spoken to one another in years, but you expect us to believe you're here now as the grieving daughter in search of an imaginary killer that nobody believes exists. No, you're playing some angle and using our personal losses to further your own agenda. I just haven't figured out what that is yet."

Parker struggled to hold her tongue, so she re-directed her focus elsewhere. "Is that what you believe, Mr. and Mrs. Emerson? That talking to you is some kind of ploy?"

Mary Emerson looked at her husband before responding. "You seem like a nice person, Miss Highsmith."

"Please, call me Lynn," Parker said, choosing to ignore the surname confusion.

"Lynn. It's just that this entire business with the book and the event at the bookshop… it's just so upsetting. It cheapens the memory of our daughter… of all our daughters. Your mother's book has taken their deaths and erased all that they were as human beings and turned their lives into pliable instruments of some sinister play. I do struggle to understand what part you play in that."

Tina Pool returned with the drinks and took a seat next to her father.

"I understand your apprehension, all of you, I really do, so let me make myself clear. I have no connection with the book. None whatsoever. Or the event at the bookshop. I have no idea why Penelope wrote the book. Like Mr. Pool so bluntly pointed out, I have not been in Penelope's life for a long time. My grief, on whatever level, is my own and, frankly, no business of yours. I did, however, speak to Penelope a few months ago, and she told me of her intention to make public during this book launch something she's kept a secret for a long time. The timing and location of this so-called revelation right here in Willow's Bane makes me believe it had something to do with the murder of your daughters, which is why her supposed suicide makes little sense to me. She wouldn't have ended her life before she said what she had to say. So, no Mr. Pool, I do not believe Penelope's killer is imaginary. Someone saw to it that she would never be able to reveal her secrets. Whether she was killed because that person was upset about her stirring up painful memories, or they wanted the secret kept quiet, or some other reason entirely I'm not sure, I'm going to find the person responsible. That is the only reason I wanted to talk to any of you."

"But what if you're wrong?" Greg Pool asked. "What if Penelope just snapped and ended it? What you're doing right now, talking to us and others, the longer it goes on, the greater the chance that the media will pick up on it and the circus will start all over again. Have you thought of that?"

An image of the words *Forgive Me* popped into Parker's mind.

"I have. I've weighed the possibilities and keep coming back to the same conclusion. But let me ask you something, Mr. Pool. What if I'm right and somebody took Penelope's life? Even though I know you didn't care for her, or her book, could you sleep at night knowing that someone had gotten away with murder?"

Greg Pool sat back in his chair and crossed his arms. "The world is filled with what if's," he replied.

"I couldn't," Tina Pool suddenly said.

"Neither could I," Mary Emerson said. "Go ahead and ask your questions."

"Thank you. I understand that your daughter, Maddy, disappeared when she went to the library that night. Is that something she did often, go to the library?"

"No, not really, but she was writing a paper on Aztec cultures and needed to do some research for it."

"Didn't the school library have what she needed?"

A weak smile appeared on Mary's lips. "Maddy was an overachiever. She wouldn't be satisfied until she had sourced everything she could. That's just who she was."

"Did she know Penelope?"

"They were on the soccer team together, but I don't recall them ever hanging out with each other. Do you Dan?"

Dan Emerson looked like he wanted to be anywhere but in that coffee shop. He shook his head.

"How about Hutch Jamesison? Did she know him?"

Mary's forehead furrowed. "Absolutely not. He was a drop-out."

"What about you Mr. Pool, did Deidre know Penelope at all?"

"I wasn't very familiar with my daughter's social life. My wife was more in tune with such things," Greg grumbled, looking down into his coffee.

"May I ask where your wife is now?" Parker asked, lowering her voice to sound less harsh.

"We've been divorced for almost ten years. She lives in Chicago now."

"Are you still in touch with one another? Do you know how she feels about the book?" Parker asked.

"We don't communicate," Greg said flatly, taking another sip of his coffee.

"I've spoken with her," Tina interjected, which drew a sharp look from her father. "She's indifferent about the book. Couldn't care less."

"Thank you," Parker said.

"Deidre didn't like Penelope," Tina offered. "She thought she was a lesbian."

Now everyone was looking at Tina.

"So, she knew Penelope?" Parker asked.

"Only in the same way she knew all the girls on the team. Deidre had an opinion about everybody, and she wasn't shy about sharing it."

"Did she say why she thought Penelope was a lesbian?" Parker said, being sure to hide the shock she was feeling.

"Because of the way she and Vanessa Sanders were always joined at the hip. Especially after the accident," Tina said, using her fingers to rotate her coffee cup.

"Accident?" Parker asked, confused because Penelope had never mentioned an accident.

Greg Pool seemed to squirm in his chair.

Mary Emerson clasped her fingers together and laid them on the table. "Vanessa's family was involved in an accident with another car. The driver was drunk, ran a stop sign and t-boned the Sanders' car. Vanessa was hurt pretty bad, a broken leg, I think, which is why she still limps today. It was a shame, too. Vanessa was a track star. You treated her, didn't you Greg?"

Greg nodded his head. "I did. Multiple fractures. Nasty. Ruined any chance of her running competitively again. But what does any of that have to do with anything?"

"What about Deidre, Mr. Pool? She told her soccer coach, Matt Jackson, and your wife that she was going to get a ride home with another player on the day she disappeared, which turned out not to be true. I know you've had a lot of time to think about it. Do you have any idea why she did that, or who she was really going to meet?" Parker asked, trying to be as delicate as she could.

Greg Pool frowned. "The sheriff and FBI both asked us that over and over, and I tortured myself with that question for years. The plain fact was, Deidre would do that. A lot. She would make up stories about a sleepover at a friend's when she was really at a party with boys. She'd claim to be at soccer practice when she was really shopping. She could be loose with the truth when it suited her."

"That's an understatement," Tina scoffed.

"Listen, she wasn't perfect, but she was my little girl and didn't deserve what happened to her," Greg stated, running his hand through his hair. "She was a teen girl doing teenage girl things."

"Could she have been seeing a boy? Was she dating anyone at the time?" Parker asked.

Greg shook his head. "We were asked these same questions years ago and the answers haven't changed. No."

"She liked older boys," Tina said, drawing another look from her father. "College age or older."

"What?" Greg asked, shocked. "How do you know that?"

"She told me. She wasn't trying to hide it, at least not from me," Tina said.

"Why didn't you say anything back then?" Greg asked.

Tina shrugged. "No one asked me. I was just a kid myself and no one seemed interested in what I had to say."

Parker sat forward in her chair. "Nobody questioned you during the original investigation?"

Tina shook her head.

"Wait a minute. I remember sheriff Crane specifically asking me if they could ask you some questions. Are you telling me they never did?"

"No one spoke with me."

"Jesus Christ," Greg exclaimed.

"So, was Deidre seeing anyone at the time?"

"I can't say for sure, but I got the impression there was someone. But again, it was just a feeling, which is why I didn't push the issue and say anything."

"Could it have possibly been Hutch Jamesison?"

"What! No way," Greg scoffed.

"I'm sorry, I just don't know," Tina answered.

"I understand. Was there anything else you would have said if someone had questioned you back then?"

Tina considered her answer. "No."

Parker took a deep breath. She knew this next part was going to be tricky.

"Okay, now for some uncomfortable questions. Penelope said in her book that you, Mr. Emerson, were having an affair with Trisha Jamesison when her daughter was taken. I've already spoken to Trisha, and she confirmed it is indeed the case."

It was Mary and Dan Emersons' turn to squirm in their chairs.

"Was that a question?" Dan said.

"Somebody had to tell Penelope about the two of you, or she saw you together. Trisha told me you were both careful, but obviously somebody figured it out. Any guesses who?"

"What does it matter?" Greg Pool interjected. "Some crazy psychopath killed our girls and you're asking questions about who was looking through peepholes?"

Parker took a deep breath, forcing herself to remain patient.

"Mr. Pool, it may not have any bearing on what happened to your daughters in 1986, but infidelity, betrayal, resentment, all these things are well-known triggers for serious crimes and could have everything to do with what happened to Penelope now," Parker stated.

"I knew about the affair," Mary Emerson blurted out. Everyone stared at her in disbelief, especially her husband.

"Oh, Mary," Tina said.

Mary kept her eyes locked on Parker.

"I've known about all the affairs. Not who they were with per se, but a wife knows when her husband is straying. Reading about it in Penelope's book surprised me, but only because it was the first time the harlot was named, and I didn't think anyone else knew."

I stole a glance at Dan Emerson. He looked like he wanted to crawl under the table.

"Our marriage has always been... fluid. My husbands' distractions have been just that, temporary diversions. He has always returned to the fold, so I chose to ignore them. I only ever worried that his couplings would become public knowledge, and until now, he managed to keep his dalliances secret."

Parker directed the next question to Dan. "You thought your wife was unaware of your adultery?"

"I... I mean—" the man choked out. The way he was behaving convinced Parker he indeed believed his wife did not know about his past affairs.

"Who were your other affairs with?"

"I don't see—"

Mary Emerson suddenly stood up from her chair. "I forbid you from saying anything else, Dan. I will not have my name soiled with your indiscretions any further. What's done is done, but I will not allow it to go any further. I am sorry for the loss of your mother, Lynn, but we've indulged you enough. You are picking at a thread that can only result in further unraveling, but it is the wrong garment."

With that, Mary Emerson marched out of the coffee shop without bothering to see if her husband was following. He was... meekly. He kept his eyes cast downward, afraid to meet anyone's gaze.

Greg and Tina Pool watched the Emersons depart, then turned back, shock still on their faces.

"I hope you're happy," Greg said.

"You think I'm responsible for their dysfunctional marriage?"

"Who are you to say it's dysfunctional? It works for them."

Right then, Parker was willing to bet a year's salary that Greg Pool had cheated on his wife at least once before they got divorced.

"Dad, it wasn't Lynn's fault," Tina said. "Dan and Mary obviously have problems, and who knows, maybe confessing their secrets will be good for them."

The way Tina glanced at Parker when she mentioned confessing secrets gave Parker pause. She studied Tina's face, searching for the hidden meaning in her eyes.

"Whatever. Are you done with us now?" Greg asked.

Parker tried to think of a way to ask Tina to stay behind without alarming her father, but she couldn't think of any. "Yes, we're finished. Thank you for coming out."

The Pools stood up from the table and made their way to the exit. Parker began to bus her table and when she looked up again, she spotted Tina Pool still standing by the door, gazing in her direction. The morning sunlight streaming in from outside made her appear smaller. It was Tina's demeanor that made Parker pause.

To Parker, it was an expression that said... *please.*

Eighteen

It was still early when Parker left the Morning Jolt, and she was confident that Kat would still be asleep. The book launch event wasn't until later that afternoon and, with so much free time, she decided it would be a good idea for her to zip over to Lewiston. Maybe she could worm some information from their police department and doing it in person gave her the best chance. She conveyed her plans in a text to Kat, then pointed her rental car towards the highway.

The drive to Lewiston took just over ninety minutes and Parker spent the time listening to several episodes of Samantha Trimble's podcast—Lewiston Unsolved. She found the series very well produced, albeit a little sparse on the type of drama usually attributed with those kinds of podcasts. Samantha's voice was articulate, measured, and well suited for narration, much different from the way she came across in real life. The manner in which she laid out the facts and sprinkled in bits of observational commentary differed greatly from how Penelope approached the same type of subject. Penelope's writing was wistful and full of emotional impact, whereas Samantha's presentation was unemotional and analytical. Parker was torn in deciding which approach she preferred. She enjoyed listening to the series, even though she learned nothing new.

The city of Lewiston was slightly larger than Willow's Bane population-wise, but pulling into the parking lot of the Lewiston police station, you'd think it was twice that size. The building itself took up most of a city block and the parking lot was full of police cruisers. Parker made her way to the reception area, tucked behind a thick sheet of clear plexiglass, and asked to see a detective regarding the murders that took place in 1984-85. While the male officer called someone to check availability, Parker scanned the waiting room. It may have been twice the size of the one in Willow's Bane, but it was also twice as nasty and reeked of stagnant body odor. The yellowing white paint was dingy, the floor tiles chipped. Even the officer looked like he had seen better days.

The officer replaced the handset of his phone and looked at Parker with a weary expression.

"The detective said he would talk to you, but it might be a brief wait. Do you still want to see him?"

"I do," she said, and when the officer nodded his acknowledgement, she moved to the cleanest chair she could find to sit on.

After settling, Parker removed the copy of Malignant Doubt from her backpack and flipped to the chapter that focused on the forensic evidence, of which she remembered from reading it the first time. It was a short chapter.

All three girls were found naked floating in the Snake River, which meant there were no fiber, fluids, or DNA evidence recovered from the bodies. There was nothing to suggest sexual assault either, but because of the immersion in the river, the results were inconclusive. The injuries on each girl, which were viciously delivered around the head and neck region, were inflicted with some form of a blunt object, like a piece of rebar, resulting in extensive tissue damage. The book included a retrospective study of the injuries and characteristics of each girl, complete with an artist drawing detailing the location and severity of each wound on the body. Two of the girls suffered skull fractures. Parker wondered if this might be what Abner Crane had been referring to when he said that one murder differed from the others, but he thought it was a fourth victim. She contemplated how much weight she should place on the retired sheriff's dementia afflicted memory.

The psychological analysis of the way the girls were killed was even more interesting. Statistically, only nine percent of victims of serial killers died via bludgeoning. Historically, most serial killers preferred "easier" methods. Using brute force was a sign of deep emotional rage and lack of control, which would often-times result in messy and forensically fruitful crime scenes. That wasn't the case with these murders.

Maddy Emerson's car, left in the library parking lot she disappeared from, was thoroughly examined. They found nothing of relevance. They also searched the parking area adjoining the soccer practice fields, which was the last known location of Deidre Pool. They found nothing from that scene either. The rooms of all three girls were gone over with a fine-tooth comb, hoping to find signs of a secret romance that might lead to a suspect, but that came up empty as well.

The police had conducted thousands of hours of interviews involving the girls' friends and any adults who may have interacted with them. But nowhere could Parker find a record of anyone talking to Deidre's sister Tina. That bothered Parker. It was a big miss. Penelope had been critical of the investigation in her book, and it looked like she had good reason.

Then there was the way Tina had looked at Parker in the coffee shop. The woman obviously had something she wanted to say, but not in front of her father. Parker would have to pay the woman a visit, and soon.

The *Eye of the Tiger* ringtone emanating from her cell phone interrupted Parker's thoughts. She pulled out her phone, already anticipating what the caller ID would read. Sure enough, Chuck's name and number glowed back at her. She declined the call, wondering how much longer she could go on ignoring her friend's calls.

"Miss Parker?"

Parker looked up to find a man in a gray ill-fitting suit standing in a door next to the reception desk. The man was short and pudgy, with curly brown hair. His eyes betrayed his annoyance at having to talk to her.

"That's me," Parker responded, putting away her book and standing.

"Detective Brown. You want to follow me?" He waved his small chunky hand towards the hall.

Parker followed the detective into a room with half-a-dozen desks. There was only one other person in the room, a man sitting in front of a computer monitor in the corner with his suit jacket draped over the back of the chair he was seated in. Detective Brown lowered himself into a chair behind the closest desk to the door, grimacing as he did. Parker took the seat adjacent to the desk.

The detective took a small pillow that had been resting on his chair and positioned it against the small of his back. "Sciatica. A real pain," he said.

"I imagine," Parker replied, offering him a brief smile.

The detective flipped the pages on his legal pad until he reached a blank sheet, then clicked his pen. "You have information about the murders that took place in 1984-85, I understand."

"Not exactly. I was hoping to ask some questions and clarify a couple of points about the murders."

The detective unceremoniously dropped his pen and sat back, grimacing again. "You didn't say you were a reporter."

"I'm not. Not at all. My mother was an author who recently passed away in Willow's Bane, and she wrote a book about—"

The detective's eyebrows sprung upwards. "Penelope Highsmith?"

Parker couldn't suppress her surprise. "Yes, that's her."

"You're Penelope Highsmith's daughter?" The detective leaned forward eagerly.

"Yes."

A huge smile broke out on the detective's face. "My wife and I are HUGE fans of your mother's books." Then the smile softened. "I'm so sorry to hear what happened."

"Thank you."

"It always surprised me at how well she depicted police procedures in her books. Very accurate, which isn't always the case in the other books we read, but she nailed it. Her plot twists were real doozies. Those sorts of things rarely happen in real life, but are still fun to read."

"Did you read her newest, Malignant Doubt?"

The detective made a face. "True crime isn't really my thing. I see too much of it here at work."

"It's kinda why I'm here. I've been told that Penelope missed some facts about the Snake River murders in her book that relate to the prior murders here in Lewiston. I'm just trying to clear those facts up."

The detective frowned. "What does it matter now? The book is published, right?"

"It is. We're holding a promotional event for the book's release this afternoon and I wanted to be prepared to answer these types of questions should they come up. But also, it's for my own peace of mind."

"Look, I'd really like to help, but even though these murders happened a long time ago, it's still an open investigation, and I'm not supposed to comment on them."

"Not even to confirm or deny? I wouldn't mention your name and you wouldn't even have to speak. Just tap your pen on the legal pad once for yes, and twice for no."

Detective Brown pursed his lips, glanced over his shoulder at the person still typing near the back of the room, then picked up his pen.

Parker smiled. "Is it true the Lewiston police had a suspect at one time with connections to Willow's Bane?"

The detective tapped his pen one time.

"Was that person officially questioned?"

The pen tapped one time.

"Was that person ever eliminated as a suspect?"

Two taps.

"When the murders in Willow's Bane began, was this suspect's name passed along to the investigators there?"

The detective hesitated, then tapped his pen twice.

"Why not?"

The detective dropped his pen. "Okay, Miss Parker, I've been more than cooperative, but that's enough. I won't say anything else."

"What about the fact the last victim here in Lewiston was found without clothing, just like the bodies that were eventually found in Willow's Bane?"

A dark scowl came over the detective's face, and he leaned in closer to Parker. "Now you're testing my patience, and I think you should go before I lose it."

"So, it's true a link exists between what happened here and the Snake River murders?"

"You've been talking to that podcaster chick, haven't you?" the detective growled.

Parker leaned forward also, almost coming nose to nose with the detective. "The name of that podcaster chick is Samantha Trimble."

"You amateur detectives are all the same. Everything is a conspiracy and actual detectives have brains the size of walnuts. We're done here."

"You're right, we are," Parker said as she stood. "I can show myself out, so don't bother to get up. I wouldn't want to aggravate your back any further."

Back in the rental car, Parker sat with both hands white knuckled on the steering wheel, doing her best to control her temper. She didn't know why she was so angry. Her expectations of garnering new information from the Lewiston Police were low before arriving, so why did the detective's response bother her so much? Was it his complete dismissal of outside help, or the way he disrespected the relative of a victim?

Parker's cellphone rang, and she saw that the call was from Kat. She took a couple of deep breaths to calm herself, then answered.

"Hey," Parker said.

"Are you still in Lewiston?"

"I'm heading back now. You finally awake?"

"Please… I've been up for an hour."

"Room service woke you, didn't they?"

"I'm neither confirming nor denying that."

"Thought so. Get this, Greg Pool and his daughter, Tina, showed up with the Emersons this morning, and I found out that the police never talked to Tina back in 1986. A total whiff."

"What? They must have had the keystone cops working the case. Did she have anything to spill?"

"A little. She said her sister hated Penelope. Thought she was gay. She also said she thought Deidre was seeing someone older but didn't have any proof of it. Just a hunch. I got the impression that she and her sister didn't get along."

"Did she dislike her enough to beat her to a pulp?"

"I've heard of stranger things, but it wouldn't explain Mikayla and Maddy's deaths. Oh, and Mary Emerson knew about her husband's affair with Trisha. Well, she was aware he was cheating on her, just not who it was with until she read it in Penelope's book. That woman is off somehow."

"Do you believe her about not knowing who her hubby was boinking?" Kat asked.

"I'm not sure."

"Do you still consider her a suspect?"

"Dan Emerson had multiple affairs, and his wife was adamant that those other names not come out, so maybe she was afraid that Penelope knew those names and didn't want them publicized. It doesn't explain why Penelope didn't include them in the book though. It's a theory," Parker said.

"Yeah. You also haven't talked with Trisha's husband yet. Maybe he was pissed at Penelope for exposing his wife's affair and dragging his name through the mud?"

"That would be easier to believe if he went after his wife or Dan Emerson, but not Penelope."

"Yeah, I suppose," Kat said. "You get anything from the Lewiston police?"

"A headache. I went through all the forensic material in Penelope's book while I was waiting to see them and couldn't find anything that would make one murder different. Two of the girls had their skulls fractured, and the third didn't, but I don't think that's what Abner Crane meant when he said one of the murders was different."

"I know Penelope was quick to discount the three murders that happened in Lewiston years earlier, and so did the investigators back then, but maybe everyone dismissed the idea too quickly. The killer, who might be this person the podcaster mentioned, could have been working his way up the river."

Parker shook her head. "I'm still not sure. Those murders happened over the course of eighteen months. The victims were older, and different sexes. Other than the last body being found naked, the circumstances were completely different. On the other hand, I confirmed there was a person here in Lewiston who was never eliminated as a suspect, but they didn't give his name to the Snake River investigators, despite having some kind of connection there. It's tenuous."

"Well, I'm out of ideas. When are you going to be back? I'd like to get something to eat before we go to the bookstore for the launch?"

"I'll be back in about ninety minutes, and the place I had coffee at this morning was fantastic. They serve sandwiches too. Wanna try that?"

"Sounds good."

"I'll call when I get close."

After saying their goodbyes and hanging up, Parker's obnoxious ringtone immediately began ringing again.

"Hello?"

"Do you know who this is?" the nasally voice asked.

Parker glanced at the caller ID. "According to my phone, you're unavailable."

"Cute. I'm going to assume you do know who this is and the reason for my call."

Parker reached into her backpack and rummaged through the side pocket, extracting a small device. She put the phone in hand-free mode, then pressed a red button on the device.

"Let me guess, you want to sell me an extended warranty for my car?"

A soft chuckle came from the phone. "I can see you're not taking this seriously, Miss Parker."

"It's Mrs. Parker."

"My apologies. Your levity is most unfortunate, because we are willing to offer you a lucrative sum of money to secure your services."

"To not testify against your client? Isn't that what you mean?"

"The employment contract we're talking about has a much broader scope."

"Interesting. Would I have to relocate to Chicago?" Parker asked.

"Your base of operations can be wherever you choose."

"Is there a job description I might look at? I'm unclear about what you think I would do for your organization."

"That's something we prefer to work on together after you're onboard."

"After the trial, you mean?"

"You seem to keep focusing on that aspect of the proposal, which I believe is short-sighted on your part. You've not even heard about the compensation package yet."

"Look, Mr. Unavailable, I don't need to know how much your bribe is because I fully intend to testify against your client when the time comes and see him go to jail with the other low-life's. I appreciate that you have a job to do, but you're wasting your time."

There was a long pause before, "I'd really hoped you'd respond to the carrot, Mrs. Parker."

"Is this where you threaten me with your big stick?"

Parker detected another chuckle. "We don't talk about such things... and you know why that is?"

"Do tell."

"Because that way... you'll never see it coming."

The call went dead.

Nineteen

After returning to Willow's Bane, picking up Kat from the hotel, and enjoying a leisurely lunch, Parker and Kat parked up the street from Book Ends. They stepped into the shop, mildly surprised at the size of the crowd browsing the shelves. The place was positively bustling compared to the first time Parker had been here. People, mainly women, wandered around, strolling through the aisles, engaging in casual conversations.

As promised, someone had replaced the broken window from the other day and restored the Malignant Doubt display, though they only exhibited a single copy of the book in the showcase now.

Parker was surprised to see Van, the owner, talking with Deputy Bonner behind the checkout counter. The deputy noticed Parker and Kat, tilted his head upward as acknowledgment, then walked away towards the rear of the shop. Van waved the two of them over.

"Hi," Parker said, gesturing towards a group of customers nearby. "Looks like you're going to have a big turnout for the launch. You should be thrilled. And I see you arranged for some security."

"Better safe than sorry. It's exciting, isn't it? I was skeptical when Susan and Trent suggested we go ahead, but I guess there's no predicting what will stir people's interest."

"I guess so. Oh, this is my friend Kat Anderson. Kat, this is Vanessa Sanders. She owns this shop."

"It's Van. Nice to meet you."

"Ditto," Kat replied. "Do you carry any Manga?"

"Absolutely. We have *Demon Slayer*, *Chainsaw Man*, all the popular titles."

Kat grinned widely. "I already like this place."

"I'd show you where they are, but my leg is really bothering me today," Van said, rubbing the upper-thigh of her damaged leg. "A change in the weather does that sometimes."

"That's okay, just point the way," Kat replied.

"It's about a third of the way down the center aisle, row twelve on the right."

"You'll know where to find me," Kat said as she walked away. She passed by Penelope's agent, Susan Reynolds, who was on her way towards Van.

"I'm glad to see you here, Lynn. Quite a turnout, wouldn't you say?" the literary agent asked.

"It is."

"There are even more people in the back already grabbing seats, even though we still have thirty minutes before we kick things off. Your Aunt Trudy is back there."

"Oh, good, I'll go find her. I hate myself for asking this, but how are book sales?"

"Phenomenal," Van replied. "I've had to rob the books from my display and request a second shipment already."

"It's the same all over," Susan added. "Malignant Doubt is selling like hotcakes. I really wish Penelope was here to see."

Parker found it improper to note that the book was selling so well because of the author's purported suicide, and more people than she cared to admit were morbidly fascinated with that fact. The tabloids were probably all over this news, spreading one fake rumor or another, creating even more buzz.

"To be honest, this is the first time I've taken part in a book launch without the author present, and I wasn't sure how it would go. I'm pleasantly surprised," Susan said.

"Let's hope there are no more surprises like yesterday," Parker said.

"Don't worry. The deputy is patrolling the area," Susan said. "That should deter any troublemakers."

"If I'm being honest, I think that window breaker actually helped with the turnout today," Van said. "The whole town knows about it and some of them came out just to see what all the fuss is about."

Parker glanced sideways at Susan, wondering if the agent or the publisher might have been behind the stunt for that very reason. Susan's expression remained stoic, staring expressionlessly at Van, her eyes never wavered or changed.

The bell above the entrance jingled to announce a new arrival, which Parker recognized as the woman and her companion from the coffee shop that morning. The woman flashed a bright smile when she noticed Parker, then she and her friend began examining the new release stack.

"What are you going to say when the time comes?" Parker asked.

"Well, we're going to let Van start things off with some introductions and remarks about her history with Penelope. Then I'll go next. I'm going to use the same comments I had planned at the original launch before… well, when Penelope was simply retiring. I'll talk about her legacy in the publishing world, some of her achievements and highlights, and all that. Then I'll switch to the reason we're here today, Malignant Doubt, and the way Penelope really put her heart into the book. I'll also speak to how she felt strongly about the way the tragedies affected Willow's Bane. Then Trent will take over and preview some titles coming down the pike from Monolith Publishing this year. I asked Trudy if she wanted to say anything, but she declined. Said she wasn't much of a public speaker. I don't suppose I could convince you to step up and say something?"

"Not a chance," Parker replied sharply. "And besides, what I would say isn't what these people want to hear. They want to remember how wonderful Penelope was and how entertaining her books are. I'm going to stick to the back of the room and observe. I would appreciate it if you didn't even mention I'm here." Then turning to Van. "I really don't want anyone knowing I'm in town."

Van's face flushed. "I'm sorry. I didn't realize it was hush-hush."

"Don't worry about it, but please don't tell anyone else."

Van pursed her lips and made a gesture with her fingers of turning a key in front of them and tossing it over her shoulder.

"I'm going to make my way to the back and see if I can find my aunt. Good luck with the presentation," Parker said, as she turned and walked away.

Meandering towards the rear of the shop, she was again amazed by the number of people she had to slip past on her way. Then again, maybe she shouldn't be surprised. Penelope was a hometown success story. Someone from their small community who had made the big time. Even though her life ended tragically, it wouldn't prevent them from recognizing her accomplishments. For them, it deserved recognition.

So what if she was a shit mother?

Parker overheard varied conversations as she walked by the many shoppers.

"It's like a circle of life type of thing. Penelope was born here, so she decided to die here."

"I heard they were going to make a Netflix series based on the book and the girl who stars in Stranger Things is going to play a young Penelope."

"This is all a publicity stunt with a giant plot twist. Penelope is really alive."

Parker's own feelings were mixed, both anxious and unsettled. Would anything unexpected unfold during the event, and if it did, would she be prepared if things turn confrontational?

Stepping out of the stacks at the rear of the shop, Parker discovered a wide-open area the size of a large conference room. There were metal folding chairs arranged in rows in front of a small podium and three additional chairs behind it. Off to the side was a large poster of Malignant Doubt positioned upon an easel. A poster of Penelope stood on another easel, the same smiling, vain photo from the back of her books. Flower tributes were placed around the photo. A tiny office was visible through a slightly ajar door on the back wall.

The publisher, Trent Carson, was sitting in one chair near the podium, conversing with Penelope's personal assistant. Willa seemed agitated, using quick expressive gestures, her eyes rolled, and her lips sneered.

Almost half of the people had taken a seat already, and people were standing around on the side waiting for things to begin. A section of the front was roped off for the media, with a throng of people Parker didn't recognize. Parker assumed that many of them close to the front were members of the media. Samantha Trimble was among them. Parker hoped to talk to the woman again, thinking about her trip to Lewiston, but the podcaster was surrounded by a group of people. Parker would have to wait until she could get Samantha alone.

Parker spotted a man who was standing off by himself in the back corner of the room who wasn't your typical book aficionado. He was leaning against the wall with his head down, causing his long, dark, shaggy hair to obscure his face.

A waving hand caught her attention, and she saw Trudy sitting in the back row. Parker was about to join her aunt when instead the elder woman rose from her chair and came to meet Parker. Trudy was wearing an outfit very similar to the one she had on when they met in the sheriff's office.

"I was hoping to see you here," Trudy remarked, taking Parker by the elbow and leading her into an unoccupied aisle. "I'm disappointed that you haven't come to see me."

Parker double-checked to make sure no one could overhear their conversation. "I'm sorry, but I've been busy trying to find out who would want to kill your sister and why."

The expression on Trudy's face grew stern, her jaw tightened and eyes turned steely. "I appreciate that, but I've given you enough rope. It's time that you tell me the truth."

Parker's face fell. "I don't understand."

Trudy crossed her arms. "It's been a long time and you do look alike, but I know what my niece looks like, and you aren't her. So, who in the darn blazes are you?"

PART TWO

TWIST

Twenty

Eight Months Earlier

Bonnie Parker sprinted the final one-hundred yards up the lane, coming to a stop at the bottom of the stairs leading up to the condo. She continued to walk back and forth with her hands on her hips, getting her breathing under control. Using the stairs to stretch the muscles in her legs, she dipped as far as she could bear to gain the maximum amount of flex. She grabbed her right heel, bent her knee, and kicked the heel up towards her right glute. Her left hand remained by her side. Then she repeated the process with the other leg.

She pulled the zipper on her warmup suit down halfway and took a seat on the stairs. The sun was just now peeking over the horizon, and she could already tell it was going to be another scorcher.

Parker pulled in one final deep breath, and when she blew it out, the sobs came.

Running usually helped her deal with the anxiety and smorgasbord of other emotions she'd been experiencing lately, but it had become harder and harder to keep them in check. She knew how crucial a positive attitude was to the treatment plan, and she kept a brave face in front of the others, but after this last doctor's visit it was becoming difficult. She could sense hope slipping through her fingers and felt helpless to do anything about it. It was a new sensation. One that left her feeling vulnerable… and scared.

When her emotions were back under control, she wiped her eyes, rose, then jogged up the flight of stairs to the condo door. After letting herself in, she tossed her keys into a bowl on a table by the door and meandered through the dark room to the refrigerator in the kitchen. She grabbed a bottle of water, took several long pulls of the cold liquid, then started moving towards the bedroom for her shower.

"How was your run?" a soft voice came out of the dark.

Parker jumped and put her hand over her heart. "Shit. You scared me, Lynn."

A lamp came to life on a table next to a recliner, revealing a woman wrapped in a light blue robe with her feet tucked beneath her.

The soft glow of the light did little to diminish the extent to which the months of chemo and radiation treatments had done to Lynn's ravaged body. Her cheeks and eyes had hollowed, and her neck seemed to struggle to hold her head up. She had lost so much weight that she looked like a child in a grownups robe. The pink beanie the hospital had supplied was covering her bare head.

"What are you doing out of bed?" Parker asked, her heart aching once again. "Do you need me to get something for you?"

"I got a phone call earlier, and I just had to get up and move around afterwards. I ran out of energy and this is where I landed."

Parker glanced at the wall clock. "You got a phone call before six in the morning?"

"It was my mother. She forgot about the time difference. It's nine o'clock there."

Parker sat on the coffee table near the recliner. "Your mother? And you spoke to her?"

Lynn nodded. "I figured if she was going to keep calling, I may as well get it over with, so yeah, I spoke with her."

"I'm kind of surprised."

During the first four years of their relationship, Lynn had refused to talk to Parker about her parents, and when she finally did, Parker almost wished she hadn't. The father had disappeared from Lynn's life before she turned two, leaving Lynn with just her mother. The stories Lynn told Parker about life with Penelope Highsmith made her seethe with anger. The alcohol and drug abuse, the screaming fits, the constant belittlement, the neglect. She wondered how the woman hadn't been reported to child protective services. Lynn had cut ties with her famous author mother as soon as she could and never looked back. Until now, that is. Parker worried that Penelope's re-appearance would only cause more emotional turmoil, something her wife was in no shape for.

"You're surprised that I talked to her?" Lynn asked.

Parker nodded.

"Yeah, well, reaching the end of your sell-by date changes the perspective a bit."

Parker's shoulders sagged. "Please don't talk like that."

"Parker, darling, you need to start making—"

"Don't," Parker said as she went to her knees and took hold of Lynn's hand and held it against her cheek. "You are the strongest woman I know, and all we need is just one break to turn this around. It can happen, I know it. You believe it too, don't you?"

When Parker looked into Lynn's watery eyes, she had her answer.

"I do," Lynn said, but it wasn't what her eyes were saying.

"Okay then," Parker said, returned to her seat on the coffee table. "What did you and your mom talk about?"

"Well, I'm not sure how, but she knows about the cancer."

Parker made a face. "How did she find out?"

Lynn shrugged her shoulders and, when she did, she broke into a coughing fit. Parker took her hand again, wishing that there was something she could do to help. But she'd witnessed these kinds of spasms enough times to know that all she could do was provide comfort until the coughing subsided. When it finally did, Lynn appeared drained, but she quickly shook it off.

"She wouldn't tell me how she found out, but she told me some extraordinary things about her past. Things she's kept secret for a long time. Things that happened before I was even born. Parker, what she told me was really shocking. I'm still trying to process it, but it explains so much."

"Don't tease me. What was it?"

"I'm sorry, but they're Penelope's secrets and not mine to tell. She plans on announcing her retirement soon because she wants to spend more time with me, but before she does that, she's going to publish one last book, and that's when the secrets will come out in it. She said she hopes it will be one small way to make up for our past together and would really like to see me there for the launch."

Parker felt surprised, and a little disappointed. The promised revelations sounded like just more Penelope drama, but Lynn was optimistic and that was something that had been rare recently. But the fact Lynn wouldn't tell her about her mother's secrets was something that had developed since her treatments had begun. A shift in her perceptions of things and a tendency to being less open. It was disheartening.

Parker shook it off and let a flash of hope find its way to her eyes as she continued to talk.

"Then we'll make that happen. So overall, it was a pleasant call?"

"It was. I think what Penelope is doing is for me, and telling the truth has real consequences. For the first time in a very… very long time, my thoughts of her are positive."

"Good. Having a goal, something to look forward to, is a good thing."

"I am looking forward to going."

"Great," Parker said, then stood. "I'm gonna jump in the shower. Want me to help you back into bed?"

"No. I think I'm going to rest here some more," Lynn said, closing her eyes.

"Okay. I'll be out shortly, and I'll make us some breakfast."

Lynn smiled weakly. "Don't use all the hot water."

"No promises," Parker said, as she disappeared into the bedroom.

Back in the recliner, the smile on Lynn's face slowly disappeared.

TWIST

Twenty-One

Present Day

"Who in the darn blazes are you?"

"Come with me," Parker said as she took Trudy's hand and led her towards the front of the store. Spotting Kat, she motioned for her friend to follow, then ushered the three of them outside, drawing a confused look from Van on the way out the door. The threesome walked up the street and entered Parker's rental car, with Trudy in the passenger seat and Kat in the rear.

"Can you answer me now? Who are you?" Trudy asked.

"My name is Bonnie Parker."

"Why are you pretending to be my niece? Where is she?"

Parker adopted a somber expression. "I'm sorry to break it to you this way, but Lynn died three weeks ago."

Trudy looked like someone had slapped her. "Died? What do you mean? What happened to her?"

"Cervical cancer," Parker answered softly. Emotions she had been suppressing for so long began bubbling to the surface. She felt the un-shed tears building, clogging her throat. She swallowed before she could talk again. "She… she fought it like a soldier… but… we caught it too late."

Trudy's shock turned into confusion. "I don't understand. Why didn't Penelope say anything to me?"

Parker wiped the tears from her eyes. "I don't know what to tell you. We got word to Penelope when Lynn passed and provided the funeral arrangements, but she never showed up."

"I don't know if I should believe you."

"I wouldn't lie about something like this. Weren't you aware that Lynn and Penelope hadn't been close for a long time? They didn't speak to one another."

"What? No. Whenever I spoke to Penelope she'd tell me that Lynn was doing great, and things were good between them."

"When was the last time you actually saw the two of them together?"

Trudy considered her answer. "Lynn must have been ten. I visited them in New York. I wanted to see more of them, but Penelope wouldn't come to Willow's Bane and I hated New York. Terrible city. Full of heathens and degenerates."

"How did Lynn seem to you, then?"

"Too skinny for my taste. And she was painfully shy. It was a chore to get her to talk."

"Lynn told me stories of what life was like growing up with Penelope as a mother, and it wasn't pretty. When she wasn't being neglected or mistreated by Penelope's assistants, they terrorized her. They would lock her in her room, withhold food, pull her hair, berate her, spread rumors about her on social media. It was relentless. She broke away as soon as she could and had nothing else to do with Penelope."

Trudy was staring off into space.

"I'm sorry to be the one to tell you all this."

Trudy seemed to shake herself out of a trance and stare at Parker. "So, how do you know all this? What was your relationship with my niece?"

Parker held up her hand and wriggled the finger with her wedding ring. "We were married. Lynn took my surname."

Trudy's expression grew sour. "Lynn was a lesbian?"

"Yes," Parker stated.

"That is a sin in the eyes of our lord," Trudy sneered.

"Oh jeez. Did we just jump back in time ten years?" Kat said from the back seat.

Parker could only recall a couple things Lynn had mentioned about her Aunt Trudy whenever they would talk about Lynn's upbringing. The one that stood out the most, Trudy's ultra-religious nature. "We'll have to agree to disagree on that point," Parker said.

Trudy seemed to digest this. "How long had the two of you… been… together?"

"Six years," Parker said.

"And you live in LA?" Trudy said, her eyes turning away.

Parker nodded. "I do."

"No wonder. Another godless city. And the reason you are here, pretending to be my niece is?"

"It's like I said when we first met in the sheriff's office. I want answers. Lynn spoke to Penelope several months ago. It was the first time they had talked in years. Your sister wanted to reconcile. Lynn was hesitant at first. Then Penelope told her things about her past, things that Penelope said shaped the way Lynn was raised. Secrets buried for years. I think it was her attempt at explaining why she was the way she was and a failure as a parent."

"What secrets?"

Parker sighed. "I don't know. Lynn never told me. She said they weren't her secrets to tell. But whatever skeletons Penelope had in her closet were supposed to be detailed in this new book. However, there was nothing significant in the advanced copy Penelope sent Lynn. When Lynn asked Penelope about it, the only thing she would say was that circumstances prevented her from telling the complete story in the book, but she was still looking for a way for it to come out. Unfortunately, Lynn passed before she could see that happen.

"Last week I came across an online ad about Penelope's book launch. I almost scrolled past it, but then I saw the event was being held here in Willow's Bane, and it made a big deal about how Penelope would be making a major revelation at the event. I assumed this was how she planned to reveal her secrets and keep her promise to Lynn. When I read about Penelope's so-called suicide, it just felt… wrong."

"We agree on that. But what I'm still having difficulty understanding is if Lynn was already gone, why would you drop everything and come all the way out here, adopt this charade, to investigate Penelope's death. There must be more to it."

Parker opened her mouth to say something, but no words came out. She shook her head and pushed the palm of her hands into her eyes. When she pulled them away her eyes were pink, but there were no tears.

"The day before Lynn passed, she made me swear that I would look after Penelope."

Kat laid her hand on Parker's shoulder. "You never told me that."

Parker glanced at Kat. "I'm sorry. I should have. Lynn was worried about what might happen to Penelope after she was gone. That surprised me. After everything that woman put her through, in the end Lynn still loved her mother deeply. She said that when her mother's secrets finally came out, she was going to need all the support she could get, and Lynn trusted me to do just that. But between mourning Lynn, my own work, and if I'm being honest, not being thrilled about babysitting someone who had caused my wife so much misery, I failed to follow through on my oath. Maybe you can see why I owe it to her now to find out what really happened to her mother, and why I came out here."

"That I can understand," Trudy said.

"I knew if I showed up asking questions as Bonnie Parker, nobody would have given me the time of day. But if I pretended to be Lynn, then people would take me seriously and be more open. We were similar enough in appearance and I was familiar with most of the people in Lynn's past. And given the fact that nobody in Penelope's world has seen Lynn in years, I thought we could pull it off. Obviously, we didn't fool you. Tell me, why didn't you give me away that first day when we met?"

"I'll admit it shocked me when I heard the deputy being called to the front desk to speak with Penelope's daughter," Trudy said, eyeing Parker carefully. "Then when I saw you, I knew right away something was up. I figured I'd play along and see what your intentions were because I wasn't getting anywhere with the deputy anyway. I guess that was a pretty good call on my part."

"It was, and thank you," Parker said, grinning lopsidedly.

"How do you fit in this?" Trudy directed at Kat in the backseat.

"I'm friends with both Lynn and Parker. Lynn was originally my social worker, but we ended up becoming friends."

"Are you also a homosexual?"

"Nope. Straight as a razor's edge," Kat said, sticking her tongue out.

"Hmmmm," Trudy turned back to Parker. "Okay, well, since you're not Lynn, tell me who you really are, aside from Lynn's wife."

Parker chose to ignore Trudy's feeble attempt to hide a sneer when she said the word *wife*.

"For one," Parker stated. "I'm an investigator for a high dollar law firm in LA, so I know a little about what I'm doing. Second, besides you, I'm the only one in this town motivated enough to look for the truth."

"Are you having any luck?" Trudy scowled.

"Somebody tried to kill me by running me down, so I must be doing something right," Parker stated bluntly.

"Oh, dear," Trudy sighed.

"How close were you with your sister growing up?" Parker asked.

"I'm ashamed to admit, not especially," Trudy said, looking down at her hands. "I was wrapped up in my church groups, and she was more interested in her social life. Penelope has always been obsessed with popularity. I thank the almighty that cellphones or things like Facebook or TikTok weren't a thing back then because she would have been unbearable to live with."

"Were there any interactions between her and the three murdered girls you are aware of?" Parker said, watching Trudy carefully.

Trudy shook her head. "No. Dan Emerson, Maddy's father, did the taxes for our parents, but that's the only connection we had with any of them. Neither I nor Penelope knew their daughter Maddy."

"Back in Book Ends, there was a man standing in the back by himself. Long hair, thick jean jacket, dirty jeans. Know who he is?"

"I've lived here all my life, there's nobody I don't know. Bill Jamesison is who you're talking about, Trisha's ex-husband. Not very well liked. He's a mean drunk, and he drinks often. He's become a bit of a vagrant," Trudy answered.

"I thought he looked out of place," Parker said, staring off into the distance.

"The only time that man picks up a book is to use it to kill the cockroaches in that filthy place he lives."

"Why do you think he's here tonight?"

Trudy thought about her answer. "Maybe to see Penelope?"

"Huh?" Parker gasped. That was the last answer she was expecting.

"Bill has a bit of a recluse since he went on disability. Bad hip. He's known to dumpster dive at some of the local businesses around town. I doubt that he has a television, so he might not have heard Penelope was dead and expected to see her there," Trudy stated.

"The man doesn't own a radio?" Kat remarked.

Trudy shrugged. "He has a radio, but I'm told he mostly listens to talk shows."

"Why would he want to see Penelope?" Parker asked.

"No idea. Maybe he wanted a handout," Trudy said.

"Do you know why he and Trisha got divorced?" Parker asked, continued to digest all this new information.

"Their marriage fell apart after their daughter died," Trudy said, adopting a self-deprecating grin. "It takes a powerful union to survive something like that, and theirs wasn't."

"Is there anything else you can think of that would explain why your sister wrote that book or what secrets she might have been holding onto?" Parker said.

"After listening to you describe Penelope's relationship with her daughter, I'm wondering if I ever knew my sister at all. I will tell you this, after the murders, Penelope became a different person. More withdrawn, less outgoing. She even spent less time with Vanessa. And she remained like that all the way through graduation. When she went off to college, that was the last this town saw of Penelope. She never returned. Whenever our family wanted to see her, we had to travel to her. She never brought Lynn here and didn't even come home for our parents' respective funerals. So, for her to hold her book launch in Willow's Bane was huge."

"I see what you mean." Parker's voice took on a gentler tone. "I need to ask you a favor. Let people continue to think I'm Lynn for a little bit longer. I know you probably feel like you need to mourn her right now, but it could give me an enormous advantage while I'm trying to find out what's going on."

Trudy nodded. "That will be difficult knowing what I know now, but I'll do my best. And if there's anything else you need, just come see me."

Parker smiled. "Thank you. Now, we should probably get back in there, don't you think?"

"You believe the person who killed my sister could be in there right now, don't you?" Trudy asked, looking at the store front.

Parker nodded. "I think it's a distinct possibility. If someone killed her to keep her secrets hidden, then that person might want to make sure they succeeded by listening to what's said here today."

"Kinda gives you chill bumps, don't it?" Kat remarked.

The three women exited the car and strolled back into the shop. Parker noticed a makeshift sign draped across the top of the cash register as she passed by. The sign read EVENT IN PROGRESS. The women made their way to the rear of the store, where it was now packed with people. Parker scanned the spot of the room where she had previously seen Bill Jamesison standing alone, but the man was no longer there.

Susan Reynolds was at the podium speaking. Van Sanders and Trent Carson were seated in the chairs behind Susan. Willa was nowhere to be seen.

"After Penelope sold her first book, *That's All She Wrote*, she went through a brief dry spell where the doubts and apprehension all writers struggle with consumed her. Was she just a one-hit-wonder or the real thing? And it doesn't matter what I or anyone else tried to tell her, she had to answer that question for herself. And boy, did she. Soon she started churning out best seller after bestseller and took the literary world by storm. Together we had a terrific ride, all thanks in part to people like you in this room right now. Her fanbase was second to none, and she adored all of you," Susan said, a wistful smile on her face.

Restrained applause rippled through the room.

"Penelope had become the queen of plot twists. No one did it better than her, though many tried to mimic her style. But little did I know she was about to spring a real-life twist on me. On all of us. When Penelope told me she wanted to retire, I was frankly floored. This was a woman at the top of her game, in the prime of her life, telling me she'd had enough. I couldn't understand it. I mean, we had just negotiated an extension to her contract. We argued about it until Penelope did something that finally convinced me she was serious. She picked up the preliminary contract we had drafted and said—*Remember the golden rule of writing, show, don't tell*—and then she tore the contract in half."

The gathered crowd laughed softly.

"I could see then how serious she was, and I began to look at things from her point of view. She was on top of the writing world, and what better time to step away than when you are on top? She was secure financially. She had won every award imaginable. Of course, us, her fans, would miss reading her fascinating stories and delightful characters, but for her, that chapter of her life was over."

The room was silent as Susan pointed to the poster of Malignant Doubt.

"Except Penelope had one final epilogue planned. Malignant Doubt was her labor of love. It documents a time in her life that obviously left a significant impression, but also resulted in long-lasting repercussions for this city. I believe the title itself says a lot about the story she has written. The lack of resolution for these horrible murders — the unease, distrustfulness, trepidation — all have left a cancerous residue in Willow's Bane. Just as Jack the Ripper left a stain on the Whitechapel district in London, we can say the same for Willow's Bane. Yes, the content in her book is dark for someone who made a living telling cozy mystery tales, but the feeling behind her words is just as powerful.

"I cannot explain why Penelope ended her life the way she did. Can anyone understand it? All I can say is that she had faith in this book and would be thrilled to see how her hometown has embraced it. Thank you, everyone."

The applause this time was more enthusiastic. Susan began introducing the next speaker, Trent Carson, but Parker was lost in thought. Something that Susan said during her speech had tweaked a memory, but she couldn't pin it down.

She had a sinking feeling it may already be too late.

TWIST

Twenty- Two

After all the remarks had concluded and the event came to an end, the guests started heading for the exit. Parker tried to find Samantha Trimble in the crowd, but the woman had already slipped away. Disappointed, Parker and Kat decided to head back to their hotel to regroup. They drove back in silence, each consumed by their own thoughts.

Kat waved a greeting to the hotel's night manager, Belinda, on their way in. Parker kept moving down the hall when Kat turned towards the elevators.

"Where are you going?" Kat asked.

"I wanted to take another run at Willa. See if we could get her to spill more information about Penelope's recent activities. Plus, I want to ask her about the lawyer and agent you said she was in touch with."

Kat remained standing where she was. "What does it matter? You can't think that has anything to do with Penelope's death."

Parker came to a stop. "Maybe not, but I learned a long time ago that seemingly insignificant threads can surprise you."

Kat glanced at the elevators. "Yeah… but… I don't know."

Her friend's sudden hesitancy concerned Parker. Their first interaction with Willa sprung to mind, and Kat's uncharacteristic silence. "What's the problem? You have somewhere else you need to be?"

Kat still looked indecisive. "No."

"Then come on," Parker said, and continued down the hall. Kat followed behind at a slower pace.

Willa opened the door after the second knock. "Lynn. What can I do for you?"

"Hi Willa. I was wondering if I could ask you a few more questions."

Willa's eyes darted to Kat walking up behind Parker. "I'm not sure how much more help I can be… you know… NDA and all."

"I don't think we'll need to worry about that. Can we come in?"

"Um… sure," Willa said.

A large suitcase was open on the bed when they entered the room, various clothes lying beside it.

"I'm in the middle of packing," Willa stated.

"Returning home?" Parker asked, cocking an eyebrow.

"In the morning. I have an early flight. I like to have everything ready, so I don't have to rush."

"That's smart, and efficient," Parker said.

"I like to be. Oh, I should tell you I've made arrangements to have your mother's remains transported back to New York. She has a plot set aside there. I'll text you the funeral details once they're finalized," Willa stated.

"Thank you for doing all that."

"It's no problem," Willa replied, continued to fold clothes and place them in the suitcase.

Parker pretended like she was surveying the rest of the room. "I didn't see you at the bookshop this afternoon for the event. Wait… I take that back… I did see you earlier, but you weren't there for the speeches. You left early?"

"Yeah, I already knew what everyone was going to say, so I didn't stick around," Willa stated.

"Then why go in the first place?" Parker asked, focusing her attention on Willa.

Willa's neck was turning a subtle shade of red. "I'm not sure I understand."

"If you had no intention of listening to the remarks, then why go down to the shop at all? That's not very efficient," Parker said calmly.

"You know… to be supportive. Penelope may be gone, but I was with her for a long time," Willa grumbled.

"You call that being supportive? Walking out before anyone says a word?"

"I'm not sure I need to justify—"

Parker decided to steer the conversation in a different direction. "I saw you talking with Trent Carson, and that conversation seemed rather intense. What was that about?"

Willa stepped to the other side of the bed and started re-folding clothes. "That's none of your business."

"Did it have anything to do with the lawyer you've contacted to break your NDA?"

Willa's gaze shifted to Kat again, remaining there for a moment or two, before returned to Parker.

Parker smirked. "Tell me, Willa, were you trying to broker a book deal with Trent to go along with the movie you were hoping to produce about Penelope's life with your Hollywood agent? I'm sure Penelope's lawyers would love to hear all about that."

"You little bitch," Willa snapped, raising her voice, but she was no longer speaking to Parker. She was looking directly at Kat.

Parker felt surprised and confused. She looked at Kat, who refused to meet her eyes. "What is she talking about, Kat?"

"It's not what you think, Parker," Kat replied, backing up and crossing her arms against her chest. Parker felt as if the ground had shifted beneath her feet as the realization struck her in the gut. Guilt was plastered all over Kat's face.

Willa pointed a finger at Kat. "She's been working for Penelope for almost a year, feeding her tidbits of information about her daughter's life. Penelope thought I didn't know, tried to keep it from me, but I'm no idiot. I intercepted the updates before she read them, then passed them along."

Parker's mind was racing to catch up with this new information while simultaneously suppressing the fury building inside her. How could Kat betray Lynn like that?

"So, you knew I wasn't really her daughter?" Parker mumbled, giving voice to something she was just realizing.

"Of course. I guessed who you were right away, but I didn't dare say anything. When Penelope heard that the real Lynn was dead she was a basket case, though she did her best to keep it from me and everyone else," Willa raged.

"If she cared so much, why didn't she come to the funeral?" Parker asked.

Willa shrugged her shoulders. "If I had to guess, she either didn't want to expose you to the media circus that usually follows her around, or she didn't feel like she had the right to be there."

Parker tried to take it all in, but she was struggling to accept one part.

Looking at Kat again, "Why?"

Kat kept her attention focused on her feet. "Does it matter? You'll be pissed at me no matter what I say."

Parker opened her mouth to say something, then decided against it. She turned back to Willa.

"So, how long have you been planning this coup d'état?"

Willa picked up a sweater from the bed and slammed it into her suitcase. "Since I found out Penelope was quitting and had no intention of keeping me around. I wasn't lying when I told you I discovered that by reading it online. She didn't even have the decency to tell me to my face. When I confronted her about it, she told me all good things must come to an end and she was confident I'd land on my feet somewhere. The witch had been promising me that she'd critique my manuscript and help me get it published, but she kept stringing me along and putting me off. Then suddenly, nothing. You have no idea how much shit I had to swallow working for that woman."

Parker recalled the stories Lynn had told her about her mom's assistants and how hateful they could be. Parker could envision

Willa filling that role perfectly. The assistant was seething now, pacing back and forth next to the bed.

"The ridicule and belittling I endured was soul-crushing, and then to find out I was being thrown away like a spent tampon — so, yeah, I started looking for a way to recoup what I was owed," Willa wailed, the veins in her neck sticking out. "The lawyer I contacted said I had an excellent case, too. Our NDA stated it could be terminated if she let me go without cause. Penelope must have forgotten about that little detail."

"But you weren't let go. She died."

"I recorded her with my phone, saying she would have no further use for my services after the book launch. The lawyer says that's enough."

Parker wasn't quite so convinced, but she'd take advantage of Willa's ignorance, anyway.

"Okay, then I want to know everything. Why did Penelope suddenly decide to retire?"

Willa seemed to regain some of her composure. "I don't know it for a fact, but the retirement talk began when her daughter was diagnosed. That's when everything changed."

"What about the missing chapter from her book? Do you know anything about that?"

Willa shook her head. "She was always very private with anything to do with her writing. She'd never left her laptop unattended and never allowed me to be in the room when she talked about her books over the phone with Susan or her editor. Everything was digital, no printed copies. She was even more paranoid about this last book. She had someone come in and install some sort of security software on her laptop, and she changed her password to something with sixteen digits. If there is a missing chapter, I'm sure it's on that laptop, but you're never going to get at it."

Parker sat in the chair by the desk. "Somebody could make a strong case for you being the one who killed Penelope. You despised her, she shafted you, you had easy access to her room and the pills that killed her. And with her dead, she wouldn't be around to contest your effort to break the NDA. They have convicted people with less."

"That's ridiculous. If I was going to do something like that, why would I wait until now? Why not kill her in New York?"

"You could use her recent changes in behavior that people have noticed to your advantage. All the emotions she was experiencing returning to her hometown for the first time in decades, coupled with the stress of the book launch, it would create a believable narrative supporting the idea of suicide."

Willa showed Parker a nervous smile. "I think you're giving me too much credit."

"You're right, I am. I don't think you killed Penelope."

"Then why—"

Parker's *Eye of the Tiger* ringtone interrupted them. She answered the call.

"Miss Parker, this is Tina Pool. I was wondering if we could talk."

Hearing Tina's voice threw Parker for a second, but she quickly recovered. "I was hoping to talk to you as well. Where would you like to meet?" Parker said.

"Would you mind if we talk in the pub attached to the hotel? I really could use a drink." Tina said nervously.

"Sure. No problem. Fifteen minute's enough time for you to get here?" Parker asked.

"Yes. I'll meet you in the lobby," Tina said.

Parker disconnected the call and looked at Willa. "I have to go, but Willa, I suggest you get a second opinion about that NDA before you get yourself in a legal mess."

Parker started towards the hallway, then turned and addressed Kat.

"Go home."

"I can't. I lost my room key," Kat whispered softly.

"No, I mean go home to LA. I don't need your help anymore."

Twenty-Three

Soon after Parker walked past the elevators and headed towards the entrance to the pub someone stumbled in front of her, blocking her path. She stepped back, blinking her eyes into focus. She didn't recognize the man in her way initially, then her memory clicked.

"Mr. Jamesison, what can I do for you?"

The first thing that Parker registered about Bill Jamesison was the smell. It was a combination of alcohol, pungent body odor, and something akin to sour milk. His long hair hung loosely around the face, and she could now make out a scraggly beard behind it. The man's jacket was in tatters and there were brownish stains around the knees of his jeans.

The man had seen better days… but not a shower recently. A part of Parker pitied him, thinking about the tragedy that had befallen his family.

"I heard you paid a visit to my ex," the man said, causing Parker's eyes to water from the liquor fumes in his breath.

"I did, and I was planning on spending time with you as well. Just haven't found the time," she said, taking a step backward to avoid the stench.

"That's good, because… because… I know things," the man said as he struggled to maintained his balance. He rocked to the left, catching himself right before he tumbled.

"What things do you know, Mr. Jamesison?" Parker asked, raising an eyebrow.

"But you have to leave Trisha alone. Hear me. She ain't deserving to be hounded like that," he grumbled as he swiped his hand across his mouth to remove a bit of dribble.

Parker spotted Tina Pool walking in the hotel entrance. "I'm not hounding anybody, Mr. Jamesison. I would like to talk to you, but I'm meeting someone else right now. Can we speak tomorrow?"

Bill Jamesison didn't seem to comprehend what she was saying.

"Is tomorrow okay with you to talk?" Parker repeated.

The intoxicated old man simply nodded.

"Where can I find you?"

"I'm usually at Rory's Saloon around noon."

"I'll see you then. Have a good evening," Parker said, then stepped around the drunken man and went to meet Tina Pool.

~

"Thanks for coming out to talk to me," Parker greeted the woman. "Shall we?"

Knights Pub was attached to the lodge via a separate door adjoining the main hotel entrance. The inside of the tavern was a sharp contrast to the sleek and modern hotel it sat beside. The room was brightly lit with adornments such as college pennants, license plates from all over the world, and a vast collection of neon lights sprinkled throughout. The owners had strategically distributed huge digital televisions around the bar, each one displaying a different sporting event. An expansive wooden bar ran three-quarters the length of the room before curling back towards the kitchen entrance.

The pub was busy. Parker spotted two unused chairs at the end of the bar and navigated Tina towards them. After settling down, Tina ordered a seven and seven, while Parker ordered a bottled beer.

"This is quite a place," Parker said, looking around at the plentiful embellishments. "Have you ever come here?"

Tina nodded. "Every now and again. The pub was here first, and they added the lodge. The pub is actually well-known for its food. Hard to find a seat at lunchtime."

"I'll have to try it out before I leave. So, I got the impression this morning at the coffeehouse that you wanted to tell me something." Parker tilted her head, quietly observing Tina.

"I did, and I do. I'm just not sure if I'm doing the right thing."

"What makes you think it could be the wrong thing?" Parker asked.

Tina began wringing her hands. "It could hurt people. I'm not even sure if telling you this will even make a difference or help you find out what happened to Penelope."

A movement behind Tina near the restaurant's entrance caught Parker's attention, causing her heart to skip a beat. Her friend Chuck was standing by the door, casually waving his hand.

"Uh… before we get started, I really need to use the restroom, so hold that thought, okay?" Parker said before stepping away from the bar. She caught Chuck's attention and discreetly pointed to the hall leading to the restrooms, then made her way there. When she turned around, Chuck was right behind her.

"What are you doing here?" Parker growled. "How did you find me?"

Chuck was a couple of inches taller than Parker, average build, with dark close-cut hair. He possessed one of those expressionless faces that made it difficult to tell what he was thinking, which matched perfectly with his dry sense of humor. When he replied, it was with a deep southern drawl.

"I'm FBI Parker. It's what we do," Chuck said, stoically.

"I'm not going back, not yet."

"You testify on Monday, so you have to go back. They have ordered me to put you on the plane."

Parker crossed her arms across her chest. "Not happening, Chuck. Tell them to get a continuance because your witness is ill or something, but the only way you'll get me on a plane is if you knock me out and carry me on."

"Come on, Parker, don't make this difficult."

"It already is. I'm not leaving until I find out who killed my wife's mother."

"I figured that's why you were here. Listen, we've been friends for a long time, and I know you don't want to hear this, but you need to let the locals handle it. You have more important fish to fry."

"Chuck, it might appear that way to you, but the sheriff in this town is less than useless and what I'm doing is time sensitive. You and your FBI buddies could help me, you know."

"You know I can't do that… we can't do that."

"Then maybe I should accept the job offer I received from Tony Isola?"

Chuck took a step back. "He contacted you?"

Parker took the digital recorder from her pocket and handed it to Chuck. "One of his stooges did. There's nothing incriminating on it, but I figured you want it, anyway."

Chuck slid the device into his own pocket. "Did they threaten you?"

"Of course, in a backhanded way. It doesn't matter. I will testify when I've done what I've come out here to do."

"Parker—"

"Chuck, you know me. Take a close look at this face," Parker said, her hand circling her face. "Do you really think I'm going anywhere with you?"

The FBI agent tilted his head to the right as he scrutinized Parker, then shook his head.

"It would speed things up for me if you could find out the name of the suspect the Lewiston police questioned who had a connection to Willow's Bane. Maybe also see if you can locate Hutch Jamesison. That's not too much to ask, is it?"

"Parker—"

"Fine. You tell them whatever you must in order to delay things, and I'll be in touch."

"But I—" Parker heard Chuck say, but she had already turned and walked away.

Parker slid back onto her bar stool next to Tina and took a long drink from her beer, allowing time for her racing heart to slow.

"Sorry about that. So, back to what you were saying. Without knowing what it is you want to tell me, I can't really make any promises, but if what you say doesn't pertain to Penelope's death, then I'll keep that information to myself. Fair enough?"

"I suppose so."

"Then tell me what's bothering you?"

Tina stared into her drink for a long while. "When I told you that the police didn't talk to me when the murders happened… well… that wasn't exactly true."

Parker looked confused. "I don't understand, did they, or didn't they?"

"Well… I saw the deputy… we just didn't do much talking."

Realization struck Parker like a beer bottle over the head. She felt an unease grow in her stomach at the same time heat started radiating from the back of her neck. "You were sleeping with sheriff Weber… when he was a deputy? But you were in high school. Seventeen?"

Tina nodded. Her eyes were still locked on her untouched drink.

Parker lowered her voice. "So, when you were talking about Deidre having a thing for older men this morning, you were really talking about yourself."

"I was talking about both of us."

"Did your sister know?" Parker asked.

"About me and the deputy?"

"Yes. Could she have known about the two of you?"

"She never said anything, but she caught us talking at the skating park once."

"Talking?"

Tina frowned. "Yes, just talking, but we were standing kinda close."

"If she suspected something was going on between the two of you, do you think she would have told anyone else? Mikayla, for example."

Tina shrugged her shoulders. "Like I said this morning, Deidre had an opinion about everyone and wasn't shy about sharing it."

Parker thought about this for a moment. "Did you tell Penelope this when she interviewed you for the book?"

"No, not about me and the deputy, but I told her about the police not asking me questions."

"Let me guess, Deputy Weber is the one who volunteered to question you. He did that in order to prevent anyone else from talking to you, thinking you might accidentally reveal your relationship. He was scared about what you might say."

"He told me it was routine, anyway. I didn't really have anything to say."

"Tina, sometimes you don't know what you know until somebody asks the right questions. You were never really questioned properly."

"You're not going to get the sheriff in trouble, are you? He has a wife and kids now and I have a husband. I know what we did was stupid, but it was so long ago, and it didn't last long."

"You mean what HE did, don't you? You were a kid. He was an adult, and a deputy to boot. What he did was technically rape."

Tina shook her head vigorously. "No, it wasn't. He wasn't that much older than me. I'm not a teenager anymore and I'm telling you right now that we both knew what we were doing. See… this is why I hesitated to tell you."

Parker could see that Tina was growing upset and she didn't want the woman to shut down. Still, she had one last point to make. "Don't worry, I won't say anything. The statute of limitations has long passed, anyway. But let me ask you this, would you feel the same way if you had a daughter the same age as you were back then and an older man, an authority figure, started a sexual relationship with her?"

Instead of answering the question, Tina took a long sip from her drink.

"I thought so," Parker said, taking a pull from her beer. "I want to ask you some questions that should have been asked years ago. Are you up for that?"

"It was a long time ago."

"Try to do your best."

"Okay."

"Great. You said that your sister Deidre hated Penelope because she thought she was a lesbian. Do you recall if her bosom buddy Mikayla felt the same way? Did Deidre ever say anything about that?"

"I think so. Seems like I remember them together saying something. They had what they called rip sessions, where they'd take turns talking shit about kids at school. Boys and girls both. Deidre was bad enough, but when the two of them got together, they could be really cruel."

"Did it ever lead to a confrontation between them and Penelope?"

Tina thought about that. "No, but I remember hearing about a screaming match in the locker room between Vanessa and some other girl. Never heard what it was about or who the other girl was, but it could have been about Penelope. The two of them were close."

"When did this happen?"

"Ummm… I can't really remember. Earlier in the year, I think."

"What about Maddy Emerson? Did she feel the same way about Penelope?"

"I don't know. Deidre didn't hang around with Maddy, nor did Mikayla."

"Okay. On the day Deidre disappeared, she lied to her coach and your mother about who she was getting a ride home with. Do you know who she was really waiting for? Was it Hutch Jamesison?"

"I don't know, that's the truth. If I had known, I would have made sure someone knew about it, despite my relationship with the deputy. My sister was difficult, but I loved her, and I would have done anything to get her back."

"I'm sure. But if you had to guess who it was?"

"If she wasn't already dead, Mikayla would be that person. The two of them were like Thelma and Louise, with a mean streak."

"I'm getting that impression."

Tina tinkered with the napkin beneath her drink. "There is something else."

"Go on."

"I'm not sure I should say this because I'm really not positive I saw what I saw. It was so long ago."

"I promise I won't say anything to anyone if I can't verify what you tell me."

"Okay. I read Penelope's book. Malignant Doubt. It might surprise you to hear that was the first time I've ever paid attention to the details of what happened back then. I mean, really paid attention. I was just a teenager when it happened and they kept the specifics from me, but **really** I just didn't want to know."

"What are you trying to say?"

"In the book it said the soccer coach Matt Jackson was the prime suspect. I guess I sort of knew that, but I didn't believe it. Anyway, it said during the time the third girl went missing, Maddy Emerson, he was jogging out on highway 41, but nobody could confirm that."

"So?"

"So, around that time I was on my way to church with my parents… and… I think I saw Coach Jackson in the city."

Parker felt the skin on her forehead tighten. "Are you sure it was him?"

Tina shook her head. "No, that's just it, I'm not. It was a quick glance, and I only saw the man from the back. But it stuck in my mind."

"Where was he when you saw him, and what was he doing?"

"He was about to enter a house."

"Do you remember whose house he was entering?"

Tina nodded. "That's the other reason I remembered this."

"Why's that?"

"It was the Highsmith's house."

Parker considered this for a moment. "It could have been a coincidence. The Highsmith's probably had a visitor who resembled Coach Jackson."

"But the Highsmith's weren't there. They went to the same church my family went to, and they were at church when we arrived."

"Was Penelope with them?"

"No. If that was Coach Jackson, then why would he say he was out running?"

Parker was asked herself the same question, as well as one other. "Or why would Penelope not say anything?"

Twenty-Four

Walking back into her hotel room and pausing just inside the door, Parker felt a pang of sorrow, followed immediately by a flash of anger. Although Kat was nowhere to be seen, her belongings were still strewn haphazardly throughout the room, which wasn't a surprise if you knew her. When it came to her work with computers, Kat's mind was extremely logical, orderly, systematic—but everything else she touched was a tornado of random emotional acts. Parker still hadn't reconciled herself to the fact that their friend had betrayed her wife the way that she had. It was a huge blow, and right now she didn't want to think about it. All she wanted was to take a hot shower, crawl into bed, and try to sleep.

Stepping further into the room she dropped her phone on the dresser top, then froze. Something was wrong. She wasn't alone. She spun around and right away she perceived a man standing with his arms crossed, up against the wall that separated the restroom from the sleeping area.

The stranger was middle-aged, tall and slim, dressed in a faded red western-style shirt with black embroidery covering the shoulders and front yoke, torn jeans, and a large silver belt buckle that screamed look-at-me. His hair was shorter, the long side-burns were gone, and he had acquired a scar above his right eyebrow that left a significant gap, but the huge Adam's apple told Parker all she needed to know.

"Hutch Jamesison, I presume?" she stated, trying not to let him see how rattled she was. Out of the corner of her eye she scanned the counter top for a possible weapon. The only item within reach was Kat's hair dryer.

"You got it in one. Congratulations."

Parker crossed her own arms. "How did you get in here?"

Hutch showed her a crooked smile. "Let's just say I have friends in low places."

Parker sized up her visitor. He acted innocent enough, but there was this menacing quality about him. He had a couple of inches on her and maybe a few pounds, but she figured she was faster and more agile. The hair dryer wouldn't be much of a weapon, but it was hefty enough to get in a couple of good blows.

"What can I do for you?"

"Well, darlin, I hear you've been asking questions around town, about me specifically, so I figured I'd come pay you a visit and ask some of my own."

"That's considerate of you. How long have you been back here in Willow's Bane?"

"Damn girl," Hutch said as he pushed away from the wall and started walking towards the end of the bed. Parker tensed, but didn't move as the man sat down on the bed. "Don't you ever stop asking questions? Are you a reporter or something?"

"I'm a social worker," Parker replied, deciding to stick with the Lynn cover story.

Hutch shook his head. "Nah, I don't think so. Why are you asking questions about me?"

"You know why. You overheard me talking with your mother."

Hutch smiled, but it wasn't a pleasant one. His teeth were stained yellow and sorely in need of braces. "Yeah… yeah, I did. Your ma jammed me up good, doing what she did to bust my alibi."

"Truth hurts."

"Is that what you think? I wasn't where I said I was, so therefore I must have killed my sister and her friends. Why else would I lie… right? Well… I guess that's what most folks are going to think now. Pin it all on the drug dealer so this town can finally sleep at night."

"Why did you lie?"

"For the record, I wasn't the only one who lied. Parnell did his part, that's the owner of the farm where I worked. I was supposed to be fixing fences with some other fellas, but I had this deal I needed to take care of, so I slipped away."

"A drug deal?"

"There's no need to get into specifics. Anyway, when the police asked Parnell if I was working that day, he backed my story because all of the taco eaters I was supposed to be working with were illegals. Parnell didn't want to get into trouble and have all his work hands deported, so he lied. And of course, the person I had business with wasn't going to alibi me, was he."

"It still doesn't look good for you," Parker replied trying to hide her disgust over his racist comment.

Hutch clenched his fists at his side. "Because I argued with my sister? Tell me what brother and sister don't argue. Sure, we hollered at one another, but I would NEVER do that to her. And I had no reason for killing those other girls."

"I've been told that you had a thing for younger girls back then."

"Who told you that? Listen, I had a thing for all sorts of girls when I was that age. Young, old, Black, Hispanic, you name it I was game for it. If that makes someone a serial killer then you'll have to lock up most of the male population."

"Were you seeing Deidre Pool?"

The man bounced off the bed and blocked the path to the door into the hall. Parker's hand inched closer to the hair dryer.

"You're back to asking questions again, and I've had enough of it. You need to pack up and head back to LA. You've worn out your welcome in Willow's Bane."

"Curious that you should say that, because I'm wondering why you came back. Maybe to silence Penelope once and for all?"

Hutch grinned. "You are like your momma… seeing things where there ain't any. In a way, I did come back because of her. I needed to let ma know the truth about where I was that day, after what Penelope wrote. Didn't want her to have any doubts. I wanted to check in with a couple of my old flames while I was here too."

"You couldn't call?"

"I don't carry a phone."

"Pay phones are still a thing."

"I was in the area anyway."

"What day did you arrive?"

Hutch shrugged his shoulders. "A couple days ago."

"You sure it wasn't sooner than that, like the day before the book launch?"

"I'm certain. Anyway, I didn't know your momma had busted my alibi until after the book was released, so why would I be here any earlier than that?"

"Why indeed."

Hutch dipped his head and shook it. When he looked up again his expression was stone cold. He reached behind his back with his right hand and when it came back it was holding a black .9mm pistol. He pointed the gun at Parker's head.

Parker's insides went numb.

"I am doing you a favor, so you'd better listen. Leave Willow's Bane and don't look back. This is your last warning."

Twenty-Five

The next morning, Parker returned to her room drenched in sweat after a rigorous run on the treadmill in the hotel's exercise room. This was the first time since arriving in Willow's Bane that she felt the desire to work out. She needed to escape her own thoughts about everything she learned in the last twenty-four hours and burn off leftover adrenaline from her encounter with Hutch Jamesison.

Normally she didn't like running indoors, preferring the fresh air and distractions of the outdoors, but her unfamiliarity with the area and the fact that someone had already tried to run her down once made it a requirement. At least the exercise room was empty on a Saturday morning, allowing her to push herself as hard as she wanted without drawing curious looks.

She pulled out her ear buds and tossed them on the bed, staring at the other unslept mattress next to the window. Walking over to the other bed, she sat down and swept her hand over the comforter. Kat's belongings were now piled in the middle. Her gaze next found the spot Hutch Jamesison had been standing when she first entered the room last night. Even though her heart rate was still elevated from her rigorous workout, she could feel her pulse quicken.

The man's visit, and subsequent threat, made little sense to Parker. If he was telling the truth about where he really was all those years ago, then why the heavy-handed attempt to make her leave town? Lack of a verifiable alibi isn't enough for an arrest, just as it wasn't for Matt Jackson, so why the threat? There had to be something motivating Hutch that Parker wasn't seeing.

Parker let her eyes drop to the floor where she noticed a pair of sandals sticking out from underneath the bed. She sighed deeply as her mind shifted gears. Even as angry as she had been about Kat's betrayal, part of her still felt a sense of regret over the empty bed.

How could Kat do what she did? How could she betray them both?

Her friend knew as much as anyone that Lynn's feelings towards her mother were a flash point. There was no middle-ground. Lynn wanted nothing to do with Penelope and her occasional attempts to wiggle herself back into Lynn's life. That changed after they diagnosed Lynn with cancer and things became bleak, but Kat's transgressions began long before that.

But why did she do it? Was it money?

Kat made a decent living as a programmer and kept her life simple, a learned behavior from the way she grew up. A financially motivated reason was unlikely.

Could Penelope have threatened her? Kat had plenty of things in her past that could be used as dirt, but was Penelope the type of person to employ blackmail? Parker found that easier to believe.

As Kat's social worker, Lynn knew everything about Kat, and the two of them only grew closer as their relationship changed from one of dependency to outright friendship. That's what made Lynn such a good... and bad... social worker. She would run through walls for the kids in her charge, but could also get too close, blurring her objectivity. Kat turned out to be one of those cases. Her many brushes with the law, which Parker still believed were intentional to drive Lynn away, wouldn't deter her wife. When Kat finally realized that Lynn wouldn't ever give up on her, that's when the wheel turned and a deep friendship started forming. Parker found it hard to believe that Kat would ever do anything to hurt Lynn, which made finding out about the behind-the-back communications even harder to accept.

As angry and hurt as Parker was by Kat's actions, she knew she had to swallow it and lock it away with all the other emotions she had been holding inside since this whole thing began. It was the only way she'd be able to function and remain focused. She was good at compartmentalizing her emotions, always had been, but that was something her wife Lynn continuously warned her wasn't healthy if she never took the time to process them. Healthy or not, it was effective, and that was all that mattered right now. She needed to concentrate and rely on her experience as an investigator to unravel all the twisted threads surrounding Penelope's death.

Parker had followed a predictable and traditional career path, at least initially. Both her parents were successful lawyers in her hometown of San Diego, so naturally, it was a foregone conclusion that both their children would follow in the footsteps left by their well-polished shoes. Her brother Chase was ten years her junior, but Parker was totally on board with her parent's plans at first. She graduated high school at the top of her class, got her BA in three years, and graduated law school in another three. But it was during that last year of law school where the future laid out for her, and her own interests, diverged.

Parker had always been physically active, so as school was ending and thoughts of taking the bar exam loomed, the idea of being stuck behind a desk or in a courtroom day in and day out filled her with dread. She still loved the law, but wished there was a way she could be part of that arena and not sacrifice her craving for more action (or throw away the money she'd invested in her education). That's when legal investigative services caught her eye. As a legal investigator she would act like a private investigator but report to a specific lawyer or law firm. She'd be responsible for conducting investigations for the purpose of uncovering information useful in building a case. Investigators analyzed case law, evidence, and discovery materials. They would visit crime scenes and obtain evidence, interview witnesses, and testify in court as experts when needed. It was a perfect fit, except that investigators typically earned WAY LESS than lawyers, which didn't sit too well with her parents when she broke the news to them.

Despite her parents' disappointment with Parker's career choice, they used their influence to get her a job as a junior investigator at a rival law firm, provided she didn't try to influence her younger brothers' own legal ambitions. It wasn't long before she made a name for herself as one of the firm's most dependable investigators, and they dropped the junior from her title. A couple of years later, she moved to LA to take a similar job for significantly more money and exposure. That same year, she met Lynn while working on a case. Despite being an obvious cliché, they both claimed it was love at first sight.

After the three years of mandatory experience requirement, Parker passed her Certified Legal Investigator examination and became a certified investigator. The following year, they promoted her to senior investigator at the firm. It was one of the happiest days of her life, followed twenty-four hours later by one of the saddest days. That was the day Lynn was diagnosed with stage four cervical cancer.

Her lowest day came less than a year later. That was only three weeks ago.

The growling of Parker's stomach interrupted her introspective thoughts. She was hungry, but she didn't feel like going out. Tina Pool's comments about the quality of the pub food popped into her head, and a quick check of the room service menu confirmed they offered a full breakfast. She would order something from room service, then pop in for a quick shower while waiting for delivery. While eating, she would devise a plan for the day, and Van Sanders would be at the top of that list.

After ordering a Western omelet, hash browns, buttered toast, orange juice, and coffee, Parker quickly undressed and headed for the shower.

Fifteen minutes later, just as she was pulling on a long-sleeved shirt, a knock came at the door. Parker greeted a young female hotel employee, pushing a cart full of food. After placing the dishes on the table near the window and getting Parker's signature for the meal, the server departed. Parker pulled up a chair and breathed deeply through her nose, taking in the mouth-watering aroma. She reached for the coffee first, then realized she had failed add creamer. She went to the small hotel refrigerator, retrieved the small container of non-dairy creamer she always made sure she had with her on trips, and added it to her coffee.

As she ate, she went back over her conversation with Tina Pool from the previous night. Learning that Sheriff Weber—Deputy Weber at the time of the murders—was sleeping with a high school student was a significant revelation. If Tina's sister Deidre had known about her sister's involvement with the older man and somehow let that information slip to Mikayla, could the deputy have gotten nervous about their secret getting out? Could he have acted on it? If people had found out what he was up to, they would have certainly removed him from his job and probably charged him. If he killed Mikayla and Deidre, then how was Maddy Emerson's death explained? Maybe she found out about the deputy's exploitation of Tina some other way. It would certainly explain the sheriff's refusal now to consider Penelope's death anything but suicide. Could he have silenced Penelope because he feared her secrets involved him?

Then Parker thought about Tina's assertion that she might have seen Matt Jackson entering Penelope's home when he was supposed to be out running the back roads. How reliable should she consider that piece of information? Tina admitted it was just a glimpse, and why would Matt Jackson be visiting Penelope, or rather, why would either of them lie about it?

Then, the nugget of information retired Sheriff Abner Crane mentioned pushed into Parker's thoughts. A fourth victim? The same as the others, but different. It made no sense. There were no other unexplained deaths during that period, so what could it mean? Anything? Only Abner's tortured brain knew for sure.

Parker's phone began ringing. She didn't recognize the number but answered it anyway.

"Hello?"

"Miss Parker, it's Deputy Bonner."

"Deputy. What has you up so early on a Saturday morning?"

"Well, we think we found the blue van that tried to run you down."

Parker's back straightened. "You're kidding."

"I'm not, but before you get your hopes up, let me tell you it's been set on fire."

Parker felt her expectations fading. "That so?"

"The van was locked in an old barn outside of town and someone burned the entire structure down with the van inside. They removed the license plate and scratched off the VIN numbers, even in the locations few people know they exist. Somebody was very thorough."

"What do you think about my near miss now?"

"Definitely not an accident. Have you noticed anyone else following you?"

The memory of Hutch pointing a gun at her flashed through her mind. "No."

"How much longer do you plan on staying here in Willow's Bane?"

"Until I find out who needs to be put in one of your jail cells for killing Penelope."

The deputy chuckled. "Well, you and your friend need to watch each other's backs until that happens."

Parker's heart sank at Kat's mention. "Will do, and thanks for the update."

She disconnected the call and stared at the phone. As hard as it would be to do, she had to push Kat's disloyalty aside and focus on the tasks at hand. That meant she had to get moving and her first visit was going to be to Van Sanders. The bookstore owner was overheard in a heated conversation with one of the murder victims and she was Penelope's closest friend. Surely, she had more to say.

Parker got up from her chair and a sudden wave of dizziness swept over her, causing her to clutch the edge of the table. When the vertigo failed to go away, she fell back into her chair. Something was wrong. She was in excellent shape and in tune with her body, and this was something way out of bounds for her. She felt hot, weak, and it was becoming difficult to breathe. What was happening to her? Her gaze fell upon the table and the empty plates, and a terrible thought struck her.

Without hesitation, Parker jammed two of her fingers down her throat, causing the entire contents of her stomach to spew out across the table. Where was her phone? On the bed? Another wave of lightheadedness struck when she stood. She stumbled forward, her vision becoming narrow and blurry, the sound of a roaring freight train in her ears. Stretching for the bed, she rummaged frantically for her phone. Where is it? Then it was in her hands and she quickly dialed three digits.

"911, what's your emergency?"

"Knights Lodge… poisoned… room 3—" Parker managed to get out before collapsing to the floor.

TWIST

Twenty-Six

Parker's eyelids flitted briefly, then opened wide. Bright light caused her to squint as she attempted to take in her surroundings. She was lying on a strange bed and a blurry figure was standing at her feet. After a couple more blinks, the figure came into focus. It was Kat.

"Where am I?" Parker asked. Her voice was hoarse.

"The hospital in Willow's Bane," Kat said, biting her lip nervously. "You scared the shit out of me. It was a lucky thing the EMT recognized what was going on and used Narcan on you. He said you were smart to induce vomiting, too."

A shiver passed through Parker. Her teeth chattered and gooseflesh covered her arms. She felt a chill deep in her bones despite being fully clothed. "I'm cold."

"It's one side-effect of Narcan," a male voice to Parker's side said. Turning her head, she could see Sheriff Weber sitting in a chair against a curtain divider. "It'll pass soon enough."

Parker looked around at her surroundings. She was in a curtained off area with medical monitors to her left. "I was poisoned, wasn't I?"

The sheriff rose from his chair. "Were you? Or did your partying go a little too far?"

Parker shifted to face him and felt a painful tug on her arm. Looking down, she saw her sleeve had been pushed up and an IV tube led to a pole beside the bed. "You might be an asshole, but surely you're smarter than that."

The sheriff grunted. "My deputy is at the hotel now with other officers talking to the kitchen staff and their servers. He says the woman who delivered the food never left the cart unattended. Whatever put you in that bed, we're not sure how it got there."

"Hutch Jamesison paid me a visit last night."

Kat stepped closer to the bed. "What?"

Sheriff Weber's face had gone slack for a moment, but he recovered quickly. "You saw Hutch, here in Willow's Bane?"

"Got into my room somehow. I take it you didn't know he was back?"

"No. What did he want with you?"

"I'm not really sure, but he was almost as eager for me to leave Willow's Bane as you are." Parker took a moment to shake off the cobwebs still lingering in her mind. "I... I keep creamer in the small fridge in the room. The container was already open. Someone could have put it in that."

"Hutch?" the sheriff asked.

Parker shook her head. "He was more direct than that. Had to be someone else."

"They would need a key."

Parker looked at Kat. "You said you lost your key. Do you remember when?"

"Thursday, I think. I didn't sweat it because I always let you open the door, anyway."

"I'll have them check the creamer," the sheriff said.

"Are you ready to start a proper investigation into Penelope's death now?" Parker growled before another shiver coursed through her body.

The sheriff remained unconvinced. "What happened to you could have nothing to do with your mother's suicide."

Parker raised her head, then banged it back on the pillow. "I take it back. You're either dumb as a rock or stubborn as hell. I'm not sure which is worse."

"We don't even know if they drugged you with a fatal dose yet. Someone might have been warning you to leave the folks of Willow's Bane alone and go home."

"It was fatal," Kat said flatly. "I was there when they revived her. If she didn't have an on-the-ball EMT, she'd be dead right now."

The curtain next to Kat slid open and a doctor in a white coat with a stethoscope draped around his neck stepped in. He bent over as he looked at the chart in his hand. He was accompanied by a nurse who went directly to the medical monitors.

"Ask him. He'll tell you," Kat said, pointing to the new arrival.

"Ask me what?" the doctor asked. He was in his mid-forties and already balding.

"Do you know what they gave me and if it would have been fatal?" Parker asked, feeling the pressure on her upper arm as the blood pressure cuff inflated. Her fingers started to tingle as the pressure built.

"An opioid of some kind, and most definitely fatal," the doctor said, his glasses sliding down his nose.

"Told ya," Kat said. "Attempted murder."

"Am I to understand that this wasn't self-administered?" the doctor asked.

Parker shook her head. "I don't do drugs. It was slipped into something I ate or drank."

"Well, there goes my speech on the dangers of drug abuse," the doctor said as he pointed his pen light into Parker's eyes. "Probably a good thing. We don't get many overdoses here and I'm rusty."

"It's my first," Parker said, giving the doctor a smile.

"I'd advise getting better friends or dumber enemies. This was a close call," the doctor said as he looked over at the monitor. "Your blood pressure is still elevated slightly, but everything else looks good."

"No offense, doc, but I really can't stand hospitals. When can I get out of here?"

"We need to keep you for another hour to be safe, then we can cut you loose," the doctor instructed, pushing his glasses up.

"Thank you," Parker said.

"I guess you'll be wanting our lab results when they're back, Lou?" the physician asked the sheriff.

"We'd appreciate it."

"Anytime," the doctor said as he started to leave. "Be safe, Ms. Parker."

When the doctor and nurse left, Parker and Kat stared at the sheriff. The man tweaked the tip of his massive mustache with his forefinger.

"If your mother's body hasn't left Willow's Bane yet, I'll have the coroner perform a full autopsy, and we'll pull the CCTV footage from the hotel," the sheriff said with a scowl.

"Her personal assistant was catching a flight to New York this morning, and I'm sure you'll want to interview her. Maybe you can catch her in time?" Parker said, deciding to limit how much she revealed to the man. He needed to draw his own conclusions, or else he'd continue to shut her out.

The sheriff adjusted his hat. "I'll be in touch," he said without looking at either woman, then left.

An uneasy silence hung in the air between the two women. Kat toyed with a knob at the end of the bed. She was wearing a baggy t-shirt displaying some new age rock group across the chest and a pair of sweatpants. Her hair was more disheveled than normal.

"That's some look you got going on there," Parker finally said.

"Yeah... well... I didn't have much time to plan my formal outfit for the day."

"I thought you went home," Parker said, picking at the tape holding her IV in place.

"Did you really want me to?" Kat asked, still directing her attention anywhere but towards Parker.

Parker hesitated before answering. "No."

The hush between the curtains returned.

"Where did you stay last night?" Parker asked.

"I slept in the car," Kat answered. "When I heard the sirens and saw the EMT unit show up—I just knew you were in trouble. I led them to your room."

"Thank you."

Kat sneaked a glance at Parker. "I know you told me to keep my cool here in this podunk town, but I had to yell at them. They were moving so damn slow."

Parker half-smiled, but then it melted away. "Why did you do it, Kat?"

Kat left the foot of the bed and moved over to the medical monitors. She started pushing icons on the screen.

"Don't play with that stuff."

Kat dropped her hands but kept staring at the monitors.

"Kat?"

"It wasn't for the money."

"I guessed as much, but then why?"

"You won't understand."

"Please let me try."

Kat took a deep breath and looked at Parker. "I understand what Lynn went through as a kid, probably better than anyone. I get it. But I grew up with no one. My parents, whoever they are, left me at a fire station like a donation to the Salvation Army. You can't imagine what that feeling is like, knowing that there is NO ONE out there for you. No one to love you. No one to care for you. No one to teach you how to ride a bike or braid your hair. And no matter what anyone says, the people who are paid to look out for you can't replace the feeling of having someone who loves and cares for you naturally."

For the first time that Parker could remember, there were tears in Kat's eyes.

"So, when I was contacted by a lawyer who represented Penelope and asked to send her simple updates about how her daughter's life was going, I balked at first. I didn't want to piss off Lynn. But then the more I thought about it, the more I felt—here is a mother with a genuine interest in her daughter's life, something I would give anything for, so what's the harm in passing along some trivial information? Just tidbits. I wrote about her relationship with you and how close you were. I wrote about boring everyday stuff, the type of stuff people routinely post on Facebook and Instagram nowadays. Also, I know how people can change, which I thought Lynn would understand and depend on, given her profession."

"Not in this case. She put up a wall, a tall one."

"I think they approached me because I was the former delinquent with suspect morals who would do anything for a buck, but that's not why I did it. I did it because I saw a mother who was desperate to connect with her kid, even if the kid was being a snot."

Parker shook her head. "Lynn would have been so pissed if she knew."

Kat gripped a section of the sheet on the bed and began twisting it. "She knew, Parker," she said softly.

Parker's eyebrows drew together above her squinted eyes, and then her eyes grew large. "What?"

Kat looked away and her face flushed. "Lynn knew I was passing along stuff to Penelope. She caught me sending one of my emails."

Parker was bewildered now. "I don't understand. She was aware you were doing this? Didn't she want you to stop?"

Kat shook her head, still focusing on something at the end of the bed. "No. She was upset at first, but then she told me to keep feeding Penelope information."

Parker struggled to make sense of this new revelation, but wasn't having much success.

"Why? And why didn't she tell me?"

Kat looked at Parker. "I don't know for sure why she changed her mind. She never told me, but she didn't want me to tell you because she knew how you felt about her mother and didn't want to cause any friction between you."

"I ... uh ... I don't know what to say."

Kat took a couple of steps closer to her friend. "I really wanted to tell you what was going on after Lynn found out, but she was adamant, and you know how intimidating Lynn could be.

I kept working on her, even after Penelope phoned her. I just ran out of time."

"Yeah, we both did," Parker said quietly.

Silence filled the room.

"I miss her," Kat said softly.

Parker allowed herself a moment to reflect on her lost love. She could only do this sparingly, as it was too painful otherwise, and she couldn't function when she did.

"You and me both, kid," Parker replied. "I knew her attitude towards Penelope softened after her mother called, but it started before then, didn't it? It hurts me to think she didn't feel like she could tell me."

"I think, maybe, she was just being cautious. The relationship could have gone south again."

Parker shook her head. "It was because of me. And she was right. She knew how I felt about Penelope because of what she put her through, and I would have reacted badly to any reconciliation. I didn't blow up when Penelope called because of what Lynn was going through at the time and it gave her something positive to focus on. That's what hurts. I should have been a better partner and not got between them."

"For what it's worth, I thought you were a great partner. Lynn thought so, too."

"Thanks," Parker said, smiling weakly.

"So, are we good?"

"I wouldn't say good just yet, but not bad either."

Kat snapped her fingers, "I just remembered. Last night, I dug up something interesting on Van Sanders."

"I did as well. You first."

"You told me that Penelope called Van out of the blue about hosting the book launch and that they hadn't been in touch for years."

"That's what she said."

"She lied. Besides the four years she attended Washington State University, she's lived in Willow's Bane her whole life. She was married for a dozen years before divorcing, had one child, and worked in various clerical jobs before she opened the bookstore in 2004. But I've found correspondence between her and Penelope going back decades. I still can't get into Penelope's laptop, but what I could tell from stuff on Van's PC is that she was heavily involved with critiquing Penelope's books."

"Does that include Malignant Doubt?"

"No. There was nothing related to that."

"That's very interesting. Tina Pool told me she heard Van was yelling at Mikayla Jamesison before Mikayla was murdered, though I don't know about what."

The women stopped talking for a moment. Kat moved to the side of the bed and laid her hands on the side rails. "You really scared me, Parker."

"I know."

"That's the second time somebody has tried to kill you," Kat pointed out solemnly. "And now a strange guy shows up in your room. I can't lose you too, Parker."

"I'm not going anywhere, Kat."

"Don't blow me off with some shoo-fly remark like you're in total control of everything because you're not. And don't treat me like a kid. Lynn wouldn't want you to die over this."

Parker paused before responding. "Okay, I hear you, but it's something I gotta do, Kat."

"But why? I know you promised Lynn you'd look after Penelope, and you feel like you let her down, but this is a lot."

Parker could feel the emotions creeping up on her. She pinched her lips together and shook her head. Even if she tried, she doubted the words would get past the lump in her throat. Swallowing hard, she tried to push the thoughts away.

"Parker, it's me. Why is this so important?" Kat asked again.

This time, it was Parker's eyes that glistened. "I let her down so many times, Kat."

"What? Who? Lynn?"

"I knew something was off with her early on, and I should have pushed harder for her to get a checkup. I let her placate me with empty promises because I didn't want to get in an argument about something that could have been nothing. But then when she finally went in and she was diagnosed, I trusted the doctors. Trusted the treatments. I trusted in my absolute belief that together we would get through it all. I was wrong. We were wrong."

Parker's breath shuddered when she inhaled, and she pulled her arms and legs up into a ball.

"By the time I realized how wrong we were, it was too late. I should have fought harder for her. Pushed for an alternate plan. Some experimental trials. Anything. I should have done more, but I didn't."

Kat placed a hand on her friend's shoulder. "Parker, there was nothing anyone could have done. The cancer was too aggressive."

Parker shook her head again, fighting against the helpless feeling. "I let her down. But I won't let her down on this. I can't. She was so pumped knowing her mother was finally moving in the right direction, and she wanted me to keep her on track. I know she would want me to find out who killed her."

"Okay, but do you think Sherriff Weber is going to catch this person before they try to kill you again?"

Parker glanced at the curtain. "I didn't want to say anything to the sheriff, but there's a slight chance it was someone else who tried to poison me."

Kat's eyebrows furrowed. "What? Who?"

"I'm supposed to testify regarding a case I was working for the firm. I witnessed something… something that happened more than a year ago… before Lynn got sick… but it's just now coming to trial. The guy I'm testifying against is part of a mid-level crime family and his goon's sort of threatened me."

"Jesus Christ, Parker. Why didn't you tell me this before?"

Parker dipped her chin and rubbed the back of her neck. "Well, the threat is recent, and I don't really think it means anything. I know these guys. They're mostly bluster. I'm only telling you now because I want to be completely honest. Whoever is after me, I'm not going to stop."

Kat gave Parker a hard stare before her next remark. "We're going to pay another visit to the bookshop, aren't we?"

"Damn right," Parker said, looking at the IV in her arm. "Just as soon as they let me out of here."

Twenty-Seven

Parker put her hand on Kat's shoulder to stop her from entering the bookshop. A chilly evening breeze blew Kat's hair across her eyes as she turned back towards Parker.

"I need you to do something for me when we get in there," Parker said.

Kat shoved her hands inside her jacket pockets. "Name it."

"There's an office in the back. I noticed it yesterday. I need you to see if you can get in there while I talk to Van. Look for anything interesting."

"Like what?"

"Like that missing chapter, for example. We know Van lied to us because she and Penelope were talking regularly, so who knows what else she could be keeping from us? Are you okay with that?"

"Let me get this straight… you're encouraging a former juvenile delinquent to break into a private office?"

"It's for a good cause."

Kat tilted her head to the side. "I'm not sure Lynn would approve… corrupting me like that."

Parker thought about that for a moment. "Lynn would trust me, and you as well, to do what's right."

Kat grinned in a way that let Parker know she was excited for the challenge. "Okay. I'm on it."

Walking into Book Ends, the bell chime ringing overhead as they did, Parker could only see a single customer. The customer was an elderly woman camped out in front of the biographies section, reading the inside cover of a potential purchase. Van was behind the register with her back to the door, opening a cardboard box. A teenage girl was sitting on the stool next to her, reading a paperback.

Parker hesitated. Other shoppers were likely meandering through the aisles, and even though it would be ideal for her conversation with Van to go undisturbed, Parker couldn't delay the two hours until the store owner closed the shop. There had already been two attempts on her life. She needed to get some answers sooner rather than later. It was tempting to wait until the lone customer she could see checked out, but at the pace the woman was browsing, it didn't look like that would happen soon. Parker decided to take her chances.

She nodded at Kat, and her companion casually moved off to the right and into the stacks. Parker waited a few seconds, then walked over to the counter and cleared her throat. Van turned around and smiled.

"Lynn, you're back," said Van. She was wearing a yellow sweater underneath her Book Ends apron.

"Hi, Van. I wonder if we could talk."

"Sure. What can I help you with?"

"Um… in private," Parker said, her eyes cutting to the girl on the stool. "If you don't mind."

Van bit her lip and glanced first at the woman test-reading the biography, then the girl. "Sure. Things are slow this afternoon, anyway. Bridget, can you watch the register for me?"

"That's what you pay me for, Miss Sanders," the girl responded without taking her eyes from her book.

Van collected her cane, then led Parker slowly towards the rear of the store.

"Kids nowadays," Van said as they walked. "Whatever happened to a simple yes, ma'am? Snark has become the first language of this generation. Know what I mean?"

Parker stopped when she realized they were headed towards the back of the store and possibly Van's office. "I do. My friend Kat is quite versed."

Van turned when she noticed Parker had stopped. She reversed course and joined Parker in the empty aisle. "I bet. So, I'm curious. Why the sudden secrecy?"

"Because you haven't been completely honest with me, have you, Van?"

Van's forehead furrowed. "I don't know what you mean?"

"You told me you and Penelope hadn't been in touch for some time, and her asking you to host the book launch came as a complete surprise."

"That's right."

"But I've since learned that you and Penelope have been in contact with each other regularly for years. You've even helped her with some of her books."

Van's eyebrows lowered and eyelids squinted. "You've been reading my emails? That's an invasion of privacy."

"Sue me. Why would you lie to me about that?"

"I'm not talking about this," Van said brusquely, turning on her heel and limping away. The space at the back end of the shop remained set from the previous day's book launch festivities, and Van navigated around the chairs, heading towards the open door and leading into the office. Parker rushed forward and grabbed Van by the shoulder, spinning her around.

"Van, the sheriff is going to question you and it will come out anyway, so why not be truthful with me?"

"Why would the sheriff want to question me?"

"Because the sheriff has opened an official investigation. I'm not the only one saying Penelope was murdered anymore."

Van's demeanor softened. "Well, I'm happy to hear about the sheriff coming around, but this was between your mother and me. It didn't concern you or anyone else."

"I beg to differ. Everything about Penelope concerns me now. Please tell me."

Van seemed to be thinking it over, then deflated. "I need to sit down," she said, making for one of the chairs surrounding them. "My leg is killing me."

After both women were seated, Van sighed deeply as she massaged her leg. "I don't know how this is going to help you."

"Let me decide that. Why would you want to keep your correspondence with Penelope a secret?"

"She insisted on it."

"Because you critiqued her books?"

Van shook her head.

"Then why?"

The shop owner was now looking downright uncomfortable. "You can't tell anyone this."

"Tell anyone what?"

Van lowered her voice when she replied. "I was doing a lot more than critiquing for Penelope. I was her ghostwriter."

Parker was shocked. "I don't understand. Penelope didn't write her books?"

"We had more of a collaboration, I would say. After she published her first book, *That's All She Wrote*, Penelope developed an awful case of writer's block. She couldn't come up with an idea for a follow-up book. She struggled and struggled. There was a lot of pressure on her to deliver another bestseller, which only worsened things. Finally, after multiple false starts, she reached the end of her rope and contacted me for help. We had always worked well together in school. She knew I had a degree in English with a minor in Creative Writing and had my own aspirations of becoming an author. Anyway, she told me what was going on with her, so I mentioned an idea for a book I'd been experimenting with, and she ran with it. It was a hit, of course. Things just sort of developed from there. I was the one who came up with the stories and plotlines. Penelope handled the character development and exposition. Her writing style was so effortless."

"So, all those plot twists she was so famous for, that was you?"

Van grinned. "Most of them. Penelope had a few of her own. She was a gifted writer, after all."

"But your name isn't mentioned in any of her books."

"That was Penelope being Penelope. She insisted I say nothing about our partnership. She sent me money to compensate and even helped me open this shop, but my name was never to be included anywhere on her books."

"Did she have you sign an NDA?"

Van shook her head. "She wanted me to, but I told her I wouldn't. We had been friends forever, and no piece of paper was going to dictate my behavior. I gave my word that I wouldn't say anything, and she could bask in all the fame and glory she wanted. I reminded her I had never broken a promise to her before then, and I would not start."

"Sitting in the shadows and watching her grandstand must have been hard."

Van shook her head, smiling. "I was perfectly fine with our arrangement. I never aspired to be part of the grind of press and marketing, and as you know, Penelope thrived on it. Seeing my talent validated was enough for me."

"But nobody else would know."

"Penelope and I knew, and that was enough."

"In all those conversations the two of you had over the years, did she not mention me at all?"

The corners of Van's lips pulled down. "She didn't, Lynn. I'm sorry. Anytime I tried to bring up anything besides writing, she'd turn me off. It could be infuriating."

"Did the help you provided include material for Malignant Doubt?"

Van shook her head. "That was all Penelope. She wouldn't even let me critique it."

"But why did she write it?"

Van considered her answer. "I don't know. I'm still baffled by it. We were all shaken by the murders back then. Who wouldn't be? But I thought Penelope bounced back faster than most. Her decision to write about that time perplexed me."

Parker removed a folded picture from her back pocket and showed it to Van.

"This is a picture from your high school yearbook. You can see Deidre Pool and Maddy Emerson there, and if you look closely, you can see Penelope behind them. She seems to stare daggers at one or both of them. Do you know why that is?"

Van drew a deep breath. "Lord, I had forgotten all about that. How stupid and insignificant it seems now. Deidre had been spreading a rumor that Penelope was gay. It was juvenile. Just your typical high school bullying."

"Is that why you were heard yelling at Mikayla Jamesison? Was she spreading the same rumor?"

Van's head slumped, ashamed. "Yes. I walked in on Mikayla telling some girls in the locker room that Penelope and I were lovers. I blew my cool and went off on her. I ended up apologizing to her later."

"Did Maddy Emerson ever spread the same rumors?"

"No, not that I ever heard. Why are you asking about all this?"

Parker ignored the question. "You're telling me it's just happenstance Penelope had a problem with two of the three murdered girls?"

"Hell, I had a problem with them too, but that doesn't mean I killed them. Half the student body had a problem with Mikayla and Deidre. They were acid-tongued bitches. Penelope did their parents a favor with how she portrayed them in her book—made them look almost angelic. But, like I said, it was juvenile cruelty. I know how that sounds, and it doesn't excuse what Mikayla and Deidre did, but I really don't see how that has anything to do with the murders."

"I'm looking at every detail that links Penelope to those murders because the fact of the matter is, she wrote this book for a reason, and she was hiding something. That something is most likely what got her killed, so I'm exploring every piece of information I uncover, no matter how small or irrelevant."

"Fair enough."

"How was Penelope's relationship with Matt Jackson, her soccer coach?"

"I don't know. She didn't talk about him. Why?"

"I've heard from a witness that said they saw Coach Jackson at Penelope's house the day Maddy Emerson disappeared, at roughly the same time."

"What? Who said that?"

"It doesn't matter. Do you think it could be true?"

"No, because I was with Penelope that afternoon, and neither Coach Jackson nor anyone else came over."

"You seem sure? It was a long time ago."

"Of that, I'm positive. Whenever one of those girls disappeared, you couldn't help but remember what you were doing when it happened because you would secretly wonder… what if it had been me?"

"Did Penelope talk with you about the affair between Dan Emerson and Trisha Jamesison?"

"No."

"Why not? Isn't that the type of gossip you'd share with your best friend? How do you think she knew they were seeing each other?"

Van looked as if she was becoming frustrated. "I don't know, and I don't know why Penelope kept it from me. We were friends, but we still had our own secrets."

"What was yours?"

Van looked at Parker hard. "I used to make myself throw up when I felt too full. No one knew that. Not Penelope. Not my parents. No one. Like I said, we all had our secrets."

"I'm sorry. I didn't mean to pry."

Van bit her lip and gazed downward. "I don't know why I told you that. It wasn't anything serious. I grew out of it."

"I'm glad to hear that."

"Are we done?" Van asked, looking impatient.

"Did you or Penelope know Hutch Jamesison?"

Van frowned. "We knew of him, but we steered clear. He dealt drugs. We were never into any of that."

Looking over Van's shoulder to the office door, Parker saw a hand extend outward, giving the OK gesture.

"I just have one more question for you." Parker followed Van towards the front of the shop. When she saw Kat out of the corner of her eye zipping up the side aisle towards the front of the store, she tapped Van on the shoulder. "What was your impression of Lou Weber? He was just a deputy back then, right?"

"That's an odd question."

"Did you know him?"

"I knew of him, but that's it."

"There was no gossip around school about him?"

"What sort of gossip would there have been?"

"I take that as a no, then."

"Yes… I mean… No. There were no rumors about Deputy Weber."

Parker's cell phone began reverberating its Eye of the Tiger ringtone as they reached the storefront. The words **Willow's Bane Police Dept** appeared on the screen.

"Speak of the devil." Parker asked Van to wait by holding up a forefinger and answered.

"Hello?"

"Miss Highsmith, this is Sheriff Weber. I need you to come down to the station."

"How many times do I need to say it sheriff, the last name is Parker? Why do you need me at the station?"

"There's been a development."

"A development?"

"Of sorts. Bill Jamesison has been found dead."

A chill ran up Parker's spine.

"He's been beaten to death."

Twenty-Eight

Parker had just stepped out of the bookstore to catch up with Kat when a hand fell on her shoulder.

Pivoting and jumping backward at the same time, Parker detected someone wearing a dark overcoat. Whoever it was raised his hands.

"Whoa," Chuck said.

"Shit's sake, Chuck… you scared the piss out of me," Parker yelled, looking over her shoulder to see if anyone else had noticed her reaction. Thankfully, no one else was on the street, as Kat had quickly tucked herself away in the car.

"Sorry Parker. I was waiting until I could get you alone."

Parker put her hands on her hips and looked skyward, taking a deep breath. "I told you I'm not going back, so why are you still here?"

"You won't answer my calls, so I'm here to tell you two things. The first is the prosecutor is throwing a conniption fit over you not being available Monday, and I'm doubtful he'll ask for the continuance."

"Not my problem."

A pained expression crossed Chuck's face. "Parker, we both know that without your testimony corroborating the other evidence, his case falls apart. You're his key witness. Without you, a very bad man could walk."

"The prosecutor has his bad man, and I have my own to catch. Chuck, we both know he could get a continuance if he wanted, but he hates it when he's not in control. It's a power thing. He'll just have to figure it out."

"What will your law firm think when they find out you're burning bridges like this?"

Parker crossed her arms. "You said you had two things to tell me?"

Chuck stared at Parker, then shook his head. "The man the Lewiston police questioned about the murders was named Landon Reed, although now he goes by Landon Green and lives in California."

The podcaster Samantha Trimble had lied to Parker. She had said the man was dead.

"In 1984, he worked for a company that re-stocked vending machines for the school system. The investigators questioned him because he was a drinking buddy of the first victim, and he had a shaky alibi for all the murders. He loosely fit the profile; was a bit of a loner, had trouble holding a job, and had minor run-ins with the local blue lights. But you'll be most interested in knowing that he also restocked the vending machines for the schools here in Willow's Bane. I already checked. His employment records show he was in Willow's Bane during the first two disappearances but not the third. He had already quit and moved to San Francisco by then. He's not your guy."

Parker digested this new information. "Chuck, I—"

Chuck put up his hand. "I sure hope you know what you're doing because from where I'm standing, it doesn't look like it will end well."

Without saying another word, Chuck turned and walked away. Parker watched until he turned the corner, and then she headed back to her own car.

"Who was that?" Kat asked when Parker closed the door. "Who?"

"That guy you were talking with outside the bookstore?"

Parker glanced over her shoulder as she started the engine. "Oh, him. He was just another Penelope fan offering his condolences." As they pulled away from the curb, she asked, "What did you find?"

"There was a bookcase in the office with nothing but binders. In each binder was a printed copy of one of Penelope's books with handwritten notes all over it. It looked like Van was making suggestions for her."

"It was more than that. Van was the brains behind the books, and Penelope handled the composition."

"Like Elton John and Bernie Taupin… music and lyrics."

Parker glanced at Kat. "You know Elton John?"

"Gotta tip your hat to the egg man."

Parker chuckled. "Find anything else?"

"No missing chapter. Nothing about Malignant Doubt at all. I saw nothing else suspicious. One kinda weird thing… she had a lot of old medals, trophies, and awards, all from running track. It felt like I was in a schoolgirl's bedroom."

Parker nodded. "She was a track star before hurting her leg."

"While I was going through her office, I got a call from the guy helping me crack Penelope's laptop."

"And?"

"It's a good news, bad news deal."

"Let's have it. Good news first."

"Well, he got in and gave me access."

"That's it? That's all the good news?"

"Sorry, yeah. I did a quick scan using my phone, but I didn't find any record of a missing chapter. Someone could have deleted and scrubbed the missing chapter from the hard drive.

"Shit."

"But get this, I found one interesting thing. You remember how Willa told us Penelope wouldn't print any of her work because she was so paranoid?"

"Yes."

"I found evidence of a print job in her spooler file, which happened the day before Penelope flew here to Willow's Bane. It was fifteen pages long."

"That could be the missing chapter. Nobody searched her belongings after they found her body. Her bags are still unpacked. It could be in there."

"Or whoever killed Penelope could have taken it with them."

"True. We need to get our hands on her belongings."

For the first time, Kat looked out of the windows at the passing buildings. "Where are we going, by the way?"

"Sheriff's office."

"Why for?"

"They found Bill Jamesison dead."

Kat considered what she'd been told before responding. "I don't suppose he died of a heart attack or choked on a chicken bone or something?"

"He was beaten to death."

"Ouch. That sucks for him, but why does the sheriff want to talk to you?"

"We're about to find out."

Parker pulled into the Willow's Bane Police parking lot, and minutes later, the two women entered the building just as they had three days earlier.

"Sheriff Weber is expecting me," Parker told the same female officer who was manning the information desk. "Lynn Parker."

The officer picked up the phone, said a few words softly, then hung up.

"He'll be right with you."

A few minutes later, Deputy Bonner appeared in the doorway leading into the rear of the building. Parker could tell from the way the deputy avoided making eye contact that something was wrong.

"Come on back, Ms. Parker," the deputy said.

When both Parker and Kat began walking for the door, the deputy raised his hand.

"We only need to speak with Miss Parker. You'll need to wait out here."

"Screw that," Kat snapped.

"Kat, it's okay. I won't be long," Parker said, reassuring her friend.

"She better have all her fingernails when she comes back, deputy dog."

Parker followed the deputy to the same room she had been in on her first visit. Sheriff Weber was already sitting, tapping his fingers on the table.

"Where was Bill Jamesison's body found?" Parker asked as she took a seat.

"We can't discuss the details of an ongoing investigation," the sheriff replied.

Parker glanced at the deputy across the table. He still refused to meet her gaze.

"Then why am I here?"

"We'd like to know where you were last night between midnight and two AM?"

Parker looked at the deputy again, but he was staring at the tabletop.

"You've got to be kidding me. You're treating me like a suspect?"

"Can you please just answer the question, Miss Highsmith?"

"God damn it! My name is Parker! Why do you need to know where I was?"

"You were seen speaking to Bill Jamesison last night at your hotel. Mind telling me what that conversation was about?"

"He wanted me to leave his wife alone."

"Witnesses say he seemed upset."

"He was drunk."

"They also saw him at the book launch yesterday. Did you speak to him then?"

"No."

"Do you know why he was there?"

"Maybe he's a fan?"

"This is not a joking matter, Miss PARKER."

"Oh, on the contrary, this is one big joke, the fact you think I had anything to do with his death. Maybe you should find his son and ask him these questions."

"We are pursuing all relevant leads," the sheriff replied.

"Have you done anything on Penelope's investigation?"

Neither of the two men responded.

"Have you?" Parker almost shouted. The rage coursing through her made her hands tremble.

"We've taken back possession of Ms. Highsmith's body, and it's scheduled for a full autopsy," the deputy said calmly, looking at Parker for the first time.

"But we have more pressing matters now," the sheriff said. "I have another witness who's seen you in possession of a retractable police baton, the same type of weapon that was used to murder Bill Jamesison."

"Your witness is mistaken. I've never owned such a weapon." Technically, it was not a lie, but Parker knew she was splitting hairs.

"Can you answer my original question? Where were you during the hours of midnight to two AM?"

"I was in my room, asleep."

"Can anyone confirm that?"

Parker thought about Kat sleeping in their car that night. "No, but it's a fair assumption that the hotel keeps track of when a room key is used. You'll see I didn't use my room key until early morning."

"You could have left the door ajar to prevent using the key when you returned."

"Jesus Christ. Tell me, SHERIFF, what is my supposed motive for killing that poor man?"

"He was harassing you - why, I'm not sure yet - but he followed you to the book launch and then to your hotel."

Parker crossed her arms across her chest. "This is unbelievable."

"We'd like to take your fingerprints to—"

"Not happening."

"We can get a court—"

Parker could feel the veins popping out on her neck. "No, you can't. You don't have enough. Nobody saw me speaking to him at the bookstore because I didn't. I had a casual conversation with him in the hotel later. I never threatened him or felt threatened by him. No judge would give you a court order based on that flimsy premise."

The sheriff stared at Parker for a long time. "Deputy, I need to speak with Miss PARKER alone."

Deputy Bonner looked surprised. "Sir?"

"The two of us need a moment."

The deputy flashed Parker a concerned look, then rose slowly from his chair, confused. He closed the door behind him as he left the room.

"I understand you've been talking to Tina Pool?"

"That I have. She had some very interesting things to say."

"Did you know she's been on and off antidepressants for years? Greg tells me she's a real basket case."

"Let me guess, you and Greg are golfing buddies."

The sheriff's mouth formed a smile beneath his massive mustache—an ugly smile filled with malice. His eyes glared at her from across the table, telling her all the despicable thoughts she had about him might be true.

"Golf's a stupid sport… if you can call it a sport. But Greg and I do like a good poker game now and then."

"You think he'd still be your buddy if I told him you were screwing his daughter when she was seventeen?"

The sheriff's smile faded quickly. "Making false allegations like that wouldn't be very smart. I think you've seen how difficult I can make things for you here, and I've not even put my mind to it yet."

Parker knew her threat was empty because Tina Pool would most likely deny the relationship ever happened, but it was enough to put the sheriff on the defensive.

"I was wondering what you might be capable of—other than statutory rape, that is—if you thought your secret might get out.

Tina couldn't be sure her sister Deidre was in the dark about the two of you. No telling who she might have told. Mikayla? Maddy?"

"Your way off base."

"Am I? Funny how you just mentioned a police baton. That could be a perfect match for the weapon used to kill those three girls."

"I'm warning you."

"Message received, as long as you understand it goes both ways. I will find out who killed Penelope, no matter where that trail leads."

The sheriff stared at Parker with dark eyes. "You and your mother have done nothing but bring havoc to Willow's Bane since you arrived. This was a peaceful city going about its own business, people living their lives and staying out of other folks' affairs, and now two people are dead."

Parker rose from her seat. "You know what, sheriff? I think Penelope was right about this town. There is a malignancy here. Beneath this façade of normalcy you're so proud of, there is a deep, unhealed wound, something twisted and rotten, and all Penelope did was expose it. She paid a price for that, and I'm going to finish what she started."

"Get out of here."

Parker turned, then hesitated. "Isn't this where you tell me not to leave town?"

Daggers of detest shot out of sheriff Weber's eyes.

"I didn't think so," Parker said, then walked out

Twenty-Nine

"I knew I should have gone back there with you," Kat exclaimed after listening to Parker recap her meeting, pounding her open palm on the dashboard.

"You can't be pissed because I'm already pissed enough for both of us."

"I can tell. That was a red light you just blew through."

Parker's eyes snapped to the rear-view mirror, and lifted her foot off the gas pedal.

"We can't both be pissed at the same time. One of us must stay level-headed," Parker said.

"Okay, I'll let you have this one, but you know me, level-headedness isn't my strong suit."

"I mean, in my job, I've seen incompetence in law enforcement before, but this takes the cake. How does a man like that even keep his position? Elections? Politics? Whatever happened to investigative integrity, a working knowledge of criminal justice, problem-solving skills, hell… common sense? Did you know you only need a high school diploma to be a sheriff? If you're friends with the right people or enough people, anyone can wear a badge. It's maddening."

"Maybe I should drive if you're going to be the pissed one? The speed limit here is thirty-five."

Parker looked at the speedometer and saw that it read over fifty.

"Shit," she said, and the car decelerated once more. "Sorry. We're almost there."

"Maybe we should look at the bright side. They have Penelope's body and will do an autopsy. That's something."

Parker's eyes kept alternating between the road ahead and her mirrors.

"That's not much of something. I doubt the autopsy will find evidence to overturn the previous ruling. Penelope was compelled somehow, but she swallowed those pills voluntarily."

"Then why did you push so hard to have them do an autopsy?"

"Because I wanted the investigation to be official, which usually begins there."

Kat looked out of her passenger-side window. "Ummm... that was our hotel you just passed."

"I know. I think we're being followed."

Kat's head and upper body swiveled around to look out the rear window.

"Which car?"

"The Z28 with the rusted hood. It ran the same red light I did, and it's been matching my speed."

"What are we going to do?" Kat's voice betrayed her nervousness.

"I have an idea who it might be, but I didn't want to confront them at our hotel. There's an empty lot up ahead."

Parker pulled their car off the road into a gravel parking lot. She drove in a little way, then made a 180-degree turn so they were facing the road. Just as she slid the gearshift into park, the red Z28 entered the lot and stopped thirty feet away.

"Don't get confrontational. Just let me do the talking," Parker said.

Kat pouted. "But we just decided I'm supposed to be the levelheaded one."

Parker regarded her friend. "You think you can handle this? Like you said, this isn't your strong suit."

"Won't know until you try, right?"

Parker smiled. "Okay. It's all yours."

When Kat and Parker opened their doors, the driver-side door of the Z28 also swung open. Belinda's unhappy ex-boyfriend Todd climbed out.

"Sure you don't want to change your mind?" Parker asked Kat over the roof of the car.

Kat twisted her head to one side, a bone popping somewhere in her neck. "Nah, I got this."

Todd walked to the front of his Z28, leaned back against the hood, and crossed his arms. He was wearing a denim jacket with its arms torn off on top of a gray hoodie. How unoriginal.

"You owe me something," Todd announced.

"Yeah, what would that be?" Kat replied.

Todd pointed his finger at Parker. "Your mother's the one who told Belinda she needed to dump me. She had no right. She didn't know me. Who is she to be telling someone she barely knows who she should or shouldn't be dating?"

Kat looked at Parker. "He kinda has a point," she said in a hushed tone.

"Ask him what he wants," Parker replied in the same manner.

"So, what do you think we owe you?" Kat asked.

"I know your mother croaked, and I guess I'm sorry about that, but now you got to make right what she wronged."

Kat looked at Parker again. "I don't understand what he wants."

"I think he wants you to get him back together with Belinda."

"But we don't want to do that, right? He's a creep."

"Just as Penelope should never have gotten in the middle of their relationship, neither should we."

Kat nodded her head like she understood. Then addressing Todd, she said, "No."

Todd pointed his finger at Parker again. "Why aren't you talking to me?"

"Because I'm pissed."

That made Todd grin. "Aren't we all?"

"Listen, Todd, whatever Penelope said to Belinda was wrong. She had no right to give advice. But neither do we. If you want to patch things up with Belinda, you're going to have to make that happen on your own," Parker stated.

Todd seemed to deflate. "Can't you say something to her? She won't even answer my calls anymore. Belinda is the best thing that's ever happened to me, and I know I screwed up. I feel like I won the lottery when she started going out with me. I've been looking for a break ever since I made it out of high school, and now I have this new job. It pays well too. So, all I need is for her to give me another chance. Can't you help me… please?"

Parker and Kat exchanged a look.

"Todd, you put your hands on Belinda in anger, and then you threatened us," Parker said. "That's something I can't get past, so like my friend said, the answer is no."

Todd's disposition suddenly changed. He stood up tall, arched his shoulders, and clenched his fist.

"You bitch!"

Parker could almost feel Kat's muscles tense up beside her.

"I don't think I can be level-headed anymore, Parker," Kat said.

"That's fine. Listen, Todd, you said that Penelope didn't know you because she had never met you, and that's true, but you know what… I have. Twice now, and the thing is, I know you. You're no different from the dozens of other men I've come across in my life. In seconds, you went from begging for our help to calling us nasty names. You have anger management issues, fella, and until you deal with that, you don't deserve someone like Belinda or any other woman."

Todd's eyes were almost black. "If you were a man, I'd rip your head off and piss down your throat."

"Thanks for that delightful imagery. Are you through now?"

Todd ran his hand through his greasy hair. He stomped back to his car door, opened it, and reached for something behind the seat. When he straightened up, he was holding a tire iron.

"I might not take to beating on women, but your car's another matter."

"Oh, I think you're perfectly fine beating on women. But the car, it's a rental."

Todd started moving forward, pumping the metal rod up and down as he did. "You'll still be responsible for the damage."

Out of the corner of her eye, Parker saw Kat adopt a protective stance, something they had both learned in self-defense classes.

"You're not touching this car," Kat breathed.

When Todd was only ten feet away, another car pulled into the lot from the street, making Todd freeze. The white Toyota coup parked to the side of both vehicles, and the driver's door swung open.

"What are you doing, Todd?" Tina Pool asked as she exited the Toyota.

Todd lowered the tire iron and hid it behind his back. "Just havin' some fun, Miss Pool."

Tina Pool removed her sunglasses and placed her hands on her hips. "I remember your idea of fun, Todd. You'd better not be bothering these women."

Todd lowered his head. "No, ma'am."

"You know, Todd?" Parker asked.

"He was one of my students when he wasn't in detention or suspended. Todd, I think you need to get on with your day now," Tina stated sternly.

Todd opened his mouth to say something, then thought better of it. "Yes, ma'am."

The man walked to his car and threw the tire iron in the back seat.

"Todd, please try to stay out of trouble," Tina called after him.

Todd smiled weakly, then got in. The car's engine roared to life and almost immediately spun out as it sped off, sending gravel flying everywhere.

"What a tool," Kat observed as they watched the Z28 race away.

"Such a waste," Tina sighed. "The boy isn't stupid. His home life wasn't the best growing up, though."

"Thanks for stepping in," Parker said.

"Don't mention it. I'm afraid you're getting a negative impression of our little town."

"Attempted murder and random assaults tend to do that… not to mention the actual murders," Kat said.

"Somebody tried to kill you?" Tina asked, shocked.

"You didn't tell me that your father was tight with the sheriff," Parker replied, ignoring Tina's question. "Doesn't that make things awkward for you?"

Tina's expression went flat. "No, not at all."

"Did you know that Hutch Jamesison was back in town?"

"Why should I care about that?"

"Just curious. It's interesting, though, that you're a teacher. What grade do you teach?"

"High school."

"I'm curious. If you discovered one of your seventeen-year-old students was having sexual relations with someone much older, what would you do about that?"

"You think a seventeen-year-old girl is that different from an eighteen-year-old?"

"I didn't say it was a girl, but to your point, it's well established that the brain does not fully mature until twenty-five years of age. It is still undergoing a rewiring process. So much physical, cognitive, and emotional development is happening during that time that serious trauma or stress can cause lifelong issues. The age of eighteen may seem like an arbitrary number for determining legal age, but it is a line in the sand for a reason, a legal one, and crossing it should have consequences."

"I guess we'll have to agree to disagree," Tina said, replacing her sunglasses. "Enjoy the rest of your day."

Parker and Kat watched the schoolteacher climb into her coup.

"Still pissed?" Kat asked, watching the car pull away.

"Livid," Parker replied.

Thirty

Belinda, the Knights Lodge night manager, caught Kat and Parker's attention upon their return to the hotel.

"I wanted to inform you that the police have released your room. It's no longer considered a crime scene. We've issued new keys and sanitized the room completely. The owner has also comp'd your stay and offers his apology for your troubles."

"Cha-ching," Kat commented.

"That's generous, but you should know I don't hold the hotel responsible."

Belinda smiled weakly. "Knights Lodge appreciates that, but we all feel bad just the same."

Parker considered informing Belinda of their recent encounter with her ex-boyfriend Todd but decided to keep it to herself—there was no point in making Belinda feel even worse.

"Kat will need a new room key. Can you take care of that for us?"

"Certainly, oh, that reminds me. Penelope's personal assistant left Penelope's belongings here for you. I hope you don't mind, but we put them in your room. They were taking up a lot of space in our storage area."

Parker grew excited. "That's fine. Thanks, Belinda."

Making their way quickly to their room, Parker found four large suitcases, two medium-sized cases, and a travel bag that doubled as a purse right inside the door.

"The sheriff's office will want to go through these, but I want the first crack at them," Parker said.

"Isn't that messing with evidence?" Kat asked, plopping down on the bed and eyeing the luggage.

"Only if we tamper, alter, destroy, or conceal anything we find. So, don't do any of that."

One by one, the women placed the suitcases on the bed and removed all the contents. Parker examined jewelry, designer skirts, blouses, dresses, and shoes. All of it was pricey, which in her mind didn't mean someone was classy, only that they were wealthy enough and stupid enough to spend money on a flashy label. They checked every piece of clothing carefully for anything hidden away. When they finished with the two smaller bags, one for makeup, the other for jewelry, and the travel bag, they stood back and stared at the mess they had created.

"Zippo. No missing chapter," Kat said.

"I thought for sure we'd find it here."

"So, the killer must have taken it."

"If it was even here in the first place," Parker said, standing with her hands on her hips. "Damn it. Alright, let's put this back together."

After returning the luggage to its original condition and pushing it all to the rear of the room, Parker and Kat lay flat on their backs on their respective beds.

"Let's go over what we know. Break it down point by point," Parker said.

"Okay, where do we start?"

"Where this whole thing started, Penelope's book."

"The book that says a lot about what happened here thirty-eight years ago but offers no actual answers, that book?" Kat asked.

"That's the one. It's also the book that Penelope told her daughter would reveal some dark secrets, but that didn't happen either. However, from what her agent and her publisher have said, we're fairly sure one chapter is missing, and that could be where those answers lie."

"And we think Penelope printed that chapter before coming here."

"But wait a minute, back up. Penelope didn't include the chapter in her book when she published it. Why?" Parker asked.

"She changed her mind."

"But why? Why did she change her mind? She knew that excluding that chapter would be a problem for her publisher, but more importantly, it would disappoint Lynn tremendously, and that was a big thing."

"Ummmm… maybe the *truth* she intended to reveal involved unfounded accusations that she couldn't prove yet. She decided to wait."

Parker thought about that. "Possible. But then she does an about-face and tells the world she will announce a significant revelation at the book launch and purposefully arranges it to take place right here in Willow's Bane. Why do that?"

"She found the proof she was missing?" Kat guessed.

"Or something changed. Between the time she submitted the manuscript and the notice of the book launch, circumstances changed. It was too late to alter the book because it was at the press, so she decided to reveal the contents of that missing chapter in person at the launch."

Kat sat up in bed. "I got it! She was being threatened or blackmailed. That's why she didn't turn in the chapter. Somebody suspected what she intended to do and stopped her."

"But who? Van? She collaborated with Penelope on all her other books."

"But there wasn't anything in her office to suggest she'd done so this time. Besides, it was no secret Penelope's next book was about the Snake River Murders. Anyone involved could have predicted she might spill the beans then."

"Then let's consider the podcaster, Samantha Trimble. She said Penelope left something out of the book that linked the Snake River murders to the Lewiston deaths. Maybe something else in the chapter does just that, and Samantha blackmailed Penelope to prevent the information from spoiling her podcast."

"But how would Samantha know what Penelope was going to write?" Kat asked.

"Penelope could have interviewed her as research for the book, and Samantha let something slip. Then she changed her mind and forced Penelope to suppress the chapter."

"It's possible, I guess, but is any of that motive enough for murder?"

"No, you're right. So, who are our actual suspects?" Parker asked.

"Sheriff Weber is at the top of my list. It's possible he killed those three girls because he was scared that news of him boinking Tina would ruin him. Even if he didn't kill those girls, he still could have killed Penelope because he was afraid she'd reveal his connection to Tina at the launch. And he's a sheriff, so he knows how to get around security cameras and how to make murder look like suicide. Plus, he was dead-set against an investigation."

"A strong candidate. I'm torn between Hutch Jamesison and Matt Jackson, the ex-soccer coach. Penelope dismantled Hutch's alibi so he could be out for revenge, but now that I've met him, I don't think that faking a suicide is his style. Jackson, on the other hand, is a different story. They never charged him back in eighty-six, and they never fully cleared him, either. And there's also Tina Pools' claim that she saw him at Penelope's house at the time of one disappearance. I know Van says she was with Penelope then, and no one showed up at the house, but I think she might be covering for her, though I don't know why. There's a connection between Jackson and Penelope somehow."

"His wife, Poppy, could have killed Penelope to protect her husband," Kat pointed out. "She already admitted being in Penelope's room that night after we caught her on camera. Maybe she suspects her hubby is guilty, but she's one of those *stand-by-your-man* chicks."

"I've heard of stranger things."

"I have an out-of-the-box suspect for you... Trisha Jamesison," Kat said.

"Interesting. You think she killed her own daughter?"

"What if she and her lover Dan Emerson had a pack with each other? You kill my kid if I kill yours."

"Why... and what about Deidre Pool?"

"Deidre was tight with Mikayla, so she probably knew something or saw something that put a kink in the lovebirds' plans. The why... they wanted to run off together, but they didn't want the entanglement of kids complicating things."

"Then why didn't they run off together after it was all said and done?"

"One of them changed their minds… who knows… but it would also explain why Bill Jamesison was killed. Once Penelope's book revealed his wife's affair with Emerson, he put two and two together and confronted his wife, so he had to go."

"Fascinating theory. You think that is what Penelope was going to reveal?"

"Why not? She had already put the teaser out there by exposing the affair. The last chapter would be the bombshell."

"You know what I just thought of? That tire iron Todd threatened us with… the sheriff said Bill Jamesison was beaten to death with something similar. Do you think Todd could have been involved somehow?"

"Motive?"

"Maybe Bill caught Todd hanging around the hotel the night Penelope was killed?"

"Penelope crapped all over Todd's love life, but I can't see him faking a suicide either."

Parker sat up and swung her legs off the bed. "Maybe we're overthinking this. Perhaps a psychopath who spent time in Willow's Bane murdered those three girls before moving on to his next killing ground. Penelope's secret had nothing to do with the murders but instead, a person or persons who did something to her back then?"

"Then why write the book at all?"

Parker punched her bed. "Damn it… I don't know." She rose, snatched her copy of Malignant Doubt from the dresser top, and shook it at Kat. "Missing chapter or not, this book is the key somehow."

"Maybe we should read it again… this time the actual book? What we read was an earlier version Word document. It may have been edited since then."

"Maybe so."

Kat bounced off her bed and headed for the door. "I need a snack. Want anything?"

Parker shook her head. After the door closed behind Kat, Parker sat back on the bed and flipped through the book's pages.

She was turning pages when Kat returned, munching on a chip from a bag she'd bought.

"Somebody ought to sue these friggin' food companies for false advertising," Kat growled. "A buck fifty for a bag that looks like it holds a ton of chips, but you open it up, and there's maybe six or seven. Not cool."

Kat's comment registered in Parker's mind, but instead of filing it away, it continued to float there. There was something about what she said. The thought collided with another thought. It was a notion she had filed away several days ago because it bothered her. Like a bolt of lightning, clarity suddenly sprung forth when the two thoughts combined.

"That's it!" Parker blurted. She turned the book pages in her lap back to the beginning, then started flipping forward again, one by one. When she came across the page she wanted, she froze. Her eyes darted back and forth across the page.

"Kat, can you get me Penelope's publisher's cell number? Trent Carson."

"Sure," Kat responded, opening the lid of her laptop. "What do you need his number for?"

Parker didn't answer the question and waited anxiously.

"I've sent it to your phone," Kat said after a short time.

Parker sprung from the bed, the book in hand, and headed for the door. Her mind was reeling.

"Where are you going?" Kat asked.

"Just keep your laptop fired up and wait for my call," she said as she opened the door.

"Seriously? What are you up to this time?"

Parker turned around and smiled. "I'm going for a drive," she replied, then closed the door.

Thirty-One

The sun hovered on the horizon as Parker strode through the hotel parking lot. It was almost as if the burning ball of gas was saying its last goodbye before giving way to the impatient night sky. Parker smiled at the thought. That was how Lynn had phrased it once. She remembered how her wife loved sunsets and sunrises, calling them the universe's way of hitting the reset button.

Parker thought about what Lynn would say now if she were here with them. *This is getting too dangerous, and we need to back off, reassess, and find a different approach that doesn't involve putting anyone in danger.* Surprisingly, she was the pragmatic one in their relationship. Cautious, practical. Together, they made a good pair because when they first met, Parker tended to be more impulsive and free-spirited. Lynn tempered those feelings in Parker and forced her to be more rounded. Parker helped Lynn become less controlling and more uninhibited. Both women's methods of approaching difficult obstacles worked in their own way, but only one was better suited when time was a factor, which was why Parker was about to drive off with no clear destination in mind.

After leaving the hotel via the back entrance, Parker heard somebody else use the same door a few seconds behind her. She paid little attention to the coincidence, but as she approached her car, those trailing footsteps seemed to be gaining on her. Her heart felt as if it had moved into her throat, pounding away. She held her keys in her palm and angled the more significant key to extend from her pinky finger at a 90-degree angle. She clenched her fingers in a tight fist around the keys and pressed her thumb down hard on her index finger. When it sounded like whoever was following her was almost upon her, she twirled, raised her key hand above her head, and then froze.

Chuck stared at her like she had just told him an awful joke.

"Really, that's what you're using for self-defense after a serious crime family has threatened you?" Chuck laughed sardonically.

Parker dropped her hand and relaxed, waiting for her blood pressure to return to normal before speaking.

"First off, I rushed to leave the room and forgot my bag. Second, we both know the Isola family never follow through on their threats."

"There's always a first time."

Parker pointed her finger back and forth between the two of them. "This is getting old."

Chuck pulled out his phone and started dialing. "I have someone who wants to speak to you."

"I don't have time for this, Chuck. Tell whoever you're calling that—"

"Sir, this is Special Agent Teller," Chuck said into his phone.

Parker stood impatiently and listened to the conversation.

"Yes, sir. I have her with me right now. I'll put her on."

Chuck extended his phone towards Parker. "You're going to want to take this."

Parker gave Chuck a sour look as she took the phone, putting it to her ear.

"Hello?"

"Mrs. Parker, I apologize for pulling you away from whatever you might be doing," said a voice Parker immediately recognized. She had only met the man a handful of times, but his deep baritone voice was unmistakable. It was the senior partner of the law firm she worked for.

"Mr. Threadmore. This is a surprise."

"An unfortunate one for both of us, I'm sure. I won't delay you any more than necessary. I received a rather unpleasant phone call from assistant DA Jefferson this afternoon, and I'm sure I don't need to tell you what the purpose of his call was."

"I'm sorry to put you in that position, Mr. Threadmore, but if you'll let me explain the details of what I'm facing, you'll—"

"Mrs. Parker, I don't have the time or the patience to listen to your excuses. This firm's association with the District Attorney's office impacts hundreds of cases we handle with them yearly, and anything that might jeopardize that relationship… well… we just cannot allow that to happen."

The line went silent. Parker assumed the man was waiting for a response, but she decided to remain quiet.

"Jefferson informs me you are to testify as a witness in his court on Monday regarding a matter only tangentially connected to our firm."

"That is correct, sir. Our client is being represented for tax fraud, but during the investigation I came across some evidence relating to more serious charges against a third party. That is what I'm supposed to be testifying to."

"Then you'll need to be there on Monday to do just that."

"That is my hope, Mr. Threadmore, but I—"

"Again, with the buts. This isn't a request, Mrs. Parker. It's a directive. You will be in that man's court on Monday morning. Is that clear?"

"And if I'm not?"

"I'm not sure you appreciate the gravity of the situation, Mrs. Parker?"

"Oh, I do, but I don't think you appreciate the gravity of my situation, Mr. Threadmore, and that's a shame. I enjoyed working for your firm."

"Mrs. Parker, let me be clear—"

Parker disconnected the call and handed the phone back to Chuck.

"Tell me you didn't just quit your job over this," Chuck said.

The expression on Parker's face hid the rage inside of her. "Shut up, Chuck. I should throat punch you for making the murder of my wife's mom sound so trivial. You've done your job, and I need to go."

"Jobs not quite done," Chuck replied, reaching around to his back. When his hand came back, it was holding a pair of handcuffs.

"You're shitting me," Parker exclaimed loudly.

"I did what I could. I'd hoped your boss might convince you, but the DA told my boss that if you're not in his courtroom Monday at 9 AM, heads will roll, mine included."

"That prick didn't even try to ask for a continuance, did he?"

"I told you he probably wouldn't, but it doesn't matter."

"But Chuck, I'm close. I feel it. And I know you know what that's like. I've almost got that last tumbler to fall into place, and I'll crack this thing. I just need another day."

Chuck held up the handcuffs and jingled them. "No can do, Parker. I really am sorry."

Parker looked down at the pavement, and when her eyes returned to the FBI agent, they were sad. She hoped it wouldn't come to this, but he was leaving her with no other option now.

"Then I'm sorry too, Chuck. If you make me go back now, I'll have to tell your boss about the documents," Parker said, looking him dead in the eye.

Chuck's face fell and turned a shade of white one step above corpse level. "What? You can't."

Parker didn't flinch. "You're leaving me no choice, Chuck. I can't go back now."

Eighteen months ago, Chuck had leaked classified documents to the press. He had a good reason for doing what he did. Accusations of fraud had been leveled against several high-ranking social services members, Lynn included, causing the agency to face severe public scrutiny. The FBI investigated, and although the accusations were ultimately disproven, no one at the bureau could be bothered to issue a public statement to that effect, allowing Lynn's reputation to remain tarnished. Chuck got ahold of the documents needed to lift the cloud of uncertainty and secretly got them into the hands of the press. One night, after too many drinks, he told Lynn and Parker what he had done, which they quickly admonished him for.

"Parker, you're talking about ruining my career."

"Now you're getting how serious this is to me—balls in your court. You have a choice to make. I told you I just need one more day. I'll wrap this up and take the red-eye back to LA to be in court on Monday, as I promised. But if you put those cuffs on me, I'll do as I said."

Chuck pointed his finger at Parker, his face red and the veins on his neck extended. "Our friendship means that little to you?"

Parker shook her head. "The promise I made to my wife means more. Always will."

The mention of Lynn seemed to take some of the steam out of the FBI agent. "You are so goddamned hard-headed; you know that," he barked.

"I've been told."

Chuck paced back and forth, then held the handcuffs out toward Parker. "Here, you'd better take these, then find a random car to cuff me to."

"Why do I need to cuff you? Just tell them you couldn't find me."

Chuck made a tired face. "Because they'll never buy that I couldn't locate you, but they will believe you'd pull some stunt to get the drop on me. You need time… this is the way to get it. Here's my phone. Leave it somewhere close by. I don't want to go through the hassle of getting a new one."

Parker took the cuffs and the phone. "Thank you for this, Chuck."

"Don't you thank me. You're blackmailing me into this, and I'm not sure if I can ever forgive you for that."

The pair walked one row over, and Parker handcuffed Chuck to the door handle of a white Ford Explorer. She placed the phone on the roof, well out of his reach.

"I really hope you'll try to forgive me for this, Chuck."

Chuck refused to look at Parker. "Get out of here. Go catch your killer."

Thirty-Two

Parker could feel her frustration building. She had been driving around for almost an hour, cruising up and down the country roads right outside of Willow's Bane, but not finding anything that matched the layout she was searching for. The certainty she felt when leaving the hotel was beginning to dim, along with the light, making her task even harder. Had she guessed wrong? Was her theory simply another case of an overactive imagination out of control? Even with the second-guessing, she refused to let the doubt reach the feeling in her gut. The feeling that she was right. It was only a matter of finding it.

Pulling off onto the side of the road, Parker looked at the map on her phone. If her assumptions were correct, what she was after had to be northwest of the city, but she had been down each road twice already. Deciding to take a different tack, Parker changed the display option of the phone's app to satellite view, allowing her to see actual photographs of the surrounding landscape. When the screen updated, she zoomed to the red pin on the map indicating her current location, then slowly began raising the view's altitude. After a couple of clicks, she spotted something that drew her interest. Re-positioning the map so it centered on the area she was interested in, she clicked to zoom in. Her excitement grew. That could be what she was after, a clearing surrounded by dense forest, but it was far from the main road with no obvious way to reach it.

There was only one way to find out. She put the car in drive and sped off in that direction.

Reaching the stretch of road that ran parallel to the lot of barren land she was seeking, she slowed to a crawl, placing her headlights on high beams. The car had traveled a hundred yards when she noticed a dirt road partially obscured by dense tree branches. That was something she missed on her previous trips down this road. She swerved onto the road and continued down the eerie trail, the headlights from her car casting freaky shadows ahead.

She had driven almost a mile before the trees disappeared, replaced by an area of wide-open space. A small wooden cabin sat in the center of the grounds, with a smaller shed off to the side.

A pang of excitement shot through her chest. *This is it. It has to be.*

A circular fire pit made of large rocks sat in front of the cabin, next to a couple of folding lawn chairs. The cabin was dark, and the firepit was empty. Parking her car angled so that her headlights illuminated both the cabin and the firepit, Parker turned off the engine but left the lights burning.

She exited the car and did a slow scan of the area. The night air was cool but not uncomfortable, even if the humidity caused Parker's breath to form a misty cloud when she exhaled. She pulled out her phone and dialed Kat's number.

"Where the HELL are you?" Kat answered on the first ring.

"I've been looking for something, and I think I found it."

"Jesus, Parker. You can't go disappearing like that for hours. People are trying to kill you, you know."

"I'm sorry, but I need you to look something up for me."

"Oh… sure… shave ten years off my life by stressing me out, and now I'm just your personal Wikipedia?" Kat growled.

"Hey, don't forget I'm still kind of pissed at you for what you did behind Lynn's back. This is important," Parker said.

After a brief pause, "Sorry. What is it?"

"On Route 29 just outside of town, between Canal Lane and Highway 22, there's a cabin about a mile off the road. I need you to look up the land records and find out who owns it."

"That's all?" Kat replied, using her best sarcastic tone.

"Kat, I think this is the key to everything. Please. And hurry."

Kat's voice became more serious. "Transmission received. I'll call you right back."

Parker slid her phone into her back pocket and walked towards the firepit. In the pit she could make out partially burned trash, beer cans, and charred wood. A wooden six-foot pole was stuck in the ground a few paces away, with a metal hook screwed into the pole near the top. An open can of beer rested in the mesh cup holder on one of the folding chairs. Parker picked it out of the holder and shook it. It was a quarter full. Replacing it, she moved towards the cabin.

From what she could see from the car lights, the small single-room cabin looked to be somewhere around three hundred fifty square feet and old. The entire structure stood on solid posts three feet off the ground. A single window, boarded up, stood in the building's front, and a narrow porch with three steps led to a seemingly newer door. The roof was metal and slanted downward, providing cover over the porch, with a small chimney sticking out of it.

Walking around the entire cabin, Parker noted that the window and door in the front were the only way in and out. The cabin had a small internal fireplace, but no pipes hooking it to any water or sewage, or power wires. At the cabin's rear, a half-full firewood bin was attached to the wall a few feet off the ground.

The separate shed stood twenty feet to the right of the cabin door. Parker tried its door and found that it opened freely. Using the flashlight on her phone, she looked inside, finding tools for cutting firewood, a shovel, a couple of gas lanterns, and several cans of gasoline. She picked up a lantern, intending to use it to light the area by the firepit, but then she remembered she didn't have a lighter. Scrutinizing the inside of the shed closer, she found a pack of matches lying next to the can of gasoline. She pocketed the matches and left the shed with the lantern.

Retracing her steps back to the firepit, Parker hung the lantern on the hook extending from the wooden pole. After a couple of tries, the lantern sprung to life with a burst of flame and, with some adjustment of the gas flow, gave off plenty of light.

Parker then climbed the steps to the cabin and tried the door. It was locked.

She was halfway through exploring the rest of the grounds when the ringtone on her phone caused her to jump.

"I found what you were after, but you're not going to believe it," Kat said when Parker answered her phone.

"Go ahead, surprise me," Parker replied. She went silent when Kat said the name.

"Did you hear me?" Kat said when her friend didn't respond.

"Uh… yeah… you're right… I don't believe it."

"It's got to be some mistake, right?"

"I don't think so," Parker said, her mind racing. *Was she in the wrong spot?*

"What are you going to do now?"

"I'm not sure. I'll call you back," Parker said, disconnecting the call despite Kat's voice expressing displeasure.

Parker paced for several minutes, trying to fit the pieces in place, but the more she tried, the more confused she became. This was like trying to put together a puzzle with all the pieces facing down.

Finally, she made a decision and dialed a number.

When her call was answered, she said, "Do you know who this is? You need to meet me at your cabin right now. This isn't a request."

She hung up before the person had a chance to respond and began pacing again. This wasn't going as expected. She thought she'd be getting some answers, but she was only turning up more questions. She was sure about one thing… she had discovered where the answers were hidden… metaphorically speaking.

After retrieving Penelope's book from the car and switching off the headlights so as not to run down her battery, Parker took a seat in one of the folding chairs. She flipped through the book's pages in the lantern light while she waited.

Fifteen minutes later, a dark-colored sedan started making its way up the trail. It pulled up beside Parker's rental car and came to a stop. The engine died, and with it, the sedan's lights. The car door opened, and someone stepped out, then made their way into the light.

"You want to tell me why I'm out here—" Deputy Bonner asked, "—and how do you know about this place?"

The deputy was dressed in plain clothes—a green hoodie and jeans.

Parker held up the copy of Malignant Doubt she had taken from her car. "I know about it because of this."

"I'm not following."

"Why don't you take a seat, and I'll explain," Parker said, gesturing to the other chair.

Tate Bonner slid into the other chair.

Parker tapped the book. "When I first read this as a Word document - an advanced copy, not polished like it is now - the version I read didn't include this drawing of Willow's Bane and the surrounding region, highlighting the relevant locations where crucial things related to the murders occurred. I've read books with maps like this before but rarely notice them. To me, they are in the wrong part of the book. They're almost always in the front of the book like this one is. You can flip back and forth between the text and the map, but typically you'd only do that if something about the logistics in the story was confusing. But if the map has no real value, most people won't give it a second look. That's the way I am.

"But this map is different, and you know why? Because there's something on it that is never mentioned in the book. When I first picked up this final version, I believe I subconsciously noticed the difference between the map and what I had read in the Word document, but it was only recently that my friend Kat helped me put it together. And you know what, there's a spot on this map that shows a cabin and a fireplace pit just like this."

Parker turned the book towards Tate with the map page facing him. She used her finger to point to a spot on the map.

"Right here. There's no label describing what it represents, and nowhere in the book does Penelope talk about a cabin. So, I asked myself, why would she do that? Why put this on her map and not talk about it? Seems kind of random, doesn't it, to do something like that? But Penelope wasn't that sort of person. She wasn't random. She did everything for a reason. Then I remembered that there was a chapter missing from the book. A chapter she held back at the last minute when she turned the manuscript in to the publisher. It took me a while, but I finally came up with an explanation for why this cabin is on the map… she must mention it in that missing chapter. She just forgot to update the map when she decided to hold back the chapter… or maybe she purposefully left it there… we'll never know. I called Trent Carson, the publisher, and he told me Penelope commissioned the creation of the map herself and turned it over to them before providing them with the rest of the manuscript. So, my assumption makes sense.

Something significant must have happened at this cabin back in 1986. That is why she included it on the map. I think it's related to the deaths of those three girls. Some secret that Penelope kept for all those years that she was finally ready to tell."

Tate Bonner's expression had remained neutral during Parker's explanation, and it was beginning to irritate her.

"Do you know what happened here, deputy?" Parker asked.

"I don't. I wasn't even born yet."

"Who did you buy this land and cabin from?"

"This land and everything on it has been in my family for years."

"But you must—" Parker stopped speaking when she heard another vehicle coming down the road. She rose to her feet when a familiar Toyota parked behind Tate Bonner's sedan.

"Did you call someone else?" Parker asked, looking over at the deputy when she failed to get a response. The man was staring at the ground.

A minute later, Van Sanders, leaning on her cane more than usual, limped into the light. She was wearing a black fleece jacket and dark slacks.

"Thank you for calling me Tate," Van said.

"What are you doing here, Van?" Parker asked, her mind racing again.

"My son, Tate, called me. Thought I might help him understand what you're doing out here."

Parker turned her attention to Tate. "Your son?"

"She thinks the cabin has something to do with the Snake River murders, Mom," Tate said.

Van looked up at the stars and exhaled.

"I guess it's time that the truth finally comes out," Van said forlornly.

"What truth is that, Van?" Parker asked.

"Yeah Mom, what truth?" Tate Bonner asked, looking confused.

"That Penelope Highsmith was the Snake River killer," Van said slowly. "Or at least one of them."

TWIST

Thirty-Three

Parker let herself ease back down into the chair, stunned. "What?"

"What are you talking about, Mom?" Tate Bonner asked.

Van began wringing her hands. "I can't tell you how good that feels, just saying those words."

"Mom, you need to explain yourself." The deputy seemed taken off-guard.

"This is so hard. I also played a role in what happened, and you do not know the burden Penelope and I carried in our hearts for all these years."

Tate stood up and offered his mother the chair. After she took his seat, he perched on a big rock outlining the fire pit.

"Maybe you should start at the beginning, Van," Parker prompted.

Van nodded. "A couple of weeks after they found Deidre Pool's body, I received a call from Penelope. It was late in the afternoon. She was calling me from the gas station up the road from here, clearly upset and hardly making sense. She needed me to come out here as soon as I could. This was my father's cabin and his father's before that. We would have parties out here sometimes, but mostly, Penelope and I would come out here when we wanted to be alone and vent about how cruel the world could be. Anyway, I drove here as quickly as I could, and when I arrived, there was Maddy Emerson, dead, lying next to the fire pit."

"What happened?" Van's son asked.

"Penelope told me she had learned that Maddy's father, Dan Emerson, was having an affair with her mother. We already knew the scum bucket was sleeping with Trisha Jamesison, so it wasn't a big surprise to me. Back then, Dan was kind of a hunk for someone his age and a horndog, but we ignored all that until he started seeing Mrs. Highsmith. Penelope was afraid Dan was going to bust up their family. She was scared and furious at the same time. She said she intercepted Maddy at the library and convinced her to take a ride. They ended up here."

"Why?" Parker asked. "What was Penelope planning?"

"She wasn't planning anything, not really. She said she just wanted to talk to Maddy about what her father doing and see if Maddy could pressure him to leave her mother alone."

"But it didn't go as planned?" Tate asked.

"No, not at all. Penelope said Maddy got really upset and denied her father was sleeping around with anyone, much less Penelope's mom. She started calling Penelope all sorts of names and demanded she take her back to town. But Penelope wasn't giving up so easily, and that's when things became heated. The two of them began pulling at one another, and when Penelope pushed Maddy away from her, she tripped on a piece of wood and fell backward, hitting her head on one of these fireplace rocks. When Penelope noticed the blood and saw that Maddy wasn't breathing, she jumped in the car and drove to call me."

After a brief silence, "That's not the end of the story, though, is it?" Parker asked.

Van's head dipped. "No. It isn't. When I arrived, I checked Maddy, but there wasn't a pulse. She was indeed dead. Penelope was beside herself. She was ranting about how she had killed someone and her life was over. I tried to convince her it was a tragic accident. The police would understand, but she wouldn't listen. Then she told me about this crazy idea she had."

"Let me guess… the two of you could make Maddy's death look like a Snake River victim," Parker said.

Van nodded slowly.

"Oh, Mom," Tanner said. "If Penelope had turned herself in, she would have probably only been charged with involuntary manslaughter. She might not have served any time."

"You don't understand what it was like, what was going through our minds. We didn't know. A girl was dead because of her, and somebody had to go to jail. Penelope was desperate for a way out of a tragic situation."

"What did the two of you do?"

"We remembered what we read in the paper about the other two murders and then set about making Maddy's death look the same. The hardest part was beating her body, as we read about. Penelope could only manage a couple of swings before she broke down, so I finished. Then we stripped her clothes off and burned them in the firepit, then put her body in the back of my car. Penelope followed me to an isolated spot by the river, and we dumped her body in the water and drove away."

Nobody said anything for a moment; the only sound was a slight breeze blowing through the trees.

"After Maddy's body was in the water, we both promised never to talk about what we had done. We kept that promise until Penelope told me about Malignant Doubt and her plans to come clean," Van said, her eyes downcast.

"She told you?" Parker asked softly.

Van nodded. "Yes."

"Did she explain why she was doing it? After all those years, why now?" Parker asked.

Van sighed. "She only said that she had to, but she said she wouldn't mention my name. She would write that she arranged the whole cover-up by herself."

Parker held up the book. "But nothing about that is in here."

"That's right. She contacted me again to tell me she reconsidered and wouldn't reveal what happened after all. I felt disappointed in a way. I was ready for all the secrets to end. She wouldn't tell me what changed her mind when I asked."

Parker held up the book that had been resting in her lap. "Then she contacted you about hosting her book launch here in

Willow's Bane and spread word of a special revelation at the launch. Was she finally going to tell the truth about Maddy's death?"

Van shrugged. "I do not know, she wouldn't say. Possibly."

"No offense, Van, but we only have your word about this."

Van sighed. "Yes, it is only my word, but you also have Penelope's actions. What do you think this last book was all about? Why did she write it in the first place? It was her guilty conscience. Remorse about what she had done. What she had done to Maddy's parents. It ate at her like a cancer, ate at both of us. I know you think someone killed her to keep this from coming out, but I really believe she did indeed take her own life. The shame of it all finally caught up with her. I think she desperately wanted to confess… but she was too afraid. Afraid of what her adoring fans would think of her, and that internal struggle caused her to take her own life."

Parker thought about Belinda's copy of the book with the Forgive Me inscription. Could Van possibly be right about Penelope's last night? Replaying everything she had learned so far in her head, she tried to match up all the facts.

Parker tilted her head. "Mikayla and Deidre's deaths were a convenient smoke screen you took advantage of?"

Van nodded. "They were murdered by a psychopath who thankfully ended his spree at two. Who knows, maybe what Penelope and I did scared him away. Maybe the thought of somebody copying his kills infuriated him, and he moved on to greener pastures. I just know we took advantage of an unfortunate situation… and I'm embarrassed to admit that it worked. It certainly ended the affair between Dan and Mrs. Highsmith."

"But mom, think about what you put the Emersons through," Tate growled, his normally stone face buckling with emotion.

Van's jaw clenched, appearing irritated with her son. "It was an accident, Tate. Maddy was dead. We were two kids trying to make the best out of a bad situation. It's not like we threw her body down a well or something. Her parents got to bury her properly. Do you think they would have felt any better knowing how she really died? Did Penelope's life deserve to be ruined because of it?"

"But it was," Parker stated.

Van looked confused. "What?"

"Penelope's life was ruined," Parker said.

"Not from where I'm sitting, it wasn't."

"That's because you weren't her daughter," Parker said, sighing. "It makes sense now. What the two of you did that night haunted Penelope her entire life. It poisoned her soul. She left Willow's Bane as soon as she could and never returned... for a reason. She couldn't bear to be around so many things that reminded her of what had happened. It's no wonder she turned into a functional alcoholic, an emotional vacuum, and a terrible parent. None of her successes, accolades, all the time in the spotlight, or even the unconditional love of a daughter could heal the darkness in her heart. Instead of facing up to what she did and dealing with the consequences, which might have been a couple of months in juvenile hall, you helped her run from them and burdened her with a life sentence."

Van stared at the empty fire pit, absently twisting the top of her cane. "In hindsight, of course, I wish I had tried harder to talk her out of it. Absolutely."

"Are you certain you've never mentioned that night to anyone?" Parker asked.

"Positive. Penelope is the only person I ever discussed it with, and I was always alone when I did."

Parker looked at Tate, who raised his hands.

"Hey, I'm just as shocked by this as you are. I had no idea," Tate said defensively.

"Then we still have a problem," Parker stated.

"How's that?" Van asked.

"Let's not forget that somebody in Willow's Bane has tried to stop me from investigating the murders and Penelope's secret, twice. Maybe it's the person who murdered Mikayla and Deidre, I don't know. Maybe Penelope had another secret we've not uncovered yet. Van, are you positive you and Penelope were alone out here that night?" Parker asked, tapping her leg as her thoughts drifted from one theory to another.

"Yes. As you can see, there's only one way in, and at night, it's easy to spot anyone coming," Van said, her hands gesturing broadly.

"What about before you showed up?" Tate asked. "Did Penelope have anyone with her she didn't tell you about? You said she drove to the gas station to call you after the accident. Maybe she dropped somebody off there before she returned and met you?"

"I... I guess it's possible," Van said, hunching her shoulders.

Parker could sense where Tate's mind was heading so she asked, "Are you certain Maddy died the way Penelope described it? Did you see blood on the rock she supposedly hit her head on?"

Tate stood up and began pacing. "I pulled the old case files on the original investigation when I found out you were almost run down. I read the autopsy notes on the injuries and —" Tate stopped talking, and his face suddenly went blank.

Van's forehead furrowed. "Are you okay, Tate?"

"I ... I'm—"

Parker was becoming concerned. Tate's expression had quickly shifted from vacant to bewilderment to now displaying a hint of sorrow.

"Mom, what did you and Penelope use to beat Maddy's body with after she was dead?" Tate asked calmly.

Van appeared shocked. "What? Why would you want to know that?"

Parker asked herself the same thing. Where Tate was going with this.

"Just answer my question. What did you use?" Tate stated.

Van became flustered. "For goodness' sake... I don't remember that. It's been thirty-eight years since that night, honey."

Parker's interest spiked. The object you used to beat a person savagely... already dead or not... isn't something you would forget. Van was lying for some reason.

The hint of sorrow on Tate's face morphed into full-on anguish.

"I'm not buying that. I need you to tell me what you used."

Van stared at her son. "A piece of firewood," she said flatly.

Tate shook his head. "The coroner's report stated that the weapon was a blunt object, like a piece of rebar or steel rod."

"Tate, please let it drop," Van pleaded.

Parker suddenly knew where Tate's questions were leading. "Shit. It also said that the same weapon was used in all three deaths. No mistake."

Both Parker and Tate locked their eyes on Van's walking stick.

Thirty-Four

"God damn it, Tate," Van snapped, slamming her cane against the stone firepit. "Why do you always have to pick at things? Since you were old enough to talk, it's been nothing but why… why… why. Now you've really gone and done it."

Tate kicked the chair, knocking it over. "What did you do, mom?"

Parker told herself she needed to remain calm, but it was proving difficult.

Van got her emotions under control and looked at her cane. "Hard maple with a walnut stain finish. One of the strongest woods around. My grandparents immigrated from Germany and at one time it was my grandmas."

"You killed Mikayla and Deidre?" Parker asked evenly.

Van shrugged her shoulders.

"I can't believe this," Tate said, looking lost. "But why?"

Van looked at her son and smiled. "There you go again."

"Just explain it to me… please," Tate said.

"Did you know I had set three state records and accumulated enough medals to fill a grocery store shopping cart by the time I was a junior? A junior! I would have become one of the fastest runners this state has ever seen. The Olympics were next on the horizon. People would tell me how I looked like a gazelle when I ran. Effortless, but lightning quick."

Van paused and rubbed her damaged leg. "The Jamesisons ended that dream for me in a blink of an eye. They were heading home from a party. It was just Bill and Trisha, and Bill was driving, and naturally, he was drunk. He ran a stop sign and t-boned us as we were headed home from my track meet. I was the only one hurt. My leg broke in three places. Crushed is a better description. Four surgeries and countless hours of physical therapy, but it was never the same. In a heartbeat, I went from graceful gazelle to a lame racehorse — one bullet away from being put down."

"When did the accident happen?" Parker asked, letting her curiosity take over.

"About a year before the murders. The worst year of my life."

Parker's *Eye of the Tiger* ringtone interrupted the conversation. She answered it quickly.

"What the hell is happening, Parker? I've been waiting—" Kat began.

"Not now, Kat," Parker said, then disconnected the call. Looking at Van, she said, "Go on, please."

Van's eyebrows furrowed, and her nostrils flared. "Mikayla Jamesison was a snobbish shrew who made a habit out of verbally dissecting anyone she didn't like or refused to bow down to her. She thought she was too good to play for the high school soccer team and constantly berated those who did, except her best friend Deidre, of course. I can't tell you how sickening it was to hear everyone lie about how kind and special she was after she was dead. It was pathetic. Even Penelope treated her with kid gloves in her book. That bothered me."

"Did Penelope know what you had done?" Parker asked.

Van laughed. "Of course not. I never talked about that with her. What happened was between me and those two girls."

"So, how did it happen?" Parker asked.

Van stared at the top of her cane. "One day before PE class, I was in the locker room, and my bad leg got tangled in a big swim towel a member of the swim team left lying on the ground. The more I fought with it, the more unbalanced I became. I fell. Mikayla and some of the other girls were there and saw it happen.

Instead of helping me up, Mikayla laughed. She stood over me and laughed! Then she started making snide remarks about how the mighty have fallen and things like that. I lost it. I started screaming at her, and she screamed back."

"That's the yelling match I asked you about? It wasn't about Penelope being gay after all?" Parker asked, trying to corral the million thoughts racing through her mind.

"Hardly. I told Mikayla exactly what I thought of her, what a lot of kids thought of her before the coach broke it up. But the one thing you need to understand about Mikayla is that you didn't show her up in front of her friends, especially if you were a gimp. She wanted revenge. So, we agreed to meet a week later to settle things."

"Why a week later?" Tate asked.

"Oh… she wanted to do it right away, but I insisted we wait," Van explained.

"Why?" Tate repeated.

"Because she already knew what she was going to do," Parker interjected. "She needed there to be time between their argument and what she intended to do next."

"That's right, but there was another reason as well," Van said with a hint of satisfaction. "There was this creepy guy who filled the vending machines in the school cafeteria once a week. He was always drooling over us girls, making lewd remarks. I could tell from the side of his van that he was based out of Lewiston."

"Why was that important?" Tate asked.

"Because of the unsolved murders in Lewiston the previous year," Parker said. "She planned on making him the scapegoat. Isn't that why you removed the clothes from the bodies?"

Van frowned. "You're both interrupting my story."

"I'm sorry," Parker said. "Please go on."

"Well, the next week, when I knew the vending guy was in town, I told Mikayla I'd meet her at a park near the campus after school. I knew she walked to and from school, so I met her midway in my car and offered to give her a ride the rest of the way. I drove her out here, and that's when I killed the bitch."

Tate put his hands on top of his head and turned around in a circle muttering.

"As you've already alluded to, the murders in Lewiston the previous year were still fresh on everyone's minds, so I thought I could make it look like the same serial killer had moved into Willow's Bane. The last body they found there was nude, so I did the same to Mikayla. It worked too, because the first couple of news reports mentioned the link to Lewiston."

"It wasn't publicly announced that the woman's body found in Lewiston was naked. How did you know that?" Parker asked.

Van grinned. "You'll love this. It came from a girl who played on Mikayla's travel soccer team. Her dad was a cop in Lewiston, and he was at the scene when the woman was found. The brass may have kept it out of the papers, but that didn't stop him from talking about it at home. His daughter overheard and told some girls on the soccer team, Mikayla included. Mikayla blabbed it to some girls at our school, which I overheard. Ironic, isn't it?"

Parker glanced at Tate, who looked like he had a severe case of food poisoning, then back at Van.

"I think I already know the answer to this, but I'll ask it anyway. Why?" Parker asked.

Van smirked. "Why did I kill her?"

Parker nodded.

"It's simple. Her parents stole my future... so I took their future away from them. They would suffer just as I was suffering. It started out as a bit of escapism really. I'd create all these scenarios of how I could make her family pay as I agonized through my physical therapy sessions. It was the only thing that gave me the strength I needed to get through it all. But they were only harmless fantasies, until Mikayla laughed in my face. That's when something snapped in me, and it sealed her fate," Van replied, stomping her cane into the ground.

"And using the cane?" Parker asked.

Van twirled the cane with her fingers. "A bit of symbolism, really. Plus, it felt fantastic. I can still remember Mikayla's face when I struck her the first time. It was a combination of disbelief and fear. Precious."

"Then Deidre?" Parker asked.

"Well, once I killed Mikayla," Van said with a sigh of satisfaction, "then, of course, Deidre had to go as well. Her father, Greg, was almost as responsible for my infirmity as the Jamesisons. He was a shit doctor, though no one knew it at the time. It's amazing how the man kept his license as long as he did, considering the number of malpractice claims filed against him. His negligence and medical ineptitude torpedoed my future as much as that accident did. He robbed me, and I was going to do the same to him. It was just a bonus that Deidre was a supreme bitch and Mikayla's best friend."

"So, it was you who Deidre got a ride with from the soccer fields that day," Parker stated matter-of-factly.

"It was. I picked a day when the vending guy was in town, and I bumped into her and told her I'd pick her up after practice because we needed to talk, but not to tell anyone who she was riding with."

"Why would she do that? You two weren't exactly friends."

"Because I told her if she didn't, I would tell Mr. Wattford she'd cheated on his last algebra exam."

"And you knew this because—" Parker said, pausing for dramatic effect.

Van chuckled. "—I saw her do it. We were in the same class, and she always did it. All you had to do was compare her answers to Gwen Doline's, the girl who sat to Deidre's right, and he'd see they were exactly the same. Even the wrong answers."

"You picked up Deidre, and then what?" Parker prompted, even though she already knew the answer.

"It went the same as it did with Mikayla. Easier even. Deidre didn't even put up a fight. That girl was all mouth and no action."

"Then a month goes by, and Penelope calls you in a panic."

Van became more animated, moving her hands as she talked. "I couldn't believe it. I mean, what are the odds? There's Maddy Emerson laid out right there where you're sitting, and Penelope's crying like a three-year-old. Mind-blowing. If I'm being truthful, Penelope came to her senses and wanted to call the sheriff. But I talked her out of it."

"Why would you do that? Why not let her do the right thing? You weren't involved," Tate asked, begging for an answer that made sense.

"No, but Van couldn't afford to have the police crawling around the campsite," Parker stated.

Tate's face screwed up in confusion. "Why? What am I missing?"

"Because this is where she killed Mikayla and Deidre. There had to be evidence everywhere," Parker said.

Tate looked from Parker to his mother. She nodded.

"My god," Tate groaned, putting his hands over his face. "I've brought my kids to this cabin."

"But making Maddy's death look like the other two ruined your plan to incriminate the vending machine man, right? Because he wasn't in town that day," Parker said.

Van's eyelids drooped, and the corner of her lips dipped. "That was unfortunate. It really was a good plan. I even hid a pair of panties in his delivery van, hoping the cops would find them if they searched it, but either they weren't able to get a search warrant, or the creep found the panties himself before they searched it. No matter."

"Tell me, Van, that night, was Maddy even dead when you got here?"

Van seemed to reflect on something before she answered. "I guess it doesn't matter anymore. She had a weak pulse."

"You could have saved her?" Tate almost cried.

"I couldn't take that chance, honey. If we called an ambulance to save Maddy, which was a longshot, it was just as likely that a patrol car would come with it. They usually did. It was a risk I wasn't willing to take." Van's eyes were imploring Tate to understand.

Tate's eyes grew wide. "So, you killed her instead."

"To be fair, Penelope did most of the damage. I just put her out of her misery."

"I think I'm going to be sick," Tate said, rubbing his hand over his face.

"You are a monster, lady," Parker said.

Van stuck her chin out and tapped her cane on the ground. "I'm sure you and others will see me that way. However, I consider myself a victim of tragic circumstances."

"It was you who tried to kill me, wasn't it?" Parker asked.

Van straightened her back, more alert. "No, that was not me. I know you don't have a reason to believe me, but I also don't have a reason to lie. I'm as confused about that as you are."

"I'm sure. And what about Bill Jamesison?"

Van slumped back in her seat, silent.

"What? You killed poor Bill?" Tate cried, anger in his voice now.

"He was trying to blackmail me. The deadbeat had been scrounging in the trash at Knights Lodge the night Penelope died and saw me sneaking in."

Tate's eyes narrowed. "So, you did kill Penelope?"

"No, I didn't, I swear. I'll admit I went there to talk her out of spilling our secret, but no one answered the door. I was serious before when I said I think she ended things on her own terms."

"If you didn't kill her, then why kill Bill?" Parker asked.

Van frowned. "Like I said, he was trying to blackmail me, and I knew how it would look if he talked. You were so persistent, and my presence there would only lead to questions I couldn't answer. The man was human garbage anyway."

Tate walked a few steps away, his hands on his head again. Parker could only imagine the emotions he was experiencing. Everything he thought he knew about his mother and his life with her had been upended and perverted.

Parker turned her attention back to Van. She was sitting in her chair with a blank expression on her face. She appeared so innocent, so vulnerable, this middle-aged bookstore owner, dutiful mother, and brutal multiple-murderer.

Parker shook her head, struggling to understand it all. Then, one more question popped into her head.

"Van, do you know why Penelope pulled her last chapter from the book?"

Van nodded. "I forced her to."

"Forced her? How?" Parker asked, her eyes turning hard.

"I tried to talk reason into the woman, but she was determined. She told me she would keep my name out of it, but I didn't trust her. Lying was second nature for her. If my involvement in Maddy's death came out, then someone might make the connection to the other deaths like Tate did. So, I hinted I would hurt her daughter if she went through with it. She gave me no choice."

Parker's nose scrunched into a sneer. "You knew where Lynn was?"

"Of course. Just as I've always known who you really were," Van stated.

Tate stepped back to the pit, confused. "Wait a minute. You're not Penelope's daughter, Lynn?"

"No, I'm not. My real name is Bonnie Parker, and I'm Lynn's widow."

"Lies, lies, and more lies. Everybody around me is telling lies," Tate said.

Parker connected the dots in her head. "When Lynn died, your leverage against Penelope disappeared, and that's when she made the arrangements for the book launch here in Willow's Bane and planned to reveal the secret you tried so hard to keep buried. Your only option left was to kill her that night as a last-ditch effort."

A flash of annoyance appeared on Van's face. "Again, I'll admit I went there to do just that, but no one answered the door."

"Excuse me if I don't believe you," Parker scoffed.

"Have it your way," Van said. She struggled to stand up and then looked at her son. "Tate... darling... there is still a way out of this mess."

Tate looked bewildered. "What?"

"I have a way we can put all this behind us and move forward."

"You really are nuts, lady," Parker said.

"Mom… there is no way forward. You are going to jail for multiple murders, and my reputation in this town is garbage. End of story," Tate said.

"What if I told you I have a different ending in mind, one where we can go back to our lives, and you can still be sheriff one day?" Van asked, smiling innocently.

Tate shook his head. "You're not making any sense, Mom."

"It might be better if I show you," Van said, then limped back to her car.

Parker hesitated before following the mother and son, unsure of what the woman had up her sleeve. Van had been extremely forthcoming about her actions, which led Parker to assume Van had resolved herself to answer for her crimes. But how she talked now made it sound like she was anything but remorseful. Parker considered what actual evidence still existed that could link Van to the murders she had just confessed to. Other than her admission, what was there? Parker was suddenly concerned and stepped quickly to catch up with the pair.

Van popped the trunk of her Toyota, then stepped to the side. Tate and Parker stepped together to peer inside.

Laying inside the trunk, bound, gagged, and unconscious, was Matt Jackson.

When Parker looked up at Van again, a 9MM pistol appeared in her hand.

"Here's our new ending," Van said, grinning.

Thirty-Five

"Mom, what are you doing?" Tate snapped, staring at the handgun. Parker took a step backward.

"Don't move, missy. Hand me your cell phone," Van demanded, holding her empty hand out.

Parker followed the woman's instructions while considering her possibilities for escape. Everything depended on Tate's reaction. Parker needed to understand where the man stood regarding his mother's actions before committing to any action.

"Mom, don't compound things by doing something stupid. Just give me the gun," Tate said, extending his hand.

"Tate, honey, I need you to listen to what I have in mind. It's a way out, I promise, and it's so simple," Van said, smiling.

"I'm not listening to anything you have to say with a gun pointing at me," Tate stated.

"Oh, it's not pointed at you. It's for her. And I won't hesitate to shoot her unless you listen to what I propose."

Tate glanced at Parker. "Fine. What craziness are you up to now?"

Van nodded her head in the unmoving Matt Jackson's direction. "We pin everything on Matt. He didn't have an alibi back in 86, and half the people in Willow's Bane still think he did it, anyway. It'll be an easy sell. The story will be that Parker confronted him out here. He shoots her, then turns the gun on himself, but not before he sets the cabin on fire with them inside. It's perfect. The sheriff couldn't investigate himself out of a paper bag and you can help steer everything else in the right direction."

"My friend Kat knows I'm out here," Parker said.

"But she doesn't know who you're out here with, does she? You called my son Tate asking questions about the cabin, and we'll say he told you that Matt Jackson uses it a lot. Has for as long as Tate could remember. That's when you called Matt and asked him out here. I have your cell phone, so it'll be easy enough to make that call happen. There will be no one left to dispute it."

"Where's Matt's car? If he supposedly drove out here, where is it?" Parker asked, stalling for time.

"Oh… this is Matt's car. I left mine at the abandoned gas station where I met him. I injected him with 10cc of GHB after tasing him. He'll be out for a while. Tate will give me a lift back to my car when we're through here."

"The taser burn will show up in the autopsy," Parker stated.

"Thus the need for him to burn in the fire. I've been writing mysteries for years; you think I can't anticipate every scenario?"

"What were you going to do with him if your son hadn't figured out what you'd done?"

"He was going to disappear," Van said matter-of-factly. "It still made sense. The renewed interest in the murders got to him, and he fled. I know a spot in the river to drive the car in, and no one will ever find it or him. But that doesn't matter because I know Tate will do the right thing."

Tate's eyes widened, and his mouth fell slack. "You actually think I'd go along with any of this?"

Van frowned. "Honey, do you want your mother to go to prison? Because that's what's going to happen unless we do this. And your hope of becoming the sheriff is gone as well. Both our lives end if you don't help me do this. Take a step back, peel away the emotion, and look at this logically. This is the right thing."

The expression on Tate's face told Parker he was struggling to understand his new reality.

"How can you talk about killing these people in cold blood so dispassionately? Who are you? This isn't the mother who raised me… taught me right from wrong… instilled in me the need to make a difference. Where's that woman?" Tate asked, searching her face.

"I'm right here, darling," Van said sweetly. "Can't you see that I'm doing this for you?"

Tate's shoulders slumped. "Oh, Mom. You know what bothers me the most," Tate said, taking a step forward. "Is that you actually believe I would help you."

"Tate, son, stay back. Why can't you see that this is the only way?"

"Gimme the gun." He took another step, causing Van to back up more.

When Tate lunged for the gun, Parker bolted. She wasn't taking any chances that the deputy could wrestle the gun away from his mother. The woods were too far off to make a run in that direction, so she headed towards the cabin. She had just cleared the cars when she heard a shot ring out.

Without looking back, Parker sprinted past the firepit as a second shot shattered the night, splintering the pole holding the lantern. She leaped up the steps and threw her shoulder into the door, demolishing the flimsy lock on the inside and sending the door flying open. Slamming the door closed behind her, she scanned the dark room. A wooden chair sat under a nearby table, so she reached out and grabbed it, wedging it between the door handle and the floor. She put her back against the wall and tried to catch her breath and slow her heartbeat, but she was having little success. Her breath came out ragged as she tried to come up with a plan.

Moving to the boarded window, she peered through the slats. Van was the only person she could see standing in front of the cabin.

"You selfish bitch," Van screamed into the night. "Look what you made me do. You're ruining everything."

"Is Tate hurt bad?" Parker yelled back.

Van looked over her shoulder. "He took one in the shoulder. He'll live, which is more than I can say for you."

Parker's eyes adjusted to the dark as she looked around the inside of the small cabin. It was sparsely decorated, with a cot, a table, a second chair, a throw rug, numerous canned goods lining shelves mounted on the wall, and a bin full of firewood next to a tiny fireplace.

The sound of footsteps mounting the steps was followed by the door rattling against the wedged chair.

"Give it up, Vanessa," Parker yelled out. "Your plan has all gone to shit, and the best thing you can do now is turn yourself in."

"Not before I make you pay. You're the cause of all this, and I didn't even kill your mother-in-law. Penelope killed herself, and now you've destroyed my life as well. Remember that when the flames start melting your face."

Parker watched Van disappear off the porch, then heard the door to the shed open. A minute later came the sound of liquid being splashed against the cabin walls. Van planned to burn Parker alive in the cabin or shoot her point-blank if she made a run for it out the door. Not much of a choice.

Parker remembered the matches in her pocket and prayed that Van didn't have a lighter. The whooshing sound of erupting flames and the glowing light emanating from one corner of the room dashed Parker's hope. The cabin was old, and Parker knew it would burn quickly. Finding a way to escape couldn't wait. She moved to the farthest corner next to the firewood bin, away from the growing flames, looking for any kind of weakness in the rear wall.

The entire wall next to the door was an inferno now, with smoke filling the room quickly. The intense heat from the blaze caused perspiration to bead on Parker's brow. She dropped to her knees and covered her nose and mouth with the crook of her arm, continuing to scan for any way out. The flames made it easier to see inside the room despite the smoke. Parker glanced at the fireplace, thinking that she could possibly cram herself inside the opening, but it was much too small. That's when she looked closer at the firewood bin. She remembered the external firewood box on the outer wall and had a thought. The inside bin was in the exact location on the inner wall as the outside box, so maybe they were connected?

Working feverishly, the heat from the fire becoming more profound, she started grabbing wood out of the storage bin and tossing it behind her. Her FBI friend Chuck was an avid hunter, and she remembered him mentioning something about campsites where the cabins could access the firewood without going outside. Parker ignored the pain from the splinters digging into her hands, hoping beyond hope that this was a cabin Chuck would approve of. Her arm muscles were screaming as she worked. Suddenly, she saw a piece of sheet metal in the wall at the back of the bin, held in place by a hinge. Doubling her efforts, she cleared away the last few pieces of wood, grabbed the edges of the metal sheet, and pulled. It came up easily.

The opening was small, but she made herself fit through it. Flames were now nipping at her shoes as she crawled into the bin and wedged through the gap. There was still wood stored in the outside bin, which she pushed ahead of her as she maneuvered her way through. She wriggled and struggled until she was finally clear, tumbling out of the exterior box and landing on the wood she had dumped out ahead of her.

After she struggled to her feet, her first instinct was to get to the woods and run for help, but she remembered that Matt Jackson was still unconscious in the back of his car. She couldn't take a chance of leaving him with Van. That psycho woman could still want to submerge him in the river. Parker had to get him away from her.

Vanessa was surely standing on the other side of the cabin, waiting to see if Parker would make a desperate attempt to run through the flames to escape death. Parker's only move would be to disappear into the woods, then make her way around the open grounds, sticking to cover. Then, hopefully, she could surprise Vanessa and wrestle the gun away from her.

Parker had only taken a couple of steps toward the trees when a new sound made her freeze. There was another vehicle coming up the trail. Parker backtracked, slid around the side of the cabin entirely engulfed in flames now, and peeked at the road. Vanessa had her back to the cabin and was staring at the arriving car. The headlights of the new arrival came to rest behind the Toyota and just sat there, engine running. When Vanessa raised her pistol and began walking towards the new car, Parker sprang into action. Sprinting as fast as she could, she heard Vanessa's gun blast away, but Parker didn't hesitate. She leaped over the firepit and closed in on her target. When she was ten feet away, she spotted Vanessa's walking cane lying nearby. She slowed slightly, swooped up the cane in one fluid motion, then swung it in a wide arc. The end of the cane struck Vanessa on the side of the head.

She crumbled to the ground like a deflated balloon.

Parker dropped the cane and picked up the pistol, taking a moment to regard the unconscious serial killer. Satisfied the woman was out cold, Parker searched for Tate. She found him right where she had last seen him, lying flat on the ground.

"Tate, are you okay?" Parker called.

Tate's hand, covered in blood, was pressed firmly against a spot right below his shoulder. "Yeah, but it hurts like a son-of-a-bitch."

Parker turned and walked over to the car Vanessa had been firing at.

The windshield of the tan Kia had three bullet holes in it. There didn't appear to be anyone behind the wheel, but slowly, a head raised up from below the dash. Kat's eyes were as big as saucers.

Parker sighed deeply. "I don't think we can return it this time."

Thirty-Six

"Keep applying pressure," Parker instructed Kat. Her friend was kneeling next to Tate Bonner, pushing an old towel they found in the car onto his shoulder. The deputy was conscious but in a great deal of pain. "The ambulance should be here any minute," Parker said.

Parker glanced at Vanessa, lying face down with her hands bound behind her back with a zip tie Tate kept in his glove box for emergencies. Even though Vanessa had regained consciousness minutes ago, she remained motionless and silent, which suited Parker just fine.

Matt Jackson was still asleep in the trunk of the Toyota. Parker carefully removed his bindings and gag, then tried to position him in such a way that would make him the most comfortable. She didn't want to take him out of the trunk by herself, fearing she might drop him and make things worse, so for right now, he would stay where he was. At least he was unaware of his situation.

Just as Parker returned to check on Tate, sirens could be heard in the distance. Shortly thereafter, flashing lights began coming up the road. An ambulance, followed by several patrol cars, came roaring up the trail, coming to an abrupt halt.

As soon as the EMTs exited the ambulance, Parker pointed to Tate.

"Ummm … he's been shot in the upper shoulder. I think the bullet exited cleanly, but he's lost a lot of blood. And there's somebody else in the back of the Toyota. He's been tasered and given GBH, but as far as I can tell, he seems to be doing okay," Parker rattled off.

"What about her?" one of the EMTs asked, pointing at Vanessa.

Parker frowned. "Tend to her last."

One EMT went to Tate, and the other headed toward the Toyota.

"What in the blue blazes went on here?" Sheriff Weber growled as he came up behind Parker.

Parker turned, put her hands on her hips, and looked over at Vanessa's prone figure.

"That's your Snake River Killer."

The sheriff studied the bound bookstore owner. "Van? There's got to be—"

"She also killed Bill Jamesison. Admitted everything, all the details, in front of me and your deputy. Then she shot Tate when he tried to take the gun away from her, tried to kill me by setting the cabin on fire with me in it, shot at my friend Kat, and kidnapped Matt Jackson intending to kill him as well," Parker said.

"Jesus Christ," the sheriff said, his eyes surveying the scene.

"Yeah, I think that pretty much sums it up. Oh… Vanessa's cane is on the hood of that Kia. That's your murder weapon for all of them."

"How did all of you end up out here?"

"This cabin belongs to Vanessa's family. There's a map in Penelope's book that detailed a rough outline of a spot like this, but it wasn't mentioned in the book. I played a hunch and found this place. I had my friend do some digging and learned who owned the property… which was your deputy… and invited him out here. He called his mother, but Tate didn't know what she had done."

The sheriff regarded Parker carefully. "I thought you were a social worker?"

Parker glanced at Tate, who was still being tended to. "What can I say, we social workers can be tenacious."

The sheriff hooked his thumbs into his belt. "What about Penelope? Did Van kill her as well?"

Parker glanced back at Van. "She claims not, but I don't believe her. She was there that night. It's why she killed Jamesison. He saw her there and tried to blackmail her."

"Damn fool."

"No arguments there."

"I'll need you to come into the office and give a full statement," the sheriff stated.

"Happy to cooperate," Parker said, looking straight into the sheriff's eyes. "Something that you wouldn't be too familiar with."

The sheriff grunted his response.

"And we're going to need to talk about that Kia."

"Fine. I'll see you back at the station," he said, then moved off towards Vanessa, barking orders to his other officers as he did.

"That guy gives pricks a bad rep," Kat commented, having strolled up behind Parker.

"How are you doing?" Parker asked, placing her hands on Kat's shoulders.

"Well, it wasn't my first near-death experience, but it was my first time being shot at."

"And?"

"Terrifying and exhilarating, but not something I would recommend."

Parker watched as the sheriff escorted Vanessa towards the patrol car. The woman's eyes locked with hers.

"I know what you mean."

Thirty-Seven

The next morning, Parker pulled the rental car in front of the tiny home in a cul-de-sac at the bottom of a hill. The house was in a subdivision crowded with older dwellings and neglected lawns.

"Tell me why we're here again," Kat asked, looking out the window at the aged house.

"I wanted to tell Trudy what we learned about her sister's death before we leave town, along with everything else we found out," Parker said, looking up at the house.

"Isn't that the sheriff's job?" Kat grumbled.

"It is, and he said he'd meet us here," Parker said. "But I figured I owed it to her since I impersonated her niece. Besides, knowing Sheriff Weber, he'll tell her as little as possible. I could have done this by myself. You didn't need to come."

Kat rolled her eyes. "Are you kidding? I'm not leaving you alone again until we have this town in our rear-view."

Parker exited the car and gazed up at Trudy's residence. It was decades old, as were all the other homes in the neighborhood, but it still looked sturdy. A large bay window dominated most of the front, with a tiny basement window beneath it. A single windowpane on the second floor was surrounded by paneling that looked like light green fish scales. The house was situated close to the road, leaving room for very little yard, and what was there was mostly dirt.

Kat made a face and pointed to a flag hanging below the mailbox that read HE HAS RISEN. As the two women walked to the stairs leading up to a small porch, Kat pointed out a large garden rock with the words JESUS IS LIFE painted on it.

"I think Trudy is a believer," Kat said.

Parker knocked on the door. "To each their own."

A few seconds later, the door opened, and Trudy smiled at them.

"Well, this is a pleasant surprise. What brings you out here?"

"Has Sheriff Weber been here yet?" Parker asked.

Trudy's eyebrows pushed together. "What would the sheriff be coming here for?"

"There is some news. Vanessa Sanders has been arrested."

Mild shock registered on Trudy's face, making Parker wonder if small-town gossip had beaten them here.

"Van arrested? What for?" Trudy asked.

"If you let us come in, we'll explain it all to you," Parker replied, softening her voice.

"Oh, yes, where are my manners? Please come in," Trudy said, backing away from the door.

When Parker stepped inside and looked around, she thought they had entered a home-based church or a boutique offering Christian adornments. The great room's wall was overflowing with various religious decorations of all shapes, sizes, and colors. Even the throw pillows on the L-shaped sectional had religious proverbs stitched on them.

Parker shot a look at Kat, who simply raised her eyebrows and smirked.

"You two have a seat, and I'll fix us something to drink. How about some hot apple cider?"

"Ummmmm… that sounds good," Kat commented.

"That does sound good," Parker added. "Thank you."

Trudy waved off the offering of gratitude. "Psssh. It's no problem at all. I was about to have some myself, anyway."

The kitchen was adjacent to the great room, separated by a bar island. Trudy began tinkering with pans and cups.

"So, tell me all about Van being arrested," Trudy called out from the kitchen.

Parker sat down on the sectional while Kat continued to walk around the room, inspecting all the decorations.

"It turns out Vanessa killed the three girls back in 1986."

Trudy stopped what she was doing and walked to the island's edge. "All three? Are we talking about the same Vanessa Sanders?"

"Yes, ma'am. She also killed Bill Jamesison and almost killed Matt Jackson, but he's fine. She admitted everything to me."

"Oh my word! That is awful," Trudy said, shaking her head in disbelief. "What possessed her to do such a thing?"

"She was upset about the accident that robbed her of a promising future running track and blamed the Jamesisons and Pool's for it. She killed their daughters in order to make them suffer. Van was one messed up little girl and probably didn't get the help she needed to deal with that loss."

Trudy returned to her work in the kitchen. "But why Maddy Emerson? You said Van killed all three."

"That's a little more complicated, and it's also where Penelope comes in." Parker paused for a moment. "Your sister had taken Maddy to an isolated spot to convince her to make her father end his affair with your mother."

Trudy came to the island again. "Our mother was having an affair with Dan Emerson?"

"Apparently." Parker found Trudy's response, or lack of one, curious. Shouldn't she be more disbelieving or shocked?

"Penelope never said anything to me," Trudy said, frowning.

"Maybe she was protecting you, or she hoped she could end it before there was a need to tell you?"

Trudy shook her head, then returned to her work in the kitchen while Parker told her the rest of it. When she was finished, Trudy emerged from the kitchen with three steaming mugs. She handed one to Kat, who was still wandering around the room, then the next to Parker before sitting next to her on the sectional.

All three women sipped from their cups.

"Wow... this is great," Kat announced.

"My secret ingredients are ginger, galangal, peppercorn, and cardamom. Adds a delicious twist, don't you think?"

"I'll say," Kat said before taking another long sip. Parker did the same.

"Let me get this straight," Trudy said, her eyes losing focus as she talked. "Penelope thought she killed Maddy by accident when she hit her head, but she wasn't really dead, and Van actually killed her. So, for forty years my sister lived with the memory of killing someone, but she didn't. And she died still thinking that she had."

Parker nodded. "I'm afraid so."

"Does that mean Vanessa killed my sister to keep her secret buried?" Trudy half-whispered.

Parker shook her head. "Van claims she didn't, but that woman has told so many lies I'm not sure I believe her."

"I'm inclined to agree with you."

"Van is the one with the obvious motive to kill Penelope, but on the other hand, she doesn't have a good reason to lie about that. It's a puzzle."

"Parker, can you come here for a second?" Kat said. There was something in her voice that drew Parker's attention. Her friend was standing in front of an accent chest, the top of which was jammed with framed pictures. Her face was pale as a ghost.

Concerned, Parker set down her drink and went over to Kat. When Parker drew close, Kat's finger pointed to a picture on the chest. Her finger was shaking.

Parker followed the finger to the picture. In it was a man she didn't recognize with a small girl on his shoulders. But it wasn't the people who drew her attention and shot a shiver up her spine. It was the vehicle they were standing in front of.

A blue van.

Parker turned quickly to face Trudy, and suddenly, the room seemed to shift. Dizziness seized her. She grabbed the corner of the chest to steady herself, knocking over some picture frames when she did. Behind her, there was a sudden thud. When she turned around, she found Kat unconscious on the ground.

"Kat?"

Turning toward Trudy again, Parker saw that the woman had risen from the sectional.

"There was one more secret ingredient I forgot to mention," Parker heard Trudy say before the edges of her vision turned black, and the world spun into nothingness.

Parker became aware of an odd sound in the distance. As it grew in volume, it morphed into something she vaguely recognized, but it was still muffled. The noise was part anguished moaning, part insistent humming. She opened her eyes, but there was very little light wherever she was. She was sitting upright on a hard surface but couldn't move. Something was covering her mouth. Her hands were behind her back and bound. Turning her head towards the noise, she saw Kat sitting in a desk chair, duct tape covering her mouth, and her hands and feet were taped to the chair. Kat was struggling to make whatever noise she could to wake her friend.

A sudden realization of their situation sent a surge of adrenaline through Parker and snapped her fully alert. Sunlight from a small basement window, the one she had noticed on their way into the house, provided just enough light to make out the room's layout. There was a slight opening between the window and the frame, but it was too small to escape through, even if they could shed their restraints. The basement was unfinished, twenty feet wide, and twice as long. Plasterboard walls were still unpainted, and the concrete floor felt grainy beneath Parker. She could see bare wooden beams in the ceiling. A heavy door in the room's corner was half-open, and the base of stairs leading upwards were visible on the other side. Stacked along the north wall were a dozen cardboard boxes and the only furniture in the room was Kat's chair and a second unoccupied chair. Parker briefly wondered why she wasn't taped to the other chair instead of left on the ground as she was.

Parker's eyes locked with Kat's. Her friend had quieted after Parker had come around, but desperation was still evident in her teary eyes. Parker nodded, attempting to assure her friend that everything would be okay… despite her own feelings to the contrary. She needed to keep her panic under control. For a fleeting moment, she wondered if this was the way Lynn felt when she was first diagnosed — needing to be strong for the ones you love.

Kat jerked her head toward the opposite wall and moaned something. Parker looked to where Kat was motioning and thought she saw something on top of one of the boxes. Raising her hips up slightly to get a better look, she recognized what it was— their cellphones.

The back of Parker's heels ached. There was duct tape wrapped around her knees, making it difficult for her to gain leverage to stand up. She started rolling onto her side until she heard steps descending the stairs outside the room. Returning to her original position, Parker glared at Trudy when she entered the room and flipped a switch to turn on the single lightbulb in the ceiling.

The woman was panting as she plopped down into the second chair.

"Phew… I haven't worked that hard for quite some time," Trudy gasped, grinning. "Gotta catch my breath. I just got back from moving your car to the next block over. There's an empty house there, and I parked it in the garage until I figure out what to do with it."

Trudy regarded Parker in such a way that it looked like she expected her to respond.

"I'm sure you have questions," Trudy continued. "And I'll do my best to answer them for you, but you'll understand if I don't remove the tape from your mouths. This room is relatively soundproof, and my neighbors are hard of hearing, but you can never take too many precautions."

Trudy took another deep cleansing breath.

"First things first… yes, I killed my sister, but she brought it on herself. In the weeks leading up to her book launch, I begged her to tell me what she planned to say, but she wouldn't. She'd only say that it would be best for everyone. What a laugh. Penelope only ever did things that were best for her. I knew she was going to spoil everything."

"I have to say I'm impressed with how you uncovered everything," Trudy frowned. In the dim light, Parker thought her eyes looked a bit maniacal. "I knew you were going to be trouble from the moment I first laid eyes on you, and I was right, wasn't I? Penelope told me Lynn had a partner who worked as an investigator, but I was still surprised. Pretending to be Lynn was a smart move. Helped you learn Penelope's secrets, Vanessa's as well, but you didn't find them all, did you. And not all those secrets were hers to tell. That's why my sister had to die. I told you I work part-time at Knights Lodge, remember? I clean rooms and do odd jobs. I have a master key that lets me into all the rooms. I'm not supposed to take it home with me, but they don't check. When Penelope's assistant called me ahead of their trip to ask me for a recommendation of where they should stay, of course, I suggested Knights Lodge. That night, I let myself into the rear entrance of the hotel. Almost ran into Poppy Jackson as she was leaving Penelope's room. That was a close call, yes indeed. I waited a minute to make sure she wasn't coming back, then knocked on Penelope's door. My sister was surprised. She knew I wasn't happy about what she was planning, but she believed me when I told her I came to make peace. I offered to hash things out over a cup of coffee. I knew which antidepressants Penelope took from the time I visited her in New York. I take the same prescription. All I had to do was crush up all my pills before heading to the hotel and slip them into her coffee, and then sit down for a chat. It didn't take too long. When she was out, I put her on the bed, took her pills to replace the ones I used, placed the empty bottle in her hand, cleaned up any evidence that I was there, and left."

Despite her interest in what Trudy was saying, Parker kept scanning the room for anything to help them. A weapon, an escape route, anything useful, but she wasn't having much luck.

"You'll be interested to know she had the missing chapter you were so interested in with her in the room. It was pure luck I stumbled across it. I was checking her bag to make sure she didn't have a supplemental stash of pills when I found it. I didn't even know it existed. I took it with me when I left. It's around here someplace. I know I should probably burn it, but I just can't bring myself to do that. I did read it though. Turns out I was right. She was going to tell my secret."

Trudy paused as she stared off into the distance.

"I had an inkling you would turn up at my doorstep eventually," Trudy continued, her gaze returned to Parker. "I tried to warn you off by leaving you that note, then used Papa's van to try to stop you, but that didn't work. I tried a couple of other things, poison being one of them, and still you kept going like some Energizer Bunny. You've had an angel sitting on your shoulder, that's for sure. But I've prayed to the lord long and hard, and we've come to an understanding. He will look away one more time to ensure my improvidence remains hidden. I'm sorry that it must be this way, but you can't be trusted, and my soul is at stake. I couldn't afford to use the last of my anti-depressants on the two of you, and all I had left was something that would knock you out. But no matter, you'll both remain here until nature runs its course, which Google says should be about two weeks. It's a lot less messy that way. Then I'll find a pleasant spot to lay you to rest. Maybe someplace near a nice patch of trees."

Kat growled through her taped mouth, pulling against her restraints as she did.

"Little girl, it's no use trying—" Trudy started.

A doorbell chime interrupted Trudy and sent a wave of hopeful optimism through Parker. Trudy's eyebrows pinched together, and she rose from the chair. She started to leave the room, hesitated, then returned to pick up the two cell phones. She slid one into each of her back pockets.

"I have this huge kitchen knife upstairs, and if I hear a peep out of either of you, I'll kill whoever is at my door," Trudy growled.

As soon as the door closed, Parker began pushing with her feet, forcing her back up the wall. Her thighs screamed in pain as she inched her way up the wall. When finally upright, she hopped over to the wall beneath the tiny window and listened.

"Sheriff Weber," Parker heard the muffled voice said. "What brings you out here?

"I come bearing some news about Penelope's case. Has her daughter been out here to see you?" the sheriff said.

"No, she hasn't," Trudy replied.

"Hmmmm… I told her I'd meet her here, but I'm running a little late. Let me just call her."

A brief silence followed; then suddenly Parker's *Eye of the Tiger* ringtone began playing.

"Uh… that's her ringtone. Do you have her phone?"

Trudy chuckled. "Oh, she left it here earlier, and I haven't had a chance to return it to her."

"But you just said she hasn't been here," the sheriff said, doubt evident in his voice.

"I meant she left it here yesterday," Trudy said.

"Trudy, I know for a fact she had her phone with her late last night. What's going on?"

"I… uh… it's—"

"I think I need to come… AAARRGHHH!"

The sheriff's painful scream was followed by a loud thump. When the sound of running steps started pounding down the stairs, Parker hopped as fast as she could to the far side of the door. She knew she would only have one chance at this. The door flew open, and Trudy burst into the room, bloody knife still clutched in her hand. When she noticed Parker wasn't where she left her, she spun around just in time to see a forehead coming at her. It was difficult for Parker to accurately direct her attack with her hands tied behind her back, so her blow landed against Trudy's cheek. The elderly woman stumbled backward, the pain temporarily blinding her. Parker blinked several times, stars in her eyes and a throbbing ache spreading through her head, but she forced herself to hop after the woman. She drew back and head-butted her again. This time, the blow landed directly on Trudy's nose, and the woman cried out in pain, staggering. Parker ignored her own agony as she followed Trudy once more and, with a muffled primal scream, smashed her head into the woman's temple. Trudy fell back against the wall and then crumbled to the ground.

Parker puffed heavily through her nose, teetering over Trudy. A sound behind her made her turn.

FBI Chuck was leaning against the door frame, breathing heavily, his gun out.

"Damn, Parker ... I was right ... you are hard-headed."

Before a crooked smile could fully form beneath the duct tape on Parker's mouth, she passed out.

Thirty-Eight

"How are you doing?" Parker asked when Tate Bonner looked up from his hospital bed.

"I should ask you the same question," Tate replied, struggling to sit taller in the bed. A thick bandage covering his shoulder was sticking out from beneath his hospital gown. "I hate to see the other guy."

Parker's hand instinctively went to her temple. She had almost forgotten about the decolorization around both her eyes. The blood-red hue around each iris underscored her skin's purple, yellow, and green shading. She looked like a sleep-deprived raccoon.

"It looks worse than it is. How are you feeling?"

"Like an ignoramus," Tate replied with a half-smile. "But other than that, not bad. I have wonderful drugs."

It was the second time Parker had been to Willow's Bane General Hospital, neither under pleasant circumstances, adding to her long list of terrible memories accumulated from time spent in medical facilities. On the flip side, Tate's room featured a large glass window, letting in lots of sunshine.

"You shouldn't beat yourself up. Your mother had a lot of people fooled, myself included."

"I get it ... but ... I know it's stupid ... but I kind of feel responsible. Not that she did what she did—I wasn't around then—but that she got away with it for so long. I keep going back over my life for the past twenty-four years and trying to remember anything that would have given me a clue to who she was."

"Well, no matter how long it took, you closed four murders. I just wanted to come by to see how you were and to thank you for saving my life."

Tate tapped his shoulder. "I did a half-assed job at that as well. You almost got burned alive."

"You stepped in front of a bullet and gave me a chance. That's all I needed, and for that, I thank you."

Tate fidgeted with his sheets. "You're welcome."

"No hard feelings then … me pretending to be Penelope's daughter?"

Tate's forehead wrinkled briefly, then relaxed. "I probably should be upset, but I'm not. I understand why you did it. Probably would have done the same, given the circumstances. How long has she been gone… your wife?"

Parker took a deep breath. "Almost a month."

"We're the two of you alike?"

Parker grinned at the thought. "Not at all. We used to joke that if I were a hard-boiled egg, she'd be sunny-side up."

"Let me guess, your friend Kat would be scrambled."

"Totally," Parker replied, laughing. "The three of us were an odd trio, but it worked. We worked."

"You must have cared about her a lot to do what you did."

"I still do. Anyway, thanks again for understanding."

"I have one last question. Why did Trudy do it? Why did she kill her sister?"

Parker debated her response. "The answer is in Penelope's lost chapter, which is back at your station now. I'll let you read it and decide for yourself."

"Fair enough. What now? Heading home?"

Parker took the sunglasses hanging from the front of her shirt and put them on. "Kat and I are being escorted to the airport right now. We'll be back in Willow's Bane for the trial, of course."

"You gonna stop in to say goodbye to the sheriff? I hear he's just down the hall?"

Parker smiled. "I'll pass. I never told him who I really was."

"Surely you had to sign a statement about what happened that night."

"I did, and I signed it, Bonnie Parker. He never even noticed. That reminds me… I gave a lot of credit for what we found out to an FBI agent who happened to be here. I kinda owed him. I'd appreciate it if you didn't act surprised when you read about it in my statement."

The deputy looked confused. "There was an FBI agent in Willow's Bane investigating Penelope's death?"

"No, he was actually here for me."

"Somehow, that doesn't surprise me. Were there handcuffs involved?"

"Well —"

Tate shrugged his one good shoulder. "Never mind. It's one more thing that will tick off the sheriff, so it's fine by me."

"For the record, you're the actual law in this town."

Tate smiled. "So, I can count on your vote when the time comes?"

"I don't live here, so I can't vote here. But if you need someone to help hand out election fliers, call me." She gave the deputy a pat on the leg. "Take it easy."

Parker walked down the hall and entered the elevator. When the doors opened on the ground floor, Kat and Chuck were both standing there, waiting.

"How's he doing?" Kat asked.

Parker tipped her head to the side. "Better than I would be, given the shock of discovering what his mother had done."

"Makes you wonder if there are other dead bodies in this town nobody knows about. I mean, the woman killed three people without batting an eye; surely that killer instinct didn't just go away," Kat said.

"It didn't, not entirely, because she did kill Bill Jamesison and almost killed the two of you," Chuck pointed out. "But it's not so hard to believe that she could live a relatively normal life after killing those three girls. The BTK killer, Dennis Rader, murdered victims until 1991 and then ended his spree prior to being captured in 2005. It's a myth that serial killers are unable to stop—because they can."

"Forgive me if I don't take any comfort in that," Kat frowned.

"You're forgiven," Chuck said.

"Can we go now?" Parker answered.

"Do you think it's smart checking yourself out of the hospital? They said you could have a mild concussion," Kat pointed out, concern in her voice.

"I'm fine. Besides, Chuck would have a fit if we delayed anymore."

"You got that right," Chuck said. "Let's get out of here."

The two women and the FBI agent exited the building. As they walked down the sidewalk to the parking garage, Kat looked at her friend.

"Can I ask you something?" Kat asked tentatively.

"Always."

Kat furrowed her eyebrows. "Do you think Lynn would be happy with how things turned out, or should we have left well enough alone?"

"You mean leave a murderer free to enjoy her freedom?" Parker said.

"You almost died … three times." Kat held up three fingers. "And me twice. A man did die. Bill Jamesison."

"Bill would have become a victim whether we came out here or not. His greed cost him."

"Okay, but knowing what we know now, was it worth it? Do you think Penelope told Lynn everything?"

"You're talking about that last chapter?" Parker asked, lifting an eyebrow.

"Yeah."

"That's a tough one," Chuck remarked.

Parker stopped walking to consider her answer. "Lynn wouldn't want to put you or me in danger. That was my choice alone. I'm sorry you got dragged into that. Truly. But Lynn was all about the truth. Her truth … and her mother's truth. Penelope desperately wanted to tell that truth as she knew it and Lynn wanted that for her … regardless of how hurtful that truth was. So, to answer your question … yes. I believe Penelope told her everything."

"Even the part about her not—"

"Yes," Parker replied. "Even that."

After walking a few more steps in silence, Kat added, "Do you think Lynn forgave her?"

"I know she did," Parker answered immediately.

"Good," Kat replied after a brief pause, "And for the record, I'll always have your back regardless of what you drag us into."

Parker looked at her friend, laughing. "Ditto."

"Who's got my back?" Chuck asked.

"You have your G-Man buddies. Don't be needy," Kat said.

Minutes later, Parker's rental car followed Chuck's SUV, leaving the Willow's Bane city limits on its way to the Portland airport. Her *Eye of the Tiger* ringtone interrupted their silence as they drove.

"Have I told you how much I love that ringtone?" Kat quipped.

"Hello?" Parker answered, using the hands-free option.

"Miss Parker?" a woman's voice asked.

"Speaking," Parker stated.

"I don't know if you remember me — my name is Kelly Bonner. I work at Tranquility Assisted Living. I helped bandage your head after your accident."

"Oh yes. You're Tate's wife."

"I am. Tate told me what you did for him. Thank you so much for that," Kelly said, emotion in her voice.

"Nonsense. I can't thank him enough. He's a great guy and a credit to Willow's Bane," Parker said.

"I'm sort of biased, but I totally agree. But that's not the reason I'm calling."

"Oh? What's up?"

"You visited Abner Crane when you were here before, right?" Kelly asked.

A sense of unease gripped Parker. "I did. Is he okay?"

Kat's head snapped in Parker's direction.

"He's fine. But he wants to see you, and he says it is urgent. He wouldn't stop until I called you."

"I'll be there in ten minutes," Parker said.

"What's going on?" Kat asked as soon as Parker ended the call.

"Chuck's gonna be pissed, is what," Parker replied as she spun the steering wheel.

Kelly Bonner was waiting for them in the Tranquility lobby. She smiled when she recognized Parker, and then the smile turned muted when she spotted Kat trailing behind.

"Thank you for coming so quickly," Kelly said before looking at Kat with a worrisome expression. "Who's this?"

"This is my friend Kat Anderson. Is that a problem?"

Kelly tilted her head and grimaced. "It's just that Abner is having an exceptionally good day, and you can tell he is doing everything he can to stay in the now. Not to slip away, if you know what I mean. He's met you… knows you… even asked for you… but strangers can sometimes confuse people with his condition. I'm worried if your friend goes back there, he might spiral and forget what he's so desperate to tell you."

Parker looked at Kat, but before she could say anything, her friend nodded. "It's okay. I'll go keep Chuck company."

After mouthing a silent thank you, Parker followed Kelly into the facility.

As the two women followed the same path Parker had taken earlier in the week, she wondered what Abner Crane wanted to convey to her. She doubted it would be anything they didn't already know about the girl's murders or Penelope's death; all those loose ends were neatly tied. His earlier comment about a fourth victim was probably the result of the cruel disease, causing him to misremember facts of an unrelated case… or even something he watched on television or read in a book. Besides, it didn't matter anyway. She would happily take the time to placate an old man's need to feel relevant.

When they entered Abner's room, they found him ambling back and forth in front of his turned-off television. A navy-blue throw blanket drooped over his shoulders.

"She's here, Abner," Kelly announced.

When Abner looked up at them, his jaw dropped open. "What happened to your face?"

Parker smiled, one of her hands instinctively going to her eyebrow. "I sort of did this to myself."

Abner glanced at Kelly, then back at Parker. "What, are they holding an ugly contest at the Elks Lodge and you considered entering? I hate to break it to you, but you're still a knockout."

Parker could feel her cheeks begin to glow.

"Don't worry, Miss Kelly, you're still the number one babe in these parts," Abner added with a sly grin.

Kelly scoffed. "You tell all the nurses they're number one. We know your game."

Parker could tell that the retired sheriff seemed more alert today. His eye had a sparkle, and his speech was more direct.

"I understand you had some information for me."

Abner meandered towards his recliner and then plopped down unceremoniously. "Kelly told me that you've caught the Snake River Killer. Van Sanders?"

Both Parker and Kelly sat on the couch so they'd be at eye level with Abner.

"That's right."

"Van Sanders," Abner repeated.

"Yes, sir."

Abner then went quiet, staring off into space. He was still for so long that Parker shot Kelly a quizzical look.

"But it was Penelope's sister, Trudy, who killed her," Parker said, hoping to jump-start the conversation. "It was all about keeping secrets."

Abner's head snapped around at the mention of secrets. "Did you figure out what I meant the last time you were here? About the fourth?"

Parker gave Abner an apologetic smile. "There wasn't a fourth, Abner. I think you were confused about that."

Abner smiled, showing a set of pearly white dentures. "You're right. I was confused. Happens a lot nowadays. But I'm not now. There was a fourth. I'm certain of it."

Parker was now legitimately confused. "How can that be?"

Abner held out his hand. "If you help me out of this chair, there's someone I want you to meet."

Thirty-Nine

Parker heard the soft knocking at the door and went to open it. Samantha Trimble stood in the hallway, confusion evident on the podcaster's face by her pursed lips and scrunched forehead. The woman nodded at Parker as she stepped into the room, and then her eyes went to the old woman lying in the bed that everyone was around.

Samantha looked at Parker. "Why did you ask me to come here? Who is this?"

The old woman's head was the only thing visible beneath the thick bed blankets. Her hair was white and unwashed. Her eyes had receded but were clear, and large fleshy bags rested below them. Splotches of liver marks covered most of her forehead and cheeks. A lightweight tube delivering supplemental oxygen was in her nostrils.

Parker's voice was soft when she spoke. "A couple of days ago, I came here to interview the man who was the sheriff at the time of the Snake River murders. His name is Abner Crane. He wanted to be here to meet you, but unfortunately, he became over-tired and had to return to his room. Abner has dementia, and his memory isn't the best, but he recalled fragments of something at the time that he thought had something to do with those murders. Today, he remembered more of that memory, with better clarity, and he asked to speak with me."

Parker moved closer to the head of the bed and smiled down at the old woman.

"This is Amanda Potter. Before she became seriously ill, she and Abner used to spend a lot of time together in the recreation area. They became close over the years. One day, Amanda told Abner a story. It was a story that she asked him to keep secret — which he did until he accidentally let a piece of it slip to me. She told Abner this story because not only were they friends, but she knew he would understand its meaning. Today, when Abner remembered it all, he introduced me to Amanda and asked her to tell me that story, and she agreed. After listening to Amanda's story, I thought you also needed to hear it."

Parker gestured for Samantha to take a position near the head of the other side of the bed, which she did.

"Amanda, this is Samantha Trimble, the woman I talked to you about. Samantha, this is Amanda Potter," Parker said, smiling down at the woman.

"Hi, Miss Potter," Samantha said.

Amanda turned her head to face Samantha. "I'm sorry," her barely audible voice said.

Samantha shot Parker a confused look.

"Just listen," Parker said. "You'll have to get in close to hear. She doesn't have much strength."

Samantha dragged a chair closer to the bedside from the corner and sat down.

"Okay. I'm listening," Samantha said.

"It was when Teddy disappeared, that's when I knew something was wrong," Amanda said in a paper-thin raspy voice. "Teddy was our dog. We kept him outside, but he never wandered far off and always stayed close to home. Jack, that was my husband, found him a week later in the woods. He said critters had gotten to him. Jack figured Teddy had wandered off to die because he heard old animals did that sometimes, and Teddy was gettin' on, but I didn't believe it. The way my boy, his name was Carl, the way he acted when they found Teddy bothered me most. He went on acting like nothing had happened. It wasn't right."

Amanda took a deep, rattled breath before continuing.

"Jack wasn't Carl's father. I didn't really know who that was because I spent time with a lot of men back then. I'm not ashamed, just explaining. Jack and I married when Carl was five, and then he left us when Carl turned sixteen. Deep down, I think he knew what was coming, so he got out while he could. Jack and Carl never really got along, but then Carl didn't jell with most folks. He was so quiet all the time. Going off by himself. When he was home, it was like someone had sucked the emotions out of him. He'd never smile or cry. The worst was when he got angry. His whole body would shake, and his eyes … those eyes … they'd turn almost black."

Amanda paused to take a couple of breaths. Parker could see how hard it was for her to talk.

"Carl never moved out of the house," Amanda continued, a shimmer of tears in her eyes. "He didn't have an inclination to, and I didn't make him. He would spend a lot of time out in the barn, though. We lived outside Lewiston on thirty acres of land I inherited from my pappy, not good for much, farming maybe, but I didn't know how. I tended bar in town and Carl cleaned up around the bar and did odd jobs around town. We made things work, and I guess you can say we were sort of happy."

When Amanda stopped speaking, Parker looked down to see the woman's eyes were closed, but her chest was still rising and falling.

"Do you want to stop, Amanda?" Parker asked.

Amanda shook her head, then opened her eyes, looking at Samantha again.

"When the body of that young man was found," Amanda paused, a sad expression in her eyes. "I recognized his picture in the paper. That boy had come into my bar one night and had a dustup with Carl. Nothing major, but when I asked Carl about it, he acted like he didn't know what I was talking about. I let it drop, but I shouldn't have. Things might have been different if I had."

Amanda took another deep breath. "Almost a year later, Carl was growing more distant and spending more time in the barn. When I tried asking him what he was doing out there, he'd just go silent and tell me to mind my own business. It bothered me. In my gut, I knew something was wrong in that barn. So, one day, when Carl was hauling some trash to the junkyard for a neighbor, I decided to see for myself. What I found still haunts my nightmares. The most important thing I came across was a set of women's clothes."

Samantha's eyes met Parker's. Parker watched as the realization bloomed.

"The clothes I found matched the description in the paper of what the woman they pulled out of the lake was wearing. I didn't want to believe it, but I knew. I was living with a monster."

Amanda paused; her frail hands clutched at her blanket.

Parker took the opportunity to explain. "Your grandmother was the Lewiston victim Van Sanders tried to use to throw off suspicion of her crimes. Sheriff Crane's tortured brain mistakenly considered her a fourth Willow's Bane victim because of the similarities."

Samantha nodded and looked back at Amanda. "So, what did you do?"

"I did what any self-respecting mother would do. When he came home and sat down for supper, I used the gun Jack left behind and put a twenty-two-caliber bullet in his brain."

The room went silent as everyone let the meaning of those words sink in.

"Why didn't you turn him into the police?" Samantha finally asked.

Amanda shook her head. "He was my son and my punishment to deliver, nobody else's. After I did what I had to do, I buried his body out beyond the barn, then burned that barn to the ground."

Samantha snapped her fingers. "Carl Potter. That's one of the people listed as missing back then. He wasn't a victim; he was the murderer."

The blanket on the bed moved as Amanda struggled to remove one of her arms from underneath. When it was free, she reached her boney hand out and took hold of Samantha's.

"I'm sorry I couldn't stop my son sooner," Amanda said, her eyes pleading for forgiveness.

Samantha smiled. "Thank you for telling me your story. But why now, after all these years?"

Amanda returned the smile. "Because I'm dying, my dear. They can't do anything to me now. I was going to take it to the grave with me, but Abner convinced me this was the right thing to do."

Samantha looked across the bed at Parker. "Thank you for this."

"Like Abner said, it was the right thing to do."

Forty

Parker's rental car was once again following a grey SUV driven by a slightly perturbed Chuck on the way to the airport.

"What do you think will happen to Amanda Potter now?" Kat asked.

"I doubt anything will happen to her. The detectives will take her statement and turn it over to the local DA, and he or she will probably find it in everybody's best interest to just let it drop," Parker said.

"Can you imagine, though, killing your own child?"

"It's not something I want to imagine, or think about, thank you. Time to change the subject."

"You're no fun—" Kat grumbled. "Then what about you? You think you'll still be in trouble with your law firm, even though we'll be back in time for you to testify?"

"It doesn't matter. I've decided to leave the firm after the trial. I'm going to open my own agency. I'd been thinking about it for a while, and the way the firm refused to support me during all this sealed the deal."

Kat swiveled around to face Parker directly. "No foolin'? You're gonna be a private eye?"

Parker smiled. "Yeah, I think so. I can work for some other law firms. I have pretty good connections there, but then I can also take on my own cases."

Kat began bouncing in her seat. "You're going to need top-notch tech support, and I know just the person."

Parker took her eyes off the road long enough to give Kat a serious look. "Are you sure? It will be rough going at first. We'll need to bring in a steady stream of clients before I can offer you decent pay."

"Hell yeah! I have some money saved up, and I can still freelance on the side. What are we gonna call the agency?"

"Slow your horse girl. I haven't even—"

Parker's *Eye of the Tiger* ringtone interrupted them. When she saw the name on the caller ID, she pressed the hands-free button.

"Susan, did you get my email?" Parker asked.

"Yes, I received the email. I am absolutely floored. Let me start by saying how sorry I was to read about your wife, Lynn. I didn't know her well, but she seemed sweet," Susan said sympathetically.

"I appreciate that," Parker replied stoically.

"It took some guts to do what you did. Are you alright?"

"A little rougher around the edges, and Kat now believes that duct tape represents everything evil in this world, but we'll live," Parker said.

"Do you have a few minutes? I have some questions."

"We have a forty-five-minute drive to the airport, so let'em rip."

"Great. In your email, you mentioned that Tina Pool saw Matt Jackson at Penelope's house?"

"I think she was mistaken or confused about what day that visit occurred because we know now that nobody was home then."

"That makes sense. Why didn't Willa tell me who you really were?"

"I believe Willa had her own agenda, which conflicted with yours. No surprise there. But I have a question for you now," Parker said. "What are you going to do now that you know Vanessa Sanders played a major part in all of Penelope's books?"

"That's the thing I wanted to discuss with you. Do you have Penelope's last chapter with you now?"

"I have a copy. The original is with the Willow's Bane sheriff's office. I was thinking you could incorporate it with the rest of the Malignant Doubt on the second printing?" Parker asked.

"Trent and I had a different plan. The thing is … there will have to be commentary and explanation accompanying the added chapter, you know, to clarify what happened in Willow's Bane and Penelope's actual role. That would also be one way to address Vanessa's connection. Trent and I were thinking of an entirely new book … like a follow up to Malignant Doubt … and … we wondered if you might take a stab at writing it and detailing your involvement?"

Parker felt the temperature in the car rise. "I'm not a writer, Susan."

"That's not a problem. We have people who can help you with that. What happened to you and what you uncovered … combined with Penelope's chapter … it could be huge," Susan said enthusiastically.

"And no one would believe it. I sometimes don't believe it. Listen, I didn't tell you about this so you and Trent could make more money from it. Penelope and her daughter, my wife, both wanted the truth to come out. People shouldn't have to buy two books to do that."

Parker's phone went silent.

"Susan?" Parker said.

"I'm sorry you feel that way," Susan finally replied. "But I think that's the way we're going to proceed."

"That's going to be difficult to do without that last chapter."

"I own the rights to it," Susan said coldly. "It was part of Malignant Doubt."

"Bullshit. Your contract with Penelope ended when she submitted the book without that chapter, and Trent published it. That chapter belonged to Penelope. If she willed her estate to Lynn, and I'm betting she did, then it would pass on to Lynn. My wife left everything to me in her will, so I'll be able to say what happens to it."

"I'll take you to court."

"You could try, and you'll lose. And when you lose, I'll find a true-crime podcaster and give them the entire story for free. I have a podcaster in mind. Anyway, you'll miss out on the rest of Penelope's story. Or you could do as I suggested, include it in a 2nd printing of her book and post a link on both Penelope's website and Monolith Publishing's website, offering a free download of the missing chapter for the people who've already picked up a copy. You'll come away looking like a hero instead of a villain."

The extended silence that followed caused Parker to look at Kat.

"We'll talk again soon," Susan said, and the call disconnected.

"What do you think she'll do?" Kat asked.

"I think she and Trent will talk to their lawyers, discuss the pros and cons of a lawsuit, and maybe they'll come to their senses and do the right thing. If they don't, then Samantha's podcast will gain a lot more followers."

Kat put her feet up on the dashboard. "It sure is a lot of fuss."

"It's quite a final chapter."

Malignant Doubt - Chapter 50

Reader—this is Penelope Highsmith speaking to you directly now. I realize that I'm breaking the fourth wall by doing this, but it is necessary. It's my guess that right about now, you're contemplating throwing this book across the room or setting it on fire. If so, please let this final chapter be my attempt to change your mind. You're probably thinking … "I've read this whole stinking thing, and I'm no closer to knowing who killed those three girls than when I started." That's because I've saved the best for last, though I hesitate to label it 'the best.' Answers are coming … at least some answers … I promise.

But first … it's confession time.

Writers. We're an odd sort. We can recall the tiniest detail of an imaginary world with characters who could populate a small village … but we can't remember to pick up the milk we've been out of for a week when passing by the local grocery store. We live in two separate worlds… one that encompasses our actual day-to-day, hour-by-hour, minute-by-minute existence … and the one we constantly have swirling in our heads, waiting to find a place on the page. If we're any good at what we do, those two worlds rarely align. We often borrow inspiration from real-life events or things happening around us to use in our imaginary worlds, but we still maintain that division. It's important. Maybe even essential. Allow me to quote Arthur Conan Doyle, who said, "Life is infinitely stranger than anything which the mind of man could invent." It's scary how much truth is in that statement.

Writers escape into fiction … to make the unbelievable believable. I sometimes wonder if fiction is a destination for us writers or a prison. Are we trapped by our imaginations? I'm sorry if I'm rambling or being too obtuse. There is a point I'm trying to make. Please be patient.

When I first sat down to draft this book (which I did initially in 2019), I had different intentions. It was never going to be about who killed Mikayla, Deidre, and Maddy. My goal was to merge the two separate worlds I mentioned above—fiction and reality. I planned on writing about the events that played out in Willow's Bane from the first-person point of view of a young girl included in the possible victim pool. A unique POV for sure. How did that feel at the time? What was running through our teenage minds while a madman got his jolly's beating the life out of our classmates? At the same time I wanted to comment on how the murders forever altered the DNA of Willow's Bane. That transformation didn't happen overnight, nor did it end when the murders stopped. I was taking a risk that this book would only perpetuate the aura of despair the town had grown accustomed to because of what happened in 1986 (or what didn't happen). Some believe that people, places, and things can personify evil. In my own way, I wanted to illustrate how Willow's Bane personified something else… impotency.

That was how this book started out. My motivations, however, have changed.

You … my reader … have spent a day, a couple of days, maybe even a week, reading about the Snake River Killer. I've lived with this story for most of my entire life, though I've rarely allowed myself to think about it. I pushed the true story of what really happened down into my imaginary world. It existed there as fiction. I did that—subconsciously—in order to live my life in some semblance of peace.

It didn't turn out that way.

I entombed the truth. Buried it deep. And when you drive these kinds of truths that far down in your mind, it creates a debt. One way or the other, you must pay for turning your back on those truths. And that debt comes with interest. We don't realize (or choose to ignore) that the debt isn't always picky about how it's paid. Repayment can also affect the ones you care about the most.

What you've read so far, and what you're about to read, is an atonement. It won't come close to undoing what needs undoing. That can't ever happen. But why now—you ask? Recent developments have grabbed me by the head and forced me to reflect on my life. You may be shocked to learn that I didn't care for what I saw. The clock was ticking, and I hadn't much time to make things right.

There's a popular saying that goes, *the truth will set you free*. What a crock of shit! This truth will set no one free, but it will explain a lot. That's not freedom … it's insight. It's what people are owed … and what I am offering you right now. Here it is.

On the evening of May 6th, 1986, I killed Maddy Emerson.

That wasn't even the worst mistake I made that night.

Two weeks had passed since the murders of Mikayla Jamesison and Deidre Pool. Of course I was frightened, the whole town was, but something else consumed my thoughts that day. I had just learned the previous week that my mother was having an affair. It was with Dan Emerson. From the preceding chapters, I revealed Dan Emerson was already having an affair with Trisha Jamesison—Mikayla's mother. The man apparently was incapable of keeping his penis in his pants, and now my mother was becoming another notch on his belt. I had seen the two of them together as they were leaving the motel out on Lincoln Street. Technically, they didn't leave together. Dan went first, then fifteen minutes later, my mother left. I was across the street watching this because I had skipped school and followed my mother. I suspected something was going on with her for a while. She was distant, away from the house more than usual, and sometimes when she returned, she smelled different. Dad didn't seem to notice. In his defense, he was working a lot of hours and never was the most observant man. He didn't even notice when I had my ears pierced and started wearing large, gaudy earrings. So, I took it upon myself to do something. My suspicions were confirmed when my mother pulled into the motel parking lot that day. But what was I to do?

For a week, I contemplated my next step. I considered confronting my mother, but ultimately, I tried to fix things differently. As you've already read, I was on the same soccer team as Maddy Emerson. We weren't close, but I thought I could convince her to talk to her father about ending the affair. To me, asking Maddy to tell her father he was embarrassing her in front of her friends seemed reasonable.

In the early evening of May 6th, I surprised Maddy at the library (I followed her) and asked her to take a ride with me. She wasn't keen at first, but I can be convincing when I need to be. I drove her out to Vanessa Sanders' family cabin. Van and I sometimes went out there when we wanted to be alone. The spot was isolated, so no one would interrupt Maddy and me.

Our conversation didn't go as I expected.

Right from the start, Maddy denied her father was sleeping around WITH ANYONE. She was in complete denial. Her refusal to accept reality rapidly turned to anger … directed at me. She accused me of starting rumors about their family to get in her head. When I asked why I would do that, she said so I could get more playing time on the soccer team. The distraction of what was going on at home would cause her performance to suffer, thus giving me the chance I would need to get on the playing field.

I laughed. Her rationalization of what I was telling her was so ludicrous I couldn't help myself.

That's when she slapped me.

Recalling that moment now, I should have had a better understanding of what was going on. I was destroying Maddy's idyllic world, and emotionally, she couldn't handle it. She was your quintessential daddy's girl, and here I was, this relative nobody and closet homosexual (according to the rumors around the school), threatening to piss all over the man she adored. She reacted harshly, though not unexpectedly. I should have been more compassionate. But we were kids. And because we were so young … I did what I thought was right.

I slapped her back.

It quickly devolved into a full-on fight. I won't bore you with the blow-by-blow details only to say that it ended with a shove.

I pushed Maddy away from me. She stumbled, tripped on a piece of loose firewood, fell over backward, and her head struck a rock surrounding the fire pit. I waited for her to cry out in pain … but nothing came. Not even a whimper. She didn't move. I went over to check on her, and that's when I saw the blood. Panic rose in me. I shook Maddy, desperate for a response, but there was none. She wasn't breathing, either.

It's difficult to explain the numbing dread that seized me. I didn't know what to do. Another human being had died because of me. I felt faint. I needed help. Guidance. So, I called the one person who would know what I should do. My best friend, Van Sanders.

Like I said, I was young … and stupid.

When Van arrived at the cabin, the first thing she did was check on Maddy. She confirmed what I already knew. Some of my sanity had returned by then, and I blurted out that we should call the sheriff's office. Van surprised me by listing multiple reasons that would be a bad idea. She was one of the most logical and grounded people I knew, so what she said made sense to me (even though it really didn't). She asked if anyone had seen me pick Maddy up from the library, which I was sure no one had. Then, she came up with a plan that shocked me at first, but I eventually accepted because it offered me a way out.

We would make Maddy's death appear like she had become the Snake River Killer's third victim.

Once I agreed, Van took charge of everything. Since the Snake River Killer had beaten the previous two victims to death, we had to make it look as if Maddy had met the same fate. Van handed me her cane to go first. My hands were shaking so badly. Even though I knew Maddy was already gone, I couldn't do it. Van snatched the cane back from me and started pounding away. I should have been bothered by how enthusiastic Van seemed to be at performing such a horrific task, but I think I was still in shock. When she was finished, we removed Maddy's clothes, set fire to them in the firepit, and then carried her naked body to the back of my car. The two of us drove her to a spot by the river away from any main roads with plenty of trees, then carried the body to the edge and dropped it in. I ran back to the car as soon as the deed was done, but Van remained by the river for a minute, staring at Maddy's body as it floated away.

Back at the cabin, we made sure no signs of Maddy's presence remained, and then we drove back to our respective homes. When I got home, I went straight to my room and cried. I cried throughout the entire night. I didn't want to go to school the next day, but I made myself go. Van had stressed that we needed to act the same as we always did, so I went. It was hard. It never got easier. Never.

Thanks to our actions, the Snake River Killer claimed a third victim, and a fresh wave of fear descended on the city. Like the loss of a child, the pain associated with that loss never goes away. The parents—if they can—learn to live with it. That happened with Willow's Bane's fear. It persisted, and to this day, its residents ... though they'll never admit it ... still look over their shoulders.

As for me, I simply existed during the rest of my time in Willow's Bane. When an opportunity for me to leave came, I left. I never returned and refused to think about the events of that fateful night ... until several years later.

Unfortunately, the story doesn't end there. This is where I will tell you about the worst mistake I made that night. I can hear you now, my loyal reader ... I killed someone ... how can there be a worse mistake?

Maddy's death was an accident. It was devastating for everyone, but it was not intentional.

Bringing my sister Trudy with me that night was intentional ... and a colossal mistake.

Trudy shared my concern about our mother's affair with Dan Emerson, so she agreed to come with me to talk to Maddy. Two against one. But my sister just listened to my conversation with Maddy and contributed very little. When the fight between Maddy and me broke out, Trudy yelled at us to stop but didn't intervene. After Maddy fell and hit that rock, Trudy's only reaction was to pray (my sister is uber-religious). Before Van showed up, I instructed Trudy to hide in the cabin because Van and Trudy didn't get along. Van constantly ridiculed Trudy's religious fervor, and I couldn't handle them squabbling when something so catastrophic had already happened. Trudy watched everything unfold from the cabin window, and after we dealt with Maddy's body, I came back to pick up Trudy, and we returned home.

I fully expected Trudy to reveal what happened at the cabin to our parents… it was a sin, after all… and people needed to pay for their sins. But she held her tongue. Like me, Trudy never said a word about what had happened. Maybe she realized it was just a terrible mistake, and since there was no malice behind what I did, I could be forgiven by her spiritual overlords. I don't really know why she kept quiet. I wish now that she had turned me in. What she did instead was much worse.

Years later, I had graduated from college, been married for a year, and was working on my first book when Trudy called. She rarely called. We weren't that close before the incident; afterward, we went our separate ways. When I heard her voice on the other end of the phone, I was taken aback, but nothing could have prepared me for what she was about to say.

This is how that conversation went, to the best of my recollection.

Trudy – "I'll get straight to the point. I'm pregnant."

Me – "What?"

Trudy – "Before you ask, the answer is no, I'm not married, and I'm not telling you who the father is."

Me – "Okay. Well, I'm happy for you, I guess."

Trudy – "I'm not keeping it. The shame of having a child out of wedlock is unthinkable."

Me – "Oh. But being a single mother doesn't—"

Trudy – "I'm not keeping it, and that's that. I'm not due for a couple of months, and I've been able to hide my condition from others so far. But now I need somewhere to stay until I can deliver the baby and hoped you would accommodate me."

Me – "Uh … well … sure. You can stay with Sam and I."

Trudy – "Excellent. There's one other thing."

Me – "What's that?"

Trudy – "I want you to adopt the child."

Me – (after a prolonged silence) "Trudy, Sam and I have only been married for a year and the subject of kids hasn't even come up. We're not ready for a commitment like that, so it wouldn't be a good fit. But there are plenty of adoption agencies. We can find one to take the baby to, and they'll find it a suitable home."

Trudy – "Penelope, I want the baby to stay in the family."

Me – "But you want no part of it."

Trudy – "That's right."

Me - "I don't understand."

Trudy - "It is my flesh and blood. It shares a piece of my soul. I cannot bear the thought of having it under my roof, but handing it over to strangers isn't an option either. You'll need to see to its needs."

Me – "Then I'll have to say no. We're not ready."

Trudy – (after a long pause) "If you don't agree to adopt my child, I'll tell the police the truth about Maddy's death."

It was as if I was standing in front of the firepit in Willow's Bane again, staring at Maddy's unmoving body. The dread was back in full force. I tried begging and pleading with Trudy to think about the child and realize I wasn't ready to be a mother yet, but she was unmoved. Take the child, or the truth will come out, and I knew my sister well enough to understand she meant what she said.

So, without telling him the complete story, I convinced my husband Sam that we needed to adopt Trudy's baby, and that's what we did. I became a parent to Lynn Highsmith.

I may have become a parent, but I was no mother. It turned out that Sam wasn't a father either, and we divorced a year later. It was just Lynn and me from then on. Little did I know that when I killed Maddy Emerson that night, I would end up destroying two lives.

Hard fact—I was a deplorable mother. That sweet child had been forced upon me, and I neglected her, especially when she was young. When my writing career took off, I attempted to reinforce the wall between my two worlds—fictional and reality—with alcohol and other mind-altering substances. I robbed Lynn of the simple need of feeling safe, secure, a sense of self-worth, enrichment, and spiritual growth. Most importantly, I did a piss-poor job of letting that child feel a mother's love.

I do not know who killed Mikayla Jamesison or Deidre Pool. We may never know. I, on the other hand, committed a terrible crime, accident or not. I covered it up and dog-piled on top of a city that was struggling to survive a series of murders that shook it to the core. I ran away and flipped Willow's Bane the middle finger on my way out. But none of that compares to the injustice I laid at the feet of my adopted daughter.

When I started this book, it was to tell the story of a city and its population shaken by a series of unsolved murders (that I had a firsthand experience with) and how that lingered and affected it long-term. While this is still that, it is also a confessional, and an apology.

I have recently informed Lynn that she was adopted and who her real mother is, along with the countless other facts I withheld from her. I played a part in what happened to Willow's Bane. It's taken me three decades to take responsibility for my actions. I'm doing that now.

To my daughter Lynn … I apologize profoundly for how this has impacted you. I failed to show you just how much I cared for you. Just how worthy of love you were and are. How we were brought together wasn't ideal, but I have loved you since the beginning. I have much to regret as a pathetic mother, but number one on the list is allowing you to believe that I didn't love you. I do… so very much! I hope this book proves that.

I gave this same apology to my daughter last week, though I expect it fell on unreceptive ears. I wanted… no… I needed to reiterate it here.

I'm not seeking forgiveness. That would be true fiction… even for me.

But what a twist that would be.

Acknowledgments

I always struggle with this part.

Numerous people have been instrumental in my development as an author along the way, so I feel it is only right to mention them in every book I publish. Their influence, however slight, has contributed to who I am as a writer today. I always fear leaving someone out, so if I unintentionally do that… please accept my apology.

I'll start with the folks who took the time to read my drafts… regardless of what book I was working on… and provide insight into how to improve. Critique Partners, Alpha Readers, Beta Readers, Friends, the list goes on and on. Their efforts over the years have molded me into what you see today. Thank you, all! In alphabetical order – Angela Brown, Patricia Burroughs, Lindsay Carlson, Alexia Chamberlyn, Crystal Collier, Julie Dao, Patti Downing, Melissa Embry, Elise Falson, Chris Fries, Sierra Godfrey, Christy Hinz, Donna Hole, Liz Larson, Lori Lopez, Laura Maisano, Linda Masterson, Alex Perry, and Nancy Williams.

In one way or another, each of the following individuals has kept me moving in the right direction and boosted my self-confidence when I needed it most. A most heartfelt thanks to

Brianne van Reenen, Lisa Regan, Dianne Salerni, Barbara Poelle, Sarah Negovetich, and Tina P. Schwartz.

Special recognition is reserved for everyone who contributed specifically to TWIST. Kelly Apuzzo, Caitlin Bell, Tina Czappa, Kristine Donahue, Davlyn Evans, Heather Lorenzini, Taylor Rabette, and Mandy Simon. They helped me shape this book into something that I'm extremely proud of. Thank you for the guidance!

And then there is my wonderful editor and cheerleader extraordinaire, Shelly Stinchcomb. This is the third book of mine that she has edited for me and I continue to bask in her knowledge and expertise. I would not be where I am today without her guidance and support. Thank you, Shelly!

I took a different approach to publication for this book. I used a service called Kickstarter, which is a way to fund the expense of publication by finding backers willing to take a chance on it…and me…ahead of time. These are the individuals who helped me fund the book, for which I will be eternally grateful. They are: Mike from Arkansas, Amy B, Melanie B, Tina Czappa, Matthew Dawson, CD DiFore, Zack Fissel, Bria Gabriel, Ayla Genesky, Marina Giverts, Robert Glasscock, Ella Graff, Charlie Grayson, Cody S. Hammons, Jaime Hammons, Greg H, Joseph Hedrick, Katie Hunsaker, Rachael Jent, Zarlina Josefsson, Elizabeth K, Tetiana Kocherhan, Robert Kotowich, Meike L, Samantha Lane, Claire McCown, Lisa A. Moore, C. Niehot, Miss Pastel, McKenna Quan, Gerry Sage, Denise Scheen, Becky Seely, Valerie Anne Sizemore, Melodie Simard, Mandy Simon, Andy Stone, P Syros, Dustin Taylor, Marc J. Waters, Lindsey Watson, and Marie Wikle.

Last, but most assuredly not least, are my family—my children—Cody, Jaime, and Casey—and especially my best friend and wife, Kim. She has always owned the first read, the last word, and my heart. Thank you for believing in me and allowing me to pursue this dream. It means the world to me. Love you all!

Oh... wait… there's one more! You, my faithful reader. I can't forget about you. Thank you for choosing this book and keeping me firmly seated on this rollercoaster ride. Stick around… there's more to come.

Much love!

A Letter From DL

I want to say thank you for choosing to spend some of your hard-earned income on TWIST. If you want to keep up with my future plans, as well as some keen exclusive material, consider signing up for my newsletter at the link below. I also use my newsletter to recruit ARC (Advance Reader Copy) readers for future releases, so if that's something you'd be interested in, you're one click away. Your email address will never be shared, and you can unsubscribe at any time.

https://dlhammons.com/

Also, if you enjoyed this book then I'd really appreciate it if you'd leave a review or recommend it to a fellow booklover. Reviews and word-of-mouth recommendations are CRUCIAL for authors, especially Indie Authors, and the best way to introduce new readers to one of my books for the first time. No joke. These things make a difference. It doesn't have to be much. Even something like This book ROCKS is enough.

I'd also like to hear from you. You can usually find me hanging out at one of the social media places below, as well as my website listed above. Tell me what your reading experience was like, or just say HI. I don't bite (unless you're covered in caramel — then all bets are off).

https://www.facebook.com/DL.Hammons
https://www.goodreads.com/DLHammons
https://www.instagram.com/dl_1956/
https://www.tiktok.com/@dl_books4us

www.ingramcontent.com/pod-product-compliance
Lightning Source LLC
Chambersburg PA
CBHW071344300726
48976CB00006B/1769